MURDER IN THE
LINCOLN WHITE HOUSE

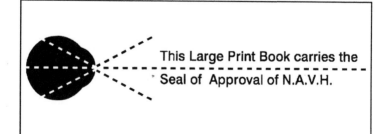

This Large Print Book carries the
Seal of Approval of N.A.V.H.

MURDER IN THE LINCOLN WHITE HOUSE

C.M. GLEASON

KENNEBEC LARGE PRINT
A part of Gale, a Cengage Company

GALE
A Cengage Company

Farmington Hills, Mich • San Francisco • New York • Waterville, Maine
Meriden, Conn • Mason, Ohio • Chicago

Copyright © 2017 by C. M. Gleason.
Lincoln's White House Mystery.
Kennebec Large Print, a part of Gale, a Cengage Company.

ALL RIGHTS RESERVED
Kennebec Large Print® Superior Collection.
The text of this Large Print edition is unabridged.
Other aspects of the book may vary from the original edition.
Set in 16 pt. Plantin.

**LIBRARY OF CONGRESS CIP DATA ON FILE.
CATALOGUING IN PUBLICATION FOR THIS BOOK
IS AVAILABLE FROM THE LIBRARY OF CONGRESS**

ISBN-13: 978-1-4328-4555-1 (softcover)
ISBN-10: 1-4328-4555-1 (softcover)

Published in 2017 by arrangement with Kensington Books, an imprint of Kensington Publishing Corp.

Printed in Mexico
1 2 3 4 5 6 7 21 20 19 18 17

For Steve

ACKNOWLEDGMENTS

There are so many people to thank for their support and assistance on this book — first and foremost, my editor, Wendy McCurdy, who whispered the breath of an idea that became the fleshed-out story of Adam Quinn and the others in this world of Lincoln. Without that little seed, I would never have come up with this concept — and I have grown to absolutely love the setting and history related to early 1861 Washington, D.C.

I am also very grateful, as always, to Maura Kye-Casella, my tireless agent, who knows me frighteningly well and is always willing to turn on a dime for me.

The team at Kensington has been wonderful, and I appreciate all the work on behalf of this first Adam Quinn book — including the perfect cover for their edition of the book, as well as sales and marketing efforts.

As always, I am indebted to the brilliant

and ever so dry Dr. Gary March, my main resource for all things medical. I must also give a shout-out to my son, who, in a conversation on the way to college, gave me the idea of the weapon and how it could be done. I knew there was a reason I had a mystery-lover and gamer for a son!

I also appreciate the support of Tammy Kearly and MaryAlice Galloway for their feedback about the first draft of the book — and during the busiest time of the year! Thank you so much for your thoughtful critiques.

CHAPTER 1

The day to which all have looked with so much anxiety and interest has come and passed. Abraham Lincoln has been inaugurated, and "all's well."
— *New York Times,* March 5, 1861

Inauguration ballroom,
  March 4, 1861, 10:45 p.m.
"Please welcome . . . at last . . . the president of the United States. Mr. Abraham Lincoln!"

The five-piece Union Band slid swiftly into the tune of "Hail Columbia" as nearly three thousand people stood, applauded, and cheered the entrance of the newly inaugurated president.

The grave, imposing man stepped up onto a dais and into the hall. The building had been erected as a temporary structure behind City Hall and was crafted with fine yellow pine flooring perfectly suitable for dancing. Lincoln, who removed his stove-pipe hat to give a brief bow amid thunderous applause and violent cheering, was flanked by his vice president, Mr. Hamlin, and Senator Stephen Douglas — the man with whom he'd argued politically for years, as well as being a former suitor of Mr. Lincoln's wife, Mary. A low murmur of appreciation and surprise swept the room when the attendees realized the president's escort also included Mr. Seward, one of the men he'd beat out for his party's nomination.

Though many of the ball attendees had seen the swearing-in earlier today in front of the half-completed dome of the Capitol Building, and still others had waited in long lines at the Executive Mansion to personally congratulate him afterward, there was still an arresting sort of sigh that overtook the room when he came into full view.

Taller than nearly every man in the area, with a head of incorrigibly thick walnut hair, a long, carved face, and heavy beard, Lincoln should have appeared austere and homely. Perhaps even off-putting. But to a man, those who met or spoke with him since his election in November registered not the angularity of his face nor the prominence of his forehead but the intelligence, warmth, and compassion in his eyes. They felt the intensity of his personality and the personal connection he made with most everyone he met.

As Mr. Lincoln and his wife, who'd entered with Senator Douglas and now walked holding her husband's arm, promenaded down one side of the hall, the sense of hope that had simmered among the Republicans since his election swelled into something almost tangible. Despite the ugliness between the Northern and the Southern states, and the almost certainty of war, the people who filled the hall tonight — and, indeed, most of those 30,000 people who'd thronged the streets of the District of Columbia earlier to witness the inauguration — were relieved that the day had gone off without a hitch; that the man they hoped would somehow keep the Union intact had been installed in the highest office in the land; and that he, now here in the flesh, was the humble, friendly, and calm individual they wanted him to be.

While Mr. and Mrs. Lincoln took their time greeting and shaking the hands of everyone possible as they made their way along the length of the hall, chatter and laughter buoyed the air. The band moved into a new piece, continuing to play the schedule of songs listed on the dance cards. Though the presidential couple had not officially "opened" the dancing, many couples eased onto the floor and began to waltz as the Lincolns greeted their admirers.

The enthusiasm and activity of those in the room were vigorous enough to cause the buntings and flags decorating the walls to shift and billow and flutter. It was as if the decor itself, along with the dancing gaslights studding the ceiling, was celebrating this new president as a new hope. A last chance for unity.

Beneath all of the celebration, however, was an underlying nervousness. A sense of stark awareness of how easily things could go wrong — not only here tonight, but beyond the limits of this capital city that represented a Union threatening to shatter.

In silent acknowledgment of this, most of the guests had pinned ornate blue and white cockades to their evening dress. The flower-like ornament with trailing ribbons indicated loyalty to the Union and was a response to the growing number of secessionist cockades being sported on coats and bodices throughout Washington.

Adam Speed Quinn, recently from the frontier city of Lawrence, Kansas, and now installed in what he understood to be a temporary role on Mr. Lincoln's staff, had brought up the very rear of the inaugural party as it made its way into the ballroom. He stood on the entry dais next to his uncle, Joshua Speed, who was the new president's oldest and most trusted friend. Along with them was the aged and withered General Winfield Scott, commander of the military, and Allan Pinkerton, the head of the president's security team. The four watched as the crowd parted below to allow the Lincolns to make their way in a sort of promenade along the edge of the hall.

This making way for the inaugurated couple was easier said than done, for the room was crowded enough with mere individuals but was made even more of a crush because of the wide, inverted teacup skirts worn by every woman present. Each skirt, held to its shape by a cage-like frame, created a circle around its wearer that made her take up a space three to four times wider than she was without her gown. The ladies in their skirts looked like a mad collection of handbells in pink, yellow, blue, and white.

Adam, who'd come from the rough and bloody Kansas frontier, hadn't ever seen this many hoopskirts in a room — and certainly not packed in as closely as they were now. He watched with both amusement and amazement as whenever a woman attempted to move or was jostled a few steps in one direction or another she was forced to tame her stiff, willful skirt. The hoops tipped, tilted, swayed, and required the pressure and direction of her hands to keep it from revealing too much ankle, or from being crushed between other skirts, persons, or, even worse and less yielding, a table or doorway.

"How the hell do they manage it in the outhouse?" he muttered. "How do they even get through the door?"

Unfortunately, Pinkerton heard him and bellowed out a great laugh as Adam grinned with chagrin at being overheard. Fortunately, his uncle and the general were engaged in their own conversation and hadn't seemed to notice.

"Still carryin' on with frontier manners I see," Pinkerton said, clapping him on the back even as his eyes continued to survey the room. "Not too many outhouses here in the city anymore — except for those for the slaves. The indoor necessary's a luxury you'll get used to, Quinn, and I reckon you won't complain about not having your stones froze off in the middle of winter."

Now that the inauguration was concluded and the party had begun, Pinkerton's tension had eased considerably from earlier today when they had been outside — in gunshot range, with people crowded elbow to elbow for streets on end. Nevertheless, there'd been a barricade constructed between the Capitol Building and the street to put distance between the president and his admirers, and any detractors that might also be in the area. General Scott had even ordered watchful sharpshooters onto rooftops to be at the ready.

All of this had been done in light of the many death threats Lincoln had received since his election. The platform on which Lincoln had taken his oath had been guarded since the night before, due to a rumor that secessionists planned to wire explosives to it.

In fact, the president-elect's arrival in Washington had been a day early and unexpectedly furtive because Pinkerton had been alerted to a well-planned assassination attempt in Baltimore. With difficulty, he'd convinced Mr. Lincoln to circumvent his route and come into town two days early on a midnight train. The press had gleefully latched onto the story that Lincoln slinked secretly into town out of fear, instead of boldly and in the midst of great fanfare — but today's festivities had certainly put those criticisms to rest.

"Well, Honest Abe's a frontier man himself, which I reckon explains a whole hell of a lot about your connection," Pinkerton commented to Adam.

Actually, it explained only a small portion of the reason Adam Quinn had been suggested by Joshua Speed to become an aide to the new president. Adam's uncle had pointed out that Lincoln could employ the thirty-year-old Adam to act as a "jack-of-all-trades" during the travel from the Lincoln home in Springfield to Washington. And that Adam, who had recently recovered from a tragic injury sustained on the Kansas frontier, could use something to "do."

"One only knows what tasks or eventualities might cross your path," Speed had said to his good friend Abraham Lincoln. "You've never been president-elect before; therefore, how can you know everything that must be done? And after what happened in Kansas . . . well, I need say no more, do I, Abe?"

Lincoln obviously had concurred, for he'd offered Adam a job — but likely for a number of considerations he kept to himself.

The fact that his duties had not been particularly well defined caused Adam no small concern, though he had a number of excellent motivations of his own for accepting such a position. He was relieved Lincoln hadn't expected him to be his social and correspondence secretary, for though Adam was well educated, writing anything was no longer his strong suit. Thus, he happily left the president's letter writing, social engagements, and documentation organization to the organized and enthusiastic Misters Nicolay and Hay.

Adam was about to reply to Pinkerton when he noticed a person — a man — edging along the side of the hall behind the crowd. Something about the figure struck a false chord with Adam. The way he moved, the way his attention fixed on the president. The furtive way he seemed to scan the room.

"Excuse me," Adam said, as the same instinct that had once saved a man's life — though cost Adam an arm — propelled him to act. That time, he'd dove to push his best friend out of the way of a pro-slavery thug, just as the man raised his rifle to shoot. The bullet had missed Adam's torso, but lodged in his left forearm, shattering the bone.

This time, a sense of foreboding about the man edging along the side of the room lifted the hair along Adam's remaining arm in a warning, prickling sensation.

He stepped off the dais, right hand moving smoothly to touch the pistol he'd been allowed to wear beneath his open coat. The heavy, tailored dress coat, which was a cutaway and worn unbuttoned and open, was a formality he found unpleasantly restrictive in the shoulders and chest after the soft, loose buckskin jacket he'd worn out west. His new black shoes were tight and shiny, and they reminded him of their virginity as he pushed his way through the field of hoopskirts and stray walking sticks — which were prevalent and nearly as much an obstacle as the framework skirts.

Down here among the crush of revelers, it smelled of tobacco and flowers, for the women not only seemed to bathe in floral scents, but most of them wore elaborate headbands decorated with roses, lilies, and other blossoms. It was also uncomfortably warm and very loud. Despite the crush, because he was nearly the tallest person in the room (besides Lincoln), Adam was able to keep his eye on the suspicious-looking gent who had paused at the edge of the crowd.

The man was slight and wiry and sported a large golden-brown mustache and generous sideburns that met at his chin in a neat beard. It was only as Adam drew closer — with a mere two dozen people between them now, instead of the hundred when he'd stepped off the dais — that he realized why the figure had caught his attention. It was his attire. Every other man in the room was wearing the requisite white shirt, dark neckcloth and waistcoat, topped by a black, cut-away dress coat with long tails. Each wore or carried a top hat of varying heights as well as a walking stick. They also wore gloves.

And if a male wasn't dressed in the stark black of formal wear, he was a servant or slave, hatless and wearing a white coat. Or he was a man in military uniform.

This man who'd drawn Adam from his bird's-eye view was none of the above. In a sea of formal finery, he wore a daytime derby hat of brown, a white shirt, plain dark waistcoat and neckcloth, but no dress coat. Instead, he was garbed in an informal topper — such as the coats worn by the office seekers and well-wishers who had been calling on Mr. Lincoln during the days leading up to the inauguration.

And there was something else: the way his eyes darted around, the way he seemed to be trying to stay out of sight of someone. Yes, the man's movements were furtive, as if he were constantly repositioning himself to stay unnoticed by someone.

The president?

Or someone near him?

Now there was a clear path of sight, if not mobility, from Adam to his quarry, thanks to a sea of hoopskirts lined up so that he could see between the shoulders of their wearers, all the way to the wall. His remaining five fingers tightened as he saw the man sliding a hand beneath his coat, eyes fixed in the area of the president. Behind his mustache and sideburns, the man's face was shiny and flushed with determination.

Adam's heart surged. He squeezed past two ladies in pale pink and yellow, stepping over their companion's walking stick as he eased his own pistol free, while doing his best to keep it out of sight. He didn't want to cause a scene, but he'd do whatever he deemed necessary.

The man's arm moved and he withdrew it from beneath his coat. Adam halted in midstride.

It was a *notebook.* The man had retrieved an innocent notebook, and as Adam watched, the strange gent slipped out a pencil from beneath his hat. Even as his eyes continued to dart about, he began to write feverishly. A journalist.

Feeling more than a little foolish, Adam took a side step and suddenly realized he was at the edge of the dancing floor, surrounded by people who only a moment earlier had been nothing but obstacles in his path to be avoided. Now, as if he'd been dropped back onto the earth after an abrupt ascent into a dream, he looked around and discerned individuals. Faces.

One of them — right there, suddenly close — was looking at him with a bemused expression even as she forced her wide, stiff skirt into demure submission when a couple passed by. "Why, and here I thought you were rushing your way through the crowd to get to little ol' me before the next song," she said with a delightful southern lilt. "But apparently I must be mistaken, for you haven't so much as asked to see my dance card, let alone introduced yourself."

As Adam reckoned he'd never actually seen a dance card and could only guess at its purpose, he found himself at a momentary loss. But he recovered immediately, discreetly shoving his pistol back into place before taking the slender gloved hand the belle offered in a smooth motion. "That is simply because I intend to ignore whatever might be on the card and invite you to dance with me nonetheless," he replied.

21

Her smile sparkled, reaching blue eyes as he bowed briefly. At least he'd learned formal manners in his mother's home before rushing off to the wilderness where no one carried walking sticks or wore gloves, and any woman on the frontier would laugh at the sight of a hoopskirt.

Not that there were any women to speak of on the frontier.

"Adam Quinn," he added as he lifted his head from the bow, then brought the young woman's hand to his lips for a brief kiss. "May I have this dance, then, ma'am?"

She was a pretty one, without a doubt the sort of young woman who normally had reams of men clustered about, clamoring for a smile, a personal word, a dance. Beneath a fancy headdress of pink roses and blue ribbons, her hair was the color of whisky — somewhere between honey and the chestnut of a horse — and she had fair, slightly flushed skin with a fascinating mark near the corner of her mouth. Her gown was white and had a low neckline decorated with blue and pink flowers. The bell-like skirt that nudged his knee had been trimmed with pink and blue ruffles — or maybe they were called flounces. Some frilly and wavy pieces of fabric that went around the skirt in several rows near the hem, and were anchored by more flowers. Jet black earrings of tiny beads dangled and glittered as she moved.

"It's a reel," she told him, giving a brief curtsy in response to his bow. This caused her skirt to puff out a little at the bottom, bumping against his calves, before she rose. "And I'd be delighted to forgo . . . er . . ." She groped for the little pamphlet that dangled from her wrist — presumably the all-important dance card — and opened it to the center. "Mr. Tallmadge and his dance," she said with satisfaction. "I've only met the gentleman once. He's a friend of a friend's, and since I don't know hardly anyone else here except for my daddy and the Mossings" — a little moue of distaste pouted her lips — "it would never do for me to be a wallflower, so Mr. Tallmadge agreed to sign his name to several of the lines."

As if to prove her point, she dragged off the soft golden cord that attached the pamphlet to her wrist like a bracelet and offered the booklet to Adam.

"I see what you mean," he replied, looking at the number of times Tallmadge had scrawled his name on the Agenda of Songs. A "Mossing" was on there as well, for several numbers. Having arrived late, Adam couldn't tell which songs had been played yet, but he saw no reason to argue with the young lady. "Then I reckon I shouldn't worry Mr. Tallmadge will put a bullet in my arm and rid me of my right hand as well."

With a rueful smile, he lifted what remained of his left arm to indicate the gloved prosthetic hand that protruded from his sleeve. Normally, he wouldn't have made such an overt mention of his injury, but as he'd be dancing with the lady and it would be obvious that his left fingers weren't flesh and bone, he thought it only appropriate to give fair warning. She'd find out soon enough if she took his hand.

Her eyes widened, but, to his surprise, with neither dismay nor distaste. "Well, I should hope it wouldn't come to that, Mr. Quinn. It is, after all, only a reel." She gave him a warm smile and slipped her hand around the crook of his left elbow with only the slightest glimmer of hesitation.

But Adam hesitated. "Is there not someone about from whom I should get permission to dance with you?"

She shook her head, a little crease forming between her brows. "If I knew where Daddy was at the moment, it would be a different story. As it is, he went off to speak to someone and left me here alone to avoid

Mr. Mossing on my own, and I haven't seen him since. My daddy, not Mr. Mossing. Well, I haven't seen Mr. Mossing since, but that's mostly intentional." She gave him a bright smile.

"Very well, then. There's only one more matter of business before I lead you out for this reel of ours, ma'am," he said, edging them toward the lines that were forming. He was acutely aware that her fingers were curled around the sleeve covering both the live part of his skin and the artificial portion of his arm.

"And what is that, Mr. Quinn?" She smiled up once again, and the southern in her voice reminded him of a particularly fine brandy he'd once shared with Uncle Joshua: rich, smooth, and dusky.

"The matter of your name, ma'am. I might be lately from Kansas and behind the times on social proprieties, but I don't reckon I'm permitted to dance with an anonymous lady. Even if her father is absent."

She laughed. "Of course not. But I thought you must have known my name, for the way you fairly mowed down the people as you made your way to my side. I'm Constance Lemagne. From Mobile."

Good God. Mobile? Alabama? The newly

minted capital of the so-called Confederate States of America?

Adam managed to hide his surprise. At least she wasn't wearing a secessionist ribbon on her dress. It would certainly stand out from the blue and white ones worn by nearly everyone in the room. It was no wonder she didn't know anyone here. In a room filled with Northern Republicans and a few former Whigs, a Southerner was more than simply out of place. And why on earth had her father gone off and left her alone?

More to the point — why on earth was her father even in attendance at a celebration for the president, who was already being demonized by the South? Today during the inaugural parade, he'd heard a Southern lady speak, belying her genteel accents with ugly vitriol: "There goes that Illinois ape — but he will never stay alive."

Adam returned his attention to the young woman at his side. "Very well, then, Miss Lemagne," he said just as the caller announced the final lineup for the reel. "Shall we?"

Fortunately, he knew the steps to the reel, and also fortunately, the movements required only the basic use of his false hand. Perhaps he hadn't needed to warn her about it after all. Another misstep here at tonight's

26

formal occasion to be chalked up next to his mention of an outhouse. His mother would be so proud.

As he do-si-doed then watched the lead couple promenade down the center of the two lines that formed the Virginia reel, Adam took the opportunity to glance around the room. The journalist had disappeared. The Lincolns seemed to have made their way down to the far end of the hall and were on their way back, still greeting and collecting congratulations from their admirers.

Adam's uncle remained on the dais with General Scott and Mr. Pinkerton, seemingly uninterested in joining the celebratory fray. He felt a twinge of uncertainty for having abandoned his own post, but of course he had done so for a valid reason. Still, after this dance, he thought, as Miss Lemagne slipped her arm through his and they swung around gaily, he would return to the dais.

Besides, his damned feet *hurt* in their pinching shoes. And he was becoming uncomfortably warm and damp.

The lineup for the reel stretched nearly the length of the hall, so it was almost thirty minutes before the set was finished. By then, everyone was out of breath, their faces were damp, and Miss Lemagne's eyes were particularly sparkly and beautiful.

Adam had a moment of regret as the dance ended and they made their way off the floor, for it was most likely he'd never see her again. Now that the inauguration was finished and the Lincolns would shortly be settled into the President's House, surely Adam would be returning soon to Kansas. A pang of grief stabbed him at the thought of returning to a place of so much sorrow. How could he even begin to start over?

"I declare, I'm just parched," Miss Lemagne was saying as she used her dance card to fan herself. At least it had taken on some useful purpose. "Did I see a table with lemonade and tea?"

"Shall I fetch you something to drink?" Despite the desire to return to his post, Adam would no sooner ignore a woman's need than cut off his other arm. And if he did, his mother would help with the maiming.

"That would be so kind of you," she replied, gesturing helplessly to her gown with a wry smile. "It's so impossible to navigate in these hoops, and I'd probably spill the drink all over me. Or, worse, you." Her nose crinkled delightfully as she smiled.

"It would be my pleasure."

Making his way as quickly as he could

through the crowd, Adam soon found himself in an even tighter cluster of people who'd had the same thought of refreshment. He was still quite far from the long table manned by black servants who carefully ladled out lemonade, limeade, and cold tea when he realized the Lincolns had finished their promenade around the room.

They'd ended at the dais where they'd begun, and although the president had stepped up to stand next to Speed and General Scott, Mrs. Lincoln had remained at ground level and was being led out onto the floor in a dance. She waved gaily to her husband, who inclined his head in an affectionate nod for her to enjoy herself.

That was when Adam realized the president seemed to be prepared to leave the ball. And that he should not be in line fetching a drink for a sweet southern belle, but with his uncle and Pinkerton and the president.

Adam was a resolute sort, and so he made a swift decision. "Do you see that pretty woman there, with the white gown and the whisky-colored hair? Standing by herself?" he asked the nearest elderly gentleman — assuming he would be the most harmless of persons to send back to the abandoned Miss Lemagne.

"Quite a picture, quite," the man replied. "Is she your wife yet, you lucky devil?"

"No, she is not, but her father has abandoned her and unfortunately so must I, as the president requires my assistance," Adam explained, doing his best not to sound self-important, while also sounding official. "Would you be so kind as to bring her a lemonade and give her the apologies of Adam Quinn?"

"Of course, of course," the man agreed, casting a speculative glance at Adam and then toward Lincoln. Clearly, he was already calculating how this information could be of use to him.

Adam thanked the man and slipped off into the crowd, narrowly avoiding a walking stick that jutted dangerously from beneath a gentleman's arm. As he pivoted, it was just by chance that he noticed the mysterious journalist approaching the dais. The man darted as quickly and smoothly through the crush of people as Adam, but the writer was already nearly to his destination.

The men on the dais — Lincoln, Speed, Scott, and Pinkerton — were all talking together, even as the president continued to respond to greetings and comments from the crowd. But he was clearly preparing to leave after having been at the ball for less than two hours.

Adam lost sight of the journalist as he drew closer to the dais, and considered trying to capture the attention of his uncle or Pinkerton. Though the reporter seemed harmless with his everyday clothing, notebook, and pencil, there was still something about him that set Adam's senses awry. It was like being on the plains in the middle of the night, with the broad lands rolling off into infinity and the moon hidden by a cloud, and not a sound or smell or movement . . . and yet *knowing* there was something waiting just ahead. Something wrong.

He sensed it. Something was off about that man.

It took him another five minutes to get to the dais, partly because Adam got trapped behind a party of five bell-skirted ladies who seemed to have neither a destination nor a speed above a crawl. He chafed, edged one way and then another, and just as he was about to make a dash for it between two separating skirts, he saw something happening on the dais.

Something was wrong. Speed's expression had gone rigid, and he and Pinkerton were speaking intensely with a third man whom Adam didn't recognize. Lincoln seemed unaware, for he was conversing easily with

31

Senator Douglas, who'd just approached, and General Scott.

Adam dodged an oncoming hoopskirt and made for the dais on his aching feet, nearly knocking the walking stick out of an elderly man's hand as he pivoted to avoid a servant carrying a tray of refreshments. He muttered an apology, but by this time, his uncle had caught sight of him and was frowning fiercely over the heads of people. The message was clear: I need you *now.*

Whatever was happening was not good news, and Adam's trepidation grew as Lincoln turned and thrust himself into the conversation with Speed, Pinkerton, and the newcomer.

"I apologize for stepping away," Adam said. He was slightly out of breath as a result of vaulting himself up onto the dais in lieu of maneuvering up the crowded steps. He'd foolishly used his left arm, which meant the prosthetic strapped to the stump just below his elbow had not only taken all of his weight, but had shifted slightly with the movement. Pain shafted up his arm and throbbed angrily as he gritted his teeth to mask it. Even more than a year after being fitted with an artificial limb, he still sometimes forgot in the heat of the moment that all of his parts were no longer intact.

"We have a situation," Joshua said to him. Though he wasn't officially on the president's staff, he cared more about the man and his well-being than anyone else in the room, save perhaps Lincoln himself.

Adam nodded, his jaws still set against the lingering pain.

"I believe now will be the moment where our jack-of-all-trades will step forward and prove himself both versatile and indispensable."

With a jolt, Adam looked up at Mr. Lincoln, who'd spoken clearly and gravely. Very different from the relaxed, affectionate man with whom he'd sat at the dinner table and listened to story after story, or argued and joked with in the parlor for years back in Springfield. "Mr. President," he began.

Lincoln shook his head, holding up a hand. His eyes were calm yet troubled. "The last thing I want is for anyone out there to know. Especially Mary. She's been waiting for this for . . . well, years. Decades, really." His smile was both wry and sad.

Adam felt a twinge. He and his uncle had spoken long and intimately about the new president — a man whom they both knew and loved — and what a burden he would bear.

What a dangerous, heavy, important burden.

"Whatever I can do, of course, Mr. President," he replied.

Joshua took Adam's arm. "A man's been stabbed here, at the ball. Murdered."

CHAPTER 2

Shock robbed Adam of words, giving Pinkerton the opportunity to speak. "The important thing is to tend to the removal of the body without causing alarm or notice."

"And even more importantly," Lincoln said with grave tones, "is to determine how and why it happened. And who was the perpetrator." He nodded meaningfully at Adam. "While I'm certain it has nothing to do with me —"

"Don't be a fool," Joshua snapped as Pinkerton and General Scott made similar sounds of disagreement. "At your inauguration dance? Of course it has *everything* to do with you. It's a political statement, a warning, a —"

"Josh," Lincoln said quietly. "If someone wanted to kill me or to make a statement, would they have done so in a back room? With a soundless blade? To someone who has no real connection to me? No, I think it would have been something much more akin to a trumpet blast than the clang of a muffled gong."

"Unless they were trying to create a distraction. Just as they planned in Baltimore, Mr. President. Cause a big problem — for that plot, they planned to create a riot; tonight it's merely a dead body . . . *only yards away from you.*" Pinkerton's voice was dry. "Draw away the attention of your security, and when everyone is busy with the problem at hand, they act."

Lincoln sighed. "They planned to blow up the platform today on which I took my oath — surely they didn't have a second plot in mind." His gray eyes fixed on Adam. "But that is what you're going to find out — who caused this death and why."

"Of course, Mr. President." Adam said the words readily, but his thoughts were filled with protests. He ventured to voice the obvious one. "Mr. Pinkerton is the detective. . . ."

"And he is well known for being so." Lincoln turned, moving closer, so that his words were only for the ears of Adam and his uncle. "I prefer someone less known to the public to carry out this investigation. And I also require someone in whom I have complete and utter trust, whose loyalty and discretion are without question. You are one of the most intelligent and resourceful men I've come to know — who is not immersed in politics or the law." The faintest glimmer of humor lit his eyes, then faded.

Adam exchanged glances with his uncle and nodded. "I'll do my best not to disappoint you, Mr. President."

A faraway look filtered into Lincoln's gaze. "I have no doubt my future disappointments will not come from you, my friend."

Adam Quinn had seen far too many dead bodies in his thirty years, beginning with the time he'd found his father — who'd broken his neck when thrown from a horse — when he was a mere seven years of age.

It was partly due to that circumstance that he'd been sent to live with his uncle Joshua when he was twelve and his mother married a man who had five children of his own. Those five children, along with Adam's three other siblings, had their modest home bursting at the seams — not to mention stretching the larder and pantry — and Molly had sent him to stay with her favorite brother in Springfield, Illinois.

Since discovering his dead father in a field, Adam had encountered a number of other lifeless bodies through a variety of circumstances and had witnessed a sad amount of killings in person — an unforgivable number of them at the hands of pro-slavery men in "bloody" Kansas.

Thus, when Mr. Fremark, the agitated man who'd brought the alarm to Speed and Pinkerton, took him to the body, Adam felt a surge of pity and sorrow rather than revulsion or shock when he looked down at the dead man.

Fremark had discovered the body in a small anteroom that had been constructed with just as much speed and simplicity as the rest of the dance hall. It was an entryway with a small utility closet — which probably contained a coal bucket and perhaps a broom — located at the north side of the temporary building. Now that the president had arrived and the ball was in full swing, the room would be traversed only by the occasional partygoer who would walk out of the building and across the muddy square to City Hall, where retiring rooms and lounges had been arranged for the ladies and gentlemen.

Though the victim was partly covered by a tablecloth with a small bloodstain on it, Adam could see he was dressed in formal clothing like that of nearly every other male at the ball — except he was missing his dress coat. Still uncertain of his approach to this task Mr. Lincoln had set before him, he paused to say a brief prayer over the lifeless body — for both the salvation of the man's soul and his own guidance — then opened his eyes, steeling himself with determination. If he were to discover how and why this happened, it was necessary for him to actually examine the body — something he'd never had occasion to do in the past.

He carefully pulled away the makeshift shroud.

Fremark emitted a sound of protest as the victim was uncovered, but he made no further comment when Adam handed him the cloth. The two men Pinkerton had sent along to assist stood back and watched silently.

A faint scent of blood hung in the air; Adam could almost taste the iron tang of it, though there didn't seem to be very much blood. Perhaps it was his own acute memories that enhanced the scent to one so strong.

No one spoke as he looked at the sprawled figure. From the ballroom only a narrow corridor away, he could hear the sounds of celebration and music. Thus, the party went on, the revelers blissfully ignorant of the violence and ugliness only a few yards distant.

For a moment, Adam had the unpleasant sense that this scene of carnage, so very close to innocent celebration and ignorant gaiety, was a dark hint of days to come.

He continued to stand, using that perspective to take in the full view of two relatively small bloodstains on the man's shirt and waistcoat. The blood was still wet and shiny on the fabric, but no longer seeping from several wounds. Surely the murder couldn't have happened more than thirty minutes ago. Perhaps less. There was one larger stain near the middle of the waistcoat, and another smaller one on the shirt. The tear where the blade had gone in through layers of waistcoat and shirt was perhaps two inches wide. Adam found it curious that the man's cutaway coat was missing.

The victim himself looked about forty. He was well groomed with a neatly trimmed light brown beard that flowed into thick sideburns. Of course, nearly every man present tonight would have been washed, trimmed, and combed in honor of the ball.

"Do you know this man, Mr. Fremark?" Adam asked at last.

"Yes," Fremark said. "Yes, I've seen him. I don't really know him personally, but I know who he is."

"And?" Adam prompted as he at last lowered himself to the floor, settling his pinched and aching feet next to the body. "What's his name? What do you know about him?"

"That's Custer Billings," said Fremark. "He's a banker."

"You found him right here, then, Mr. Fremark?" he asked, crouched on his haunches a mere finger length away from the body as he tried to determine how to proceed.

What was important? What should he be looking for? Why the damned hell did Lincoln think *he* was capable of resolving this matter? Wasn't this a matter for the authorities?

"Yes. He was just lying there."

"Was he like this when you found him?" Adam asked.

"Oh, yes . . . oh, yes." Fremark was pacing, his slender fingers waving nervously inside their white gloves. The Union ribbon pinned to his lapel fluttered with his agitation. "I had walked over to City Hall to use the — well, I didn't want to be fumbling outside at an outhouse dressed like this. So I went over there for a moment for the necessary, and when I came back through here on my way to the ball, I came around the corner and *there he was.* Just lying there, like this. I was only gone for ten minutes, maybe fifteen. I don't understand how it could have happened so quickly.

"I — I was sure Billings was dead right away — there was blood, and he wasn't moving. I did kneel at his side —"

"And then? You didn't touch him or move him?"

"No, no, I — well, I probably shouted, and then seeing that no one was about, I ran to get help. To tell someone. I found Mr. Pinkerton right away." He gave a delicate shudder. "There was nothing like walking into a room and seeing a man with a blade sticking out of his stomach. I'm going to have nightmares."

"Did you see anyone else — wait. A blade? Sticking out of his stomach?" Adam repeated slowly, craning his head to look up at him. "You saw a blade in his stomach?"

"Why, yes, of course. It wasn't very big. It's right — it's *gone.*" Fremark's voice squeaked up a notch. "But it was right there!"

"How long were you gone after you discovered him? Did you pass anyone when you left this room to get Pinkerton? Did you *hear* anything, anyone, any sound that might have been unusual?"

"No, no. I didn't see anyone. No one at all. Wait — I might have passed someone in the hall as I went back to find Pinkerton. I-I don't remember. Maybe. Maybe someone. It was only about ten minutes, maybe a little more, from the time I found him till I brought Pinkerton back. I don't remember anything unusual — other than that I had just seen a dead body with a knife sticking out of it." He was wringing his hands now, and his voice remained at that tight upper octave. "I-I can't remember. I was just running back to the dance hall, and . . ." His hands flapped wildly.

Adam closed his eyes to think. Had the murderer been interrupted by Fremark? Had he hidden somewhere when he heard Fremark's approach, then waited until he left to take the knife out of the body? Why had he chosen this place, here and now, one of the most public places in the city, to stab the man? Why was the man's dress coat missing? And surely he would have had a hat and walking stick. . . . They were gone as well.

"All right, Mr. Fremark," he said, opening his eyes once more. "All right. Now, think for a moment. Did you see anyone when you walked through on your way to City Hall to use the necessary? Before you found

Mr. Billings? Or on the way back — either time, walking across the square? Are you certain there was no one around at all?"

Fremark had regained his composure. "I was in a hurry. The president had just arrived, and I didn't want to miss anything, so I was going as fast as I could to get to City Hall and get back. My wife was mad that I had to leave the dance; she was hoping to get a spot in the quadrille near Mrs. Lincoln, but — well. Nature calls." He gave a rueful smile. "So I came through the room here. It was empty. I-I went outside and was starting across the wooden walkway they put down, to keep the mud off, you know, and I was rushing because — hold up." His eyes widened. "*Hold up.* Maybe I did see someone there. In the shadows, right outside the doorway." He straightened up, and now there was a gleam of certainty. "Now that you mention it, I think I did see someone. Two people. Right there — they weren't on the walkway, so I didn't really pay them any mind."

"What were they doing?"

Fremark shrugged. "I-I don't know. I just hurried by, but now that you mention it, I remember voices and the impression of people standing there. Maybe I wondered for a minute why they were standing in the

mud, off the walkway, in the shadows —
maybe I thought it might have been, well,
a-a secret meeting — but I was in a hurry.
So I just went on my way."

"A secret meeting?"

"I don't know. I don't know!" Fremark
held his head in his hands, his ears protrud-
ing from between his fingers. "I can't really
remember. I don't remember anything
much. The — the sight of the body just —
it just —"

"All right there, Mr. Fremark. And when
you came back? How long was it? And they
were gone? The people you saw?"

"That's right. I came back and they were
gone. And I opened the door," he said,
gesturing to the door leading to the outside,
"and then I saw him. Right here on the
floor." His voice was going tense and sharp
again. "I went to get Pinkerton."

"And you reckon you might have passed
someone in the hall on the way to get Mr.
Pinkerton."

"Yes, yes. Maybe. That's all I know. That's
all I remember."

Adam nodded. Then, sensing he had all
the information he was going to get from
Fremark — at least at the moment — he
trained his attention once more on the
unfortunate Custer Billings. Scoring his at-

tention carefully over the body, he absorbed every detail, looking for anything out of place or disturbed. Anything that struck him.

All at once, in a burst of clarity, he realized what he was doing — what he'd been tasked to do — was hardly any different from how he'd learned to track in the woods, how to read the signs and language of nature. For when he was twenty, he'd moved to Wisconsin and met a young Ojibwe man with whom he partnered in a trapping business.

Ishkode had shown Adam the way to recognize when a stick was broken by a footstep, a paw, or a hoof. Or the particular pattern in which grasses or brush were disturbed, and how to determine the direction whatever had disturbed them had been moving. Some of it, he'd learned, was instinct: that innate sense that something was not as it should be. It was the same intuition that had drawn his notice to the journalist today.

And some of it was pure observation.

And even more of it was knowledge: the ability to identify a species or a paw print, or in this case . . . something left behind.

"Hello there," Adam said quietly when he noticed just that: several short golden brown hairs clinging to the fingertip of one of Billings's gloved hands.

"Get me a . . . an envelope. Or a napkin. A piece of clean paper," he said, speaking to the younger of Pinkerton's agents. That one had at least seemed interested in the proceedings — unlike that of his companion, who stared off into the distance. "I need something for these." He held up the finger toward the agent. Adam needed a safe way to save the hairs — and, for that matter, any other small item of interest. Who knew what might be important later down this path.

With the hairs still perched delicately on his fingertip, Adam continued his examination of the body. It was necessary that it remain, for the time being, mostly a visual one. For one hand was employed by holding the tiny clues, and the other was hardly useful for anything other than inelegantly pinching and grasping — and then only with some maneuvering to set the wooden digits into position.

"And you," he said, catching the eye of the other agent, who'd thus far done nothing but hold up the wall, "I reckon you can empty the man's pockets. Take everything out and lay it on the ground there for me to see." He'd been balanced on the balls of his feet, down on his haunches, for some time and his thighs were beginning to ache.

Nevertheless, Adam waited patiently as the agent did as he requested. Fremark stood back and watched with what could only be described as morbid fascination.

With the dress coat missing, there wasn't much in the way of personal items to find on Billings's person. Inside his waistcoat was a pocket watch, and in another small, shallow pocket was a handkerchief. The pockets of his trousers were empty of everything except a business card.

Adam held out his left arm, maneuvering his elbow close to his torso in order to twist his false hand palm up, and the agent set the card there. *Mr. Hurst Lemagne, Frenchwood Plantation, Alboit, Alabama,* it read.

Lemagne.

Constance's father? Her *absent* father, who, according to her, had been missing from the ball for some time. Adam frowned thoughtfully, then allowed the card to slide onto the floor next to the other objects.

There wasn't much blood around the body, but there were many dusty footprints from the myriad people who'd walked through the room, along with a few muddy prints that were in various stages of drying.

A wooden walkway had been laid out between City Hall and this temporary building in order to keep the guests' fine shoes from becoming dirty when traveling across the muddy square. But some people hadn't been able to completely avoid the muck — which was no surprise, as the streets of Washington were notoriously wet and dirty.

Just then, the other agent returned. He was, blessedly and miraculously, carrying a small stack of envelopes. "Borrowed them from one of the offices in City Hall," he said with a cheeky grin.

"Thank you. What was your name again?" Adam eased the minuscule golden hairs into one of the envelopes, then carefully pulled to his feet.

"Hobey Pierce, sir," replied the young man. He looked barely twenty, with no beard to speak of and a shock of strawberry-blond hair. His nose was anointed with freckles and his two front teeth were too large for the rest of them.

"Well done. Thank you."

Before Adam could say anything further, there was a dull thump from behind them. He turned and noticed the small door to the utility closet.

Without speaking, he strode over and yanked it open. A mop and a broom fell out, clattering onto the floor . . . but what was even more interesting was the pair of shocked eyes that met his. Familiar eyes, beneath a battered derby hat and just above a luxurious golden brown mustache.

"Who are you?" Adam demanded, yanking the odd journalist out from the closet. "And why are you hiding in there?"

The man stumbled as his feet landed on the ground, barely keeping his balance because of Adam's force.

"I —" he began in a voice high with fear. "I was just —"

"Mr. Quinn!" Hobey Pierce had taken the initiative and looked inside the closet. He emerged, holding a black dress coat.

As he pulled it free, something clattered to the ground.

A knife. There was blood on it.

The journalist gasped, his eyes going wide and round. "How did — I didn't put that there. I *didn't,*" he said.

Adam glared down at the weaselly little man. The only significant thing about him was his magnificent mustache. "What's your name? What are you doing here?"

"H-Henry . . . Altman. I'm a reporter." He pulled from Adam's grip and straightened up. A flash of fury replaced the initial apprehension in his eyes. His voice squeaked high with agitation. "I'm just doing my job. I didn't know there was a knife in there."

"Why were you hiding, then?"

"I told you, I —"

The outside door flew open, and a woman wrapped in a cloak came in from the night. Adam recognized her, for she'd been at Willard's Hotel earlier today — where the Lincolns, as well as he, had been staying. It was Elizabeth Keckley, a free black woman whose gray-streaked hair and delicate lines lining her forehead suggested an age of around fifty. She was a seamstress who'd been called in earlier today to meet with Mrs. Lincoln.

He immediately stepped toward her in an effort to somehow block her from seeing the obvious. The last thing he wanted was for Mrs. Keckley to carry the word to Mary Lincoln — or anyone — that there'd been a murder here at the ball. Then he would have failed at his task more quickly than even he'd supposed.

"Oh, Mr. Quinn! I heard there was a — an accident, and I thought maybe a doctor might be needed. Someone who wouldn't carry tales." She stopped, slightly out of breath, as Adam's attention turned to the man who'd followed her inside — even as he wondered how someone had already heard about the dead man.

Mrs. Keckley's companion — possibly her

son? — had dark skin, brown as a walnut. Though he met Adam's eyes unflinchingly, his steady gaze was marred by a trace of wariness. He was a well-turned-out man around Adam's age, maybe a little older than thirty, and he wore a close-cropped beard and mustache as well as a morning coat. He carried a black derby hat but wore no gloves. "I'm George Hilton. Dr. George Hilton," he said in a deep, carefully modulated voice.

"We don't need no nig—"

Adam spun, his arm coming out in a sharp gesture to silence the second Pinkerton agent. "You," he said to him, eyes narrowed with anger, "find out where Custer Billings lives, and if any of his family is present. Don't tell anyone why." Then he turned to Hilton. "You're a medical doctor?"

"Yes, sir, I am."

"Thank you for coming. Unfortunately, this man's need for a doctor is long past."

He turned back to the woman. "But thank you for thinking of bringing him, Mrs. Keckley." He itched to ask her how she'd learned of the death so quickly.

She seemed surprised that he remembered her name. "We were already here, sir. George drove me here. He knew I wanted to see Mrs. Lincoln at the ball, but there's the curfew, you know, and we . . ." Her voice trailed off as the doctor stiffened slightly, perhaps from shame . . . or fear.

"Miss Lizzie." His voice was quiet, and he watched Adam warily.

"Curfew?" Adam said, and then with a flush of disgust, he remembered. There was a Black Code in Washington City, part of which imposed a ten o'clock curfew on all Negroes — whether they be slave or free. As it was nearing midnight, obviously George Hilton was taking a risk bringing this woman — who didn't seem to be a relative, based on the way he addressed her — here. Though her skin was light and she might pass for white, the doctor certainly could not.

Adam glanced at the Pinkerton agent, who was just leaving through the interior door, then said to Dr. Hilton, "If you'd like to look at the body and see if there's anything you notice that might give us a clue to who did this, Doctor, I'd be much obliged. I'll vouch for you should anyone ask," he added.

"Of course, sir," he said, some of the wariness easing from his stance. "Thank you, sir." He removed his hat and knelt next to Custer Billings's body.

At that moment, the exterior door slammed and Adam spun around to realize

Henry Altman was gone. "Damn!"

He bolted after the little sneak, dashing through the door and out into the dark, chilly night.

To his relief, he caught sight of the journalist hurrying along the edge of the building, obviously trying to stay in the shadows while avoiding the muddy area that had most recently been part of the construction of the hall.

"Stop!" he shouted, running after him. Though he was lame in one arm, there was nothing wrong with his legs — other than the fact that they topped sore and pinched feet — and it was no hardship for Adam to catch up to the man. "Henry Altman! Stop now!"

The man glanced behind him, the hat tumbling off his head and to the ground, and increased his speed. But he was no match for his pursuer's long legs, and at last Adam got close enough to lunge for the reporter.

He caught hold of the back of Altman's coat and yanked as they both stumbled to a stop on the small area of muddy lawn between City Hall and the dance hall.

"What do you think . . . you're doing . . . ?" Adam puffed, spinning the reporter around as he shoved him up against the wall. "This is a murder . . . investiga—Mother of God," he gasped.

The mustache was hanging lopsidedly from the man's face, whatever had adhered it to his upper lip no longer in play, and the same was true for one of his sideburns.

But it wasn't that that had Adam dropping his hand and stepping back in shock. It was the soft curves he'd felt when he grabbed him — no, *her* — by the front of his shirt.

Henry Altman was a *woman.*

CHAPTER 3

"Release me at once," demanded the so-called Henry Altman, no longer attempting to disguise her gender with a false voice. She was still panting, but her demeanor was one of outrage instead of distress.

Adam had already stepped back, horrified by the way he'd manhandled the woman — grabbing her by the shirt and practically flinging her against the wall. Nevertheless, he stood such that she couldn't dart past without giving him the chance to stop her with his good arm. "Why were you hiding in the closet?"

"I-I heard people coming and I didn't want to —" She grimaced and gave a little shake of her head like she was exasperated. "There was a dead body lying there and it's *news.* I wanted . . ."

"So you wanted the story? But you can't really be a reporter," Adam said. Women didn't write for newspapers — at least other than about female topics like fashion and housekeeping. "And why are you dressed like a man?"

"I most certainly *am* a journalist. And the answer to why I'm dressed as I am should be obvious: because, according to you — and every other man — *I* can't really be a reporter. And yes, of course I wanted the story." Altman underscored her rapid-fire words by ripping off the drooping mustache and sideburns. "I was the first — well, the second — person on the scene of a crime, and it was my chance to get a real scoop."

The gaslight street lamp gave off enough light for Adam to see determination blazing in her expression. "You were the second person to find him? How do you know that?" He'd seen her in the dance hall just before Mr. Fremark arrived with his awful news, so Adam knew Altman hadn't had enough time to sneak out and stab Custer Billings herself — even if she'd had the strength and proximity to do so.

"Because I passed the man in the hall — the man who found him. He nearly bowled me over, running back toward the ball, exclaiming that he'd found a dead man."

"And so you reckoned you'd hide in the closet?"

She sighed. "I told you, I didn't want to

be noticed."

Adam didn't point out that she hadn't actually told him that. Instead, he stepped back a little. "You didn't want to be recognized, you mean. A murder would attract a lot of people, and someone might notice you weren't who you appeared to be." When she opened her mouth — to argue, he suspected — he continued quickly, "Did you see anyone else? Why did you take the coat and knife into the closet with you — so you could get the scoop, as you say? Keeping the evidence for your own story?"

"I told you, I didn't know the coat and knife were in there with me. And you don't even know whether the coat belongs to the dead man!" Now she was mad as a doused hen. "I'm not a liar."

"Except you lied about being a man," he reminded her. "And I reckon you could be lying about being a reporter too. Who do you report for anyway?"

"Never you mind." She shoved past him, stumbling a little over the uneven, muddy ground.

He didn't try to stop her, though he sure as hell wasn't going to let her go off alone in the night. But his conscience warred with the fact that he had to get back to the pressing problem of Custer Billings — namely removing him before the news of a dead body got around.

And then somehow he had to find out who'd killed him — in a town Adam didn't know, filled with people he wasn't certain he *wanted* to know.

"If you would wait only a minute, I'll get someone to see you home, Miss . . . ?"

"Never you mind about that," she said again. "I'm perfectly fine walking home. I haven't far to go." She jammed the mustache back on. Though she took a little more time replacing the sideburns, even in the dim light he could see that none of the hairpieces were convincing in their placement or stability.

"Or you could come back inside with me and maybe you could get more information for your story. And then someone could see you home."

She looked at him with bald distrust. "I don't think so. I don't know who you are or what you're doing — it's obvious you aren't a Pinkerton — but I'm not going anywhere with you. I'll take my chances walking across the mall."

"Washington City is filled with soused-up men either very happy or terribly angry over the new president — and neither group is well behaved. I can't in good conscience allow a woman to wander the streets at night alone, Miss . . . uh . . . Altman."

"Well, Mr. . . . whoever you are —"

"Adam Quinn —"

"Thank you for your concern on my behalf, but I assure you, I'll be fine. I haven't far to go. Now if you'll excuse me."

Despite his responsibility to the president, Adam turned to follow her — he simply couldn't allow a woman to go off alone, especially at midnight — but he'd taken only a few steps when a noise from behind drew his attention.

"Mr. Quinn? Are you out here?" Hobey Pierce, the resourceful Pinkerton with strawberry-blond hair, came into view.

"Yes, I'm here. I'll be right — *damn.*"

The minute he was distracted, the woman who called herself Henry Altman had taken off at a run. She was quick, and Adam's prosthetic hand didn't work well enough to grab her in that flash of a moment, and so it was with great misgivings he let her go. He was needed inside, and she was clearly the stubborn sort, as his mother used to say. Often about him.

"You," he said, "Agent Pierce?"

"Yes, sir?"

"Follow that wo— that man. The reporter. He ran toward the square — did you see him? Make sure he gets where he's going without incident."

"Yes, sir."

"And I want to know where he goes."

"Yes, sir."

"Thank you."

His conscience thus relieved — hopefully soon to be followed by his curiosity — Adam hurried back to the anteroom of the dance hall, apprehensive about what he might find.

However, the only people in the room were Dr. Hilton and Mrs. Keckley, as well as poor Custer Billings.

"He's standing guard at the door," Mrs. Keckley said. "The other Pinkerton man. He won't let no one in, but he says he can't keep them off for long without them knowing there's a problem."

Adam hesitated. He wanted more time — more time to look at everything, to think about what had happened, to imagine it — to figure out how the hell he was going to complete a task for which he was hardly qualified.

He picked up the dress coat that had been found in the closet with the knife. Why had the murderer taken the time to drag the coat off Billings and throw it in the closet? To hide the knife? There was no blood on the front of it, but that wasn't surprising, as the two wounds on the dead man's torso hadn't bled much, and the coat was in the fashionable style: worn unbuttoned and "cut away" to fully expose the waistcoat and shirt worn beneath it. Its shallow pockets were empty, and the blue and white Union cockade was crumpled and saggy. There was some blood on the sleeve, probably from when he hugged his abdomen after being stabbed.

"Sir, if I may . . . ?" The low voice of Dr. Hilton drew his attention.

"Yes?"

"You offered to allow me to look more closely at the body. With your permission, I'll have it taken to my office, and I can do my examination there. And then you can allow the people to come through here."

"Yes, of course. But how will you get it there?"

"My wagon is outside. I use it for transporting patients."

Adam didn't hesitate. He didn't know any other physicians in town to ask or trust for such a task, and instinct told him the body should be looked at carefully — and as soon as possible — before it was prepared for burial. Just as finding a mauled rabbit in the woods could tell the tale of what predator had had its way — and when and how

— so, perhaps, could a close examination of a human body. "Yes, I think that would be best, and quickly. Shall I help you?"

The two men carefully wrapped Custer Billings back in the tablecloth. Elizabeth Keckley opened the exterior door, holding it as they easily carried the body out into the night.

"Thank you," Adam said, offering his good, right hand to Hilton. The man hesitated a fraction before taking it in a firm handshake, but looked him in the eye as he did so. "I'll visit tomorrow to see if you've found anything in the examination."

Once again, Hilton seemed surprised, but just as quickly masked it. "I'm in the First Ward. Ballard's Alley. Go around Great Eternity Church to the door in the back." He hesitated, then added, "It's all right if I — well, I'll have to cut him to do a thorough examination."

"Do whatever you need to do," Adam replied, quelling a pang of apprehension. The president of the United States had put him in charge of the investigation. A man had been murdered only yards away from him. Adam wouldn't dance around sensitivities. He had a job to do.

"I'll be careful as I can," Hilton said. "Come early tomorrow. I'll be up all night.

Body's not going to get any fresher." There might have been a slight twitch of humor behind the neat mustache, or it might have been a grimace.

"I'll be there soon as I can," Adam said, glancing toward the east, which was still dark with night. "Might be dawn."

Hilton and Mrs. Keckley drove off in the wagon and left Adam to go back inside, where, as promised, the less helpful Pinkerton agent was just about to open the door to the room.

A few stragglers from the ball wandered through, but no one seemed to be aware that the room had been closed off. Instead, they were far too engaged in excited conversation about the ball to do more than chatter as they passed through, obviously en route to City Hall, where there were lounges in which to freshen up.

Adam was staring at the floor where Billings's body had been, reimagining it and its position, when he noticed a faint dark smudge.

He knelt, swiped a finger over the small black stain. No. It wasn't dirt, mud, or horse dung — all of which were plentiful in the square behind City Hall. At first he thought it was shoe black, but when he rubbed it between his fingers, he discovered it was greasy. He sniffed it. Oil.

He looked around and noticed two more traces of oil, closer to the exterior door. And there was a third one, slightly darker than the others, right next to the wall by the door.

Someone had walked into the anteroom with a trace of oil on his or her shoe. It had happened recently, for there weren't any shoe prints on top of any of the smudges except near the doorway.

He stood and looked around the room, noticing the faint trail of dusty footprints, the clumps of muddy ones near the door, and the hardly noticeable oily smudges. The swath of dusty footprints — made by the majority of traffic — were a distinct path from exterior entrance across the room at the shortest distance to the door to the dance hall corridor. Easy to tell where most people had gone.

There were traces of mud near the outside door and a few crumbles near where Billings had been found. The body had not been in the direct pathway across the room, however. It had been slightly off to one side, where there were few footprints and the regular traffic didn't pass. Where the closet was. There were some muddy traces mingling with the dusty prints, but there were also some small crumbles near the site of the body.

But it was the oily smudges that really snagged his attention. They were recent, and unmarred by overstepping prints except the one nearest the door, and the three stains made a direct path from the outside to where the body had been. Off the beaten path.

Whether the oil had anything to do with the stabbing of Custer Billings, he didn't know. But it was curious. How and why would someone have oil on the bottom of his or her shoe?

Adam frowned, closing his eyes to picture the scene and the activity around it. Just as Ishkode had taught him to do when reading natural signs in the woods, he watched the tracks being made, seeing the activity in his mind, *being* there.

He was deep in his imagination when the door slammed. Adam's eyes flew open.

"Agent Pierce. What happened?"

The young man was slightly out of breath. "Mr. Quinn . . . I'm sorry, but he gave me the slip. The reporter. He was walking past the Smithsonian building, and then suddenly he was gone."

Adam stifled a sigh. So his conscience had been eased, but his curiosity had not. "Thank you."

"Is there anything else I can do?" asked Pierce. "Since I'm not working on any case right now, Mr. Pinkerton told me I was to help you with anything you wanted."

"I don't know." Adam resisted the urge to rub his forehead. He needed to think. He needed to get away from people and think. "Maybe, to start, you can ask around discreetly to see when was the last time anyone saw Custer Billings. And if anyone saw him leave the dance hall with anyone else."

Pierce nodded eagerly, but they both knew it was an insurmountable task to try to speak to hundreds of people — some of whom might already have left the ball.

"And where can I reach you tomorrow if I think of anything else?" Adam asked.

Pierce gave him his address, which seemed to be at one of the boardinghouses in town.

The door from the dance hall opened and Adam's uncle walked in. "The president has gone home," he said without prelude, speaking to the room at large. "We thought it best, under the circumstances, that he cut his time here short."

"I'm surprised he agreed to that," Adam commented, knowing how difficult it had been to get Lincoln to agree to change his travel plans through Baltimore, despite all of the evidence of a plan to assassinate him.

Joshua pursed his lips. "Pinkerton and Scott didn't give him much choice, but I think he acquiesced mainly because he's exhausted — and he has an enormous amount of work to do. Mrs. Lincoln remains, however. I expect she'll dance till dawn. She's been waiting for this night for years." He gave a small smile that in no way indicated a sour feeling, even if there was one. He, along with Adam, was well acquainted with Mary Lincoln's longtime political aspirations for her husband. "Abe wants to meet with you first thing in the morning, Adam."

"Yes. All right." Adam swiftly corralled his scattered thoughts.

He knew his honorary uncle well enough to know that first thing meant seven o'clock, and that he would expect a well-organized, thorough report.

He just wished he knew on what he was going to make his report.

Oil on the bottom of someone's shoes wasn't quite enough to satisfy.

As the inaugural ball raged on only a short distance away, Adam reviewed what he knew about the murder from the crime scene, then set about to gather more information regarding the victim. That seemed the best place to start: What sort of man was Custer Billings, and who would want to kill him?

Fortunately, Mr. Pinkerton — who, along with General Scott and a tight contingent of soldiers, had left to escort the president back home — had already determined Billings's address and identified one of his companions at the ball. Agent Pierce hadn't returned with the results of his interviews, but Joshua Speed had some information.

"So Mrs. Billings isn't here tonight?" Adam asked. From what he'd gleaned, no woman in Washington City would voluntarily miss the celebration — especially if her husband was invited.

"She is not," Joshua told him. "But the news of her husband's death will have to be delivered to her." He looked at Adam meaningfully.

Unfortunately, Adam had had more experience with that sort of task than he liked, having brought similar news to many family members of those who'd lost their lives fighting in the Bloody Kansas wars.

It was bad enough, the battles that had raged in a single state between the proslavery men and the Free-Staters like himself and the soon-to-be Senator Jim Lane. . . . What would happen if — no, unfortunately, *when* — the entire nation went to war?

The battles on the frontier over whether to allow slavery to extend into Kansas had been brutal and ugly, violent and vitriolic. How much worse would it be when states that already allowed slavery felt their way of life threatened? Since December, seven had announced secession from the Union, and created the capital of the Confederate States of America.

The battle lines were already drawn. War would come. No one doubted, though all dreaded it, for Lincoln would do whatever must be done to preserve the Union. And when the battles began, the entire nation would surely be as brutalized as Adam's adopted home state. Kansas was only a taste of what would happen to the whole country.

"I'll pay Mrs. Billings a visit tomorrow morning, then. After I meet with the president," he told his uncle. "No need to awaken her with bad news over something that cannot be changed. Perhaps she'll get one last good night's sleep."

Josh gripped his arm with fatherly affection, unerringly choosing the limb that was actually sensate. "I take that to mean you aren't yet sleeping yourself."

"In a city like this, filled with noise at all

hours of the night?" Adam joked. "Not at all. Which is why I don't expect to seek my bed until near dawn this morning."

Perhaps by then he'd be so exhausted he would be able to sleep. Maybe it was a good thing his honorary uncle had given him this task. It would keep his mind and body busy.

"Good luck, Adam. I know you can handle this. Abe trusts you implicitly, which is more than can be said for ninety-five percent of the people in this town." His expression turned grim. "By God, if he lives out the year, it'll be a miracle."

Adam couldn't help but agree, and a pang of sorrow filled his heart as he thought of their friend's dear, craggy face. He'd seen the vitriolic letters and posters that had been sent to Lincoln since the election had ended. Threats of assassination were everywhere, even here in the capital.

Especially in the capital.

Washington was a thoroughly Southern city, filled with slave owners and secessionists, and sandwiched between the two slave states of Virginia and Maryland. And though Lincoln had given no indication that he intended to free the slaves in his new city, the fear and expectation that this was a foregone conclusion bubbled everywhere.

With a heavy heart, Adam went off to find

Mr. Billings's business associate, a man named James Delton, who he'd been told was waiting for him in one of the offices at the City Hall.

"What's going on here?" said Delton when Adam introduced himself. "Who are you? Why did that Pinkerton man tell me to wait here? My wife is going to yank my ears off if I don't get back to dance with her." He gestured with a walking stick to emphasize his frustration.

"Mr. Lincoln has asked me to speak with you about Custer Billings."

"Mr. Lincoln? What's this about Billings? Is he even still here? I thought he went home, left early. Not much of a dancer without his wife to insist on it, and — did something happen?" Delton seemed to read the gravity in Adam's face, for he calmed a little.

"Mr. Billings was killed tonight. Here, at the ball. I reckoned you should know, being his friend."

Delton's eyes widened and he sank back into the chair he'd vacated during his vociferous speech. He removed his top hat and thrust a hand into thinning light brown hair, making it stand on end. "Dear God. Poor Custer. He was killed? How? Carriage accident? Poor Althea."

"He was murdered," Adam told him.

"*Murdered?* How? Here?" Delton's face flushed above his mutton chops, then drained to the color of chalk.

"Unfortunately, yes. He was stabbed." Adam saw no reason to hide the truth; he suspected it wouldn't be long before the news got out anyway. "Do you know anyone who might have wanted to kill Mr. Billings?"

Delton shook his head, his eyes still bulging. "No," he whispered. "I can't think of anyone."

"When did you see him last?"

"Um . . ." The other man's eyes lost focus as he concentrated. "It wasn't long after Mr. and Mrs. Lincoln arrived. I shook the president's hand and introduced my wife, and then Billings and I were talking for a bit before he excused himself. Dear God. That was the last time I'll ever speak to him."

Adam had arrived with the president's party just before eleven, and it had been hardly more than an hour later when the body was found. That was a fairly small window of time.

"Did you see Mr. Billings leave the dance hall? Was he with anyone?"

"No, I didn't notice anything like that. It

was so crowded in the room. I lost track of him after a while — so many people to talk to, you know."

"Did he seem upset or agitated at all?" Adam had the same sensation he did when feeling his way through an unfamiliar room in the dark: unsure of where he was going, but determined to get there without stubbing a toe.

Delton shook his head. "He seemed the same as always — a little quiet, but cordial."

"Thank you. And — I reckon I should have asked you this first — how do you know Mr. Billings?"

"I'm a lawyer. I've handled his business arrangements. Paperwork, contracts, the like."

"And Mr. Billings? He's a banker?"

Delton looked surprised. "Why, yes. He's the Billings of Billings Bank & Trust — over there on Seventh Street. Been in business since the city was rebuilt after the Brits came in and burned it down. He liked to tell how his father financed some of the construction of the new Treasury Building."

"You said you don't know of anyone who might have a grudge against him, but I reckon I should get the names of his other close friends and colleagues. Along with people who might be in arrears with the bank, or anyone you know who did a lot of business with Mr. Billings." Adam realized belatedly that he had neither paper nor a pencil with which to write the names.

Fortunately, they were in a clerk's office, and he was able to locate a sheaf of paper in the desk drawer as well as a pencil. The lead tip was dull, but it would suffice, and Delton took it to note down the names of the people. He paused after a few lines, staring down at the list.

"Is something wrong?" Adam asked.

Delton pursed his lips but didn't look up. Then he sighed, as if making a formidable decision. "I've . . . well, I've noticed that Custer was . . . shall we say, friendly . . . with Annabelle Titus — she's married to Mortimer Titus — but I don't know that it's anything more than that. It's not even a suspicion on my part. But they — well, I've seen them together quite often. Even tonight, earlier, I saw them together."

"And if what you saw might be more than simple friendship, Titus might have had a grudge against Billings. Was he here tonight as well?"

Delton sighed and nodded, and Adam watched as he wrote *Mortimer Titus* roughly on the paper, as if it was the last thing he wanted to do. "But even if it was true, he wouldn't *kill* him. I know Titus. He's not — he wouldn't. He wouldn't do that." He thrust the paper at Adam. "I don't know that this is going to help. It was probably some random thug who saw Custer walking back to the dance from City Hall and thought he'd rob him. It's dark out there in the square, and once the president arrived, hardly anyone left the dance. They didn't want to miss anything. A thug could have sneaked up and jumped him. Custer wasn't a very big man. He'd be easy to overpower."

"Thank you. And if you think of anything else, send word to me, Adam Quinn, at Willard's Hotel." When Delton looked at him curiously, he felt compelled to add, "Mr. Lincoln has asked me to investigate the murder."

"Better you than the damned constabulary," Delton said, standing. His face was set with grief and anger. "Nice enough uniforms, but worthless for hardly anything other than whipping niggers and accepting bribes. Did you know my wife and I were almost late for the ball tonight because our driver wanted to stop so he could help the constables whip a black man?"

Adam didn't know what to say to that, but something soured in the back of his mouth. What sort of city was this? "Thank

76

you, Mr. Delton. I'm sorry for the loss of your friend."

Delton paused with his hand on the doorknob. "Does Althea — Mrs. Billings — know?"

"Not yet. I'll be paying her a visit in a few hours."

"Sad business," he said, shaking his head. "My wife will want to visit her tomorrow, I'm sure. So tragic, for both of them." He was just about to walk out the door when he hesitated once more. "Give Mr. Lincoln my regards, will you? James Delton, attorney at law." He dug out a business card and offered it to Adam. "Maybe you could pass this on to him too. Never know if he might need a Unionist lawyer who knows his way around Washington City — even being one himself." He offered a crooked smile.

"I'll do that. Again, I'm sorry for your loss."

Once Delton left, Adam looked at the list of business associates he'd provided. None of the names were familiar to him — but there was no reason they should be. Adam had been in the district for only two weeks, and he'd been cloistered with Mr. Lincoln and his personal security team — most of whom were close friends, such as Adam and his uncle — at Willard's since arriving. He'd not even ventured out to visit a pub, instead staying mostly inside at the busy hotel, which was lavishly decorated with brass, crystal, and red velvet.

With a flash of annoyance, Adam realized he'd forgotten to ask James Delton if he knew Hurst Lemagne, and why Billings would have had his business card in his trouser pocket. Lemagne's name wasn't on the list Delton had left.

Adam realized he had no choice but to brave the crush of the dance hall once again. He had to find Hurst Lemagne. The sooner, the better — for all he knew, Lemagne could be planning to follow in the exodus of his fellow Southerners and return to Alabama right away.

Which meant, Adam reckoned with a surprising niggle of interest, that he had a very good excuse to seek out the blue-eyed southern belle once again.

Constance Lemagne had the feeling something was wrong.

It wasn't just that she hadn't seen her daddy since supper — which had been served in the room adjoining the dance hall — and that he'd left her almost to fend for herself in this jam of a party. And it wasn't that he'd been so . . . tense and ill tempered lately — even for him.

No, her feminine intuition told her there was something else happening, and the back of her bare neck prickled.

Something was wrong. Something had happened.

That *something* had caused the very interesting and almost handsome Mr. Quinn not to return with the lemonade for which she'd actually been quite desperate, along with the excuse to keep him at her side for a little longer. Whatever it was had taken him and his rangy self to the dais where the president and his entourage had entered, and where a cluster of men still stood.

Constance was tall for a woman, and because of that, she'd been able to watch the even taller Mr. Quinn abruptly turn from his path to fetch her lemonade.

Instead of navigating to the drinks table, he'd turned and begun to push his way through the crowd toward the dais. The man had very nearly been running, his long legs eating up the space quickly and efficiently.

When he'd levered his lanky body up and onto the platform with hardly a hitch in his step, her stomach had given a little flutter of appreciation for the graceful movement.

And when he had been quickly absorbed into the group of men standing there with grave expressions, including that of the new president, she had been even more intrigued.

Who was he?

Everyone back home in Alabama said that Abraham Lincoln was an uncivilized railsplitter (and they used that term with derision) who would destroy the Union, and that he hadn't the first idea of how to move about in society or to entertain properly — let alone work with Congress and lead the country. The topics of secession and war had been a source of conversation at dinner since the man was elected, along with laughter and insults about the strange-looking frontiersman who thought to be president.

If the new president was considered uncivilized, Constance wondered what the ladies back home would think about Mr. Quinn. At least Lincoln didn't look as if he were choking behind his tall, tight collar, and the new president appeared quite at home — though a bit awkward in appearance — dressed in the fine clothing he wore. Constance's dance partner, on the other hand, had seemed as uncomfortable in his dress coat and top hat as a yellow-striped snake about to shed its skin.

Mr. Quinn had mentioned coming from the new state of Kansas, and his appearance was just like Constance imagined a man recently off the frontier would look: with too long, almost shaggy hair; a tan, rugged face that obviously spent much time in the sun; and an unpolished manner. The only thing that surprised her was that he sported neither a mustache nor a beard.

Why a man would make the effort to shave his face but not to cut his hair, Constance couldn't imagine. But she could also admit it suited him, with his square jaw bare, a subtle dimple in his chin, and an upper lip free of the fringe of hair common on most every other man.

He'd talked to the president and the other men up there, and then he'd left the platform. She'd stood on her toes and tried to catch a glimpse through the curtained entryway through which he'd disappeared, but she couldn't see anything. And though she had been tempted to follow Mr. Quinn, Constance had been unintentionally dissuaded by an elderly man who'd arrived with a glass of lemonade for her.

He had cotton-like white hair and a formal, erect carriage, and he'd wielded his walking stick expertly. After gallantly introducing himself as Mr. King, he'd offered Mr. Quinn's regrets at being pulled away from a "very delightful task to a less pleasant one." Constance had suspected those were Mr. King's words, not Mr. Quinn's.

But now it was more than an hour since Mr. Quinn had been summoned to the platform and disappeared, and to her regret, she still hadn't seen the dark-haired frontiersman return to the ballroom.

Mr. Lincoln had left his own celebration already — why so soon? — and she couldn't help but wonder if the elusive Mr. Quinn had gone with him.

Why had the president left so early? Something was definitely wrong.

"Miss Lemagne, I've been looking all over for you!"

As she spun, Constance nearly lost her balance, for she'd been standing on her tiptoes in hopes of seeing her quarry.

"Have you truly?" she managed to say, though inside she was berating herself for having been distracted long enough to let Arthur Mossing sneak up on her.

Mr. Mossing was the son of the man who'd been her father's close friend and business associate. Mr. Mossing Senior had died several years ago, and Daddy had bought the man's robust textile business.

That was why they were here in Washington, for he made regular trips to meet with contacts in Congress and other associates in the government. It had something to do with trade and tariffs. This was Constance's first trip accompanying him, and she'd almost begun to regret coming — for Daddy had been very blunt about his desire that the Lemagne and Mossing families should be united through marriage in the same way their businesses had become one.

That was a desire with which Constance did not concur.

Oh, drat it. Why couldn't it have been the rangy, interesting, almost scruffy Mr. Quinn who'd sought her out — instead of the prim and perfect Arthur Mossing?

"Why, Mr. Mossing," she said, "I've been here the whole time. You seem to have been the one who disappeared." She exaggerated her accent and even simpered a little, snapping open her fan to wave it briskly while she considered escape options.

"Well, it is quite a jam," Mr. Mossing said a little more firmly. He frowned suddenly and adjusted his coat sleeve, yanking it down and straightening his shirt cuff. She'd come to learn this was a man very particular about his appearance. Perhaps it was because he was a lawyer, and often spoke in front of judges and juries. Or perhaps he simply wanted to give off the impression he was richer than he was. Thus, it had been with almost malicious delight that she'd pointed out during their first (and only) dance that his Union cockade had a small stain on the white ribbon. She was only slightly mollified that he'd removed it, but why he'd even worn it in the first place while escorting them when he knew her father was a secessionist — and of course Constance was as well — she didn't know. Even though tonight was a celebration for the new *Unionist* president, Mr. Mossing didn't have to be so blatant about his sympathies.

As Constance was a Southerner through and through, his political sympathies were yet another check mark against him when it came to marriage. Well, besides his position as merely a lawyer, and the fact that his hair was always pomaded into helmet-stiff waves, and the fact that he always dominated the conversation, speaking over her. . . . There were far too many check marks against Arthur Mossing to consider him for her husband.

Having finished straightening his coat, Mr. Mossing offered her an arm — which she ignored. "I told your papa I'd watch over you tonight, and I've hardly had the chance to speak to you." His pale blue eyes glinted with irritation; then the annoyance faded as he swept his gaze over her, lingering a bit too long over her bosom and not bothering to hide the fact.

"Oh, yes, of course. I had to visit the ladies' tiring room to fix my hem," she lied, opening her fan in front of her bodice to obscure his view. "Perhaps that was when you were looking for me."

"By my count, you've missed two of our dances already."

"I didn't see you when it was time for either of them," she replied primly — not even sure when the supposed dances were.

"And who was that man you were dancing with during the reel a while back? The tall one? I was supposed to have the third dance —"

"Why, Mr. King! How kind of you to remember my lemonade!" Constance waved a little wildly, then fairly bolted toward the elderly man, heedlessly squeezing herself and her hoops between two startled gentlemen. She felt the cage holding her skirts tip up a bit and welcomed the brief gust of fresh air under the layers upon layers of fabric she wore.

Mr. King — who more than an hour ago

had brought her the lemonade Mr. Quinn had originally promised — was no doubt startled, and possibly confused, by her exclamation.

But his sharp gray eyes gleamed with unabashed delight as he handed her the cup of lemonade that had, most likely, been for himself. "Of course, Miss Lemagne. How could I forget? And who is this young man forging through the crowd in your wake?" Though surely older than seventy, with gnarled hands that shook a trifle, Mr. King obviously possessed a mind that was as crisp as a January night in Mobile.

"I'm Miss Lemagne's fiancé," Mr. Mossing said, taking her arm firmly. "Arthur Mossing, Esquire."

Constance was so shocked by his bold pronouncement that she gaped for a moment, then quickly took a sip of lemonade to collect her thoughts. Before she did, her mama had drilled southern, ladylike manners into her head. And so instead of calling him a liar outright, she contented herself with pulling out of his grip.

"Mr. Mossing, though I'm honored you should think of me that way, I do believe it's a bit premature to make such an announcement." She hooded her eyes so he wouldn't see the ire flashing there. Her mama insisted that a lady should never countermand a gentleman in public, no matter how politely she might do so, but Constance wasn't going to ignore his presumption. The pompous *duck* hadn't even asked her to marry him, let alone courted her.

Not that she was interested in entertaining either option.

"Now, now, darling . . . you know it's only a matter of formality until we do make an announcement." He smiled down at her with affection, though there was a bit of steel behind his eyes. Apparently, he sided with her mama when it came to having his statements countermanded in public. "Your father and mine talked about joining our families for years before my father died." His mouth compressed slightly as it always did when the subject of his father came up. She wondered, not for the first time, why the younger Mossing hadn't wanted to take over the family business. Perhaps he thought it would be more beneficial to be a lawyer in a city of politicians and power.

Constance glanced at Mr. King, who was watching her from beneath raised wiry gray brows as if to see what her next volley would be. "But, Mr. Mossing, you know I . . ."

She trailed off, for Adam Quinn had just

appeared at the edge of the dance floor. He seemed to be looking around the room. Was it possible he was searching for her?

Constance turned her attention back to her determined suitor and fanned herself vigorously, suddenly feeling quite warm in her cheeks. "Oh, yes, of course, Mr. Mossing. My daddy would simply *love* for us to — oh *dear*!" She jolted. "Oh, Mr. Mossing, I'm so sorry! I'm so terribly, *terribly* sorry."

It was a calculated move, one Constance had practiced and perfected many times in the company of her best friend, Betsy-Anne: a foolproof escape plan when one was trapped in a conversation one needed to exit.

One must have a glass of some libation — the larger and the more full, the better — and be very energetic and enthusiastic about the conversation topic at hand. And then, as one flung oneself into an enthusiastic speech, one did the same with the drink — smoothly, but with perfect aim — so that it splashed all down the front of the unwanted suitor.

A variation on the escape plan was to generously slosh the entire cup down one's own bodice, but that wouldn't work in this situation, and was only to be used in dire circumstances, or when the beverage in question wouldn't stain. For Constance didn't want to leave the dance — as she would have to, if she were wearing lemonade. She wanted to speak to Mr. Quinn.

Her insistent suitor was spluttering — she'd managed to get a good portion of lemonade on his chin, which was covered by a beard and would soon become sticky and smell of pungency — and Mr. King charged into the fray by whipping out a handkerchief and dabbing helpfully at the other man's soaked shirt and waistcoat. It was particularly effective, because Mr. Mossing was always so proper about his attire and the way he looked.

Despite her satisfaction with the results of her actions, Constance managed to keep a horrified look on her face while continuing to apologize profusely — though, at the same time, she was also attempting to watch Mr. Quinn's movements. She even managed to manufacture a few tears as well, though they were from mirth instead of embarrassment.

"Never mind," Mr. Mossing said tightly, stepping away from the fluttering handkerchief. He gave Mr. King a look as sour as the beverage he was wearing and said, "I'll be fine. I've plenty of shirts, though my waistcoat . . . it's new, and I don't know if it can survive, blast — er, right. But never mind, Constance dear, I'll tend to it quickly and I'll be back before you realize I was gone." He patted her hand. "Don't be so upset, my sweet. Accidents do happen. Now, wait for me here, and I'll be back soon."

"Nicely done," Mr. King murmured to her as Mr. Mossing pushed off through the crowd. "Shall I get you a replacement beverage, Miss Lemagne?" His eyes glittered with appreciation and humor.

"Oh, no thank you, sir," she replied, resisting the urge to pat down a flyaway wisp of hair at the top of his skull. Being long-legged herself, and Mr. King short and wizened, Constance had a clear view of scalp through his thinning cloud of white hair. "But I must beg your pardon now and take your leave, kind sir."

He smiled, patting her hand with a wrinkled one. "Of course you must. Give Mr. Quinn my best regards."

With pink cheeks and a smile, she started off through the crowd as quickly as she could without exposing her ankles and pantalettes to all and sundry from beneath her unwieldy cage of skirts.

But she was on the other side of the dance floor from where she'd seen him, and by the time she made it around to the opposite side, squeezing through a crowd of gossiping ladies, the rugged Adam Quinn was gone. . . .

And Arthur Mossing was just coming back into the ballroom, sleek as a groomed horse and with a determined look on his face.

Already? Drat.

If only she could find a place to hide.

If Adam had thought the hall would be less crowded now that the guest of honor had left, and since it was after one o'clock in the morning, he would have been disappointed. If anything, he thought as he stood on the dais where he had first entered in the wake of the president, the room appeared to be even more crowded. It seemed as if no one had yet heard about Custer Billings's tragedy in the anteroom, for surely if the news had spread, there would be some sort of pall over the revelry.

The music was still loud and joyous, and the partygoers were exuberant in dance as well as conversation. The crush didn't appear to have thinned out with the departure of the president; if anything, the revelers seemed even more determined to stay up all night.

Adam saw that Mrs. Lincoln was still present, smiling gaily as her former beau, Senator Douglas, led her through a quadrille in the center of the room. Though relatively short, she stood out, easily identifiable because of the glow of joy that seemed to surround her. Her genuine pleasure emanated from her own person as well as those gathered around her.

But, after staring out over the crowd for far too long in his pinching shoes, Adam realized locating Constance Lemagne in the sea of dancing headdresses and bowing black top hats would be a near impossibility. Perhaps he could even leave the ball in short order. He was a frontiersman — used to going to bed shortly after the sun went down, and getting up when it rose. It was becoming more difficult for him to hide his need to yawn, and he wanted nothing more than to get out of his pinching shoes and to unstrap his prosthetic arm.

Nevertheless, he decided he should remain until half past one; then it would be permissible for him to leave. He leaned against the edge of the dais where Lincoln had been standing when he gave Adam the seemingly impossible task of finding Custer Billings's murderer, idly watching the crowd . . . and thinking.

Adam reckoned that if the story was in the papers, perhaps the article could also include an invitation for anyone who'd seen or noticed anything around the time of Billings's death to contact him. There were too many people at the celebration tonight to interview each of them, even though Agent Pierce was doing his best to speak to at least some of them.

Adam was considering whether it would be worth his while to pay a visit to the *Daily Intelligencer* or one of the other papers to make the request when a breathless voice spoke just behind him.

"Why, Mr. Quinn. That was a very long journey to fetch a simple glass of lemonade."

Somehow, the woman's dulcet accents overrode the pomp of the Marine Band's brassy tune and the accompanying dull roar of party atmosphere, and Adam straightened from his relaxed stance as he turned to greet her.

"Miss Lemagne," he said, angling so his good hand was the one close enough to take her gloved one.

"It's a good thing I wasn't completely parched, or I declare I'd be in a sorry state, like a cotton husk waiting for you to return — all dried up and shriveled beyond recognition. Were you helping to squeeze the lemons yourself, then? Or perhaps you found a line on Miss Corcoran's dance card instead, and my thirst was forgotten?" She looked up at him from beneath thick lashes that were surprisingly dark, considering her whisky-colored hair and ivory skin. Fortunately, she was smiling and not glowering.

"I've had no interest in even looking at any other dance card tonight," he told her gravely. "Nor have I had the honor of fetching lemonade — or even tea — for anyone else. Even myself. I beg your pardon, Miss Lemagne, but I was called away on unexpected business, and only just now have returned. I made arrangements for a gentleman to bring your drink and to make my excuses."

"Oh, yes, Mr. King was extremely attentive, and he begged my pardon for you in a most earnest manner — even going so far as to claim a line on my dance card, though the poor man looked as if he'd fall over in a stiff breeze. Still, I much prefer the real thing, Mr. Quinn. Mr. King doesn't have quite the same . . . anything . . . as you do."

Her fingers were still curled around his from when he'd lifted her hand, and Adam discovered he was in no hurry to release them. She stepped closer, bringing with her a whiff of something floral. The bell of her skirt bumped against his trousers, and she groped automatically with her free hand to keep the hoops from tipping too far up.

"I had given up hope of finding you in this crush, Miss Lemagne," he replied. "And I'm not yet used to society hours. Back home in KT — pardon me, I mean Kansas — I'm usually in bed long before midnight and up with the sun."

"So you were looking for me. I'm delighted to hear that — but surely not to bring my lemonade at this late hour?" she teased, dimples flashing. "For your hands are terribly empty."

Adam's pleasure ebbed. "I'm afraid the lemonade is long forgotten, Miss Lemagne. I was searching for you for an entirely different reason."

Her eyebrows rose as she looked at him from beneath her headdress. One of its pink roses was sagging a little. "I can hardly breathe with anticipation, Mr. Quinn," she said, still in that flirtatious voice. But he thought he saw a flash of concern or fear in her eyes and her fingers tightened a little in his grip.

"I need to speak with your father. It's a matter of some urgency."

The jesting light faded from her eyes. "You need to speak with Daddy? Is something wrong?" She pulled her gloved hand away.

"Yes. Would you be so kind as to point him out to me — or, even better, to introduce us?"

"I would very much like to do that, Mr. Quinn," she replied. "But I'm afraid I cannot. I haven't seen my daddy for hours. What's happened?"

"He left you all alone for this long?"

"I'm not exactly alone, am I?" She gestured to the hundreds of people around them. "And father and I came with the Madisons — yes, *those* Madisons — and Mr. Mossing, who seems to know most everyone. I confess I've been avoiding him all evening, even though, as you saw, he signed up on my dance card." Though she continued to jest, Adam noticed the tension in her expression and that worry lingered in her eyes.

Then she seemed to realize there was no reason to continue her charade, for she continued, "I have no idea where Daddy has gone off to, and, quite honestly, I'm becoming worried. Something's happened, hasn't it? I saw you go away, and — is everything all right?"

By now, Adam had eased Miss Lemagne off to the edge of the room at a relatively quiet spot. A red, white, and blue bunting shivered against the wall next to them.

"You're worried about him. Is there a particular reason?"

She looked over his shoulder, as if to seek an answer in the crowd. "I heard him arguing with someone earlier today, before we left the hotel to come here. It sounded . . . well, the words weren't quite fit for the ears of a lady," she said with a wry twist of her lips. "Daddy seemed distracted and even worried all day. And not long after we arrived, he disappeared. I haven't seen him since."

Adam was torn between disgust with Hurst Lemagne for leaving his beautiful daughter unattended all evening — except by the unfortunate Mr. Mossing — and a growing concern that something was very wrong concerning her father. "We need to find him." He released her hand and automatically offered his left arm, purposely keeping his good one unencumbered.

"Has something happened?" she asked once again, curving her fingers around the crook of his elbow. Her planted feet and gentle grip kept him from leading her off right away, and she looked up at him. "You seem far too serious, Mr. Quinn."

He hesitated. Then, like she had obviously done, decided honesty was the best option. She'd find out soon enough anyway. "Only

97

a few people are aware, but a man was found dead tonight."

Her face drained of color. "Daddy."

"No, it's not your father," Adam said immediately. "It's a man named Custer Billings."

"Mr. Billings is dead? No. Oh, no." The southern inflection in her voice grew stronger with her distress. "But how?"

"What is it?" Adam asked. "Do you know him?"

"No, I don't know him . . . but . . . Oh, Mr. Quinn, Custer Billings was the man my father was arguing with today."

CHAPTER 4

After Miss Lemagne's unexpected announcement, Adam led her out of the ballroom. He offered to help her search for her father in City Hall and the area outside the two buildings.

They passed through the anteroom where the body had been found (which he didn't mention to her) and went outside, moving along the wooden walkway between City Hall and the dance hall. It was rather chilly out, and Adam was acutely aware of how much skin Miss Lemagne's low-cut bodice left exposed to the cool night air. Surely she was quite cold. He was about to offer his coat when she spoke. "How did Mr. Billings die? Do you know what happened?"

"He was stabbed."

She stumbled, her white face even more pale as she stared up at him. "Stabbed? Someone *killed* him — right here?"

"Unfortunately, yes. Miss Lemagne, do

you know what your father and he were arguing about?"

She shook her head. The moonlight glinted off her smooth, shiny hair and frosted the roses anchored there. A soft floral scent wafted up with her movement. "No. I couldn't quite hear them. They were —"

"Miss Lemagne! Where are you going?"

The peremptory male voice halted Adam, and he turned. His companion exhaled in frustration and probably would have kept walking on the plank path if he hadn't stopped. Though he didn't hear what she muttered, he thought it might have been something very unladylike.

"Miss Lemagne, what do you think you're doing? Where are you going? And who are you?" The man who was striding toward them appeared none too happy with the situation, and for a moment, Adam almost expected him to take a swing at him when he got close enough.

"Miss Lemagne is looking for her father," he told the man, speaking mildly. "I reckoned it would be better to escort her than to leave her wandering around City Hall and the square alone at night."

"I'll escort her." The man, who Adam had by now figured was the elusive Mr. Mossing, was tall — but Adam was taller, and therefore Mossing was forced to look up at him; something he probably rarely needed to do. He was Adam's age and had a full, neatly combed set of mutton chop whiskers and thick, shiny hair that brushed his collar from beneath his top hat. He was, Adam thought, what was known as a dandy: dressed primly and expensively, and carried himself just as stiffly as the walking stick in his hand.

Curiously, he also smelled faintly of lemonade.

"Miss Lemagne is my fiancée," Mossing added, taking her arm.

Adam managed to hide his reaction to this unexpected and completely unforeshadowed statement. The woman next to him stiffened, and he put a little more space between them. Last thing he needed was to get between a man and his fiancée. "Adam Quinn," he said, and offered his hand to shake the other's.

"Arthur Mossing, Esquire. Of the law offices of Strubert, Blackmore, and Mossing." He switched his walking stick to the other hand and offered Adam a brief, gloved handshake. "Constance, darling, I'm certain Hurst must have returned to the St. Charles. Perhaps he was feeling ill and couldn't locate you to tell you he was leaving. I know how difficult it is to find someone in this jam. Mother and the Madisons are ready to leave, and they're all waiting in the carriage. You need to be escorted back to your hotel, of course." He looked down at her with what passed for an indulgent smile and offered his arm.

Miss Lemagne drew in a sharp breath, and for a moment Adam thought she might argue. But then she gave a soft sigh of acquiescence, and, with an apologetic glance at Adam, she said, "Thank you for your assistance, Mr. Quinn. I suppose Mr. Mossing is right — most likely my father has returned to our hotel." She held his eyes for a moment too long, as if sending him a silent message.

But whatever she meant to telegraph to him, he didn't know. Adam went to tip his hat and realized it was long gone — left in the office where he'd interviewed Mr. Delton. "Good evening, Miss Lemagne. Pleasure to meet you, Mr. Mossing."

After they went off, Adam decided there was little else for him to do while it was yet dark.

Grateful for a reason to escape, he left the festivities and walked the three blocks back to the room he shared with his uncle on the second floor at Willard's. Joshua wasn't there; presumably he was with his friend at the Executive Mansion, and Adam was more than happy to take off his stiff shoes, undress, unfasten his wooden arm, and seek his bed without the need for conversation.

Though the mattress was a far sight more comfortable than the straw ticking on which he slumbered back home, and the bed coverings smelled fresh and even a little sweet, Adam found it difficult to sleep.

And when he finally did so, he awoke a short time later drenched with cold sweat, heart pounding, and his arm — the arm that had been missing for almost two years — shrieking with the agony of split skin, shattered bone, and frayed muscle.

He lay there for a while, fighting off the remnants of the dream, gritting his teeth against the raw pain from a phantom limb, wishing he were back in Lawrence — or even Springfield — where he could hear silence instead of clip-clopping hooves, shouts, and various metallic clinks and clangs at all hours . . . where he could smell fresh grass and wood smoke, and where he could look out and see nothing but shimmering switchgrass and cerulean sky for eternity.

But even back in Lawrence, it would be

strange and empty. Tom and Mary, along with their son Carl, were gone. And Adam was no longer the man he'd been when he knew them and dandled the little boy on his knee while showing him how to draw the bow over his fiddle. Of course, now Adam could no longer play the fiddle, and his grandfather's instrument sat unused, wrapped in soft cloth, and stowed in the bottom of his small trunk.

Now that he was awake, Adam heard the soft snores of his uncle rasping in the beginning of dawn's light. Apparently Josh had let himself in during the brief time his nephew slumbered. Adam took care to be grim and silent as a wraith when he slid from his fancy bed.

When Mr. Lincoln and his party had arrived at the Willard in the dead of night, a rich New Yorker had been removed from his suite of rooms on the second floor so the Lincoln party could take over Parlor Six and the rooms attached to it — which included an indoor toilet and water pump.

Still unused to such a luxury as indoor plumbing, Adam finished his morning ablutions without taking time for the water to heat. Happy to be rid of the tight shoes, stiff collar, and restrictive neckcloth of his evening clothes, he strapped on his prosthetic, then dressed as he normally did: in a worn, cowhide vest and simple cotton shirt he was able to pull on without fussing with buttons.

On the bottom, he wore black trousers tucked into worn boots. The boots at least were practical for traverse along the muddy, offal-strewn streets of the city. It had taken him some time to learn how to tie them using his false fingers, but now it was surprisingly easy.

Adam set his wide-brimmed hat on damp, unruly hair that Joshua had suggested — in vain — he cut before the Union Ball, and considered the overcoat he'd brought with him from home. Its hem was becoming frayed and a button dangled a little too much, but it had large enough pockets to easily conceal his Navy Colt so he didn't have to wear a gun belt. Plus, the fabric smelled pleasantly like prairie smoke.

Last night, he'd cleaned the knife that had been found in the closet near Custer Billings's body and wrapped it safely in an oilcloth. Now he tucked it into his knapsack. He had the idea it might be helpful for Dr. Hilton to look at it.

Adam also meant to see if anyone could identify its owner, for the end of the hilt had a distinctive design. It was an unexceptional weapon except for the simple handle fashioned of black ivory. The end of the grip was capped by a hemisphere of opaque blue stone veined with black, and it was surrounded by tiny black beads. Nice, slightly decorative, definitely unusual enough to be an obvious identifier. Easily small enough to carry in a man's boot — but no one was wearing boots last night to the ball. And the formal dress coats had no pockets, nor were they designed to be closed and buttoned, as Adam had cause to know, so the outline of a dagger could be noticed if it were sheathed and in a trouser pocket. Waistcoat pockets were barely large enough for a pocket watch. So where the murderer had carried his weapon was an intriguing question.

Had the murderer even brought the weapon with him? Or had he come upon it and been compelled to use it for some reason? Or, he reckoned, had the killer secreted it somewhere on the grounds of City Hall or the dance hall? The answer to that question could be important, for it could indicate whether the murder had been planned, or whether it had been committed in a moment of passion.

Who would *plan* to commit a murder at such a public event? The chance of being seen or interrupted would surely make it a foolish choice.

Unless it was *meant* to be public. Like an assassination attempt — or a distraction from one.

Adam's boots made soft clumps as he descended the red carpeted staircase to the high-ceilinged hotel lobby. Crystal chandeliers sparkled from above, their glass pieces clinking like faint chimes as he bounded down the steps. Since it was barely dawn and the society-loving occupants of Willard's weren't likely to rise until midmorning, the common areas of restaurant, lounges, ballroom, barbershop, and other public rooms were empty and still except for the night manager, adding up figures at his desk, and the doorman in his pristine white gloves and navy and white uniform.

Above the ever-present aroma of coal smoke, Adam smelled the faint scent of coffee, and he veered off into a small alcove where he found delicate white cups and a fresh pot of the beverage. He'd become so used to steeped chickory root out west that the real South American beans they ground here in Washington were a treat, and so far he'd never declined an opportunity to have a cup. He felt as if he should be in a hurry — though he wasn't certain why — and the coffee scalded his mouth when he gulped it too soon.

It was too early for the fancy, extensive breakfast the hotel served beginning at eight, but since Adam generally preferred fried eggs to the regular offerings of blancmange and gray slop called pâté de foie gras, he didn't much mind the restaurant being closed.

The Negro doorman greeted Adam as he went out into the brisk March dawn. His words left white puffs in the air as he said, "The omnibus don't be running yet this morning and you ain't goin' find no hackney about now, mister," looking both ways down Pennsylvania Avenue, and around the corner up Fourteenth Street. Adam followed his gaze, pleased to see that the streets were just as empty as the hotel lobby, except for a —

Adam squinted in the pale gray light. "By God, is that a *pig*? Crossing the street up that way?" Surely he was mistaken. A hog walking down Fourteenth Street, proud as you please — only blocks from the President's House and the Capitol Building.

The doorman, who went by Birch, gave a raspy laugh. "Sure be. They like to wallow in the mud behind City Hall."

"They? How many pigs are there walking around the capital?"

Birch shrugged. "Don't rightly know, there, Mr. Quinn, sir. Enough, I s'pose. Where be you headed this morning so early? Usually it's just me and them hogs out here at dawn time, and sometimes a goat too. And the bakers, up yonder on Seventh Street. That smell of bread baking sure makes my insides cry." He grinned, adjusting his cap.

"I'm going up to Ballard's Alley — it's in the First Ward," he said. "To a church."

"A church at Ballard's Alley? What you be wanting with up to there, mister? They don't got services this early, and especially not on a Tuesday."

"I have an appointment. And no need to worry over a carriage. I'll walk." And he'd be happy to do so, though he'd have been happier to ride his horse. But he'd left Stranger back in Springfield when Josh had pressed him into joining the Lincoln party, which traveled by train. Only the Good Lord knew when he'd see him again.

Adam bid Birch good morning and started off in the direction the man had indicated, albeit reluctantly.

"Don' know why you be goin' all the way up to them mad alleys instead of you havin' your appointment come down here — church or no church," the doorman mumbled. "That's what most sane folks do."

Most sane *white* folks, Adam thought as he strode along the two blocks where Pennsylvania Avenue jutted north between the Treasury Department and the grounds of the President's House. The Capitol was at his back, though he couldn't see it because the street had had to bend due to the size of the Treasury.

This was the first time he'd been out of the hotel on his own in the daylight and on the streets since arriving in the city two weeks ago. It was hard to believe it had been that long, but Josh, General Scott, and Mr. Pinkerton kept Adam and the others in the president's private security contingent occupied with keeping the hotel's suite and parlors safe for Lincoln.

On foot for the first time, Adam took in the frontier-like aspects of the city: a sewage canal that ran not far from the most traveled avenue, Pennsylvania, and contributed to its unpleasant odor; the unmaintained cobblestones and thick mud around and in between the street; and, most of all, the amount of livestock that seemed to make its way just as freely along the byways as the human citizens of the district. He saw not only pigs, but a passel of chickens and a cow as well, walking down the street as if it were a barnyard.

This was certainly not what Adam would have expected for the capital of his nation.

All along Pennsylvania Avenue to the north were houses, a few school buildings, and some churches. On the left, or south side, of the main thoroughfare were shanties and poorer structures. Toward the east, from Fourteenth down past Seventh Avenue, was the main business district of the city.

He crossed Lafayette Square, just past the State Department, and the President's Mansion was on his left. Sixteenth Avenue jutted due north from the large statue of Andrew Jackson on his rearing horse, leading into the area of the district known as the First Ward.

By the time he turned north, past the dramatic statue, the sun had risen enough to cast its mellow golden glow over the city's roofs.

The First Ward's residents were a nearly equal mix of whites, blacks — both free and slave — and a recent influx of immigrants, mostly from Ireland and Germany. The wealthiest lived in street-front homes or row houses, but the poorer ones — mostly free blacks and the abhorred Irish Catholics — lived along a warren of narrow, crowded walkways described as "the alleys." The housing they rented was poorly constructed and flimsy.

It was a strange sort of juxtaposition, for, unlike other cities, where the wealthy lived in one area while the poor were relegated to slums, and those who were neither resided in yet a different area, in the First Ward, the rich and underprivileged lived side by side. Or, more accurately, back to front.

If he hadn't been told, Adam wouldn't have suspected that behind the prim brick homes with their small patches of lawn and neat walkways were shacks and other shelters accessed by narrow roads that cut behind the facade of wealth. Some of the passageways were called blind alleys, having no entrance or exit to a main road. These narrowest of the narrow streets could be accessed only via other alleys.

Adam also discovered belatedly that none of the many alleys, blind or otherwise, were marked with street signs. It wasn't until he stopped a scrawny boy carrying a brown hen under his arm and asked for directions that he found his way to Ballard's Alley.

"Great Eternity Church?" said the lad, who was missing a front tooth and wore a coat whose sleeves reached only halfway down his forearms. His nose was red from the chill. "Aye, that's at the head of Ballard's Alley, behind K Street. You see that chimney there, mister? With the tall neck and the black cap? The church is being right in its backyard." His lisp didn't hide the fact that he was Irish.

Adam thanked him and, noting the way a big toe had worn a hole in one of the kid's boots, gave him a quarter. "Much obliged, young man."

"Gor!" he said when he looked at the coin. "Thank you, mister." The hen protested as the boy tucked the money inside his boot — it looked as if the boy squished her as he bent over. "You be still, Bessie," he warned as he straightened. "I ain't got time to be chasing on you again."

"Does Bessie lay eggs?" Adam asked.

Damn, the kid reminded him of his youngest half brother, Danny. Maybe it was the plops of freckles on his cheeks that looked like maple syrup had rained on him, and the way his mud-brown hair stuck up in the back. Unlike Danny, however, the boy didn't seem to have a coat that fit him, or shoes that held in his toes, or even a cap to keep his head warm and dry.

"When she's about wanting to," the boy replied. "Which means, not too often. My mam says she's going to be plucking her for a stew if she don't stop running away and making me have to chase her down every morning insteada doing my chores. But I told her I'm not minding doing the chasing, and that we just *can't* have Bessie for stew. She does lay eggs *sometimes.*"

Adam didn't know why he was lingering in this gray-to-golding light, but something kept him there with the boy and his struggling hen. "What's your name, son?"

"Brian. Brian Mulcahey."

"You got a job? You go to school?"

"Sometimes. Why? You be needing something done with your horses, mister? My pa useda say I got a way with horses." The hen squawked again, and Brian stroked her on the head.

"I don't know. I might be needing a messenger boy." Adam suddenly felt certain he could find use for a messenger boy. "Do you know where Willard's Hotel is?"

"Gor! That's a big place. Fancy." Brian's bright green eyes had gone wide. "Aye, I know where 'tis."

"Can you call there today at noon? And at six o'clock? Ask the doorman if Mr. Quinn left you any message."

"Mr. Quinn. Who's that? Is that you, mister? Aye, I can do that!" The hen protested once more, but Brian didn't pause to soothe her ruffled feathers this time. "Wait till I tell Mam!"

"I'll leave word for you with the doorman," Adam said, then continued on to his destination.

Now that he knew where to go, it wasn't difficult to find the correct alley. As Brian had indicated, Great Eternity Church was near the corner of the street. A white clapboard building, it boasted a large cross perched on the peak of its roof and two small windows on either side of the front door, which was accessed by five steps off the ground. The church, at least, didn't appear ready to blow over in a gust of wind — unlike far too many of the other buildings he'd seen.

Dr. Hilton had told him to go around to the back of the church, and Adam discovered four more steps — this time leading from ground level down to an entrance. Once at the bottom, standing in a small earthen entryway, he knocked at the whitewashed plank door. It rattled in its hinges, but seemed solid.

"Yes. Come in," called a voice.

Adam did as he was bid, and found himself in a spacious cellar. It was cool and would have been dark had it not been lit by at least a dozen lamps and candles.

Dr. Hilton looked up from where he stood, next to a table that held Custer Billings's body. "You're here," the doctor said, making no effort to hide his surprise.

The man wore an oiled-canvas butcher's apron to protect his clothing, and his sleeves were rolled halfway up his generous biceps. A wary look still lingered in Hilton's eyes, but he gave a sharp gesture with his chin for Adam to come in.

"I said I'd come early," Adam replied, stepping across the threshold into the cellar-turned-morgue.

It was an open space with no dividing walls except a single curtain that could be used to block off part of the room for privacy. The curtain was pulled back, exposing what probably passed for a small examination room as needed. But Hilton wasn't working in that area; he was standing at a long table in the center of the room.

Kerosene lamps had been arranged throughout the room, hanging from beams in the low ceiling, arranged on tables and shelves, and one was even suspended on a shepherd's hook–like metal rod directly over Hilton's workstation. This array of lights illuminated the room nearly as well as noon sun on the prairie, though with a hazy golden glow instead of a clean, sharp light.

Shadows spilled into the dark perimeter of the space. The floor was hard packed dirt and there were two small, high windows that allowed for a cross-breeze, praise God.

Custer Billings's naked body was arranged on the table, and he was covered from the bottom of his rib cage to his feet by a dark blanket. His ice-white skin, loose and sallow from a life of leisure, was unmarked except for the two knife wounds: a shallow one on the left side of his rib cage below the underside of a fleshy breast, and in the gut directly below the sternum.

The scent of blood was in the air, but it was faint. It mingled with that of the earth that surrounded the room, along with an antiseptic essence that made Adam's nose want to pinch.

"Early for most of your — for most people," Hilton corrected himself quickly, "is hardly before noon."

"Want me to come back on account of it being early?" Adam asked mildly.

"Oh, no, sir," Hilton said, injecting a deferent tone in his voice. "Not at all. It took longer than I thought to get the lamps set up — had to borrow a bunch of 'em — and I didn't get very far with my examination yet. I didn't want you to feel as if you wasted your time coming all the way here."

"Don't let that concern you. What else would I do at this hour of the day — seeing as all of my kind are still sleeping," Adam said in a dry voice.

Hilton glanced up warily, then seemed to relax when he realized Adam was making a joke. "His clothing and shoes are there, if you want to look through them. I've just finished an external examination and am beginning the internal one."

"Did you find anything helpful?" Adam picked up one of the lamps farthest from the table and brought it with him as he walked over to Billings's personal effects, which included the dress coat found in the closet. He wondered if there would be oil smudges on one of the man's shoes.

"So far, no, sir. I found no unusual marks on his body other than the two stab wounds in the torso. No recent bruises or other cuts. And the lividity — the way the blood sinks to the ground inside the body once it's dead — is right for him being found on the floor there."

"What do you mean?"

"I mean there isn't any sign that Mr. Billings was killed somewhere else, and then later moved to where he was found. If he had been killed somewhere and then left there for a time — at least for an hour or two — then brought to the dance hall, the way the blood pooled in his body might have been different."

"Why would someone kill him somewhere else and then move him to such a busy, public place?" Adam mused aloud.

"I don't claim to understand why people do what they do. And I don't believe anyone would have done it — though I suppose I could come up with a good yarn as to why if I wanted — but, anyway, the examination confirms that it didn't happen. He was killed there — or at least very nearby and left in the anteroom shortly afterward."

Adam nodded. All right. He could appreciate the man's thoroughness. "Was there anything else you noticed?"

"Mr. Billings was wearing gloves, so if he fought or struggled with anyone, there wouldn't be skin, hair, or any other remnants beneath his nails."

"There were some hairs on the fingertips of his gloves." Adam set down his lamp on the table where the clothing had been laid out. But the broad brim of his hat cast a wide shadow over the items, obstructing his light. He removed it and set it aside. "They were short, light brown hairs. Looked like they got stuck to his fingertips with something sticky." He dug inside his knapsack for the envelope where he'd slid the ones he'd found last night adhering to Billings's gloves.

"Mr. Billings has light brown hair," Hilton pointed out, dunking his hands in a basin of water.

"Yes. I'll take some of his hair with me — they could be from his own beard if he scratched his face; the length of them is right for facial hair — and see if I can tell whether it matches what I found. If the hairs don't match, then maybe he fought against whoever killed him." Adam put the envelope back in his knapsack; it wasn't light enough in here to try to compare the sets of hairs, and he didn't want to risk losing either sample.

Instead, he picked up one of the dead man's shoes and brought it closer to the light. No oil smudge, but there was quite a bit of mud on the sole. Billings would've had to step off the wooden walkway between the dance hall and City Hall and take at least several steps for the shoe to get that dirty. Some of the mud was scraped off near the heel.

Adam wasn't one to care about the appearance of his own footwear, but he'd been forced to submit to a good blacking of his new, virginal shoes yesterday, so he knew how important that bit of grooming would have been to a man dressed like Custer Billings.

So Billings had left the ball, and walked across unprotected ground — ruining his perfectly blackened shoes? Why would he have done that? To speak to someone?

Fremark had seen two people standing in the shadows near the door to the anteroom. "A secret meeting," he'd said. Something had given him that impression.

Adam reckoned a rendezvous would count as a secret meeting. Had Billings been with Annabelle Titus? Or her husband? Or someone else?

He checked the other shoe. More mud, but no oil smudge. He sniffed at the dried mud. It smelled like earth and animal dung. No surprise.

"I'm going to take the shoes with me."

"Extra rags over there if you want to wrap them up." Hilton showed him a small jar. "And here are samples of his hair — from his head and his beard."

Adam was pleasantly surprised by the man's preparedness — which was markedly better than his own. "Much obliged."

He was picking up Billings's gloves when a thought struck him. What was the sticky substance that made the strands cling to the gloves? It could have been anything from the meal — especially the dessert, which had been dried apple tarts and cinnamon-frosted cakes.

He stilled as another realization came to him.

Miss Henry Altman — if that were her real name, which was surely not the case — had been wearing very thick, dark blond facial hair that *had been glued onto her face.*

Damn. Now he had even more questions to ask the so-called journalist. If he could even find her.

How the hell was he going to track down a woman who'd been dressed as a man, in a city he didn't know, with people coming and going now that the inauguration was over? Would he even recognize her if they came face-to-face, thanks to last night's shadowy light?

That was another task to add to his list — besides calling at the St. Charles Hotel to see whether Hurst Lemagne had shown up, helping Agent Pierce follow up on the list of business associates Mr. Delton had given him, and, of course, reporting to Mr. Lincoln what progress he'd made on the task to which he'd been set.

And surely there were other things Adam should be doing in this investigation . . . but he wasn't certain what. He wasn't a damned detective. He was a simple man of the West who just wanted to make a living and maybe, some day, have a family.

He sure as hell wasn't happy in a town where hackney drivers stopped so they could help whip a black man, or where people slept until noon and didn't go to bed until nearly dawn. And where the noise was constant, the smells were pungent, and young Irish boys had bare toes in the middle of winter. . . .

Adam moved sharply, annoyed with himself and his mental grumbling, and his false hand bumped against the table. He felt the jolt up over his elbow and into the bicep, and then a dull throb at the base of his arm's stump, reminding him of last night when he foolishly put too much unexpected weight on the fake hand to propel himself over the dais.

Hilton eyed him as he dried his hands with a rag. "Is that a Palmer arm?"

Of all the queries Adam received about his prosthetic, that was definitely not one of the common ones. "Yes."

He didn't ask the obvious follow-up question, but the other man acknowledged it, shrugging as he spoke, "I've never seen one before, but I hear he makes a good limb.

My friend Marcus is something of an . . . expert, I suppose you'd say."

"Not bad. Better than the first one I got, which was made by Selpho. The leather socket that strapped to my stump stunk to high heaven after six months. This arm's hollowed-out willow," Adam told him. Obviously the man was a doctor and had more of a technical interest in the limb than the average person. "Light, durable, and it ages well. No leather. That's fine calfskin stretched over it, making it look as natural as possible. If I move my arm just so, the fingers close — see?" He demonstrated by rotating his upper arm and squeezing it closer to his torso. "The thumb's got a spring-loaded joint, which works if I do this." He contorted his shoulder, which moved the mechanism inside the limb.

Hilton nodded briefly, though his eyes were riveted to the false hand curiously.

"Only thing I can't really do with it is play the fiddle," Adam said. "And I reckon my writing's not as clear as it used to be, but it's passable, once I get the pencil in the right position. Can even hold a gun and pull the trigger, though my aim's pretty damned sorry with that hand." He gave a wry laugh, then sobered. "I have a gang of pro-slavers back in Lawrence to thank for all of it. They ambushed me and a friend of mine."

Hilton nodded once more, then, as if ashamed by his bold curiosity, jerked his attention back to Billings's body.

Adam was about to leave when he remembered the knife in his knapsack.

"Take a look at this, will you?" He unwrapped the dagger and brought it to Hilton. "Can you confirm this is the blade that stabbed him? There's hardly any doubt; it was found in the closet with his coat, and it had blood on it. But I reckon we should be certain."

Hilton, whose hands were still washed, took the dagger and examined it. "About two inches wide at its greatest width, four inches long," he muttered to himself. "I'd say most likely."

As Adam watched, the doctor carefully measured the dagger against one, then the other, of the stab wounds. When it seemed to match, he then carefully slid the blade into the cuts as if to ensure it fit. Each time he withdrew it, blood glistened on the blade.

"It fits the width of the wounds exactly. I didn't force it all the way through, though, and as you saw, it didn't go to the hilt. Maybe only four inches deep. There isn't any bruising next to the cuts, so that means the hilt didn't hit his skin like it would if the killer shoved it all the way in." He wiped off the blood and handed it back to Adam. "I'd say yes, this is what did it."

Adam took the knife, but he was looking at the dead man on the table. "That cut is a straight entrance, with the same width all the way across," he commented, looking at where the knife had glanced against a rib on the right. "But the other one isn't. Why?"

Hilton nodded, following his gaze to the wound just below the sternum. Instead of looking like a straight, slender line where the blade had gone in, in the middle, the cut was slightly wider, then narrowed at the edges.

"Yes, I noticed that. It could be the angle he was holding the blade, or if Billings moved at the moment he was stabbed. But . . . it looks strange to me." Hilton hesitated, looking down at the table. "The only way to know for certain is to do an internal examination," he said, as if measuring his words. "Which might explain what, if anything, caused that wound to be wider in the center. And I want to make certain there's nothing I've missed. It'll take a long while, and it'll be . . . sir, the body will be cut up inside."

Adam looked up at the other man. "I reckon you should be thorough, Dr. Hilton."

The doctor exhaled quietly. "Obliged to you, sir." Hilton straightened and gave Adam one of those wary but determined looks. "I'm truly obliged for you letting me take him back here, sir. I don't get much chance to study a whole body like this. Us'ally, I'm just trying to mend what's broke."

And probably rarely getting any payment for it. Adam wondered how the man had come by such a comfortable workshop, for his Negro patients likely couldn't pay him what he was worth. "I'm obliged you taking him for a look," he replied. "If you find anything that might help me learn who stuck him with this knife, I'd be even more obliged."

Adam wrapped up the dagger again. The president would be expecting him soon. "I'll come back later. Or, if you need to send word, I'm at Willard's. I'll reimburse you for a messenger."

Hilton didn't look up. "I got my own money."

"Suit yourself," Adam replied. "I'll be back when I can."

"I'll send word if I find anything."

Adam nodded and stepped out into the bright morning, leaving death and its mysteries behind him.

CHAPTER 5

March 5, 1861

Adam had just crossed Lafayette Square and was approaching the north portico of the President's Mansion when someone called out.

"Mr. Quinn!"

He turned to his right and saw a lone woman in a simple dress and unremarkable hat hurrying up behind him. It wasn't until she came closer that he recognized her beneath the brim of her bonnet.

"Good morning, Mrs. Keckley." He smiled but was curious as to what she was doing out and alone at seven o'clock in the morning. At least it wasn't dark any longer.

She was puffing a little, for her legs were much shorter than his. She was at least a decade older than he and also carried what looked like a heavy satchel. Her breath left little white clouds, for the morning hadn't grown any warmer and was quite damp and windy.

"Well, now," she said, looking at the sedate mansion that was bookended by stables on each end. "There it is. The president's house." She paused as if to take it all in.

Adam didn't mind, for he was able to get his first good look at what resembled little more than a large country house — certainly much larger than anything in which he'd ever lived, but nothing all that grand. There were outbuildings, stables, and what looked like a greenhouse, with the new sun glinting off walls of glass.

A large iron fence ran along the north side of the property, and there was another on the south side. But the sides of the land-scaped lawn were open with interior walk-ways to the Treasury on the east side, and the Army and Navy buildings on the west. He tensed a little, noticing how unsecured the grounds were.

"I have an appointment with Mrs. Lincoln," Mrs. Keckley told him without wait-ing to be asked. "I was supposed to come on Sunday so I could help dress her for the inauguration, but I didn't get the message from my patron, Mrs. MacLean, in time, and when I visited her at Willard's yesterday morning before the ceremony, it was almost too late. But Mrs. Lincoln told me to come first thing this morning." Still puffing some, Mrs. Keckley gave him a smile. "I think it's because she heard I used to do work for Mrs. Davis before she left to go back home."

Adam had slowed his pace and walked along companionably with the older woman as they passed a bronze statue of Thomas Jefferson that stood in the large circular drive. Her breathless chatter reminded him of his mother. "Is that so?"

Varina Davis was the wife of Mississippi Senator Jefferson Davis. From what he'd heard, the couple had been the cream of Washington society, and Mrs. Davis a very popular hostess — until she and her husband left town, along with all of the other senators and congressmen from the seven states that had seceded since Lincoln's election. Now, Jeff Davis was the president of the Confederacy.

"Mrs. Davis asked me to come with her back home," Mrs. Keckley confided as they began to climb the steps. "To Mississippi, to be her modiste. She said even though there's going to be a war, it won't last very long, and it would be a good opportunity for me." She shook her head, still a little out of breath — but that didn't seem to keep her from rattling on. "But even though

I'm a free woman now, I didn't think that would be a good idea, to go down south. I decided to stay, and — Lawsy, will you look at that?"

He couldn't help but see: there was a line of people coming out of the main entrance of the sprawling white house.

"Are they all here to see Mr. Lincoln?" Mrs. Keckley asked.

"I would say. It's been like that since he arrived in the city. They're lining up all day long — people wanting a position or help from him."

"Laws." She shook her head, then stumbled a little because she wasn't watching her step. "And standing there with the door open wide like that, letting all the damp and chill in."

Adam walked past the line, ushering the seamstress through the door ahead of him. The people standing there were of all walks of life: some in stylish clothing with high, stiff collars and neat neckties. They carried walking sticks and wore hats and gloves, while others waited in more casual working garb like loose trousers held up by braces, plain white shirts, and no waistcoat. Still others were dressed in items that were as poor and ill fitting as Brian Mulcahey's.

Unfortunately, as Adam looked around,

131

he realized that although the furnishings and decor of the President's House were of good quality, they were also just as shabby and worn out as the young Irish boy's clothing. The carpets were threadbare, and nearly every wall or wainscoting needed a coat of paint. The portraits that hung on the walls were dusty, and their frames nicked and scratched.

The queue of people extended through the foyer and down the hallway of the first floor, where it curled back around and then snaked up the stairs to the second level, which, presumably, was where Mr. Lincoln was receiving them.

"Heaven help us," Adam muttered, realizing how simple it had been for himself — and the hundreds of other people — to enter the home of the president unchallenged. He hadn't seen any sign of the tight security that had been in place since Lincoln had left Springfield.

Perhaps there were guards on the second floor. But why weren't there ones on the grounds, or even at the door? What was Pinkerton thinking?

"Good morning, sir," said a tiny, wrinkled man in a nonmilitary uniform. He stood just inside, in the center of the foyer, and seemed to be the only house staff member in sight. "I'm Mr. McManus — been the doorman here since President Taylor. And you're here to be seeing the president, are you?" He might have been in Washington for years, but he hadn't lost his Irish accent.

"I've an appointment with Mrs. Lincoln, sir," said Mrs. Keckley.

"I'm Joshua Speed's nephew, and I've got an appointment with Mr. Lincoln as well. At least he's expecting me." Adam raised his brows as he looked toward the line of people.

"Aye, then." McManus turned and pointed in the opposite direction of the queue that led upstairs. "If you walk down this corridor past the East Room — that's the big one — you'll find another stairway that leads up."

The second floor showed no more sign of security than the first, and Adam scowled as he walked down the corridor with Mrs. Keckley. Last night his uncle had said it would be a miracle if Lincoln lived out the year; with this lax arrangement, it would be a miracle if he lived out the *month.*

"Nicolay!" He called out when he caught sight of one of the president's secretaries darting from one doorway across the hall to another, evading the line of office seekers that wound up the stairs.

Up here, the queue ended with a row of chairs lined up in the hallway just outside a door, and the lucky few who sat in them seemed anticipatory as their time drew near. The chatter and conversation was slightly quieter up here, now that those waiting were closer to the man they'd come to see, but they had all turned to look when Adam spoke.

James Nicolay poked his head out from inside a room and motioned for him to approach. "He's been expecting you," he told Adam, pointing to a closed door.

"Mrs. Keckley here has an appointment with Mrs. Lincoln," Adam said. "Do you know where she'd find her?"

Nicolay gestured again, this time indicating farther down the corridor. "The family's private quarters are down there. Hay and I are bunking next to his office, if you can believe it. I don't know where Mrs. Lincoln is right now — everything is still being moved in and unpacked — but the house-keeper can help Mrs. Keckley."

Assured that the seamstress would find her way, Adam knocked on Lincoln's office door, and was immediately bid entrance.

The president was standing behind a large mahogany desk. He wore glasses perched near the end of his nose, and his long wrists stuck out from the cuffs of his shirt. He'd changed from the formal clothes of last evening — though Adam wouldn't have found it surprising if he hadn't taken the time to do so, well knowing the man and his determined work ethic.

"Adam. Come in." Lincoln gave a wry smile as he looked around the small office, which was cluttered with chairs, a long walnut table, books and boxes of more books, and stacks of paper on every surface. "Looks worse than the henhouse after a dog got in, don't it?"

"Good morning, Mr. President."

"Good God, man, there's no need for formality. I spooned parsley soup into your mouth when you had the ague and I've seen you bare-assed naked stumbling out of the outhouse the morning after too much whisky," he said. "Sit down." He gestured vaguely to a chair near the desk.

"Have you had any sleep?" Adam asked, noting the grooves that lined his face seemed even deeper than they had been only a day ago. But of course they were — the man before him had taken an oath to preserve a Union that was splintering as they stood there.

"A touch. You sound like Mrs. Lincoln. She had a wonderful time last night." He smiled affectionately. "Didn't get home until after four o'clock. I reckon her feet'll be sore as a bad tooth today."

Adam wondered whether Mrs. Keckley would be relegated to waiting for several more hours until Mrs. Lincoln woke up. "You don't have any guards stationed around here," he said. "Anyone could walk in and —"

"I've already told your uncle — and Pinkerton and Scott and Loman and everyone else — I'm not going to be watched over and smothered all the time. It will be what it will be. I've got to breathe. See this?" He gestured to a stack of packages that spilled over a table and onto the floor. "From some of my well-wishers in the South. Preserved fruit — there's apricots and plums and even some cherries. A bottle of Kentucky bourbon. Got some cakes and a pie. They've been arriving since the election and haven't stopped since."

Adam was horrified. "You're not tasting any of it are you?"

Lincoln laughed, a great, infectious, booming laugh. "Hell no. Though I was tempted to try the pecan pie — it was right sweet looking. But, alas, Josh wouldn't let me, and Pinkerton had a bottle of brandy tested. Either it was really poisoned, or it was good enough for him to keep for himself." He laughed again. "And there — see?" He gestured to a rack of pigeonholes behind his desk, many of which contained envelopes or other papers. "That slot up top is for the really bad letters — the ones Nicolay and Hay think I should see."

Adam pursed his lips grimly. "Mr. Lincoln, I —"

But the other man shook his head, clearly unwilling to hear any further remonstrance. "Now, tell me what you've accomplished with the task to which I've set you. To my knowledge, Mrs. Lincoln hadn't heard about the tragedy before she left the ball, and she's been abed since coming home. That alone is commendable."

"I don't have much to report yet, sir," Adam said, and went on to explain everything that had occurred since he examined the body. He even unwrapped the dagger and Billings's shoes, and displayed the small jar of the victim's hair for Lincoln to take a gander.

The president interrupted only once. "A woman dressed as a man? A journalist? How curious."

Curious was not the word Adam would have used, but he tempered his response. Instead, he went on to list the things he

137

intended to do today, including interviewing Mr. Lemagne and visiting Mrs. Billings to give her the unhappy news. When it came to the topic of Dr. Hilton, he hesitated, then plowed on.

"I reckon I might have misstepped, sir, but I allowed a doctor to take the body to do an examination of it."

"A misstep? That seems like a sound decision," Lincoln replied.

"Yes, sir, but . . . the doctor is a black man."

"Is he? That's quite remarkable."

"He appears to be knowledgeable," Adam said, although he had little to support this opinion other than his instinct and some brief conversations with the young physician.

He went on to explain how Mrs. Keckley had brought George Hilton into the situation, and what had transpired from there. "I'm not certain what sort of condition Mr. Billings's body will be in once he's finished," he ended. "I reckon he means to cut him up and look inside."

Lincoln nodded. "One can't argue with that — although the cause of death seems obvious, right? Stabbed in the belly. Still, I remember a case I read about — it happened in Glasgow, I believe — where a man was stabbed three times, but it turned out he'd died from drowning. They wouldn't have known that if there hadn't been an examination."

Adam couldn't help but feel relieved, yet he had other concerns. "Sir, I can't help worry that this murder was meant as a warning to you, or, worse, that it was a plot meant for you but that it went awry."

"Your uncle and Scott and Pinkerton have all said the same, and they in louder, more vociferous voices. I say, if the plot were meant for me — first, it didn't happen, and so the plot was foiled. And second, if someone meant me harm at my own party, I reckon it would have been with something much louder and wilder than a simple knife blade. After all, they were planning to blow up the platform where I stood to take the oath! But again, that's why I want the matter investigated, and in a circumspect manner. I trust you'll find the answer."

Adam resisted the urge to point out that the boxes of poisoned fruit and baked goods were even less "loud" or "wild" than a knife blade. "Should I be working with or reporting to the constabulary, or Mr. Pinkerton, or — or anyone else?"

"You report to me," Lincoln replied. "The constabulary in this city don't have anything resembling a detective agency — their only purpose is to keep the peace during the day. They might look official in their uniforms, but they don't investigate crimes. They only try to stop them while in progress.

"And the Auxiliary Guard's responsibility is solely to protect the federal buildings at night." He gave a derisive snort. "For that, we can thank Congress for their lack of foresight. Yes, I can see that creating an actual police force for the district is yet another task that lies before me, but for now, I've more urgent matters. Such as waiting for the Senate to confirm my cabinet this afternoon so I can call a meeting. And tending to the line of people filling up my house.

"Now, where did I put that . . ." He scrabbled around through the papers on his vast desk, and Adam decided it was time to leave the most important man in the nation to his joyless task of keeping it together. His heart squeezed when he imagined what it would be like to walk in Lincoln's gargantuan shoes . . . yet, at the same time, he knew there was no other person better suited for the upheaval ahead.

"Thank you, Mr. Lincoln," he said, starting toward the door. "I'll report to you —"

"I found it. Hold your horses, Adam —

this is for you." He handed him a paper a little larger than the size of a playing card. It was made from heavier stock than most of the other papers on his desk, and the words *Office of Abraham Lincoln, President of the United States of America* were engraved across the top.

Adam took the card and saw the handwritten words: *Please note that Mr. Adam Speed Quinn acts with all authority of the Office of the President of the United States, and that all due courtesies should be afforded to him in any request or action he takes.*

It was signed by Lincoln and dated today.

"There are very few people with whom I would entrust such a document," said the president. "Now, off with you, my boy. I've position seekers to placate and a disillusioned Congress to face. Down in Richmond, Virginia's about to vote to secede, and I reckon things will get even more unpleasant when that happens."

Feeling both humility and dread, Adam slipped the card into his pocket and left Lincoln to his work.

At the very least, he could alleviate some of the man's heavy load by fulfilling the task set on him . . . if he could figure out how to do so.

■ ■ ■ ■

The home of Custer and Althea Billings was located such a short distance from Willard Hotel, just off Twelfth Street, that Adam stopped at his room in order to drop off the dagger, Mr. Billings's shoes, and the jar of hair samples.

He didn't think it would be appropriate to inform the woman she'd become a widow while in possession of a sample of her dead husband's hair and the blade that had killed him.

Before leaving the Willard again, Adam told Birch, the doorman, about Brian Mulcahey. "If you aren't on duty at noon or at six, would you be so kind as to tell whoever relieves you?"

"It's only me, here, sir, from six to six or so, ever' day. Even on Sundays, and during thunderstorms or blizzards. Then Billy Mudd from six till six, though he sleeps half the night anyway and he don't like to get wet." Birch gave a deep, rolling laugh. "But I'll tell 'im."

Adam reached the Billings house less than five minutes later. Though it was approaching half past eight, he set aside any qualms about the early hour.

A middle-aged Negro man opened the door to Adam's knock. "I'm sorry, sir, but Mr. Billings is not in at the moment."

"It's Mrs. Althea Billings I've come to see."

The man shook his head gravely. "I'm sorry, sir, but Mrs. Billings doesn't receive guests. Especially not at this hour. She's not well."

"I'm sorry she's ill, but it's very important I speak to her." Since Adam had no need for calling cards of his own, he had nothing to offer but the authorization Lincoln had given him.

The servant was probably illiterate — for it was illegal to teach slaves to read, and even most free blacks had a difficult time finding an opportunity to be taught — but he seemed to recognize the importance of the card. "Yessir." He moved back and allowed Adam to step inside to escape from the dreary March morning.

As the butler — was that what they called them at fancy houses like this? — went off to speak to Mrs. Billings, Adam looked around the foyer. His first impression was a rush of shame that the Billings home was more polished and fancy than the home where the president of the United States lived.

There weren't any threadbare rugs or peeling paint here. Everything was shiny and fresh — from the polished wood floor surrounding the thick rug on which his boots dripped, to the sparkling clean glass windows, to the plush furnishings he glimpsed in a room nearby. The walls were covered with paper printed with tiny floral designs, and fresh flowers spilled out of porcelain vases. The wood trim around windows, doors, and along the wainscoting was carved with undulating vines and other organic shapes. Mr. Billings was doing very well for himself and his family.

"Mr. Quinn, if you would please come this way. Mrs. Billings has agreed to see you." The butler offered back to Adam the placard with the president's authorization on it. Adam slid the card back into his pocket and removed his hat as he followed the man from the foyer.

Instead of leading him to a sitting room or parlor, the butler started up the grand staircase that swept away from the entrance hall. They walked a short way down the carpeted upstairs hall, and though by now Adam wasn't surprised when the servant opened the door to a bedchamber, he was hesitant to step inside.

Sunshine poured through the tall windows

whose drapes had been hooked back to allow the spill of light. A kerosene lamp sat on each of the tables, and there were sconces on the walls as well. Though the fireplace was filled with unlit logs, the room wasn't cold, despite the definite March chill. Adam guessed the Billingses had installed a furnace — which, along with indoor toilets, was one of the few modern improvements that had been done to the president's home.

Mrs. Billings's bedchamber was quite large and filled with delicate, feminine furnishings decorated in pink, yellow, and pale green. Lace trim traced the hems of tablecloths, bed coverings, and the curtains. Despite the bright light that gave the chamber an airy look, there was a stuffy, medicinal scent that made the space feel close and stagnant.

"Mr. Quinn, please have a seat. I apologize that I'm unable to greet you properly in the parlor downstairs." The voice, which carried a lilt from the South, came from the bed. As he stepped toward the chair that had been arranged next to it, Adam saw Mrs. Billings for the first time.

She was propped up against a slew of pillows, her slender hands folded over the pink and yellow quilt that came up to her waist. Dressed in a lacy lemon-colored bed gown, she was lovely in an ethereal way, with pale skin as smooth and translucent as the sort of fabric women used for their summertime wraps. She had large blue eyes that followed him as he made his way into the chamber. Her hair was tucked up into a cap, which kept the color of her tresses obscured, and her lips were pale, but not bloodless, pink. Althea Billings was perhaps five or ten years younger than her husband, who, Adam had learned, was forty-five.

As he sat in the chair that had been arranged for him — a wooden one, with a straight back and a thick seat cushion trimmed with the requisite lace — he noticed a black maidservant sitting in the corner. She was doing mending, but obviously she was also present to watch over her mistress and patient. The sight of her alleviated much of his discomfort at being admitted to a woman's bedchamber.

"I'm sorry you're ill, Mrs. Billings." He settled his hat on his lap. "I wouldn't have insisted on disturbing you if it wasn't terribly important."

"The *president* sent you? Mr. Lincoln?"

Adam rejected all of the more detailed responses and simply said, "Yes." He was about to speak when Mrs. Billings beat him to it.

"Is it about my husband?"

"Yes. I . . . I regret to inform you that your husband is dead." He said the words clearly and without hesitation, having learned that was the best way to deliver such news.

"Dead?" The word was neither a shriek nor a whisper. She might simply have been commenting on the condition of a squashed bug. "You're saying Custer is dead? Are you quite certain of this?"

"Yes, ma'am. He was found, stabbed, at the — near the Union Ball last night."

"S-stabbed?" Her eyes widened, then suddenly filled with tears. She blinked rapidly, turning away. Now there was a thread of tension and shock in her voice. "You're certain, then. It's definitely him? I — I wondered why he didn't come in last night when he got home. I just thought . . . perhaps it was so late and he didn't want to disturb me. But I thought for certain he'd come in and tell me all about the ball. He knew how much I wanted to go, but . . ." She unclasped her hands in order to flutter her fingers.

The tears had spilled over during her speech, and without waiting to be asked, the maid brought her mistress a handkerchief. Also lace trimmed.

"I'm very sorry for your loss, Mrs. Billings."

"Thank you," she said from behind the handkerchief. He waited patiently until she took it away from her face, revealing watery, red eyes and a pink-tipped nose. If possible, her face seemed to have gone even more pale. "I just . . . I can't believe it. You're certain? He was stabbed? How? By who?"

Adam drew in a deep breath. "That's partly why I'm here, Mrs. Billings. To try to discover who would have murdered your husband."

"Murdered?" She jolted against the pillows as if she'd been stung. "Do you think someone really murdered him? I thought — I thought you meant it had been an accident. Are you certain?"

Adam could hardly think of any way in which a man might get stabbed by accident, though he supposed it was possible. A duel gone wrong, perhaps? But then that wouldn't have been an accident, would it? "I don't reckon it was an accident, Mrs. Billings. He was left to bleed to death in the room just outside the entrance to the ball. Apologies, ma'am, for the details."

Her eyes widened to circles and she gasped. Now a bit of color pinkened her cheeks. "But why?"

"I'm hoping you might be able to help me figure that out, ma'am. Do you know of anyone who might want to ki— who might have a grudge against your husband? Anyone who hated him, or had a strong dislike for him?"

Mrs. Billings was staring in his direction, but Adam didn't think she was really looking at him. The brief flush had subsided from her cheeks and now she was ghost white again. "Not . . . not that I can think of . . . no one that I know."

"What about a business associate? Someone he had a problem with related to the bank?"

She shook her head slowly. "I don't know. . . . Custer didn't talk much about business. He didn't like to upset me — especially after . . . especially since I became ill." She brought the scrap of lace to her face once more, but this time, there were soft but audible sobs accompanying her tears.

Adam swallowed and looked down at his hands, uncertain what to do. He wanted to ask about Annabelle Titus, but it seemed terribly unseemly and unfeeling to ask a new widow about her husband's possible lover — even in the pursuit of justice for his killer.

As Mrs. Billings's sobs became more pronounced, the maid rose from her chair and came over to her mistress, making soothing sounds and patting the ice-white, fluttering hands with her small dark ones.

"I'm so sorry," he said, speaking both to the maid and to the crying woman. He felt like a hulking lunk, completely out of place in this bastion of femininity and tears. "I'll . . . I'll be on my way now and let you rest a bit, Mrs. Billings. I'm very sorry to have brought such unhappy news."

The woman sobbed something unintelligible, and the servant nodded toward him as if to agree that he should leave.

"If you should think of anything that might help, ma'am, anything about your husband that might give a clue as to what happened, please contact me at Willard's Hotel." He was speaking to Mrs. Billings, but he included the maidservant in the conversation as well. She nodded, then turned back to her grieving mistress.

The butler was waiting in the foyer when Adam came down the stairs, and by the expression on his face, he knew the man had heard the news. *How* he had done so, Adam didn't know and didn't care. Probably had listened at the door, like any normal servant would do, he thought wryly.

Despite having grown up in a household without even the whiff of a possibility of a servant, he wasn't naive about how things worked with hired help.

"Mister," said the butler as Adam settled the hat back on his head, preparing to leave. "It's true? The master was stabbed? Killed by someone, purposely?"

Adam paused. A servant who listened might know more than he or she should — and possibly even more than the mistress of the house. Whether he could get the information from the eavesdropper was another issue. "It's true. I've been given the task of finding out who did it, and I'd like to speak with you and all of the other servants in the house. What is your name, sir?"

"James. My name is James. I'm a free man," he said, answering the question before Adam realized he needed to ask it. "All of us here, we're free, paid servants, for Mr. and Mrs. Billings. I have my papers."

"Is there somewhere we can sit, and where I can talk with all of the other staff? One by one?"

"I don't know, sir . . . Mr. Billings mightn't like that — *oh.*" He bit his lip and straightened as he realized the only person in charge now was Mrs. Billings, and she was incapacitated for the moment. "I-I think so, sir. Mebbe the sitting room here?"

"Please sit down, James," Adam said. "I'm sure it comes as a shock to you to hear about your — your employer. Can you think of anyone who might have wanted to do something like this?"

"No, sir. No, I can't. Mr. Billings, he was liked well enough, far as I could tell."

Adam hesitated. What else did he want to know? What else could help him with this puzzle?

And then it came to him. The answer settled in his mind in what Ishkode called a "knowing."

Yes, this murder investigation was quite like watching for signs in the woods of some creature that had passed by, or discerning the coming of some threat of weather, or reading the story of what had happened in a battle between two animals. But to be a good tracker, one had to have knowledge of the woods, of the earth, of the seasons, of the weather. One had to know the habits and lifestyle of nature, and how all the elements — fire, water, air, wind, earth — acted and interacted.

In order to identify the predator of a mutilated rabbit, he had to know how the rabbit lived, where it went and sought food, how it mated, what its habitat was. He knew everything about it . . . and then combined that knowledge with the traces the predator left behind: tracks, scat, and how the prey was fed upon and when, and in what condition it was left. . . .

And so it must be the same with tracking this killer as well. Adam must learn everything about *this* nature. *This* world — and everything he could discover about the victim and the life he'd lived.

So he looked at James and considered how to go about getting information he didn't know existed. Start with the basic information, and follow the trail. "Do Mr. and Mrs. Billings have any children?"

"Oh, no, sir." James shook his head sadly. "There was a child, just a year ago . . . but he died. And Mrs. Billings, she ain't been the same since. She ain't got no family either. No mother or sisters to come see to her. Just a brother."

Adam hesitated, then said, "I'm going to have to ask you some questions that might seem strange or too nosy, but it's important you answer them. Anything you tell me could help me find out who killed your employer."

James nodded, his lips firm. "I'll do my best, sir. Mr. Billings was a good man. He treats — treated — us well. Not like some other —" He quickly changed the subject. "And Mrs. Billings, she's a kind lady too. We were all very sad when the boy died. They were married almost twenty years, and there was only the one child."

"Was she sick when she had the baby?"

"No, sir. The baby was a year old when he died. Tubber — tubberlosees, they said. I don't know much about what the mistress is sick from. Lacey — she's the upstairs maid — said a growth in her middle is what's causing it, but it ain't another baby."

"You greet most of the visitors who come here, right, James?"

"Yes, sir."

"Has a man named Hurst Lemagne ever called for Mr. Billings?"

"No, sir. Not that I remember."

Adam fumbled around for another question. "Have you ever heard Mr. Billings arguing with or angry with any of his business associates or anyone else who came to the house?"

James began to shake his head, then stopped. His eyes grew wide as he looked at Adam. "There was someone. I heard them in the master's study. Their voices were loud and it sounded like — well, something broke."

"Do you know who it was? What they were

arguing about?"

He thought for a moment, staring into the space over Adam's shoulder. "I couldn't hear them. The other man . . . I don't know his name. I heard something about — about ducks. . . . Holding ducks, I think. But I don't know what that is."

"Holding ducks?" Adam frowned, turning the words over in his mind. What on earth . . . ? "Could it have been docks? Dock loading, maybe?" But even that didn't make any sense. Yes, Washington had a shipyard and a naval yard too, and plenty of docks — and probably some ducks living in the Chesapeake Bay area — but none of that made any sense.

"I don't know, sir. I couldn't hear them that well."

"Was there anything about the man you remember? Anything that might help identify him? What did he look like? Did he arrive in his own carriage?"

James rubbed his eyes wearily. "Mebbe he was forty years old. He had some curly hair, and his beard was curling too." He gestured as if he were fingering a very wiry, frizzy beard. "It was blond. Dark blond. And he come in a fancy open landau." He squinted as if trying to remember. "It was black and had a gold seal on the side. A big cross-like thing." He gestured, making a sign like a *T*. *T*. For Titus?

Adam nodded. "Thank you. That's very helpful, James. Is there anything else you can think of that might help me? And is there someone to call for Mrs. Billings? A friend, some family? She's obviously not well, and I'd hate for her to take a bad turn."

"Louise, she's going to send to Mrs. Billings's brother, Mr. Orton and his wife. Her only family now. And mebbe Mrs. Delton and Mrs. Lomax too. They be her friends."

But not Mrs. Titus? "That's good. If you think of anything else, James, I need you to send for me at the Willard."

The butler stood and gave a little bow. He started to leave, then turned back. "Sir, is it true you're working for Mr. Lincoln?" He said the name with reverence.

"It is."

James looked as if he were about to speak, then thought better of it. Instead, he straightened up as if he'd just been given some great and important task. "Thank you, sir. I'll send Louise in next. She's the house-keeper."

Adam asked similar questions of Louise. She was a clear-eyed woman of fifty with pudgy hands and short, iron gray hair. Unfortunately, she had little to add to

James's answers.

"Miz Althea . . . she's just sick about this all. Poor lamb. And she ain't never been the same since her baby boy died. Poor lamb. Waited so long for a baby, and then that."

"I'm very sorry for her loss — and for yours as well."

"She's already done cried through two handkerchiefs and a linen tablecloth." Louise's eyes filled as well. "Mr. Billings . . . he was a kind man. I know how unkind a man can be, sir, and he was not that way. He was nice to Miz Althea too, even after she got sick and didn't leave the house anymore and didn't like to come out of her room."

Being nice to his wife didn't include taking a mistress, Adam reckoned. Once again, he wanted to ask about Annabelle Titus, but he couldn't bring himself to be so blunt. Instead he tried a different tactic. "Did a Mr. or Mrs. Titus ever visit the Billingses?"

To her credit, Louise didn't answer immediately, and seemed to ponder. "That name sounds familiar, sir, but I don't know anyone calling here with that name. But Mrs. Billings wasn't accepting callers much in the last year, 'cepting her brother, who come from Baltimore sometimes. And Mrs. Delton."

157

"Can you think of anyone who might have wanted to hurt Mr. Billings? Anyone he might have argued with?"

"We heard it once — me and James. Him and a man in the study. The man was shouting like he was gon' kill him." Her eyes popped wide as she realized what she'd said. "Oh, sir."

"Do you know who it was? Did you hear what they were arguing about? Could you tell *who* was shouting?"

She shook her head. "Not really. They was just loud voices raised, somethin' about shells and cockles, I think, something that made him real mad, whatever it was. Man slammed out the door and got in his carriage and left. Mr. Billings didn't come out of his study for two hours after that." She *tsked* and shook her head.

"When did they argue? Do you remember?"

"It was . . . well, now, it was mebbe a week past. Or five days. Not very long."

"Did you see the carriage that brought the man?"

"It shore was fancy."

Though Louise was impressed by the carriage that could have belonged to Titus, she wasn't able to add any new information. Mr. Billings's manservant, Stanley, had been dispatched to take the message to Mrs. Billings's brother, so he wasn't present to be interviewed. The housemaid, Lacey, who'd been in Mrs. Billings's bedchamber, came into the room next, but as she was restricted mainly to caring for her mistress, she hardly was aware of what went on downstairs.

"I don' think Miz Althea's gone get through this," she said when Adam had finished questioning her. "She's been in a bad way, and this might just do her in." Her eyes were sad and her mouth grim. "Then I don't know what we gonna do, me and James and Louise and Stanley."

Adam felt a little tug of concern, for just this morning he'd seen the sort of living arrangements that would be available to the likes of four free Negroes in Washington. Residing in dank, filthy alleys in cramped, ramshackle housing with few options for employment, and low wages when they could find it.

Things would get even worse when the war came. They'd get worse for everyone.

CHAPTER 6

The St. Charles Hotel was closer to the capitol than the President's House, and, like most of the important buildings in the ward — at least as far as those people who ran the country were concerned — it was on Pennsylvania Avenue. It was in the heart of the business district, in the shadows of the half-domed building that housed Congress and all of its offices, a cafeteria, restaurants, and galleries.

Two wings had been added to the Capitol within the last ten years, and the new, larger dome needed to balance this redesigned architecture was only half completed. Nor were the marble wings — still lacking even stairs to access them — completed, and only three of the planned one hundred Corinthian columns had been finished with their decorative tops. A crane and scaffolding around the base of the cast-iron dome marked the activity still needing to be done in order to finish the work.

As Adam approached, a uniformed man opened the St. Charles Hotel's front door, tipping his hat with a polite greeting. When he entered the lobby and headed for the registration desk, he noticed a prominent sign on the wall:

HOTEL HAS UNDERGROUND CELLS FOR CONFINING SLAVES FOR SAFEKEEPING. IN CASE OF ESCAPE, FULL VALUE OF THE NEGRO WILL BE PAID BY THE PROPRIETOR OF THE HOTEL.

Adam stared as the words sunk in, then looked away, shocked and ashamed that such a notice would be posted in a public place.

If we do go to war, God willing the Union will remain intact, and Lincoln will do what must be done and free the slaves.

Until he'd moved to Kansas in 1855, Adam hadn't considered himself a true abolitionist. He'd grown up in the free state of Illinois, spending almost a decade living with his uncle in Springfield, and thus had little experience with what was known as the "peculiar institution." Since it didn't affect him, he gave it hardly any thought.

But then he went off to Wisconsin. There

he became friends with Ishkode and learned how to live with, comprehend, and respect the natural world. He remained there, often traveling north with his Ojibwe friend's tribe, making a living hunting and trapping for nearly five years.

Living close to the land and learning about the way the Ojibwe honored nature and all creatures gave Adam much to think about when it came to the idea of enslaving humans, and the more he thought about it, the more he became distinctly uncomfortable with the idea of that unique "domestic arrangement" — as it was also called.

After the Kansas-Nebraska Act, in which Congress voted to allow each new state to determine, on its own, whether to be free or slave, the Free State movement began in earnest in Kansas. Abolitionists — often ministers or other religious speakers — from the North encouraged enterprising young men like Adam to move to Kansas Territory, or KT, and homestead so as to garner enough support to keep the territory free of slavery when it came time to be brought into the Union.

The idea of owning his own land was all the incentive Adam needed, and he made the decision to bid farewell to Ishkode and transplant himself to a new adventure in

Kansas. Supporting the Free-State initiative while trying something new was, Adam had told himself, one way he could honor what he'd learned about respecting nature from his Ojibwe friend.

The battles between the pro-slavers — who crossed the border from slave state Missouri to vote illegally, and even set up a false government to promote their agenda — and the Free State advocates were vicious, bloody, and unyielding. Too many of Adam's friends were tarred and feathered, maimed, or even killed during the skirmishes, and the hatred and evil he experienced at the opposite end of the pro-slavery movement was more than enough to solidify his belief that slavery should be completely abolished — not simply confined to the South.

And that was three years before he lost his arm during the attack at Tom and Mary's house.

"May I help you?"

Adam was jolted from his unpleasant musings. He looked at the neatly dressed man behind the registration desk, who was eyeing his well-worn coat and the battered hat that was still on Adam's head with undisguised disdain. To the man's coat was pinned a palmetto cockade: the badge made from palm reeds from South Carolina — the first state to secede. The flower-like ornament openly announced its wearer's support for the secessionists.

"I'd like to speak with Hurst Lemagne," Adam said, deliberately taking his time in removing his offending hat.

"Who shall I say is asking?"

He didn't know if it was the man's barely concealed disdain, the palmetto badge, or the sign about slaves — maybe it was even seeing young Brian Mulcahey running around with his big toe sticking out of his boot in a coat that was too small — that got his dander up, but it was up.

Adam leaned nearly halfway across the counter, resting his crossed arms in the center. His substantial height required the other man to look up at him even from the other side. "Adam Quinn. I need to speak with Lemagne. Now. I'll wait over there." He jerked his chin toward a cluster of blue velvet chairs. A fat spittoon sat on the ground between two of them and a fern's feathery leaves spilled from a table above it.

Apparently, Adam got his point across, for the man spun on what surely were perfectly blacked shoes and hurried away to speak to a page.

Adam removed himself from the counter

slowly and deliberately, gathered up his hat, and went over to wait. Since it was still early by society's standards — just approaching ten o'clock — there were only a few people wandering through the lobby. However, he noticed a proliferation of southern accents filtering through the air. It seemed this establishment was the preferred one for those whose sympathies rested with the South.

Frowning, he rubbed his chin. Hadn't most of the Southern politicians left the city already? Seven states had seceded since the election, and from what he understood, the exodus of many people from those same states had emptied the city as well, including their senators and congressmen. But apparently some businessmen and visitors still lingered.

Which brought him to a very interesting question: What had Constance Lemagne and her father, from Alabama, been doing at the inaugural ball for a man who was loathed and despised — called evil, and an ape, and many other vulgarities — by those of their ilk?

"Mr. Quinn!"

Speak of the devil.

He rose, barely remembering to remove his hat again, and greeted Miss Lemagne.

She looked quite fetching this morning. Even more so, he thought, than she had last night, when she had been wearing yards of fabric, lace, and ruffles, along with a fussy headdress. Today, her honey-gold hair fluttered in soft, minuscule wisps around her face, and though most of her ears were covered by smooth swoops of hair drawn back into a tidy knot, he could see the delicate shape of her earlobes peeking from below.

He was rising from the brief bow of greeting when he got a better look at her eyes. "Miss Lemagne. Is something wrong?"

His mother would probably have jabbed him with her pointed shoe if she'd heard him, for asking such a question implied there was something amiss in a woman's bearing or presentation — a not so subtle criticism of her grooming or looks. But the wide blue eyes and the dark circles under them told him what he needed to know.

"Miss Lemagne, has something happened with your father?"

She sank onto the chair next to the one he'd just vacated and pulled him down into his seat. "First, Mr. Quinn, you need to know — I'm *not* engaged to Arthur Mossing. I wanted you to know that immediately."

"All right." He nodded, feeling a small flicker of warmth at the news. It was stoked further by the realization that she'd cared enough to inform him so immediately. "And about your father?"

"He didn't get back until almost dawn this morning. I waited up all night, listening for him to return to his room. It's right next to mine," she explained. "When I finally heard him at the door, I went out to see him, and —"

"Constance, what are you doing?" A loud, angry voice had both of them turning. "I thought I told you to stay in the room."

"Mr. Quinn, I need to speak with you about something," she said in a rushed, hushed voice as she grabbed his arm. "As soon as possible. Meet me — meet me at the lobby at the Kirkwood at one o'clock."

She released his wrist and rose. Though she looked chagrined, Miss Lemagne didn't appear to be cowed or frightened by the man — presumably her father. "Daddy," she began.

Adam stood to greet the newcomer. "Mr. Lemagne? Good morning. I'm Adam Quinn —"

"I don't give a damn who you are," retorted the man. His voice boomed, drawing attention from the few people in the vicinity. "And I don't care what you want. And I'll not have you bothering my daughter."

Hurst Lemagne had likely given his daughter her whisky-colored hair, but his eyes — which flashed furiously — were not the same crystal blue as his offspring's. Properly dressed — though obviously in a hurry, as his necktie was slightly off-center and he wasn't wearing a hat — the man was of average height and had a torso shaped like a barrel. He had both mustache and beard, which were neatly trimmed and slightly waxed to smooth the ends, and a long, straight nose.

The desk manager hurried out from behind the counter, clearly on his way to soothe the ruffled feathers. Adam turned toward the much slighter man and gave him a cold look. The manager spun around on his heels and skittered back behind the desk.

"Mr. Lemagne," Adam began, keeping his voice calm and even. "I need to speak with you about something that happened last night at the Union Ball." He offered the man his card from Mr. Lincoln. "The president has asked me to —"

"The president?" Lemagne's eyes bulged. He snatched the document from Adam, took one look at it, and tore it into four pieces. Flinging them aside, he said, "That damned rail-splitter's no president of *mine.* Constance." He took her by the arm. "You are forbidden to speak to that man again."

"Daddy!" she exclaimed, obviously horror stricken at his rudeness, but more appalled than frightened by his anger.

As Lemagne towed her past the hotel desk, he said to the manager, "If you see him here again, you have my permission to throw him out."

Adam watched the father and daughter leave, then looked down at the scraps of placard at his feet. He gathered them up. As he rose, he glanced at the desk clerk, who seemed to be enjoying himself while casually adjusting the straw-colored badge pinned to his coat.

"Well, I reckon there's no question where Mr. Lemagne's sympathies lie," Adam said dryly, then replaced his hat and walked out of the hotel.

Though it was several hours past dawn and the sun was high in the sky, its light was obscured by a blanket of pale gray clouds. The fact that it might rain weighed more heavily than the hope the clouds might disintegrate and offer a brighter day, so when Adam left the St. Charles he made his way directly to Judiciary Square, the stuccoed City Hall, and the makeshift building that had housed the inaugural ball.

In the daylight, he examined the plank walkway that stretched between the civic building and the temporary structure and noted more than a few dried footprints on it — most of them leading from the hall to the ballroom. Obviously more than one person had brought with them traces of dirt on their nice shoes. But that was because mud was everywhere, due not only to the recent, hasty construction of the dance hall, but also the simple fact that Washington was a city of unfinished streets, nonlandscaped parks, and unpaved squares.

Judiciary Square was finished with neither brick nor cobblestone, and Adam jolted to a halt when he saw a pig mucking in the shadow of a building. He stared, hardly believing his eyes.

Yes. There was a very happy sow snorting about in one corner of a public square bordered on one side by City Hall and the mayor's office, and less than five blocks from the Capitol Building. There were people entering the building, obviously going to their offices for work, and none of them seemed to pay any mind to the pig.

And there were people in Washington who claimed Lincoln was rustic and came from an uncivilized town?

Shaking his head, Adam put aside the irony of the situation and concentrated on the tasks at hand. He was looking for two things. One, a smudge of oil that might confirm his suspicions as to whether Mr. Billings had obtained a significant amount of fresh mud on his shoes by being one of the persons Fremark had seen in a "secret meeting" — and then possibly some indication as to who was with him. And two, the trail Miss Altman had left when she disappeared from Agent Pierce's sight last night.

Adam started with the dance hall's anteroom. The door was unlocked, and although office personnel and clerks were entering and exiting City Hall from both the square side and the Indiana Avenue side, this adjacent building was silent and empty now that its purpose had been fulfilled. Workers would surely arrive at some point to tear down the decorative buntings and put away the tables and chairs that had been used for the supper, but for now, he had the place to himself.

Once inside, Adam located the traces of oil and, with the external door open, was better able to see them in the natural light. There was a slightly larger stain just outside the threshold that he'd missed in the moonlight, and he noticed a scuff mark next to it.

He knelt to get a better look. There was definitely a scrape of mud, and he recognized it as the sort of track a shoe would make if it was being dragged. He could tell the stain wasn't from the heel, but from the side of the shoe, and when he looked around, Adam found another trace of a trail almost parallel to that one.

Yes. Someone — Billings — had been either dragged or half carried into the room. If that was the case, then logically it followed that he was either dead or dying at that time. And whoever dragged or helped him had had a smudge of oil on his shoe.

He reckoned that the "secret meeting" Fremark had half-heartedly noticed was Billings speaking with the man — or woman — who, moments later, killed him and then dragged his body inside the anteroom.

Next, he examined the closet where Miss Altman had been hidden, but there were no grease smudges inside or near the door. He did find an oil stain the size of a nickel near the wall where the closet jutted out. There was a slender, faint streak leading from the smudge — as if the drop had been made, then something had marred it slightly.

Adam scrutinized all of the marks — both

inside and outside — carefully, but he couldn't make out enough of the shape of any print to get an idea of the size of the shoe, or any marks that might identify a flaw in the footwear. None of them were more than small scrapes of grease . . . but that didn't mean there wasn't more to find where the shoes in question had originally picked up the mud or oil.

Once he traced the tracks to the door and outside, things became much more complicated. For the marks he was following mingled with the main foot traffic. Another close examination of the walkway all the way to City Hall confirmed no other oil smudges, which meant that whoever made them hadn't walked into the antechamber directly from the wooden path, but from somewhere else.

With great care and patience, Adam examined the area outside the antechamber and was rewarded when he discovered the barest trace of grease on the edge of a piece of the plank walkway just outside the entrance to the building. If he hadn't been so persistent, he might have missed it.

Satisfied he was on the right path, he continued his search in the direction from which the prints had to have come — which would have been in the shadows last night.

This was far more difficult since he was no longer looking at a wooden surface, but peaks and valleys of mud, anemic patches of grass, and small, sticky puddles. But Adam had tracked animals and humans on surfaces much more challenging than rough, damp mud, and it wasn't long before he found what he was looking for: a few indentations in the soft ground that were too new to be from the construction crews and too precise to be natural upheavals of earth.

And there was a small, crushed clump of grass with traces of black grease on it.

A rush of comprehension washed over him as he read the tracks, and the story filled his mind like a stream of sand pouring into the bottom half of an hourglass. He closed his eyes and took himself to the scene, utilizing the skill of "knowing" that Ishkode had taught him by becoming part of the story. . . .

They stood here . . . right here, rather close to the doorway.

Just as Fremark had said.

They stepped off the walkway, likely so as not to block the way of people going in and out of the building. They were within sight of anyone walking by . . . but it would have been in the shadows last night at midnight. If someone like Fremark saw them — two of them, only two of them, the murderer and Billings — they'd think nothing of it. Just two men conversing.

They faced each other, so Billings knew his killer well enough to stop and talk to him — not to just pause, but to stop and move out of the way for an extended — maybe private — conversation.

Adam continued, unraveling the story in his mind: picturing the tracks, the traces of oil, the way the footsteps had been made.

"Step over here, I need to speak to you," the murderer would have said. "Let's get out of the way of anyone walking by. It's not too muddy."

Billings would have agreed for some reason; he had no reason to fear or be wary of this person, especially here and now, in the shadow of the most public event in the city. Perhaps even Billings had been the one to make the suggestion.

Adam thought again of Annabelle Titus, wondering if she and Billings might have slipped away for a private moment.

They stood talking for a short time — it wasn't very long, for there aren't many signs of shifting footsteps. And then, when there was no one walking by, no one to see, the killer would have struck out with his knife: slash, slash.

Adam's eyes bolted open. So the killer would have had to pull out his knife from a pocket? It would have been difficult to conceal such a weapon, at least for very long.

And the assailant would have to take Billings by surprise, when at any moment someone could walk out of the building or walk by and see him? Adam frowned.

Surely Billings would have seen the knife and held up a hand or an arm to ward off the blow? There'd been no marks on him other than the two stab wounds.

And would one thrust of the knife have killed the man immediately, or would he have cried out in pain or surprise? The killer had struck twice, right here, right out in the open, unerringly stabbing his victim twice in the torso. . . .

He shook his head. So risky. Such a bold chance to take.

There was something he was missing . . . something he couldn't quite see.

Adam knelt, looking at the tracks again. Could the two men have been farther away from the entrance when the killer struck? Around the building, away and out of sight?

No. He shook his head, imagining the shoes he'd brought back to the Willard. There wasn't enough mud on them for Billings to have walked more than a few steps in this muck, and the entire perimeter of the building was of soft, wet dirt.

The tracks stopped here, right here. . . . They hadn't gone very far from the door —

Adam stilled, crouched awkwardly, balancing on his false hand. Yes, that was blood. Right there, in a small arc across the mud-stained grass. It was like a small spray, as if someone had dipped a brush in whitewash and whipped it out too quickly, leaving a trail of paint behind it.

But the spray wasn't from the white paint that covered the dance hall exterior. It was blood.

He frowned. Such a small amount of blood for a man to have died from being stabbed multiple times. No great pool of it, no other drops . . . just the small, delicate arc. Hardly enough blood.

Surely it couldn't be enough blood for a man to die. There hadn't been much more than this inside, either, where the body had been lying.

Billings had to have been killed elsewhere. Adam knew what it looked like — how much blood there was — when a man was stabbed or shot.

There just wasn't enough blood here.

It didn't make any sense.

He rubbed his eyes and looked again. He walked all the way along the side of the building in both directions, looking for more prints, for blood, for grease stains — for something that would lead him to the place where Billings had been killed.

But there was nothing more. He read the tracks again and again, and the story didn't change.

They stood here. Fremark walked by on his way to City Hall, hardly noticing them, he was in such a hurry.

As soon as Fremark was gone, the man killed Billings — here's where the weight of his stance changed, where Billings staggered and lost his balance and sagged forward, toward his killer, maybe even brushed against the outside of the building. The murderer caught him, and then he put his arm around his waist and half carried him into the building, walking side by side. If anyone saw them, he'd say his friend was soused.

But where was all the blood? A man who was stabbed would bleed out *somewhere.*

Adam stared blindly at the ground. And why would the murderer have brought him inside? Why would he have taken the risk of doing this here, where anyone could see him? Come upon him?

Because he wanted the body to be found.

It was the only explanation that made sense.

And then there were the traces of oil. The biggest smudge was just outside the door, and there was another one on the edge of the temporary walkway, right at where the killer would have stepped on it to take his victim inside.

He nodded. Yes, the oil smudge was on the bottom of the killer's — he looked narrowly at the track, imagined it in his mind — his right shoe. And the genesis of the grease stain was here in the muddy grass. There were no other traces of oil anywhere but at the murder scene and just inside the building where Billings had been arranged.

Adam knew it then. He knew it in the same way he'd read the rest of the tracks, the way he *saw* it all. The oil smudge had to be directly related to the killing — to the moments surrounding the murder.

And he had that same sense of easy comprehension he'd experienced a moment ago: learn the reason for the oil and why it was on the shoe of the murderer . . . and then he'd be able to follow the rest of the "tracks" to their conclusion.

Though he continued to look around the grounds for another twenty minutes, Adam could find nothing to negate the story he'd built in his mind.

He was right. He *knew* he was right. He just didn't know why and how.

With a sigh, he passed a hand over his face and realized that it was approaching midday, and that he'd had nothing to eat since early last night. The coffee with which he'd fueled himself had long done its job, leaving him with an empty, gnawing stomach.

Since it was nearly noon, and the scrawny Brian Mulcahey would be arriving at the Willard as directed — he hoped — Adam decided to go back and meet the young boy. He could get himself something to eat, and feed the kid as well.

When Adam approached the Willard, Birch was standing at the door in his pristine white gloves and shiny black shoes. He grinned and thumbed toward the wall behind him, and that was where Adam saw Brian Mulcahey. The boy was leaning against the bricks watching everything happening around him. Currently, a horse-drawn omnibus was rumbling down the avenue, and behind it was a shiny barouche upholstered with a plush gold interior.

Brian was so entranced by the activity on the street he didn't seem to notice Adam right away. But when Birch gave a sharp whistle and shouted at him, the kid straightened up guiltily.

"I'm here, mister," said the boy, running over to him as if afraid Adam would disappear if he didn't move fast. "What are you wanting me to do?"

"How about we get something to eat and I'll tell you. I reckon I could eat an entire cow and still want more."

Brian looked up at him as if uncertain whether to believe him. After all, Americans were strange. "Eat a whole cow yourself? How would you be doing that, mister?"

Adam shook his head and laughed. "With my Arkansas toothpick and a very big fork. Come on, boy."

"What's an Arkansas toothpick?" Brian asked, trotting along next to him, the tip of his big toe pale as a baby's backside as it extruded from his boot.

"It's a very long knife. Long as my forearm here, with a blade about two inches — this big — wide."

"Why's it called a toothpick?"

Adam grinned. "Some of the fiercer men claim they use the tip of that long damned knife to clean their teeth. Me, I know that's a load of bunk because you'd be holding its hilt way out to here in order to manipulate it without cutting off your lip." He demonstrated.

Brian sucked in his breath, his pale blue eyes wide, the freckles on his face standing out against his fair skin. "I guess you're right about that, mister."

"We wore 'em strapped to our backs out west like so." Adam showed how he could reach behind his head and pull out the sword-like knife. "There's a saying on the frontier not to let a man reach behind to scratch his neck or he might come up with a toothpick in his hand."

"*Gor!* You're from the frontier?"

"I sure am." Even as he described the Kansas frontier to Brian's litany of questions, Adam was imagining the murderer pulling out his knife in front of his victim, and how Billings would have reacted to seeing such a threat. The dagger with the blue stone on its hilt hadn't been nearly as long or wide as an Arkansas toothpick — or Bowie knife, as it was also called, though some purists argued they weren't precisely the same blade — but it certainly had done the job.

And he reckoned the killer sure hadn't had an Arkansas toothpick stuck down behind his dress shirt and waistcoat.

They went to a shop that sold meat pies, crusty bread, and other edibles, and Adam's stomach hurt in a different way than hunger pangs when he saw how round Brian's eyes became when he looked at all the food offerings. So Adam bought four meat pies stuffed with potatoes, carrots, and peas, along with two apple tarts. They stood at a small counter in the shop to eat.

"Reckon I wasn't as hungry as I thought," Adam said after they'd each eaten a pie and washed it down with water from a pump outside. "Maybe you could do me a favor and take these others to your family for me, boy. I don't have anywhere to keep them at the hotel." He offered him the rest of the food, which was in a brown paper bag.

Brian's eyes were wide as he nodded. "My mam would be happy to see them pies, I'd be guessing."

"I guess she would. Now," Adam said, wanting the boy to remember he had work to do, "I need you to go to the St. Charles Hotel. You know where that is?"

When the urchin nodded his head, but looked confused and then stricken, Adam realized he probably didn't know where the building was and didn't want to admit it, so he casually told him.

"You got anywhere you need to be today? School?" he asked belatedly. His mama would flay him if she found out he was keeping a kid from learning. She'd been so strict when they were growing up, which was how Adam came to be as well read as he was.

Brian frowned. "Ain't no schools up in Ballard's Alley, sir. My mam, she's about learning me some lettering, but she don't always have time with little Benny and Megan, and my papa being gone. But I can make my name and I can read that sign there. Louisiana Avenue. See?"

"That's a very good start." Adam was just about to give him his instructions for the St. Charles when a sleek black landau caught his eye.

It had an ornate gold design on its door that looked like a *T.* The vehicle was forced to stop behind an omnibus, which was coming from a different direction from the other they'd seen earlier. It met the description of the vehicle owned by the man Billings had been arguing with in his study. And, he reckoned, it probably belonged to one Mortimer Titus.

"Brian, do you see that carriage there? With the letter *T* on it in gold painting?"

"*Gor.* That's one right beautiful buggy," the boy whispered as the vehicle in question began to inch forward. "It looks like a king would ride in it. And look, there's a beautiful lady inside too," he added, straining to see.

Adam had seen the woman too. Annabelle Titus. He'd wager his last dime on it. "Can you follow that carriage and see if you can find out who the owner is? Learn his name, and the lady's name, and where they live if you can. Do you think you can do that?" Adam reckoned the boy would be able to travel just as quickly down the busy street on foot as the carriage would travel making its way through the clogged traffic. "If you lose sight of it, you just come back to the Willard and tell Birch at six o'clock, all right then?"

"Yes, mister. I can do that easy. What was your name again? My mam asked me, and I forgot."

"Adam Quinn."

Brian looked up at him, shifting from one foot to the other, the paper bag with the extra food crinkling with each movement. Adam was just about to point to the nearest outhouse when the boy asked, "Is it true you know the president? Mr. Lincoln? That man at Willard's, Mr. Birch . . . he was all about telling me you did."

"It's true. And the task I set you," he said, gesturing to the street toward the carriage, "is related to a secret job I'm doing for him.

185

So you want to do your best, and don't tell anyone else about what you're doing. You got that?"

"A secret job?" Brian looked like he was about to explode. *"Gor."* But this time, he whispered the exclamation on an exhale. "I will, mister. Mr. Quinn. Thank you." He was just about to dash off on his mission when Adam stopped him.

He just couldn't let the kid keep running around in those damned boots.

"Mr. Lincoln can't abide by people working for him who don't have good shoes — never know when you might have to run, or sneak up on someone. You can't be tripping over your own big toe there, son. A man's got to have a solid pair of shoes if he's going to work for the president."

The boy looked stricken again, those maple syrup freckles standing out starkly against dead-white skin. He nodded.

Adam was digging out some money for the boy when Brian shuffled his ill-clad feet. "I understand, mister. Thank you anyway."

"Wait a minute," Adam said, feeling stricken himself. "I only meant to give you this — go buy yourself a pair of boots to wear. Mr. Lincoln always equips his men." He handed him four silver dollars, which would more than cover the cost of proper footwear and a new coat too. "Next time I see you, you'd better have new boots. You got that?"

Brian nodded vigorously, the paper bag crinkling under his arm. "Yes, sir."

"Now off with you."

Adam turned away as Brian dashed off down the street in the wake of the fancy carriage; otherwise, he'd be watching him with stinging eyes. He was bemused — and hoping the kid wouldn't trip over his toe. At the same time, he was suddenly nostalgic, missing his godson Carl — who was an angel in heaven now — as well as his own little brother Danny . . . who was probably not so little anymore.

Damn it all. He wasn't certain what he was doing here — even more of a misfit than Lincoln — in Washington, among all of this ugly muck of a world.

The muck being both literal and figurative.

With a sigh, he checked his pocket watch. Nearly one o'clock: time to meet Miss Lemagne.

CHAPTER 7

"I cannot apologize enough for my daddy's rudeness this morning, Mr. Quinn," said Miss Lemagne, offering him a slender, gloved hand.

She wore a hat stuffed on the underside of its circumspect brim with pink and blue nosegays woven with lace. The wide ribbon that tied beneath her chin made her eyes look the color of a clear summer sky over the plains: bluer than blue. Her dress, though its skirt hung over a frame that kept it stiff and bell shaped, was not nearly as wide and ruffled as the one she'd worn last night, and the fabric wasn't silky or shiny, but a lightweight dyed wool. She wore a heavy cloak of dark blue that fell to her shoes, its hood hanging over her back. A rabbit fur stole covered the tops of her shoulders and crossed over the front of her throat and was pinned by a large pearl brooch.

She smiled a little bashfully when he lifted a brow at the fur. "It's much warmer back home, Mr. Quinn, and this cold dampness chills me to the very bone. It hardly ever gets this cold in Alabama, especially in March." Then, just as quickly as it had come, the sweet, demure demeanor faded into a more serious one. "Thank you for meeting me."

"What is it you have to tell me?"

She slipped her hand from his fingers and took his arm, bringing with her a waft of something light and floral as her skirt and cloak brushed his trouser leg. "Over here, where we won't be heard."

He allowed her to lead him to a small alcove in one of the public rooms of the Kirkwood Hotel. "You were beginning to tell me that your father didn't return to the hotel until early this morning."

She sat on one end of a divan upholstered in gold brocade, swiftly and expertly arranging layers of skirts, then patted the space next to her. Adam had no choice but to acquiesce, though he felt strangely awkward sitting so close to a woman he hardly knew, and in such a public place — a woman whose father had already made a scene, and whose self-proclaimed fiancé had done the same.

The last thing he wanted was to compromise her reputation in any way.

"Yes, although that's not the most important part."

"But I'd like to know about your father first," Adam said, thinking of Lemagne's business card found in Billings's pocket. "Had he been at the ball all that time?"

"I hadn't been able to sleep, so when I heard him, I came out of my room. He was walking unsteadily and I thought he was drunk — or maybe hurt. Of course, I went out to find out what happened, and to see if he needed help. It's not like him to stay out that late, or to drink too much."

"What had happened?"

"He said he went to the chambers at City Hall to wash up, and then he was standing outside having a cigar. Then something — or someone — hit him in the back of his head. The next thing he knew, he woke up alone in one of the offices in City Hall and it was almost dawn. He had no idea how he got there." Miss Lemagne's eyes were filled with worry. "I'm afraid someone tried to kill him too, but was somehow interrupted."

"I reckon he had a big lump on the back of his head," Adam said.

"I — well, he wouldn't let me look at it. He became gruff and grumbly when I tried, and said he just needed some rest. That's why he was so rude this morning, I'm sure. His head still hurt him."

"He told you his head hurt? And there wasn't any sign of a lump that you could see?"

Miss Lemagne pulled back a little and her expression cooled. "Are you suggesting he might have made up the story, Mr. Quinn?"

"No, of course not," he replied quickly. "It's just that if he was blacked out for several hours, he should have a big bump on the back of his head." And most likely one on the front, if he fell forward — which was likely if someone had struck him from behind.

Adam didn't remember seeing anything like a cut or bump on Hurst Lemagne's forehead, and the man had a receding hairline that exposed a good portion of his temples.

"He could have died," Miss Lemagne said tightly. "Whoever killed Mr. Billings might have wanted to kill him too. And I think I know who it was."

"You do?" Now she had his full attention.

"I think I overheard something important." She had a hint of chastisement in her voice. "Yesterday, after the inauguration and before it was time to get ready for the ball, I walked around the hotel to the rear-facing side. There's a little courtyard there for the guests, and I wanted some fresh air. The servants' and delivery entrance is right next to it, but it's separated by a wooden wall made from crisscrossed slats. I got a little turned around and ended up on the wrong side, by the servants' entrance, not in the courtyard. And that's when I heard some men talking.

"Of course, I wouldn't have dreamed of eavesdropping if I hadn't heard one of them say something about everything being set for tonight. Meaning, last night — not tonight."

"Yes, I follow you." He looked at her keenly. "Why did that phrase catch your attention? It wouldn't be a surprise for someone to be talking about the ball last night and everything being prepared."

She gave him a satisfied smile with a dimple that winked near the corner of her mouth. "Because, Mr. Quinn, he was speaking with a deep southern accent. A Mississippi or Alabama accent, one from way down in Dixie — not just hoverin' near it like the ones that do up here. And why would a very deeply Southern man be talking about everything being set for the ball that celebrated the swearing in of a president he surely despises?"

"I see. So you're suggesting there was no reason for a man — or men — from the Deep South to be looking forward to the Union Ball unless there was some other reason? But by that same logic, then, Miss Lemagne, I reckon I could wonder the same about you and your father."

Again she drew back a little. "Mr. Quinn, I'm not certain I like your implication."

"I'm not implying anything, Miss Lemagne," he replied, unable to subdue his male appreciation for the way her eyes flashed and her cheeks turned pink with unfeigned outrage. "I admit to being curious as to why the two of you bothered to attend the celebration for a man your father obviously despises."

"It's very simple: *I* wanted to go. I wasn't about to miss the most excitin' event in the city, and Mr. Mossing was invited, of course, and he graciously agreed for us to be his guests. Daddy consented to attend in order to make some business contacts — and because I begged him to go."

That was a reasonable explanation, Adam reflected, and it made sense as to why Lemagne spent hardly any time in the ballroom himself. But who would have hit him on the head? And why?

"You were saying, Miss Lemagne . . . about what you overheard. Was there anything else?"

"Oh, yes." Her eyes were still sparkling, but not quite as furiously as they had been. Her temperature seemed to have gone up along with her ire, for she pulled off her gloves and unfastened the fur stole from around her neck, setting the three items between them on the divan.

And then she leaned closer to Adam so he was distracted for a moment by the scent of her, and the proximity of her full, pink mouth. "First one man said things were set for the night, and then the other said something about 'splitting that damned Illinois rail to the ground.' " Her voice was low and mellow.

Adam went still, curling his right hand into itself. "You're certain that's what they said?"

"I was standin' right there, Mr. Quinn, with only a flimsy fence between us. There's not a thing wrong with my ears."

He couldn't help but glance at the tease of white earlobe peeking from beneath the smooth wing of her hair. There were no earbobs today. "Did you hear anything else at all? Or did you see any part of them through the wooden slat fence? How many men were there?"

"Three," she replied. "I could see a little bit of them through the holes. One of them was very tall, and the other two not as much. They were all of slender build. I'm afraid I couldn't make out much more; they were all wearing hats and dark coats. And, of course, they weren't exactly shouting their conversation. I did hear them say something about — what was it? About the fools in Baltimore letting the cat out, so this time they made sure the sack was tied tightly."

Baltimore. Adam's suspicions that there had been a plan to assassinate the president last night — and that Custer Billings was somehow involved — grew stronger.

Back in early February, Pinkerton had sent two of his agents to go undercover in Baltimore to flesh out rumors of a deadly attack on the president-elect when he traveled through the city on his way to Washington.

It was the thorough, patient work of Pinkerton, as well as his associates Harry Davies and Kate Warne, that gave the detective enough ammunition to go to Lincoln and convince him to secretly change his travel plans at the last minute. The president-elect's reluctant agreement caused Lincoln to arrive at Willard's in the middle of night — to the delight of the press, which had made much hay out of the way the "cowardly" man had "crept" and "slinked" into town in the dead of night.

Adam knew all of this for he'd been there when the detective had laid out for Mr. Lincoln all the details of the Baltimore Plot he'd gleaned, and had helped convince the man not to take the risk of keeping to his schedule. Although Lincoln never completely believed in the severity of the threat, he'd acquiesced to the pressure from Pinkerton and the others.

The plan in Baltimore had been simple: When the president-elect arrived at the train station from Philadelphia, he had to disembark and be taken by carriage to a different station for the train to Washington. The stations were several blocks apart, and the plan was for the plotters to cause a riot in the streets as the carriage approached. It would create havoc and distract and weaken the local police — as well as Lincoln's own security team — giving the assassins an opening to kill the president-elect.

Perhaps that same concept had been in play last night. Finding a dead body at the Union Ball might have caused great distress if Pinkerton and Joshua hadn't handled things differently and kept the news quiet.

"Mr. Quinn?" Miss Lemagne's gentle voice, and the brush of her cool, bare hand against his returned him to the moment.

He blinked, and as his attention skittered back to the woman next to him, his gaze swept up from their two touching hands and the jumble of skirts in her lap, along her spine-straight torso . . . and stopped. He stared — not at the black and white cockade attached to her bodice, but at the brooch pinned to the center of her neckline.

The simple pin had been hidden by the fur stole, as had the cockade, but now it was fully revealed and terribly familiar: the opaque blue hemisphere of a stone veined with black, surrounded by tiny black beads. It was the same design as on the handle of the dagger that had been found near Custer Billings's body.

Miss Lemagne made a soft noise, and her slender hand came up to caress the petal-like edges of the secessionist cockade. "Are you so shocked to see this, Mr. Quinn? Of course, I must support my Southern brethren."

"I was more interested in the other pin you're wearing," he said, keeping his voice casual as a number of thoughts bombarded him. "I've seen it somewhere before. What sort of stone is that?"

"This?" She fingered the brooch, her voice light with surprise. "It was my grandmama's. It was sort of a family heirloom her father brought over from Ireland. The stone is from the land he grew up on in Kilkenny and he had several pieces made in the same way."

"What other sort of pieces?"

Miss Lemagne seemed confused by his interest, but she replied, "Earbobs, for one, and I believe a belt buckle at one time, but it's long gone missing. There was an eating set too and a goblet with the stones set around the base. A dagger. Oh, and a horsehair brush."

Adam stood abruptly. "I need to speak with your father, Miss Lemagne. As soon as possible."

"Why? Whatever is wrong?" She gathered up her gloves and fur, then stood.

But Adam just shook his head, keeping his lips pursed tightly. He offered her his arm as she refastened the stole around her throat, then said, "I'll escort you back to the St. Charles. Do you reckon your father will be there?"

"I have no idea, Mr. Quinn." She pointedly didn't take his arm, frowning at him instead as she yanked on her gloves. "Just as I have no idea what's come over you with all of these unmannerly questions."

He considered telling her, but something held him back. There was something so very convenient about the way she'd overheard just the smattering of a conversation between three men — and yet there was enough detail that it wasn't ambiguous. It all could be true, but then again . . .

"I beg your pardon if I seem uncivil," he said, reminding himself that he was still his mother's son, and she still expected him to be a model of politeness in the company of a woman — even if his manners weren't as smooth and perfect as those of the society men of Washington. "But it's important that I speak with your father, and though he was unwilling this morning, I'm hoping you can convince him to give me a few moments. The president may not be his choice, but he *is* the president, and what I do is at his direction."

Miss Lemagne gave a little huff and spun away to start walking out of the Kirkwood — but not before she shot him a dark glare. "I'll do my best, but I can't promise anything."

Adam escorted her back to her hotel, promising to return in twenty minutes to speak with her father. That would give him enough time to retrieve the dagger from his rooms at the Willard and give her the opportunity to convince Lemagne it was in his best interest to speak with him. He wasn't certain what he would do if the man refused.

When Adam reentered the lobby of the St. Charles, he found both Constance and Hurst Lemagne waiting for him. The man glared at him with flinty eyes, but the presence of his daughter — whose hand remained on his arm — seemed to keep his fury at bay.

"I'm much obliged to you for meeting with me," Adam said, taking care to keep his voice neither conciliatory nor condescending. "Is there somewhere we can speak privately?"

"It depends what this is in regards to," Lemagne replied testily.

Since he didn't know what Constance had told her father, Adam replied, "Custer Billings was found dead last night." At the same time, he considered the man's build. Yes, it was possible he'd be able to carry the slighter Billings into the anteroom, although if the other man was a dead weight, it wouldn't have been easy.

"Billings? Dead?" Surprise flared in his

eyes, followed by some other emotion quickly masked. "But what do you want with me?"

Adam merely looked at him, examining the older man's dark eyes for any sign of guilt or subterfuge. He could carry on the conversation here, but he didn't think the man would appreciate it — especially when he showed him the dagger he carried in a parcel under his left arm.

"Daddy, he said you should speak alone. Why not go into the small parlor? No one will be there right now."

"If you insist."

The room Miss Lemagne suggested was small and cozy, and a wood fire blazed against the chilly March day. The single window was mottled with both drizzle and imperfections in the glass, and its golden drapes were pulled back to reveal a busy side street. There were a small sofa and two chairs in front of the fireplace with a low table between them. She led them to this seating arrangement and sank onto the divan.

"I don't know about you, Lemagne, but I reckon a cup of coffee would be in order." Adam met the man's eyes and held them meaningfully.

"I can't disagree. Constance, dear, would

you go get someone to bring us coffee?"

"But there's a bell right there —"

"It would be best if you saw to it yourself. You know how lazy the servants can be. Close the door behind you."

Miss Lemagne, who'd just finished arranging her skirt prettily over her lap, stiffened. But when her father's pointed look didn't waver, she rose with a distinct huff. Her cheeks were pink with fury, and she looked as if she were about to choke on her words. But obviously realizing argument was futile, she shot a glare at Adam before sweeping from the room with another huff.

The door closed, but not very quietly, behind her.

Lemagne turned a cold gaze onto Adam. "Now what the blazes do you want?"

"Is this yours?" Adam laid the parcel on the table between them, then flipped open the piece of cloth to reveal the dagger.

Lemagne looked down at it, then up at him. He clearly didn't need to examine it closely in order to respond. "Yes. It's part of a matched set of family heirlooms. Where did you find it?"

"It was found sticking out of Custer Billings's body last night."

What? Lemagne was on his feet, his face

suddenly the color of beets. "That's impossible."

Adam shook his head, again watching the man closely to read what was in his eyes and expression.

"Are you saying this knife was used to kill Custer Billings?"

"Yes. Last night, at the inaugural ball. The knife belongs to you, and your business card was found in his coat pocket. You were overheard arguing with him earlier in the day. And," Adam continued, though the man appeared ready to shout some more, "you were missing from the ball for several hours and no one knows where you were."

"Are you accusing me of *murdering Custer Billings*?"

Adam reckoned using a private room didn't matter after all, for Hurst Lemagne was making no effort to keep his voice down. Surely everyone in the hotel lobby could hear him, though it was a corridor away.

"On whose authority are you questioning me? What gives you the right to do this?"

By this time, the man's face was nearly purple, and Adam began to fear that he was going to collapse from apoplexy. He gestured to the sofa where the older man had been sitting in hopes of diffusing the situation.

"I'm not accusing you of anything, Lemagne. At this time, I've only pointed out some facts. And to answer your question, you know from our brief conversation this morning that I'm working under the authority of the president —"

The man's eyes bugged wider and tiny flecks of spittle flew as he responded, "I told you he's no damned president of mine! Pissed rail-splitter has no business coming in and taking away our nigger slaves. That ape bastard is nothing more than a cocklick —"

Adam had stood, and he towered over the stout man. It took all his effort to keep from grabbing Lemagne by the front of his waistcoat; his five fingers trembled with the effort of keeping them curled close to his side. "I reckon you have the right to say what you will, Mr. Lemagne, but I'll not listen to you impugn my president — who is also my friend — in such a vulgar manner. Now sit down," he said in a cold, hard voice, "and tell me where you were last night . . . or we'll have this out on the street. And I reckon you'll be the one crawling away."

"You *are* accusing me of murder," Lemagne shot back . . . but he sat. Or maybe his knees buckled; Adam noticed how quickly he seemed to drop into place.

"For your daughter's sake, I hope not," Adam replied as he took his seat again. He went silent, watching and waiting.

"I didn't kill Billings."

Adam looked pointedly at the dagger, then back up at the man, whose face had cooled to a blotchy red above his dark blond whiskers. But there was a sheen over his forehead now, and his hands were folded tightly in his lap.

"I don't know how they got the knife. Someone must have stolen it."

"When is the last time you remember seeing it? Are you in the habit of taking it with you when you travel?"

"I don't know when I saw it last. Yes, I usually take it with me when I travel. Don't you carry a knife for eating or other tasks, Quinn?"

Adam couldn't refute that; most men did carry a small knife or dagger for the random needs one might have while traveling — including eating at a small inn or public house, which often didn't have good knives. He hadn't been joking — too much — when he told Brian Mulcahey about some men using the Arkansas toothpick to clean their teeth. It had been done, though probably not with a Bowie knife.

"Where were you last night? Your daughter told me she wasn't able to find you for a very long stretch of time — the time during which Billings was murdered."

Lemagne looked at him furiously, his eyes still bulging, his teeth grinding. For a moment, Adam thought the man was going to refuse to answer, but then Lemagne's grimace eased slightly. "I didn't want to be at the damned ball for that bast— for that man," he said from between tight jaws, "but Constance was set on going. And Mossing was happy to bring us on his invitation. I've known him since he was a young boy, and his father was my friend and business associate. I only decided to attend because I have business with plenty of people in this city and thought it would be an opportunity to talk to them. But after the cursed railsplitter arrived, I didn't want to stay in the same room as him" — he looked at Adam in challenge — "and I went over to the City Hall to the men's lounge. After that, I went outside to have a cigar. I was standing there and something — or someone — hit me on the back of the head, and I must have blacked out. When I woke up, I was in an office in City Hall. It was almost dawn and

I went back to the hotel after that."

"Someone hit you on the back of the head and you blacked out . . . and fell down?"

"Yes."

"You must have some sort of knot, and even a cut on the back of your head. You probably bled too. Did you see a doctor?"

"No. I had a headache, and the bump is almost gone. I-I didn't bleed."

"And I reckon you fell . . . forward, then, right? If someone hit you from behind?"

"Yes, I suppose I did."

"But your forehead and temples are smooth and unmarked. Not even a cut from shaving around your beard. If you'd fallen, you'd have hit your head or face on something — the ground, the side of the building. . . ." Adam held his gaze. "There'd be some sort of mark or scrape."

He didn't need to say anything more; the realization was dawning in Lemagne's face. The man shot to his feet, meaty hands balled into fists, but Adam was just as quick.

"Look, Mr. Lemagne, it looks pretty bad that you killed Billings. So either you did, or I reckon someone's trying to make it look like you did." Adam wasn't certain whether he truly believed the latter, or if it was for Constance Lemagne's sake that he gave it as an option. "I've been asked to investigate and find out what happened — and I will. Even if you don't hold Mr. Lincoln in high regard, he still has executive power in this country and, more importantly, in this city. I have the authority of him and the military he commands, as well as the constabulary — such as it is — behind me.

"Someone was killed at the Union Ball, and no one is going to take the death of Custer Billings lightly, partly because of where and when it happened. Now, tell me where you really were during the ball, Mr. Lemagne."

CHAPTER 8

Constance stifled a gasp, bumping lightly against the Ajar door in her agitation. The hardware of the knob made a very faint clink, but surely no one in the room could discern it over the volume of raised voices — mostly her father's.

And she herself could hardly account for what she was hearing at any volume.

Mr. Quinn thought her daddy had killed Custer Billings.

How could he? Her father was a loud, often angry man, but she loved him nevertheless. He wouldn't hurt a fly. She *knew* he wouldn't.

Constance adjusted her ear at the seam of the door and turned the knob to ease it open once more. During her furious exit moments ago she'd fairly slammed it shut, only to stealthily crack it open immediately afterward. How dare they try to send her away! And fie on them if they thought she was just going to skip off and get them coffee. That Mr. Quinn was getting to be more than a little annoying.

"Miss Lemagne?"

She whirled, barely managing to keep from bumping the door again, and found herself looking up into the cool dark eyes of another of the hotel's guests.

"Why, I declare, Mr. Wellburg, you nearly startled me right through the ceiling," she said with a coy smile. She'd met the gentleman briefly one night in the hotel dining room when he'd come to their table to speak to her daddy.

Mr. Wellburg was from South Carolina, and he owned a tobacco warehouse and cotton export business. Apparently the Mossings had done business with them for years. Arthur Mossing might be a Unionist, but Wellburg and her daddy were not, and Constance had sat like a lump of clay when they fell into a fiery conversation about the hated president-elect, when Virginia was going to join South Carolina and secede, the rising price of cotton, and some business group called the Association.

"Didn't your mama ever tell you it's not nice to sneak up on a young lady?" she added sweetly to Mr. Wellburg. As she knew how to make her eyes sparkle, she turned on that extra bit of charm along with her flirtatious ways.

"Especially when she's listening at a doorway," he replied in a smooth southern tone. "And didn't your mama ever tell you that nice young ladies aren't supposed to listen at doorways, or at windows — or in the garden? They can overhear things they really don't want to know, and sometimes they find themselves in a peck of trouble if they do. . . ." He'd stepped closer so that one of his shoes bumped the toe of hers. "You know what they say about curiosity and the cat, Miss Lemagne."

Constance's breath caught in her throat. He sounded almost as if he were threatening her. Her eyes fixed on his coat lapel and the palmetto cockade he wore there. It had a triangular button in the center and what looked like an ink stain on one of the frayed palm fronds.

Before she could gather her wits to respond, Mr. Wellburg stepped back. He gave her a warm smile that had no trace of the warning that had been in his voice. "But surely even if you overheard something, you're far too prudent to carry tales, aren't you, Miss Lemagne? Especially when we all support the same cause." He reached out to tap the black and white ribbon she wore;

then his hand fell back to his side.

Her lungs were still clogged but she forced herself to look up at him unabashed. "I'm certain I have no idea what you're talking about, Mr. Wellburg."

"That's right, Miss Lemagne. That's exactly right. I'm so glad you understand me." He gave a brief bow and took her fingers before she could pull them away. A smile tipped his lips as he brought her gloved hand up to kiss it. "Have a lovely afternoon, Miss Lemagne. Give your father my regards."

Her heart was pounding and she felt a little light in the head — though that could be because she'd had Moppy pull her corset laces extra tight today, knowing she was going to be meeting with Mr. Quinn.

She drew in a few breaths as deep as her corset would allow and felt some of the light-headedness dissipate. But even as it did, the clamminess of fear settled over her. Was it possible Mr. Wellburg had been one of the men she'd overheard yesterday, talking in the courtyard? Otherwise known as the *garden*?

She hadn't recognized his voice, but only one of the three had been talking. And she didn't think anyone had seen her, so how would he have known she was there?

Maybe she was just making too much out of some genteel teasing. She'd been around enough gentlemen to know that oftentimes their idea of flirtatious teasing was annoying and more uncouth than they realized.

But there'd been something in his eyes just now. Something hard, something certain. Something that made her insides feel unsteady.

Constance looked at the door to the parlor, then down the empty corridor. She wasn't a coward, but she didn't want to encounter that man again. And there was too much going on inside the parlor to miss. *Mr. Quinn thought her father had killed Mr. Billings.* Even though she *knew* he couldn't ever have done anything like that, what if no one believed it?

What if they arrested her father? What if he went to jail? What would she do? She was in a strange city where she knew no one. She couldn't stay here *alone,* she didn't have any money and had no way to access any — and she couldn't go home and leave her father. What if there was a trial? What if she had to stay for months? What if war broke out, like everyone said it would? What would she do?

She drew in another ragged breath, shoved those fears aside. Nothing had happened yet. It was just Mr. Quinn talking.

Interrogating her father, like he was a common criminal.

She pushed open the door.

The heads of both men pivoted to look at her, and she felt the whiplash of tension in the room. Neither wore a welcoming expression — either for her or the other.

"Constance," her father began in a tight voice. He rose, as politeness dictated, but he didn't appear happy about it.

"I heard what you were saying," she said, forestalling any command for her to leave. "Bless your black heart if you think my daddy killed Mr. Billings, Mr. Quinn. He'd never do anything like that. He's a whole lot of bluster, you see, but he's all bark and no bite. Why, he doesn't even whip the horses."

"Constance," her father said again, this time with more underlying fury. "This is not your concern."

"Yes it is, Daddy." She glared at the frontiersman, who'd actually remembered to bolt to his feet at her entrance to the room. Now he stood, far too tall and imposing next to her poor, red-faced father. "I had no idea you would take what I told you and try to make a case against my father. For shame, Mr. Quinn."

"Please sit down, Miss Lemagne. I'm not trying to make a case against your father. I'm only trying to discover the truth. The knife that was used to kill Custer Billings is part of the same collection as the brooch you're wearing. It belongs to your family, and it was found sticking out of a dead man's chest. You must admit, that is cause for question."

"Well someone must have stolen it and used it to cast suspicion on us," she replied, and her chest felt tight once again. Who would do something like that? "It must have been a Yankee. They hate us Southerners."

But even as she spouted those unfounded words — for she hadn't actually met a Unionist who was anything but polite and friendly, even if they noticed her cockade — Constance couldn't dismiss the memory of the cold expression in Mr. Wellburg's face.

Was it possible he'd recognized her listening in on him and his cohorts and planted the knife at a murder scene in order to implicate her father? As a warning — or even in retaliation for her unintentional indiscretion? That clammy, nauseating feeling was back.

What would she do if her father was arrested for murder?

"Please sit down, Miss Lemagne. You look

a little pale. Your daughter brings up a good question, Mr. Lemagne. When is the last time you saw your dagger? Since you use it all the time, surely you'd notice it going missing."

Constance glared at Mr. Quinn. She didn't care for his tone, and the way his brows lifted in silent challenge. But she did as he suggested and sat.

"Wait . . . wait one moment. Now that I think on it, I do remember the last time I saw it," said her father. "Yesterday afternoon, it was. I had it out back by the stables. Used it to dig a stone out of my horse's shoe, if you must know."

"That's right, Daddy," Constance said eagerly. "I remember — you'd taken the carriage for a drive after the streets were clear from the oath-taking."

"Yes, poppet. And when I got back, I thought Samson had something in his shoe and so I looked at it myself. Sure enough, a damn — er, a little stone had gotten lodged in there."

"You didn't have a groom take care of it for you?" asked Mr. Quinn, who'd also, finally, taken a seat again. Still, his broad shoulders seemed too large for the ornate back of the chair on which he sat. And he appeared far too relaxed — in his clothing, and with the way his hair was all messy as if it hadn't been combed in days. He was a far cry from Arthur Mossing when it came to proper grooming. Mr. Quinn was more like a stable hand than a gentleman.

And yet . . . somehow, despite the trouble he was stirring up, the frontiersman fascinated her, with his large, tanned hand; stubbled chin; and rough manners.

"I see to my own horses, Quinn, as often as I can. Especially Samson and Delilah. They're worth more than the house you grew up in." Constance was familiar with her father's haughty tone, and felt it was fairly directed at Mr. Quinn in exchange for all of the unpleasantness he was causing.

"And so you used the knife to remove the stone . . . and that was the last time you saw it?"

The frontiersman was dogged and determined if nothing else. She had to give him credit for that. And the way his eyes remained so serious and steady. She could imagine him out on the frontier riding a horse, instead of sitting in a plush carriage, the wind blustering through his too long hair, and his strong hand holding the reins as he sat astride, tall and powerful in the saddle, moving as one with the horse. . . .

All at once, she had the desire to fan

herself. Stridently.

Constance forced her attention back to her father, whose expression had gone from haughty to one filled with concentration.

"I picked the stone out of Samson's shoe, and must have set the knife down on the ledge in the stable, because I needed two hands to examine his leg, make sure he hadn't pulled anything. I don't remember picking up the dagger again. And that's the last time I remember using it. This morning I looked for it, but it was gone."

"Someone took it from the stable," she said quickly. Her heart was pounding, for the stable was adjacent to the courtyard where she'd heard the men threatening to split the rail-splitter down. "That's what happened, and they used it to stab Mr. Billings — and tried to lay the blame on my father."

She was feeling warm and light-headed again. The timing was right: her father had gotten back from his trip in the carriage only a short time — maybe a half hour — after she'd overheard the conversation in the courtyard garden.

"Who was around the stable at the time, Mr. Lemagne?"

"I don't know. There was a groom, and maybe some other people. I don't remember seeing anyone in particular — except, oh yes, there was a man just arrived on the train from Baltimore. Was looking for someone he was supposed to meet, or something. I didn't pay attention, damn — er, excuse me, poppet. I was more concerned about Samson than anyone standing around."

"But don't you see, Mr. Quinn? Someone took the knife. Someone who wanted to frame my father for murder." Constance looked at Adam, willing him to believe her.

He nodded. "It is possible. I'll go and speak with the grooms and see if anyone remembers anyone hanging around the stable yesterday. About what time was this?"

"I was coming out for my walk around four o'clock and Daddy had already gone for his ride in the carriage," Constance replied before her father could speak. "That was about the time I saw three men standing there in the courtyard. They seemed to be discussing something very serious. Maybe they're involved."

She looked at her father, whose face had set into something pale and tight. His eyes were dull with concern and shock, so she reached over to pat his hand.

"Do you know of anyone who might want to get you into trouble, Mr. Lemagne? Someone who might have taken the knife and used it to frame you for murder?"

"There's only one person I can think of who hated me that much."

Constance looked at him in surprise. The idea that someone hated her father enough to frame him for murder was shocking, and almost beyond belief. "Who was that?"

"Custer Billings."

I went to visit a lady friend.

That was the answer Hurst Lemagne had given Adam about where he'd really been during the ball. And he'd spoken it only moments before the man's daughter had slipped back into the parlor.

So Mr. Lemagne had lied to everyone — including Constance — about where he'd been. But he'd finally told the truth to Adam. Supposedly.

Yet, when Adam had pressed him for the name of the woman he'd visited — for, it seemed, several hours — the man had clammed up. And then his daughter had walked in, effectively ending that portion of the conversation.

Adam reckoned he could have pursued the topic, but decided it was best not to do so in front of the young woman, for clearly her father wanted her kept in the dark. But that also meant he might be able to use that to his advantage, if he cornered Lemagne alone later.

Thus, after Adam excused himself from the father and daughter, leaving them in the small parlor, he went directly out to the back of the hotel where Constance Lemagne had overheard the conversation among three men. There was a service entrance near one side, facing the alley. Servants and delivery people were coming and going along the narrow walkway, which was separated from the hotel's courtyard by the fence Miss Lemagne had described.

Garbage and other refuse were piled in the alley, and Adam's presence disturbed a scrawny cat that slinked off as soon as his shadow fell onto the hard-packed ground. The stink of sour milk and other rotten food tinged the cool afternoon air, along with urine and wood smoke.

Along the walkway to the service entrance was the wooden slat fence that kept the hotel guests from having to witness the drudgery that went on in order to keep their stay comfortable and clean: refilling coal bins, receiving butchery deliveries, emptying chamber pots. . . .

On the other side of the fence was a generous, landscaped courtyard. Generous by city standards, but stamp sized to a man who'd lived on the plains. The yard was closed in on two sides by the L-shaped hotel and the fence, and the far side was bordered by the entrance to the stable. The fourth was made up by a narrow side street. In the grassy yard were two small wooden benches beneath a rose arbor. Of course, it was too early for roses to bloom, but there were spring flowers beginning to poke from beneath the dark earth. Adam was fairly certain they were daffodils.

The stable was small and sturdy and would hold only three or four horses and maybe one carriage at a time. Likely, the hotel had a livery several blocks away where it rented space for its guests' horses and buggies. Higher-paying guests might be able to pay for a stall in the on-site stable for easier access to their transportation. The small barn would also be used as a holding place for the horses between transfers to and from the livery.

As Adam walked out of the hotel and looked around, he automatically paused to examine the ground for footprints near the servants' entrance. While there was a well-trodden path where foot upon foot had pressed into the ground in layers and layers, obliterating all but the freshest ones, there were also outlying shoe marks off to the side. As he imagined Miss Lemagne standing here, next to the wooden fence, he reckoned she would move off to the side and away from the main travel pattern, if for no other reason than to distance herself from slopping chamber pots or dusty coal bins. And if she was eavesdropping on a conversation that was happening on the other side of the fence, surely she'd want to get closer. . . .

And there they were — not exactly where he'd expected, but close enough. The footprints of a female with wealth and style. Servants didn't wear shoes with small high heels that made a distinct foot mark, and they certainly didn't have the opportunity to stand in one place for very long.

So that confirmed at least part of Miss Lemagne's story: that she'd come outside and ended up in the path of the servants' entrance instead of the guest side.

She claimed to have heard the men speaking in the courtyard — or perhaps she was merely fabricating the story in order to help her father save face. Although, to be fair, Miss Lemagne had told him about the conversation she'd overheard before she knew her father was suspected of murder.

Either way, the tracks would tell. They always did. So Adam walked back and forth across the courtyard and examined the ground. If what Constance had said was correct, he should find evidence of two or three men talking. According to her, it had not been more than twenty-four hours earlier. And although there had been some drizzle, nothing that would have wiped away the footprints.

It didn't take long for Adam to realize Miss Lemagne had been telling the truth. He found three sets of footprints clearly indicating a small group conversation very close to the wooden slat fence near the servants' entrance. Adam reflected for a moment, remembering the tense look on her face as she told him about someone threatening to split the rail-splitter. She might be a secessionist, but she didn't appear to be a violent one.

The possibility that a participant in an assassination plot meant to take place at the Union Ball had been standing in the courtyard, and then discovered the knife Lemagne had left in the stable, grew stronger in Adam's mind. It would be beyond foolish for a man to stab someone in a public place and leave his personal, easily identifiable dagger at the scene of the crime.

Hurst Lemagne did not strike him as someone who was stupid enough to do something like that.

Either that . . . or Lemagne was very, very clever and assumed Adam — or anyone else — would think just that: that a murderer would never leave his weapon at the scene of the crime.

Thoughtful, Adam went over to the stable to see if he could glean any other information. A groom was inside currying one of the horses. He was spare and wiry, with flyaway gray hair unmoored by a hat, and a low, soothing voice that spoke to the gelding he was brushing. His skin was a tan-gray color and his hand was small and knobby.

"Afternoon, there, sir," said Adam as he stepped farther into the stable. A rush of sweet-smelling hay and that of horse assaulted his nostrils. That brought Adam's thoughts to Stranger, back in Springfield. Hopefully, he too would soon be home and back with his horse, now that he had helped get the president safely inaugurated and into his new home.

It was also time for Adam to decide whether to return to Kansas or to remain in Springfield. Or even to go somewhere else, new and interesting. Colorado, maybe. California?

The groom had not ceased brushing the

broad chestnut he was looking after, but he glanced up as Adam approached. "Afternoon, there, mister. You need something, sir?"

"I seem to have lost a dagger of mine. It was so long," Adam said, demonstrating, "and had a blue stone at the end of the hilt. I reckon I might have left it here in the stable yesterday afternoon. Did you happen to see it?"

"No, sir," replied the groom. "I don't remember seeing nothing like that."

"I reckon one of my friends noticed it and took it to return to me. Did you see any well-dressed man around here yesterday afternoon, late afternoon? Four o'clock or thereabouts?"

"There was Mr. Lemagne here, bringing his horses back after he took out his buggy. Had a stone in one of the shoes, and he insisted on digging it out himself — didn't want me to touch it." The groom spat out a hunk of tobacco, seeming to underscore his opinion about Hurst Lemagne. "After that, I had to take the pair back over to the livery. When I got back, I seen some other men, talking there in the courtyard and smoking *cee*-gars. Maybe it was around that time. I dunno. I warn't paying that close attention — had to muck out the stalls and see to the tack. Joey don't ever hang things up in the way I taught him, and I always gotta go back and rearrange it." He squirted another stream of tobacco into the corner of the stall, filling Adam with relief that the stalls got mucked out regularly.

"Do you remember what the three men looked like? Or did you recognize any of them?"

"I didn't say there was three men." That got the groom to pause with the curry brush and squint up at him. "Why d'you wanna know?"

"If they were my friends and one of them found the knife, I'll know who to ask," Adam replied smoothly. "How many men did you see?"

That seemed to satisfy the groom, for he returned to his work. "They was four of them, standing there talking, holding up the fence. And they all looked the same to me. One of 'em, he was from way down in Dixie. His accent was so thick I could drive a buggy over it."

Four men. Had Miss Lemagne been wrong, or had the fourth man joined the group later? "What were they talking about?"

The other man stood, groaning a little when he straightened up from his position.

"I'm gettin' too old for this." Scrubbing his lower back with a fist, he gave Adam another sharp look. "Why you asking so many questions there, mister?"

"I told you — I'm trying to figure out what happened to my knife." Adam gave him an easy smile and, on a whim, dug in his pocket for a half-dollar coin. He set it on a small shelf at eye level with the groom. When the older man looked at him in surprise, Adam was still smiling. "Just call me curious."

The man snatched up the coin and stuffed it down his shirt. "I didn't hear nothing what they were talking about, and I didn't see no knife. One of the guys was shorter than the others. Two of 'em, they had dark beards. The other two had lighter ones. That's all I can tell you. And they was all dressed fine. Mebbe guests here; I dunno. I don't see much of them; they just send out a footman when they want me to go get a horse from the livery. Mr. Lemagne, he's different. He don't want anyone to touch his horses."

"Did he say where he was going when he took his buggy out?"

"Not that I recall."

"Was there anyone else here in the stable when Mr. Lemagne was fixing his horse's shoe? Or afterward?"

"Yah. Mighta been. Man standing there smoking a *cee*-gar." He pointed vaguely toward the door of the stable that opened onto a busy side street. "I seen him before. Might be he stayed here. Musta come in from somewhere up North; he didn't have no Dixie accent." Another brown stream of tobacco.

"There was no one else?"

"Look, sir, I got a lotta work to do because that blasted Joey don't know his hand from his hind end, and that ain't no exaggeration. I ain't got time to watch who's coming in and out and standin' on the street there. People is always standing there, waiting for a hansom or meetin' someone."

"All right, then, sir. One more question. Is there anything else about the men who were talking you noticed? Would you recognize them again if you saw them?"

"Yessir, I reckon I would."

"I'd sure like to know if you do see them again. Or remember anything else." Adam would have shown the groom his paper from Mr. Lincoln, but as it was in pieces and he doubted the man was literate, he didn't. Holding the man's eyes, he placed another coin — this time a quarter — on top of the shelf. "You can send word to me at the

Willard. Name's Quinn."

After Adam left the St. Charles, he set about tracking down the men on the list James Delton had given him — ones Custer Billings had done business with. He debated visiting Mr. and Mrs. Titus, but decided to wait and see whether Brian Mulcahey learned anything from his mission. And it wouldn't hurt to see if any of Billings's other associates had noticed he and Annabelle Titus being particularly close.

Locating each of the contacts created a frustrating and exhausting rest of the afternoon, as Adam had to first try each man at his office — once he located the address — and if the man had left for the day, he had to find his home and visit there.

The worst part about it was Adam didn't seem to learn anything new, even after tracking down and interviewing three different business associates. They each said the same variations on a theme: expressed sorrow and surprise that their acquaintance or friend had been killed — at such a public venue — and that Billings was an honest and admired businessman with an amicable personality. He didn't have any enemies or rivals of note. No one mentioned Annabelle or Mortimer Titus.

"Other than what one normally encounters in business — beating out someone for a contract. But that's not something to hold a grudge on," said the last person Adam spoke to — an Elmer Garrett, a tea and spice importer who was quite pleasant and forthcoming. "And I don't know anyone who holds a grudge against Billings — except maybe a secessionist."

Adam lifted his brows in question and waited for more.

"Billings was a pure abolitionist, no question. Didn't affect his business, but it certainly did his politics. He grew up somewhere in the South . . . was it Alabama? Arkansas? I don't right remember, but it was far south of the Mason-Dixon. But something must have happened down there that made him hate slavery." Garrett shrugged. "But, like I said, he didn't let it affect his business. He loaned money to the Southerners who came knocking — and there were plenty of 'em. Too many cotton plantations down there, and not enough financiers, he'd say — then he'd take their money and charge his fees and laugh all the way to his bank."

"Althea Billings has been doing poorly for over a year," Adam said, choosing his words carefully. "I reckon that must have left Mr.

Billings with a lack of . . . well, female society." Acutely uncomfortable, he stopped there and waited to see if Garrett would take the bait.

The other man looked at him in surprise, then a lopsided smile ticked his mouth. "I'd say Billings wasn't missing out on female companionship. He cared for Althea, but a man's got needs, right, Quinn?"

Though Adam gently pressed, he learned nothing further and he dared not mention any names, for fear of tarnishing a woman's reputation unnecessarily.

By the time Adam left Elmer Garrett's modest row house on F Street, it was well past supper time. The sun was low in the sky, brushing the tops of distant trees beyond the Potomac. Drawing on a trick he'd adapted from something Ishkode had taught him, Adam raised his fist vertically toward the sunset, positioning it so the bottom of his hand aligned with the horizon. He counted three knuckles between horizon and sun, which meant there would be about three quarters of an hour left of light.

He considered stopping at a public house for an ale and a bite to eat, and as he walked south along Tenth Street, he watched for a likely establishment. But by the time he reached the end of the block, he found himself facing the long stretch of open land that was called the National Mall.

Despite its grandiose name, the mall was hardly more than a long, narrow patch of swampland that stretched from the Potomac River to the Capitol Building. There were some rudimentary walkways along one edge of the long rectangular stretch, and despite the damp, chilly evening, a smattering of people — mostly men in hats with walking sticks — strolled along on either side.

In the center of the mall, halfway between the Capitol and the river, and directly opposite the Executive Mansion, was a stunted-looking tower. The simple square projection was supposed to be a monument to George Washington. But, like the Capitol, it was unfinished and rose to only one-third of its planned height.

Construction had ceased some time ago, and now the monument sat there surrounded by scaffolding, forlorn in its abandonment, and reminded Adam far too much of his own dismembered limb. Or, maybe — and more poignantly — the abandonment of the honorarium to the nation's first president echoed the imminent abdication of the Union for which General Washington had fought so hard.

But it was the castle-like building on the south side of the mall that drew Adam's attention. Looking unlike any other building he'd ever seen — and definitely nothing like the pale stone and marble government buildings, with columns and broad sweeps of steps — the Smithsonian Institution had been constructed of a rich red sandstone. He counted nine turrets and towers thrusting up from the sprawling, fancy structure. It looked just like a fairy-tale castle, and its construction had only been finished in 1855, although the institute itself had been created in 1846. Even Adam, who'd lived on the frontier, knew the Smithsonian was the preeminent science center of America.

The Castle, as it was called, drew Adam's attention because it was near there that Agent Hobey Pierce had lost Miss Henry Altman during last night's pursuit. Adam could understand why — the exterior of the large, long building had many nooks and alcoves. And though there were some gaslights on the grounds, it would have been simple for a slender woman to duck into a corner or cranny and wait in the shadows for the Pinkerton agent to blunder past.

He'd wanted to examine the area Pierce and Miss Altman would have traversed in an attempt to follow her tracks and locate her, but it would soon be dark and shadows were already falling. Still, curiosity compelled him to at least make the effort, and he would use what little light was left. If he was lucky, maybe she'd even dropped part of her false facial hair or some other clue that might help him to follow her.

As he approached the gate surrounding the Smithsonian building, feeling rather like a hound dog ranging back and forth as he scoured the muddy ground looking for footprints and other impressions, he heard the sounds of joviality.

Two men, loud with enthusiasm, were standing at the foot of the low, broad stairway that led into the building. Behind them, light spilled from the windows of one of the first-floor rooms as a third man approached from the southeast side of the Castle. They appeared to be preparing to enter the building, which made Adam curious — for surely the institute closed, as did most businesses, by five o'clock. Most of the other windows were dark, as he would have expected them to be, except on the second floor of the easternmost towers.

"Hurry up there!" called one of them, waving to the third, slighter figure who was walking hesitantly toward them. "Stimpson's already frying the oysters!"

Though Adam wasn't usually the sort to insert himself into a group — especially where he didn't know anyone — he found himself walking closer. There was something familiar about that lone figure, hurrying along from the east side of the building.

Then one of the street gas lamps shone on his face and Adam straightened in shock and delight.

It was Henry Altman himself — or, rather, *her*self — decked out in the same fake whiskers and male clothing as she'd worn to the ball last night.

"Mr. Altman," he called, striding toward the group on his long legs.

She looked over at the sound of his voice, and he saw her eyes bolt wide and her steps hitch as she tripped and nearly fell. For a moment, he thought she might turn tail and run, but she was too close to the entrance where the other two men stood, and one of them had already reached out his hand as if to shake hers.

"Altman! So glad you could make it. We're going to have a roaring time of it."

The other had turned at the sound of Adam's voice, then waved toward him. "Are you coming to the meeting then too? The more the merrier!"

Adam decided right then and there that

he was most definitely going to be attending the meeting with Henry Altman . . . whatever it might be.

CHAPTER 9

No. Simply . . . no.

Sophie Gates caught her breath, goggling over at the all too familiar man who was just introducing himself to Robert Kennicott and Millard Richardson at the base of the steps to the Castle. She automatically reached up to ensure her mustache was still glued in place. Not that it mattered, for he'd recognized her.

She was stunned into silence — which anyone who knew her would consider a miracle.

"Mr. Altman here invited me," the tall, rangy man from last night's debacle was saying. Adam Quinn was his name, she somehow remembered through the shattering of her thoughts and the roaring in her ears.

What on earth was he doing here? *How? How did he find me?*

"Welcome, then, sir. It's Altman's first

night at the Megatherium Club too," Kennicott said. "Nice to have both of you, as Haydn and Torrey have gone off on expeditions, and Stimpson gets ornery when there aren't enough of us for relay sack races. Of course, he doesn't like to share his plate of oysters if there's too many of us, so it evens out either way."

Sophie bit her lip behind the bristling mustache to hide a sudden grin. The sack races were certainly part of the reason she'd been determined to join the Megatherium Club from the first time she'd learned about it — among other reasons. She'd just had to wait for one of the regulars to leave — which happened all the time, as most of them were naturalists and always going off on expeditions — and use his name as an entree.

Which, apparently, Mr. Adam Quinn had also decided to do . . . using *her* name. Or, rather, her fake name.

She'd caught on too late to do anything to dissuade him from being welcomed into the group, and so she had no choice but to join the other three as they mounted the familiar steps to the main entrance of the Smithsonian Institute.

Once inside, they were in the main public gallery of the building, which had been converted into a museum of sorts just over two years ago. The Patent Office had turned over to the Smithsonian an entire jumble of inventions, plans, samples, and other items that had been held in its National Cabinet of Curiosities for decades. Some of the more interesting pieces were on display in glass cases in this main hall — which was dark at the moment, as the institute was officially closed for the day. Since Stimpson, Kennicott, and the others actually worked — and lived — in the Smithsonian, they always had access to the building.

"Stimpy!" shouted Kennicott, his voice echoing in the empty chamber. "Billy Stimpson! We've got two more! Find some more cups!"

He and Richardson were already through the main hall and heading down the corridor to the Natural History Laboratory. She would have followed them if Mr. Quinn hadn't used his dratted long legs, beating her to the threshold of the corridor and blocking her way. In the darkness, with a bare frosting of light from the lab down the way, he appeared even taller and more broad of shoulder as he kept her from following the others.

Never one to easily relinquish control she hissed, "What are you doing here?"

"Apparently, I'm attending a club meeting — same as you," he said in a sort of slow, drawling voice that reminded her of honey. Honey — which was thick and sweet and far too slow for the way she was used to living, speaking, and thinking. That easy demeanor and low voice were part of the reason she wasn't afraid of him — and anyway, all she had to do was cry out or shout if she was threatened. Every noise echoed and carried in this place.

"So, Mr. Henry Altman . . . though your given name probably isn't Henry, is it?" he continued.

"Henry Altman is my pen name." She was going to take control of this situation immediately, and the best way to do that was to go on the offense. "And what were you doing, skulking about out there?"

"So you *are* a journalist." His doubt was clearly indicated now, and he edged into the light from the corridor. She followed him, wondering if there'd be a chance for her to slip past and get to the laboratory. "You never did say who you write for."

For whom you write, said her internal editor — but for once she kept such a thought to herself. "It wasn't as if we had an extended conversation last night, Mr. Quinn. But if you must know, I've submitted stories to the *New York Times*, the *New York-Herald*, and the *Daily Intelligencer.*"

Not that they'd been accepted, bought, or printed, but she'd submitted them nonetheless. So far, only the small, mostly unknown *District Herald* had bothered to print any of her stories — including the one she'd written about the body from last night. She still didn't know if Henry Altman was going to get paid for it or not.

"That explains it," he said.

"That explains what?" She glanced down the hall toward the lab, but no one seemed to have noticed they were missing.

"Your accent. I reckon you must be from New York City."

"Shall I give you a blue ribbon?"

That caused him to crack a smile, which, along with the subtle cleft in his beardless chin, made him look less rugged and more handsome than she'd first thought. This annoyed her even more.

"As long as it ain't a secessionist cockade," he replied.

She must refuse to engage with him. He had no right to be here. "You need to leave. I'll make your excuses to the others."

"Why, that's very kind of you, *Mr. Altman.* But I reckon oysters and sack races — along with whatever they're pouring in the cups they're scrambling to find — are much more appealing than walking back to the Willard."

"Why are you here?" she asked — then immediately regretted it. She already suspected she knew the answer.

"I was looking for you."

Drat. She'd been right.

"I'm investigating the murder of Custer Billings, and I have a few questions. You're a journalist. I reckon you're used to noticing —"

"Aren't you coming?" a voice reverberated from down the hall. "Altman! Quinn! We've got eggnog! And Stimpson needs you to look at — no, fill that one first, Newberry. What? I don't know what's keeping them. *Altman,* what's the holdup?"

Sophie glanced over her shoulder and saw Mr. Kennicott hurrying toward them, a cup in each hand. She turned back and, without thinking, reached out to grab Mr. Quinn's forearm. She almost released it when she realized it wasn't flesh and bone. "Please don't give me away. Please. I'll help you in any way I can, but —"

"Here you are! Eggnog for our two new members. Come on, then, brothers. Billy's getting impatient. He's got a letter from Haydn he wants to share — all the way from Colorado — and he insists we all have to be there. Even Baird is here already."

Mr. Quinn took the eggnog and, giving her an inscrutable look, turned to follow Mr. Kennicott down the hall.

Muttering under her breath, Sophie followed — after checking once more to make certain her wig and facial hair were in place. She wasn't going to let Mr. Quinn ruin the evening.

Adam hadn't had eggnog for a very long time, and it tasted good: rich and creamy, and with a glug of whisky to make it mellow.

He discovered he wasn't quite as fond of fried oysters, but the thick slabs of toasted bread served with the crispy shellfish suited him just fine, and took away the gnawing in his belly. There was also a bowl of peanuts, and a messy pile of shells next to it that grew throughout the evening.

As was his nature, he'd settled into a more observing than participatory role in this room of boisterous men — oh, and one woman. Not to forget the mysterious Miss Altman, with the soft gray eyes that had pleaded with him to keep her secret.

He'd selected a chair near the edge of a space obviously used for scientific research. The plaque next to the door read Natural

244

History Laboratory, and the jars and boxes of specimens that lined the tables and counters — along with magnifying glasses and what he thought must be a microscope — supported this designation.

Henry Altman — Adam was mildly irritated she still hadn't told him her real name — had also chosen a seat at the fringes of the group of four other men, who clearly knew each other and did not stand on ceremony. An older, more sedate man referred to as Baird looked on in a sort of fatherly, affectionate manner.

Miss Altman refused to look in Adam's direction except when she thought he wasn't looking — probably to make certain he wasn't going to expose her.

Adam wasn't certain why he'd agreed to keep her secret — curiosity maybe. What was she going to do, and why? After a dark day immersed in the problem of murder, he found the situation slightly humorous and a little fascinating. Besides, she couldn't get into much trouble if he was there, watching out for her. And as he had a number of questions for her — he reckoned she had to have seen something — he wasn't going to let her disappear before he had the opportunity to ask.

Yet though he had a crime to solve, a

puzzle to put to bed, he wasn't averse to a bit of society that didn't revolve around the new president and his security, politics, and the shadow of impending war. And, better yet, he was able to do this while putting something in his belly and having a few laughs.

By now he'd also learned the Megatherium Club was made up mostly of naturalists — their expertise being a topic with which he was quite comfortable, having spent years immersing himself in the natural world with Ishkode. And the fact that he'd been "sponsored" by Henry Altman — who in turn had apparently been recommended by one of the conveniently absent members of the club — meant that he'd been absorbed into the meeting with no questions asked.

So when they gathered around a small, clawed crustacean Stimpson produced, Adam joined in. He caught on that this seemed to be a sort of friendly challenge to club members: produce an unfamiliar specimen, and see what they could surmise merely from observation.

"What can you tell me about it?" asked William Stimpson, thumbs in his waistcoat pockets, coat nowhere to be found. If Baird was the mentor or father, Stimpson seemed to be the gang leader of this motley group of scientists, and, from what Adam had gleaned, an accomplished naturalist and artist as well. His careful drawings of labeled sea life specimens were all over the laboratory: framed or curling up in sheaves of paper.

"Come on now, boys — you've not had enough whisky to muddle your brains yet. Though I can help you with that!" Stimpson grabbed the bottle and offered a straight pour to each of them in turn as they crowded around the table.

Adam glanced over and saw that Henry Altman was still nursing her cup of eggnog and declined the additional whisky. While he agreed with her decision, he did not choose to do the same and held out his cup.

"I do believe it's a *female*," crowed Richardson suddenly, spinning around with the same exuberance that had accompanied nearly every announcement at this club meeting.

Henry Altman's eyes flew wide open and her cheeks flushed red behind the beard. She looked as if she was about to bolt from her seat, but Adam merely shook his head at her. Then he smiled when, after that startled moment, she relaxed, having realized Richardson wasn't talking about her, but about the crawfish specimen.

"A blue ribbon for Mill, then," said Stimpson as cheers erupted in the small group. He adjusted his spectacles. "And what more, gentlemen?"

"Five pairs of thoracic appendages, so the order is . . . Decapoda," said Kennicott, pushing closer for a better look. "But it's not a Nephropidae. . . . No lobster for us tonight, Newberry," he added sorrowfully. "We'll have to stick with oysters."

"Oysters! More oysters!" cried Richardson, who clearly had had plenty of whisky and who knew what else. "A man needs more oysters!"

Adam found it difficult to keep from grinning at the energy and volume of his companions. They certainly knew how to enjoy themselves. "It's a freshwater crayfish," he said, poking at the inert creature. "From the north. Lake Michigan, I would guess."

"Ring the bell for the newcomer!" cried Stimpson. "And refill his cup!"

"The man needs more oysters!" Richardson joined in, and stumbled a little as he came over to take his seat.

Adam covered his cup with a hand and shook his head smilingly. "I'm fine."

"Lake Michigan, is it? How did you know it wasn't from the South?" Stimpson demanded. "These rock heads here wouldn't have known that. I thought to fool them for much longer."

Adam shrugged, then pointed to the trace of crusty algae on the bottom of one of the crayfish's claws. "I see this all the time on the shells in the lakes up there — that green-blue edging with a crimp in it. Never seen it anywhere else." He grinned as Stimpson smacked him on the back.

"You're a good man, Quinn. Happy to have you aboard. Kenny, give the man some more in his cup."

Henry Altman was giving him a sour look across the way. Clearly, she didn't have any expertise with crustaceans.

After a bit more discussion, the crayfish was put away, and the older gentleman, Baird — who turned out to be the assistant secretary of the institution — bid them good night. "No sack races. And leave the mummies where they are," he warned with a twinkle in his eye. "I'll see you all bright and early tomorrow."

He left amid a chorus of boos and sighs, and shortly after that, conversation turned from science and madcap adventures to the obvious: the new president.

Adam, whose tongue was slightly loosened by the whisky, and whose niggling mind had been picking at him to get back to work, settled in his chair and said, "A man was murdered at the Union Ball last night."

All five of them stared at him, suddenly flat and sober: Stimpson, Newberry, Richardson, Kennicott, and, of course, Henry Altman.

"What did you say?" asked Kennicott, swiping a hank of long, dark hair away from his eye. "Murdered? At the ball?"

"I didn't hear anything about it," Stimpson said, sitting up straight.

"That's because you had your nose in a microscope all night," Richardson jested. "As usual."

"My nose doesn't go *in* a microscope," Stimpson retorted. "It goes *beneath* it — beneath the viewing hole. It fits right in there." He demonstrated.

"A microscope." Adam straightened up as a thought struck him.

He still had that envelope in his pocket with the hairs that had been stuck to Billings's glove . . . and Henry Altman was here, wearing the same damned mustache and beard she'd been wearing that night. If he could determine whether those hairs were hers, or whether they possibly belonged to the murderer, that might go a long way in helping him solve the crime.

He stood. "How about another challenge this evening, gentlemen?"

Of course, they were all for it, sloshed and exuberant as they were.

"The freshman has a challenge for us!" cried Richardson, staggering on his feet. "I wager I'll win."

"I challenge everyone here to snip this much" — Adam demonstrated a measurement with his fingers — "of his beard. I will collect them all, then offer a sixth sample of hair. This is what you must match. I won't say whose it is or where it came from, but you must determine whether it belongs to someone here." He purposely did not glance at Henry Altman. "I suggest the microscopes, gentlemen."

There was a scramble as they all moved about to snip their beards. He placed the samples on slides — including the one he covertly extracted from the envelope in his pocket while pretending to take it from the samples collected. When Henry Altman tried to slip toward the door, Adam called her on it.

"Altman, you're in this too," he said with a firm, steely smile. He blocked the door and met her eyes. "I believe Stimpson has the scissors."

"Fine," she muttered, then turned back to

the group.

Adam watched to make certain she partic-
ipated properly and snipped a piece of her
false beard. Then he sat back and enjoyed
the show as the five of them pushed and
shoved at the microscopes, drank and ate,
discussed, debated, and argued, and at last
came up with the conclusion.

"Your sample don't match anyone here,"
Stimpson said. There was a red ring around
one of his eyes from the eyepiece of the
microscope. "We all agree. It ain't the
same."

"You would be correct, then," Adam told
him with a grin. "A toast all around — this
time it's on me."

They all laughed uproariously, since, of
course, Adam hadn't brought any libation
with him to the club. However, he would
certainly send a bottle of good Irish whisky
over as a thank-you.

He was gratified that his plan had worked.
Five different sets of eyes, and minds, had
all agreed that the tiny hairs attached to Billings's gloves weren't Altman's. Which
meant they must belong to the murderer,
for they were the wrong color to be Billings's hair. He pocketed the slide with the
original sample and smiled, then sobered.

"Was there really a murder at the ball

Monday night? Who was it?" Kennicott said suddenly. His joviality had disappeared, and his eyes no longer held the glassiness of whisky mirth.

"Yes, there was. I saw the body myself."

Apparently, Henry Altman had found her voice — and a topic on which she could speak.

The others swiveled to look at her, and Adam noticed her cheeks pinkening slightly under this sudden weight of attention.

"His name was Custer Billings — of the bank. He was stabbed."

"Right there? At the Union Ball? I knew we should have gone," Stimpson moaned. Then he sobered. "Poor sot. There was no chance to save him?"

"He was dead. Very dead." Henry Altman's voice held nothing but sorrow.

"Do they know who did it?" asked Kennicott. "I didn't see anything in the paper."

"There was only one story," said the journalist. "In the *District Herald.*"

"Never heard of it." Stimpson picked at an empty oyster shell. "Why'd someone want to kill a man — and at the ball?"

"Probably a sesh— seshess — sheshess —" Richardson couldn't get the word out, so he rerouted. "Southern sympathizer. Wanted to make a scene at the ball. Make

Lincoln look bad."

"Maybe." Adam spoke up thoughtfully. "But killing someone in such a public place — where you could be found so easily . . . I don't know. Why *does* a man — or woman — murder?"

"For love, of course," said Kennicott, and the others chimed in with their own thoughts, and the words became a jumble.

"Or revenge."

"Definitely money. It's always money."

"Or power."

"Power and money and greed — they all go together."

"Hate. People would even kill the president if they could."

"Hell, they tried to in Baltimore, Kenny. Coulda."

"Anger."

"Anger and hate — well, they're the same thing, Stim," Newberry interjected.

"Protection or self-defense."

Silence fell, and Adam found he couldn't discount any of their suggestions. Feeling suddenly morbid and heavy, and a little bit drunk, he mused, "It's always about love, though, at the core. Love of oneself. I reckon every one of those ties back to love — of self. Money, power, and greed — that's all for love of self. Hatred and anger

— ridding yourself of someone who makes you unhappy, which is a reflection of the love of self. Revenge — winning over or besting someone who hurt you. Love of self once again. Self-defense speaks for itself, and I reckon love for a woman — or man — is also obvious. It's all related to self. Selfishness, self-centeredness."

His words hung there for a moment, and when he looked up from studying the table, Adam found Henry Altman looking at him. Above the brown beard and mustache, her gray eyes were sober.

He wondered how any of the men in the room — so used to looking at every minute detail of an organism — couldn't recognize that it was a woman sitting there, hiding behind patently false facial hair and beneath a wig that looked like horsehair. *People see what they expect to see.*

A clock struck eleven somewhere in the building, shocking Adam that he'd spent almost three hours with these men.

"There's the warning bell," said Richardson, groaning a little as he pulled to his feet. "Time to crawl up the steps to the tower and slumber till dawn, when Baird cracks his whip to get us up."

The others laughed and stood, replacing chairs and picking up the whisky bottles, peanut shells, and dishes.

Adam was in the thick of it, sweeping up a pile of crumbs, when he realized Henry Altman had slipped away.

He bolted out of the laboratory and shot down the hall, only to find it silent and empty. Going back the route on which they'd come, he made his way outside to where a piece of moon and a swath of stars glowed, only to find no sight of her. No moving shadows, no sounds of humanity, no indication of which way she'd gone.

Irked at being dislodged so easily — but more than that, concerned that she would be making her way home alone, at night — Adam stood there for a minute, listening and waiting.

But she'd done it — disappeared again.

He went back inside to bid good night to his new acquaintances. They'd somehow forgotten about cleaning up and were sitting around on chairs and tables singing "Buffalo Gals" in loud voices.

He joined them, and by the end, they were all ready for another round of whisky.

"Not that bottle," Stimpson said when Adam reached for one on the counter. "That's the bad stuff — we use it for preserving specimens."

"It's got copper sulfate in it," Kennicott

told him in the earnest manner of a man trying not to look drunk.

"Always got to check around here," warned Newberry. "Lots of whisky, but most of it ain't gonna go down too well. Stim keeps a stash in his room — when he can afford it. We all help him drink it."

They all laughed and Adam found the right bottle, then poured. "You all live here, then?" he asked, trying to imagine how that would be, bunking in this huge, stone castle.

"In the cold North Towers," Stimpson replied. "We get our bed and board and little more, working for Baird."

"But wouldn't have it any other way," Newberry said. His cheeks were flushed and his eyes glinted happily.

"Like brothers — to the Megatherium Club!" Richardson lifted his glass for a toast, and they all clinked.

"One more question," Adam asked. "Why Megatherium?"

"It's a sloth," Newberry said wetly. "An extinct sloth."

"To the sloth!" cried Stimpson, and they smashed their glasses together so violently two of them broke.

"To the extinct sloth — and our extinct glasses!" Kennicott shouted as they all sagged into helpless laughter, sending shattered glass all over the floor.

Adam woke with a minor headache, but also with a pained grin when he remembered why. The members of the Megatherium Club were certainly unique.

The smile faded, though, when he recalled how Henry Altman had given him the slip once again. The only clue he'd really obtained about her identity was the newspaper called the *District Herald* — which apparently published at least one of her stories. Perhaps he could track down the elusive reporter that way.

Not that he would allow it to take his attention from the murder investigation, but he reckoned he had several questions to ask her.

Joshua had already left the hotel room, and when Adam realized it was nearly eight o'clock, he fairly bolted from the bed.

Ten minutes later, he was downstairs in the lobby enjoying a cup of coffee and a honey-drenched biscuit, waiting for the hotel barber to have an empty seat. Fifteen minutes after that, newly shaven, belly full, he walked out the front door.

Birch was there, of course, standing tall and straight in his pristine uniform.

"Morning, Mr. Quinn," he said. "Looks

like you've missed half the day already." He smiled and the corners of his eyes crinkled.

"Sure feels like it."

"Did that Mr. Fremark find you?" asked the doorman.

Adam halted. "Lyman Fremark was looking for me?" Something prickled down his spine.

"Sure was. Come here yesterday, mebbe half past six. I was just getting my things together to leave, and he was talking to George, asking about you. Said he needed to talk to you — real important. I told him I hadn't seen you for a while, and he asked if I knew where you might be. I tole him I didn't know, but you was working with Mr. Lincoln and mebbe you were up there." He thumbed toward the Executive Mansion.

Adam nodded. "Thank you. He didn't leave any word about where to find him or what he wanted to see me about?"

"No, sir. He just looked like he needed to talk to someone real bad. Kinda nervous."

Maybe he'd remembered something else important about the men he'd seen in their "secret meeting." Adam looked across the avenue toward the President's House.

"He was walking that way when he left," Birch said helpfully.

"Thank you."

Adam warred with indecision for a minute, then started down the block to the big white house. If Fremark had gone there trying to find him, maybe he'd left word or other information with Nicolay or Hay.

As he strode up the walk past the elliptical-shaped horse corral, Adam saw the long line of office seekers snaking out the front door. It was perhaps even longer than the one from yesterday. Adam stifled a groan at the thought of Mr. Lincoln having to meet with each one of them, along with doing the rest of his thankless job. He wondered if either of the president's secretaries were able to help cull that line down at all.

But, no. He reckoned not. It wasn't Mr. Lincoln's way.

McManus was at his station at the front door, and he remembered Adam immediately. "Top o' the mornin' to ye, Mr. Quinn. Though it's getting well past mornin'-tide by now."

Adam shook his head. Couldn't a man have a bit of a tie-on, then sleep a little late in the morning without it being pointed out to him every minute what a sloth he was? Then he realized what he'd thought — sloth — and had a good grin over that.

"Good morning, Mr. McManus. I reckon it's a good thing I've been up and about my business since dawn, then," he said with no qualm about the lie. He paused before walking into the foyer, where the sounds of conversation from the crowd waiting to see the president echoed and bounced and filled the chamber like a dull roar. Along with the noise was an aromatic stew of everything from cigar smoke to stale body odor to fresh hair pomade. "I don't reckon you met up with a man named Lyman Fremark, who was looking for me?"

"Aye, lad, I sure did. He was here last evening, just as the sun was setting. He was about asking if you were here, and when I said I hadn't seen you since the morning, he said how it was real important he talk to you or Mr. Lincoln."

"Did he leave word where he was going, or where I could meet up with him?"

"No, sir, he didn't, because I sent him up to the second floor to see Mr. Lincoln himself. It was a real worry I was a-seeing, there in his eyes, and so I thought to myself he should get to see the president if he needed to. Anyone's got that much somberness ought to be a-laying it down as quick as he could. So I told him about how there was a back hallway — different than the one I showed you, even — hardly never used by anyone, and how he could miss the line if he went there, and maybe get to the president that way."

Adam had a moment of terror, thinking about the possibility of Mr. Fremark being an assassin himself, and slipping up to the private quarters of the president and his family without anyone seeing him.

But McManus must have read his mind, for he said, "Don't you be furrowing your brow there, lad. That back way ain't well traveled, but it's only dropping you at the west end of the hall from where Mr. Lincoln's office is, and where the family apartments are. And you're still about having to walk past all the other rooms and even the main staircase to get to him. And there's even a guard there now, at the top of the stairs, just in case. Mr. Pinkerton insisted."

Praise God for small favors, Adam thought. "When he came back down, did you see Fremark? Did he talk to Mr. Lincoln?" He didn't want to bother the president if he hadn't met the man.

"Come to think of it, did I see him coming back down? His friend come looking for him not very long after — maybe they left together in the crowd of people that was sent out when Mr. Lincoln closed up for the day. Whole loud pack of 'em, crowding through the door here. Either way, Mr.

Quinn, he didn't stop here to talk to me again."

"His friend?" Adam straightened. "A friend of Mr. Fremark's came looking for him?"

"Aye. He surely did. Sick as a dog, he was, coughing into his handkerchief and leaning on his walking stick the whole time. I'll be honest, Mr. Quinn, I didn't want to get too close to him. Sounded like he was dying. But he said he hadda be finding Mr. Fremark straightaway, and so I sent him up the way I told him and put as much distance between us as I could, as fast as I could. I ain't lived to be eighty-five by taking any chances, lad."

Adam tamped down a sense of growing alarm. "I'll just go on up and find out if Mr. Lincoln spoke to Fremark," he said. "Where exactly is this back way?"

McManus told him, and Adam went off down what could only be described as a bedraggled hallway, past the Blue Room and the Green Room, around the corner and along the side of the house. In one of the largest rooms, Mrs. Lincoln was fussing around, taking measurements and giving orders to a group of servants.

Taking the narrow steps two at a time, Adam bolted up, around a bend, then up a second flight to the next floor. The door at the top stuck a little, and when he opened it, he found himself in a short, empty corridor with a small door on each side and a larger one directly in front. Cobwebs, peeling paint, and water stains decorated the small alcove, and the single small window was coated with dust. McManus was correct — it seemed no one ever came this way.

He paused for a moment to consider again what a travesty it was that the President's House should be in such disrepair, then continued toward the door in front of him. He judged it would open into the main hallway that led across the entire floor where he'd been yesterday morning. But just as he was about to turn the knob, he noticed a dark stain on the floor.

It was leaking out from beneath one of the other smaller doors. Already knowing what he would find, he said a quick prayer and pulled the door open.

Lyman Fremark's body tumbled out, sprawling over the floor in a pool of blood.

CHAPTER 10

"A murder in my great white house," said Lincoln, looking soberly at Adam. "If it was to happen, I'd have thought it would have been me —"

"No," Adam said fiercely as his uncle surged to his feet, equally as furious, and the others erupted as well. "Don't say that, Mr. President. Don't even say that."

"Abe." Joshua's voice was sharp and hard, and lined with horror. Because they all knew — every one of them in the room: Adam and Joshua, Nicolay and Hay, Pinkerton, his young agent Hobey Pierce, and Lincoln — that it was far too close to home. Far too possible that it might yet happen.

How *easily* it had already happened. And how easily it could again — this time, with even more dire consequences.

"You think it was this friend of Fremark's. The one who was ill," said Lincoln, who looked slightly chastened by the fury and concern directed at him.

"He was hiding behind a handkerchief so he couldn't be identified. Even when pressed, McManus doesn't remember much else about him. He wasn't too tall, he wasn't too short, he had on a hat that covered his hair, he wore gloves that covered his hands . . . and with all of the other people crowding in the foyer, he didn't look at him very carefully." Adam shook his head grimly.

"And so he went up after Fremark . . . and what?" Hay pressed. "He couldn't have been that close behind him. How did he even know in the first place Fremark was coming here?"

Adam frowned. "I have the same questions, but I reckon maybe whoever it was saw or heard Fremark speaking to Birch about needing to talk to me, and heard him being sent up here. I don't reckon it's a secret that I've been tasked with finding out who killed Billings.

"And if the murderer followed Fremark up to this floor — well, there are so many people here, there's the long line waiting, and then McManus said they were all sent home. Maybe in the midst of the chaos, the murderer followed Fremark down the back hallway — or lured him there — and attacked him then. Stabbed him in the back several times. No one would have heard it happening, with all the noise and being at the opposite end of the hall behind a door."

Lincoln and Pinkerton were nodding in agreement. "If that's true," said the detective, "and it makes sense to me, then someone might have seen the murderer near the Willard yesterday when *he* saw Fremark, and then decided to follow him so he could off him as well. Bastard probably wouldn't have been holding a handkerchief then."

"Yes, I reckon I'll be talking to Birch to see if he remembers anyone loitering. Or the person might have been following Fremark anyway, already, waiting for an opportunity to silence him." Adam looked out the window. If he'd gone home last night instead of socializing with the Megatherium Club, he would have seen Fremark, and possibly prevented this tragedy. The biscuit he'd eaten churned unpleasantly with the bitterness of coffee and regret.

"Someone will need to inform Lyman Fremark's family," Nicolay said quietly. "Mr. President?"

"I'll do it," Adam said. "I . . . I reckon I should, and his wife might have some information that would help."

"Very well, young man. I'm obliged to you — for all of this."

"If you need any assistance, Agent Pierce continues to be at your disposal," Pinkerton said.

"Thank you. I'd like to take another look at the scene, and I'd like permission to have Mr. Fremark's body taken to Dr. Hilton, Mr. Lincoln," Adam said. "In case there is anything he might be able to find about who did this."

"Of course."

Adam took his leave and was accompanied by Hobey Pierce when he went back to the small alcove. The body had been covered with a sheet and removed to an empty room, which left only the traces of violence on the floor: blood, disturbed dust, a few footprints.

Lyman Fremark had been stabbed in the back several times — Adam would leave it to Hilton to determine the number. Regardless, it was a different situation from that of Custer Billings, who'd had fewer wounds and far less blood. Adam found that curious and wondered if it would mean anything helpful to the doctor.

Pierce stood to one side, his round, youthful face serious as he watched Adam examine the walls, the doors, the floor. There wasn't much to be found. A few faint footprints that had disturbed the dust, the spill of sticky blood, blood spatters on one of the walls.

"Looks like he came at him here," Adam said, demonstrating how the murderer would have laid the first blow, then pointing to the bloody spray marks on the wall nearby. "Fremark fell here — see the dust is all disturbed and there's more blood."

Though he looked around on hands and knees, propped by an awkward false hand, Adam found nothing else to help identify the culprit. Then he and Pierce did the same painstaking examination of the stairs — down and then back up — looking for even a single footprint that didn't match Fremark's smaller ones, or Adam's.

Until he found, back at the top of the stairs, on the floor just outside the door that led to the alcove, a smudge of oil. A hardly noticeable drop that had seeped into the edge of an old, frayed carpet, and smeared onto a bit of the wooden floor.

George Hilton reckoned his life could have been a hell of a lot worse if he'd been born one day earlier.

That simple bit of timing had ensured he was born a free man, because on February 7, 1829, his mother had made the last payment to her master and had been given papers that stated she was a free woman. The very next day, she'd given birth to him, and that made George Hilton free from the moment he was born.

Had he come even a few hours earlier, he'd have been born into slavery like his mama had been. She would have had to scrape and save all over again, for years and years, to accumulate fifteen hundred dollars or more to buy her son's freedom.

And if Mr. Pellman, her master, had known Callie Hilton was pregnant, he surely would have held off on signing and sending those papers that made her free until she'd delivered herself of the baby. But because the master had rented out Callie Hilton to serve his distant cousin, not only did he not know she'd gotten with child over the last year, but he also enabled her to save the money to buy her freedom.

It was a common practice to rent or loan slaves out to other families — especially in Washington, where people came and went with the seasons of government and didn't want to bring their own servants. It was beneficial to both master and slave, for there was an elite class of slaves — usually from wealthy, equally elite families that were servants with excellent reputations and work ethics — that often negotiated their own rental fees. The slave owner expected a certain amount of money, and the slave was able to keep anything he or she negotiated above that fee.

And servants who were particularly sought after — like Callie had been, because she was a brilliant seamstress and because she was from the greatly admired Pellman family — could make enough money doing extra side work as well. It had taken her five years to save the money for her freedom, and that was a relatively short amount of time because the master had set a low price on her head when she made the request — simply, and, as it turned out, fortunately, because she was sickly and not expected to survive.

It was because of all those quirks of fate — and others to come later on in his teens, as if the bricks of his life's path had already been laid so neatly — that George had figured he'd best make the most of this blessed life into which he'd blundered. His mama was dead and gone five years now, but she'd nearly been replaced in his maternal affections by Miss Lizzie Keckley, who was so much like Callie Hilton that George couldn't help but wonder if his mother had somehow come back in the other woman's shell. Hell, she was practically glowing over the fact that Mrs. Lincoln had hired her to sew the dress for her very first levee on Friday night.

All of that was why George had returned to Washington a year ago. Returned to the place of his birth, though he'd lived here less than a year after he was born before Callie took them to the safer, Northern city of Philadelphia. For, even as recent as ten years ago, Washington City was a very dangerous place for free Negroes: they could be captured and sold as slaves at the whim of anyone who chose. There had been outdoor slave markets in the shadow of the Capitol Building as well as the President's House. And even George well knew there was a dais adjacent to Judiciary Square where black men like himself were stripped and whipped for any infraction perceived or imagined. Even though the slave *trade* of bringing in people from outside the country had been abolished in Washington, slaves could still be bought and sold — and were, in reputable auction houses like Williams & Green.

And though he was a free man, there was still the danger of being "taken" and sold into slavery. It was a subtle awareness George lived with every day. An underlying suspicion and wariness he couldn't quite subdue, especially whenever he met some-one new. Someone who was white, that is.

There was the ugly Black Code that restricted his life and movements, and that, if he'd never left Washington, would have prevented him from becoming as educated as he was.

Despite all of that, he'd come back here because he knew he was needed. His people needed him — because, by God, there was no one else to help them. Because, by the same quirky twists of fate — or, more likely, set forth from the Good Lord, as his mama had told him — that had helped him leave the capital city, he'd become something a black man in America could hardly dream of: a medical doctor.

Negroes weren't permitted to aspire to such professional positions as doctor, law-yer, or teacher. And even if they did, gain-ing admission to a medical school or even paying for it were insurmountable barriers.

George figured he owed it to the Good Lord — and whatever angels had brought him from Washington to Philadelphia to medical school in Montreal and now back again — to help his people.

To help any people.

He lived in the same small boardinghouse Miss Lizzie did, over on Connecticut Avenue — where it was a little clearer, cleaner, and brighter than in Ballard's Alley, a few blocks above Lafayette Square. But he spent most of his time in the cellar beneath Great Eternity Church, seeing patients who couldn't afford to pay him and, as of early yesterday morning, performing a postmortem on a dead body.

He didn't know what had possessed him to offer such a service to the sober Mr. Quinn, but there he had, and here he was. The number of lamps he'd needed to borrow and buy — and the kerosene for them — had set him back some dollars, but for now, he had the money to do it. He figured the Good Lord had made things happen the way He did because He expected George to take care of things down here for Him.

If caring for the sick and helping to find a murderer were some of the tasks on his brick path, so be it.

"Now, there we are, Mrs. Brown," he said to his patient as he helped her off the examining table. He steadied her until she got her bearings, then handed her a crude crutch her husband had made. "You need to keep yourself off that foot for another week, you hear? That stinky green mess coming out of that lacera — that cut — is gonna come back if you don't keep it wrapped, and with this salve on it. Hot water and the salve — three times a day, there, Mr. Brown. She'll need your help. You understand?" He gave the husband a firm look. "Otherwise, that foot's gonna get infected again, and it's going to end up coming off. And then where will you be?"

"Yessir, Mr. Hilton, sir," said the husband, sliding a dark, spindly arm around his much rounder, equally dark wife. "Thank you, sir." He managed to jam a hat onto his head while steadying his spouse.

"I'll be by to see you, Mrs. Brown, and I'll know if you've been walking around on that foot," George warned as they hobbled their way to the door.

As they did, the husband glanced curiously at the white sheet that divided the long, rectangular room in half, and George was thankful no one could see the cut-open corpse on the table there, even though it was properly covered from head to toe. Though, he supposed, everyone could probably smell it: the scents of blood, of death, of imminent decay.

He took a moment to wipe his face and dunk his hands into a pump-sink before turning to his next patient. That convenience had been the deciding factor in using this location as his medical office: an internal water source with a sink. The fact that it was a cellar, and therefore cooler than aboveground offices, hadn't been a factor at all — but now that he'd turned half the space into a morgue, it was obviously a benefit. Still, he'd had to move everything behind the sheet before opening up to patients this morning, and it was more crowded and darker back there.

There were three chairs lined up along the wall near the door, and although at seven o'clock this morning they'd all been full — with two more waiting — now there was only one patient sitting there. George spared a moment of relief that he could attend to Mr. O'Malley's stitches rather quickly (they only had to be removed and the wound cleaned), and then he'd be able to get back to the puzzle of Custer Billings's body.

The minimal amount of blood from the stab wounds on Mr. Billings continued to niggle at him. There'd been no blood to speak of on the floor where the body had been lying, and George knew he was correct when he told Mr. Quinn that the body hadn't been killed and allowed to bleed out somewhere else.

Until he got a more thorough look at the man's insides, he wouldn't have answers to that puzzle. And he might not even have an answer then.

"Have a seat here, Mr. O'Malley," George said, wiping his hands.

As the broom-slender Irish man loped over to the examination table, he too glanced at the white dividing sheet. "What're you about doing back there?" he asked, sliding onto the counter. "Smelling real bad. Like a bloody butchery shop." He wheezed a laugh at the joke.

"A man died two nights ago," George told him, lest the man begin to suspect him of butchering a patient. He was, after all, a black man — and O'Malley was not. "I'm preparing the body to be laid to rest." He figured that was as good an explanation as any.

"Smells real bad," said O'Malley, then winced as George used forceps to drag a thread from the stitched-up slice on his palm.

"Sure does," George replied cheerfully. "That's why I'm going to get you fixed up and out of here as soon as I can."

He was just finishing up, washing the wound with water he kept heating at all times, when someone knocked on the out-side door, then called for him.

George stifled a grimace of frustration;

he'd been hoping for a break from patients so he could get back to his work on Billings.

"Office is open," he called needlessly, for the door had begun to ease wide.

There seemed to be a lot of movement outside, as if someone was managing a heavy or awkward parcel. The door thudded against the wall as a man backed in, carrying one end of something long and wrapped in a blanket.

George stared for a moment, then recognized the man as the younger Pinkerton agent from the night of the Union Ball. The one who'd been helping Mr. Quinn. And it looked as if he was on one end of a body being maneuvered through the small doorway.

"You're all set here, Mr. O'Malley," George said hastily, nearly dragging the man off the table by his wrist. "Keep it wrapped up, and feel free to pour a bit of your favorite Irish whisky on it whenever you have an urge for a little sip yourself." He smiled, but his attention was on the two men who were making their way carefully through the door, with what could only be a body sagging between them.

O'Malley gawked at the sight of the shroud, likely noticing the blood seeping through the layers of linen in which the body was wrapped.

"By my eyes," muttered the Irish man, staring as he walked past. He stumbled a little when he bumped into the edge of a chair. "Looks like you're about turning yourself into a funerary home, Doc."

"What's all this?" George asked as soon as he closed — and locked — the door behind O'Malley. Any new patients would have to wait, at least for a few minutes. "Bring it — well, to this table here for now."

"Adam Quinn sent us. He said he'd be obliged if you'd take a look at Mr. Fremark here," said the Pinkerton agent.

George was already peeling away the wrappings on the body, which the men had placed on the table. "What happened?"

"Man was found stabbed to death inside a closet at the President's House."

"At the *President's House*?" A chill rushed through his body.

"Quinn says he was the man who found Billings's body the night of the ball, and he thinks someone killed Mr. Fremark in order to keep him from telling something he might have seen."

"All right, then. Tell Mr. Quinn I'll take a look." He didn't add a thank-you to his message — it just didn't seem right to be grateful for another mystery to solve. Yet, George found himself both intrigued and determined to have a go at this second challenge.

Hardly noticing when the two men left, George turned to the remains of Mr. Fremark, carefully easing away the shroud to expose the man and his clothing.

One thing he already knew: this man had bled enough for both of the dead bodies he now had in his office.

Chapter 11

By the time Adam began to make his way back to Willard's, it was nearly five o'clock in the afternoon. His prosthetic was bothering him, for it had been strapped on for nearly ten hours without relief, and yesterday it had been more than eighteen.

But his discomfort was nothing compared to that of Mrs. Lyman Fremark, whose face had crumpled with disbelief when Adam had delivered the horrible news. He'd gone to her directly after leaving the Executive Mansion.

"No . . ." she had whispered, staggering back as she placed a hand over her heart. "Not Lyman. He's such a harmless man . . . such a nice and harmless man. He wouldn't hurt a fly! Who would want to do such a thing?"

"Please, sit down, Mrs. Fremark," Adam had said, helping her to the small parlor off the main entrance to the Fremarks' tiny row house on Eighth Street. "I'm hoping to find out who would do that to your husband."

One of the servants was hovering, wide eyed, in a doorway, and Adam had suggested she make some tea for her mistress while he tried to calm her enough to ask a few questions. The servant, a matronly woman with mahogany skin and a cheerful face, had offered to send for Mrs. Fremark's sisters and grown daughter.

Mrs. Fremark had nothing helpful to share. She was overwrought, and barely coherent. But, no, she could think of no one who'd want to hurt her husband. And no, he hadn't told her much about finding the body at the ball — she'd been there too, of course, wearing her new rose-pink frock and with a filled dance card too! They'd gone home soon after — but Lyman hadn't spoken of the incident since. He felt it was unbecoming for a woman to think of or know about such things. He had been more quiet than usual since then, and he had woken abruptly from a dream the night before, but he wouldn't talk about it with his wife.

And as far as Adam could reckon, wading through her weaving dialogue, Fremark hadn't told his wife or even hinted at why he would have needed to speak to Adam urgently.

After a few more minutes of listening to Mrs. Fremark sob and ramble, he had excused himself and taken his leave. There was nothing more he could do for her except find the person who'd shattered her life. And even that, Adam well knew, would make little difference in stemming the grief and loneliness — and keeping the bills paid.

There were still others on his list to speak to — more of Billings's business associates, including the Tituses. Agent Pierce had little new to report based on his interviews but would continue with his task and send word to Adam if he learned anything relevant.

Adam also intended to find the offices of the *District Herald* in hopes of tracking down the elusive Henry Altman.

With a lingering guilt over Fremark's death, Adam duly went about his business of interviewing the people on his list, and found more of the same: Custer Billings was well respected, and though being an open abolitionist, he was fairly well liked. No one seemed to have any reason to want him dead. None of the men he spoke with gave any hint of a relationship between Billings and Annabelle Titus — or that Billings stepped out on his wife at all. Adam began to wonder whether Delton's impression was simply wrong.

Neither of the Tituses were home when he called at their ostentatious home on Third Street, and Adam was reluctant to leave a message with the servants. He did ask the butler, who had coal-black skin and a stiff, uptight manner, whether the Billings ever called there.

"I'm not permitted to divulge any information," he replied with an unfamiliar accent and a sneer. And he very nearly closed the door on Adam's boot.

Adam was beginning to wonder if the death of Billings had simply been a random act perpetrated by a group of Lincoln haters who either wanted to send a warning to the new president or simply to make a statement by ruining his celebration.

But more likely the murder — with the victim once again a random choice — had been meant as a distraction to give them the opportunity to actually strike at Lincoln himself. Their plot was foiled when there was no hullabaloo about the crime, and their target left the ball early.

What had become obvious, however, was that Fremark's death was not only related to the murder of Custer Billings, but it had been handled in a completely different manner. Instead of leaving his body in a public place where it would readily be found, the killer had hidden it. Was that important in itself, or merely a matter of convenience for the culprit?

Adam stewed over these thoughts and more as he made his way around the city, on foot and via the omnibus when he could.

Tracking animals in the woods and discerning their stories was a hell of a lot easier than investigating a murder, he decided. Animals generally acted as they were created to do: hunting, hiding, fighting, mating, traveling — all in the same way each species had done for thousands of years. They simply didn't deviate from their basic nature.

The same could not be said for man, who lied, manipulated, and acted on emotions like greed, anger, love, and hate.

Speaking of love . . . that reminded him to wonder again about the identity of Hurst Lemagne's lady friend. If she'd been a fancy girl in one of the brothels — many of which were conveniently near the Capitol — surely the man wouldn't have balked at giving out her name. The fact that Lemagne hadn't owned up to it suggested either he was lying or the woman was married and he didn't want to ruin her reputation any more than he wanted to ruin Annabelle Titus's.

And then there was greed. Adam hadn't reckoned over that very much in the way of motives, but Billings had been wealthy, to be sure. What would happen to his business? His wife would inherit any money and property —

"Mr. Quinn! Mr. Quinn!"

Adam stopped in the doorway of the hotel and exchanged a smile with Birch as Brian Mulcahey tore up to them from somewhere down the block.

He was, Adam noticed immediately and gratefully, wearing new boots.

"I'm surprised you can run in those," he told the boy. "Ain't they a little tight, being new and all?"

Brian was puffing a little, and his pale cheeks actually had some color in them from the effort. "They don't hurt. But they squeak something awful." He dug into his pocket, still breathing heavily, and the next thing Adam knew, he was plunking two silver dollars into his hand. "I been trying since yesterday to give them to you, but Mr. Birch said on as how you ain't been here very much."

"What's this?"

"My mam said the president was about giving me too much money for only a pair of boots. So here, it's back. And she liked

286

the pies, and so did little Erin, though *she* spit out the peas."

Adam gravely took the coins and slipped them back in his coat pocket, next to the Colt that weighted it down. "Erin's your little sister? What addles her that she doesn't like peas?"

Brian shuffled and shrugged. "She's only four, but she's a girl. And so I gave them to Bessie. She didn't care they had Erin's spit all over 'em. I wonder if inside Bessie's eggs will be greener now."

Adam kept his face straight with great effort. Behind the boy, Birch wasn't quite so successful, guffawing silently.

"And what about you, son? What did you find out about the fancy buggy with the *T* on it?"

"I followed it yesterday, like you said, until it stopped at one of those shops where they sell lace and ribbons." Brian didn't seem any more thrilled about that than he had been about little Erin's disdain for peas. "Girl things. But a pretty lady got out of the buggy and went inside. While she was being in there looking at lacy things, I got myself up by the driver to look at the horses. Two matching bays — *gor,* Mr. Quinn, I ain't ever been seeing none so perfectly matched. I don't think no one but the

287

groom could tell 'em apart, they were just alike. The same height and everything. I was talking to 'em real nice, like I know how to do, and the driver — he asked me to *hold* them. He even gave me a *penny.*"

"A whole penny?" Adam nodded as he spoke, his voice filled with nothing but interest and admiration. "That's very generous."

"Aye, he gave me a *penny* to hold 'em while he went into the pub next block for an ale. Said as how Mrs. Titus would be in the shop buyin' her frilleries for longer than two ales — but he said he'd only be gone for one, and not to let Silver and Tate get too prancy. That's what he said — 'prancy.' " Brian's face screwed up with bafflement over the man's word choice.

"And so you learned the woman in the landau was Mrs. Titus. I reckon Mr. Titus is represented by the *T* on the side of the carriage?"

"Oh, aye, sir, Mr. Quinn. When the driver come back — and he was right, he only stayed for one ale, and that Mrs. Titus was still in the shop looking at *ribbons* and fake flowers." Brian took no care to hide his disgust over such a waste of time. "And Silver and Tate — the bays — they were so sweet, and they nuzzled on my shoulder, too. I think they liked me. I wished I had an apple core for 'em."

"Can't see why they wouldn't like attention from a polite young man," Adam replied. He realized that simply speaking with the sunny young man had lifted a bit of the black cloud over his mood. "And when the driver came back . . . ?"

"Aye, when he came back, I remembered what you said about finding out things for Mr. Lincoln. But I didn't go right out and ask the driver, mister. That wouldn't have been the right way to go, because he was wearing a — what are they called? A cock . . . cock — a ribbon. Those ribbons like flowers?"

"Cockade," Adam prompted. At the same time, a thought struck him.

Cockade. Like cockled?

Had that been what the servants at Mr. Billings's house had overheard during his argument with the visitor — who'd been driving the fancy barouche with the golden *T* on it? If Billings was an abolitionist, maybe he'd had words with a Southern sympathizer like Titus.

Or . . . cuckold. Titus could just as likely have been yelling at Billings about being cuckolded. Adam really needed to speak to the man and his wife. At least he could gauge their reactions if he was able to question them.

"Aye, that. I saw the driver was wearing one of those cock . . . *ades,*" Brian said carefully, "they're about wearing if they don't like Mr. Lincoln, and so I was thinking because of that, he wouldn't want to be hearing nothing about Mr. Lincoln. Or nothing nice, anyways. So I wasn't gonna be saying that name, but I just started talking to the man. And he got talking back to me, just like I wanted, and that's when I started asking him questions — just as easy as pie." His grin was wide and very pleased, making his freckles appear to expand in size.

"And what sorts of things did you learn?" Adam was surprisingly impressed by the young boy's intuitive actions.

"Mrs. Titus, she likes to shop. All the time. Every day." Again, the disdain was heavy in his words. "Or she likes to visit her friend. At the . . ." He screwed up his face, thinking. "A house place."

"A house place?"

Birch, who'd been listening, edged closer. "Britton House? Munderly House? Latney House?"

"Oy, that's it! Latney House."

Birch glanced at Adam knowingly, but spoke to Brian. "That's like a resting house.

A hotel. Not so fine as the Willard, though, there, boy."

A hotel. Annabelle Titus visited her friend at a hotel. "Did the groom say anything about Mrs. Titus's friend? Anything at all?"

"No, sir."

"What about Mrs. Titus? Did her groom say anything about maybe her being sad yesterday, or upset?" If Annabelle Titus had been romantically involved with Custer Billings, Adam reckoned she might not be feeling herself today. Especially if her husband had gotten involved.

"He didn't say nothing about that. But I did see her holding a handkerchief at her face in the carriage. And Mr. Titus, he makes a lot of money. They're *rich* — rich as kings! And they live over on Third Street. I saw the house. *Gor,* it's big!"

"You followed the carriage all the way to the Tituses' home?"

"No, I wasn't about doing that — waiting around for them. I walked over and looked for it m'self. Mrs. Titus was still shopping."

Adam hid a grin. "Very nice work, there, young sir." He handed Brian a half-dollar coin. "You come back here again tomorrow at noon, and we'll see what else I might have for you to do."

"For Mr. Lincoln?"

"That's right. Now take that home to your mam and practice your reading and writing tonight. Someday, I reckon it'll come in handy. Mr. Lincoln's mother also taught him to read, you know, and he puts great store by anyone who takes the time and energy to learn his schoolwork."

"*Gor.* His mother taught him too? Wait'll I tell my mam!"

Adam watched him dash helter-skelter down the block, then turned to Birch.

The older man was smiling fondly, looking between both of them. "He's one hell of a firecracker, that kid," he said in his grating voice. "I think you picked a live one there, sir."

"You're telling me. As it's almost six o'clock, I reckon I'll see you tomorrow morning, Birch." He started, then turned back. "You ever hear of a newspaper called the *District Herald*?"

The doorman thought for a moment. "Can't say as I have, Mr. Quinn."

Adam frowned. "No one seems to know it. I've been asking around all day. I begin to wonder if it even exists."

"There's lots of papers in Washington," Birch said. "And some of 'em are even real." He laughed, the corners of his eyes and mouth crinkling.

Adam went upstairs and was hardly through the door to his hotel room when he was shrugging out of his coat.

"You're back."

He looked over to see his uncle standing next to the bed. He had an open carpetbag sitting there and appeared to be packing.

"You going somewhere?" Adam asked, dragging off his shirt and tossing it onto a chair. With nimble fingers, he flipped open the fastening for the wide harness-like strap that went around his chest and under his good arm, giving a soft groan of relief when the prosthetic's tight binding released.

"That's how your aunt sounds when she unlaces her corset." Joshua glanced over, grinning. "Or when I do it for her. Says it's the first time all day she can take in a full breath." His expression was filled with affection.

Fresh air cooled Adam's skin, and as he unbuckled the rest of the bindings, the wooden arm fell away from its tight position. He sighed again and rubbed the end of his stump and the upper part of his arm because it felt good.

As he did so, he mused on what his uncle had just said, for it hadn't really struck Adam how much more strictly women had to be bound: through their entire rib cage, and then shaped into an hourglass form. He reckoned that must be worse than to have a few straps around his upper torso and upper arm, no matter how uncomfortable wearing a prosthetic was. He could choose to go without wearing his contraption at any time, but for a woman to do so would be quite unusual. Though, he guessed, out on the frontier maybe they were more lenient about fashion. He'd not really had the opportunity to find out.

With that in mind, he reckoned he could maybe understand a lady's desire to dress as a man.

As he rubbed a lavender-scented salve on the scarred, rounded end of his stump, he looked meaningfully at Joshua's bag and asked again, "Where are you going?"

"Back home."

"Home? To Springfield?"

Joshua lifted a brow. "Yes. I can't stay here forever. I've got a store to run and a wife to manage. I've been away from your Aunt Sarah for far too long. She's getting impatient, and her time is coming near as well. I have to be home before the baby arrives."

Adam smiled in return, but at the same time he was aware of a gentle pang of something painful deep in his gut. "I reckon I'm ready to go home too. I just . . . I don't reckon I know where home is anymore. I thought it was Lawrence, but now . . ."

His uncle paused in his packing and looked at him with quiet understanding. "I know it's been a difficult two years for you since all that ugliness with Tom and Mary and Carl — and your arm. That's why I thought it would be worthwhile for you to help Abe these last few months — and now here in Washington. I hoped it would give you time to think about what you want to do and where you want to go."

Adam gave a short, bitter laugh. "I still don't know that. Nothing seems to hold much appeal. There's always California. Or Colorado."

Somewhere away from people and city and *politics*.

Joshua nodded. "You'll figure it out. Eventually."

Adam replaced the top to the tin of salve, frowning. "I don't want to stay here in the city, Uncle Josh."

"I'm sorry to hear you say that. I'd stay if I could, just to be near Abe. To support him, protect him. He's . . ." He shook his head, a grim, humorless smile flattening his lips. "Hell, he's the smartest man I know, but he's got an open heart that's far too trusting sometimes. He's going to need people he can trust — but, more importantly, people who don't want or need anything from him. You — and I — are two of the few who can say that."

"Damn, but you're right about that," Adam muttered. "The last thing I'd ever want is a job in politics or with the government — or even in the damned city." Only now that he'd relieved the stress on his half-arm did he turn to the next best thing: removing his boots and stockings.

"You also have a task that's been given to you," Joshua said, stuffing a waistcoat into his carpetbag. "I don't suppose you're going to leave until you've finished that, will you, Adam?"

"No, of course not." Especially now that there was a second death laid on the doorstep.

Yet, he felt a pang of uncertainty. What if he never solved the murders? Everything seemed so murky, and his brain was filled with a lot of disparate pieces of information, snatches of conversation, and what felt like an infinite number of solutions . . . and none at all.

"Well, you'd best get washed up and dressed or we'll be late," Joshua said matter-of-factly.

"Late? For what?"

"For supper. At the President's House. Oh, you must have been gone when he mentioned it. We're both expected to attend. And there's to be a levee — a reception — Friday night, so you'd best plan on that as well. It's Mary's doing, of course," Joshua added without a hint of inflection in his voice. "I, of course, will be halfway to Springfield by then."

Adam looked grimly at the wooden limb from which he'd just freed himself. "What time are we expected tonight?"

"Seven."

A glance at the clock on the fireplace mantel told him he had slightly more than an hour before supper. It would take less than fifteen minutes to walk to the President's House. That gave him more than thirty minutes to close his eyes and think — as well as a breather for his arm. He might even doze off.

"If I'm not up, wake me at half past six," he told his uncle, and laid full out on his narrow bed. "I'll be ready to leave on time."

Though the end of the mattress cut into him midcalf, leaving his bare feet dangling, he was used to being too tall for most beds and that didn't keep him from drifting off into a light doze as images and voices from his day accompanied him.

His dreams were permeated by thoughts of blue-stoned daggers and oil-patch footprints, ladies dressed as men with bristling mustaches and house-wide hoopskirts, . . . and a hen with a fondness for peas that laid green-tinged eggs.

And murder.

Blood. Violence. The wide, shocked eyes of Custer Billings as someone thrust a dagger into his belly. His mouth gasping silently, his body shuddering and jolting at the force of the attack.

It was someone close. Someone who moved toward the victim, walking into an embrace or to shake his hand. Someone who came near enough to be able to maneuver a weapon so quickly and precisely that the man had no time to react, to step back or hold up his hands in defense. . . . But he did hold up his hands, and with a vicious swipe, the murderer used his dagger to slice off not his hand, but his entire arm.

Sharp, fiery pain roared through his arm, radiating up through his shoulder and torso as he cried out —

"Adam."

His eyes bolted open and he looked up into his uncle's concerned face. Adam's mouth was dusty, and his body damp with sweat. Deep beneath the skin, his muscles trembled, and he felt shamefully nauseated from the sudden jolt back to reality.

Adam shook off the dream, sitting up too quickly for his ratcheting heartbeat — but the expression on Joshua's face had made him determined not to show how boggled his mind had gone. How hard his heart was pounding.

"I reckon I got pretty deep in my sleep," he said with a laugh. His legs were a little shaky when he stood, but that was due to the residual of the dream. And his arm — the one that was missing — hurt like a son of a bitch. So much so that he found himself gritting his teeth.

But he wasn't about to show that either.

"I reckon there's no sense asking if you're all right," Joshua said. He was still watching him with fatherly eyes, and that made Adam feel even more foolish.

"I'll be right back." He left the room with no other explanation, going down the narrow hall to wash up.

Splashing cold water on his face and on other important areas of his body did wonders to shock away the lingering disorientation. He ran his hand through the ragged mop on his head, reflecting that it was almost as thick and wild as Lincoln's more famous one, which was part of the reason people called the man an uncivilized rail-splitter.

Adam didn't mind the comparison himself. But he desperately needed a shave — and though he briefly considered the option of just letting his beard grow in, he once again decided not to bother. He'd get a proper shave tomorrow, for there was simply no time to maneuver that now. Shaving himself was one of the more difficult things he'd had to contend with since losing his arm, and so whenever possible, he paid for it to be done for him.

Yet he hated facial hair: the way it itched, the way food and other debris got caught in it, the way a man had to shave around the edges to keep its shape neat. A man might just as well shave off the whole of it instead of dancing around the edges.

His opinion *might* have had something to do with Mary Elizabeth Letterman from back home in Springfield. She'd had a particular liking for the cleft in his chin, and had told him so when he was fourteen. She'd even touched it, ever so lightly sliding her fingertip over the little depression. And since she was the prettiest thing he'd ever laid eyes on, with her dark brown eyes and coronet of raven black braids — and the fact that a girl who wasn't his sister or mother had *touched* him — he surely wasn't going to disappoint her.

Though she and her family moved away shortly after, Adam had never quite gotten over the idea of Mary Elizabeth liking the dent in his chin. And since his facial hair was very sparse right at the front, and his chin looked, to his eyes, like nothing more than the behind of a porcupine when he did grow in his beard, he figured that was enough reason to keep his face bare.

Adam drew in a deep breath, looking at himself in one of the clearest mirrors he'd ever had the pleasure of using. The memory of Mary Elizabeth had helped to banish the last bit of pain from his missing arm, as well as the swirl of ugliness from his dream.

Despite the pall that hung over the house, due to the horrible death in the second-floor alcove, supper at the President's House turned out to be more enjoyable than Adam had anticipated.

Meals with people he didn't know, or didn't know well — especially formal ones — could be uncomfortable due to the awkwardness of manipulating his false hand and arm in order to cut his food and feed himself. However, he'd dined with the Lincolns and the others many times during the trip from Springfield, so there wasn't the least bit of discomfort to be had.

Despite the fact that the living arrangements for the Lincoln family were still in some disarray, the cook and serving staff hadn't been disrupted when the Buchanan household moved out on Inauguration Day. Thus, though it was by no means as expansive as the dinner at Monday night's Union Ball, the meal was as complete and delicious as anything Adam had eaten since joining Lincoln's entourage.

The family dining room was located on the first floor, just down the hall from where Mrs. Lincoln had been measuring the parlor this morning. And the group that surrounded the table in the State Dining Room was a relatively small one, considering the number of people who had been crowding and lining up to obtain entrance to the Executive Mansion since the oath had been administered. The diners included only Mr. and Mrs. Lincoln, her sister Mrs. Edwards and her cousin Mrs. Grimsley, the two secretaries Nicolay and Hay, Joshua Speed, Adam, and Ward Loman, a close family friend of the Lincolns.

The first course was a local specialty Adam hadn't yet sampled: terrapin soup, made from the turtles that flourished in the nearby Potomac River. There were also smoked ham, roasted potatoes, candied carrots, and hunks of pale yellow cheese and dark, fresh bread. He wasn't surprised to see a bowl containing polished red apples that had surely been retrieved from a cellar somewhere.

That simple, basic staple was one of Lincoln's favorite foods, and he used a small knife to cut one unbruised apple into thin slices as he said, "Did you happen to take note of the great pearls of wisdom President Buchanan shared with me on our final meeting Monday, John?"

The president was speaking to Hay, and when Adam looked up he saw a glint of humor in Lincoln's eyes — one that hadn't been there earlier today in his office.

John Hay, who was the more gregarious and less formal of the two young secretaries, grinned back. "Indeed I did. And I waited with such wonder and credulity to hear what momentous counsels were to come from his gray and weathered head when he pulled you aside, just before leaving for the oath taking."

Lincoln laughed uproariously at this and speared a piece of apple with the tip of his knife. "Surely it was to have been a valuable moment indeed — one of great wisdom and the passing on of the torch of knowledge, isn't that so? From one president to the next. But you were paying far better attention than I to what the president was saying — I confess, my mind was somewhere else.

"Therefore, I cannot remember, dear John, whether President Buchanan told me it was the water on the right-hand well or the left-hand one that is better." By now, Lincoln's laugh had subsided to chuckles as the others at the table looked at him with expressions ranging from confusion to shock to outright horror. "Do you remember? Tell me true now — don't mislead me on this matter of great importance!"

"It was the right-hand well," Hay replied gravely, though his lips twitched.

"Do you mean to say the ex-president's parting advice to you was to use the water in the right-hand well over the water from the other?" Joshua said incredulously. "That's all the — that's all he said?"

Adam was also grinning by now, and he knew from his uncle's expression that if there hadn't been ladies present, he would surely have said something quite emphatic that included a curse. And Adam likely would have joined him.

"Indeed it was," Lincoln replied, chewing thoughtfully on an apple slice. "And there was quite a list of information about the running of the pantry and the cellars and kitchen." He shook his head. "How fascinating that the quality of the water here at this grand house was the last thing on his mind as he left it."

"That's no surprise," Joshua grumbled. Adam knew how much he — not to mention most of the Republicans and a growing number of others — despised the former president for doing little to attempt to repair the growing schism in the nation. "He did nothing but squawk mildly in protest over the secessionists and their threats, while patting them on the head and saying that he couldn't stop them even if they went." His face was set in harsh lines as he exchanged looks with his friend.

"Now then . . . all that talk of good water does put me in mind of a murder case I once worked on — back in Illinois, near Peoria. The Goings case," Lincoln continued, clearly settling into story-telling mode, which was one of his favorite pastimes. It was fortunate he was as good at telling yarns as he enjoyed doing so, for it would have been tortuous otherwise considering how often he chose to spin them.

But since Adam had been the recipient of the older man's tales since he sat cross-legged on the floor in breeches by the wood-stove, he merely reached for another hunk of bread and slathered it with butter — despite the fact that the word *murder* had been a sharp reminder of his own looming task.

"Melissa Goings — oh, she was seventy years old if she was a day — had been indicted for murdering her husband, and I was an attorney for her defense. Now, by all accounts, Mr. Goings was a hard quarreler, and an even harder drinker, and he wasn't much liked by many, including his wife. Now, I'm certain no one at this table would know anything about strife between husbands and wives, would they?" Lincoln sent a twinkling smile down the table to his own mate, who gave a delicate little sniff as she smiled demurely.

There were people who didn't care for Mary Lincoln and her political aspirations, but no one could say she wasn't devoted to her husband, nor he to her. Adam himself most often found her charming and witty, not to mention quite well versed on things many women — Mrs. Fremark, for example — didn't generally speak on, such as politics.

"As the story went, Mr. Goings, the unpleasant farmer who was, incidentally, quite well-to-do and seventy-seven years old himself, was choking his wife when she managed to free herself. She stumbled away and took hold of a stick of wood for the stove and gave him a good, hard whale — as good, I reckon, as a rail-splitter might have done, driving a spike into the railroad tie." Lincoln's voice was grave, but his eyes were lit with self-deprecating humor. "She fractured his skull and he managed to say, 'I expect she has killed me,' just before he did indeed succumb, thus fulfilling that prediction.

"Mrs. Goings had the public in her favor — for who could blame her for defending herself, and from a brute such as he? — but who could tell what the judge and jury would say. And what a shame to put an elderly woman on public trial after such an experience. And so I had myself a talk with the prosecutor one day. Just the two of us.

"Now, when the day of Mrs. Goings' trial finally came about, she was granted time to have a short conference with me, her trial lawyer." Lincoln's expression became as innocent as a baby's.

"What happened then?" asked Mrs. Grimsley.

"Why, she left the courthouse for our meeting, and was never seen again." Lincoln looked around the table with satisfaction as he took up his glass of milk.

Adam knew the game, and so he obliged by asking, "And what did the bailiff say when she didn't return?"

"He accused me of running her off, if you can credit that," replied the president. "I said to him, 'Oh, no, Bob. I didn't run her off. She wanted to know where she could get a good drink of water, and I told her there was mighty good water . . . in Tennessee.'"

"Good for you, Father," said Mrs. Lincoln with a smile as everyone else laughed.

"Why, I have no idea what you're talking about, Mother," he replied, still chuckling as the servants brought in an apple pie as deep as the Mississippi.

That treat took up the attention of the diners, including the president — who normally hardly remembered to eat unless the food was put in front of him.

They were just finishing dinner when there was a loud thud from out in the corridor, followed by the pounding of feet.

Adam was up, spinning to ward off the threat as his hand went to the pocket where his Colt would be — but currently wasn't, as he'd left it with the doorman. He glanced at Joshua, who'd turned and bolted to his feet as well, as had Loman, just as the door slammed wide.

Two small bodies hurtled through the opening, shrieking and laughing, and began a mad dash around the dining table.

Adam's heart settled back to where it belonged and he sank into his seat as the two Lincoln boys, Tad and Willie, continued their merry chase of tag. As they wove around and under — but thankfully not *over* — the table, its chairs, and their occupants, the boys' father merely watched them with an indulgent smile.

"Now, if only we all had that much energy," Lincoln said, managing to pat Willie on the head as he streaked by.

Even Mrs. Lincoln, though she murmured an admonishment as one dashed past to "take care of the shoes, loves," didn't seem bothered by the energetic interruption.

Then, by some unknown signal, the chase changed course and the two urchins made their mad exit back into the hall just as the doorman appeared. Mr. McManus barely missed being mowed down, pivoting to the side with only a whisker of space to spare.

Nevertheless, nearly being flattened by the two little devils did nothing to rattle the doorman's composure, and he announced, "I have a message for Mr. Adam Quinn. It come by way of the Willard."

Adam began to rise, but the doorman gave him a horrified look at this apparent breach of etiquette. "Allow me, sir," he said, bringing a small folded paper to him.

"Thank you, Mr. McManus." Adam unfolded the note and read the very short and neat message: *Come soon. Hilton.*

CHAPTER 12

Adam didn't take his leave immediately, but when the men rose to seek out the study for after-dinner cigars and brandy, he explained the message to Lincoln.

"Of course, you must go when you like," the president told him, waving his knobby hand easily. But his eyes were sober. "No need to stand around jawing with us. How does the investigation go? I must ask how is Mrs. Fremark, though I reckon I know the answer."

"She's not very well, I'm afraid, sir. Her sisters and daughter were coming to stay with her when I left."

"Family is important at a time like that," said the president. "I've already asked Nicolay to help prepare letters of condolence to both her and Mrs. Billings. I would that I could do more." He looked at Adam closely. "But that is a task that's fallen to you, young sir. And I'm grateful for your help in the matter. Now, is there anything more with which you can enlighten me?"

"I'm flattered by your trust, sir. And I've identified the owner of the dagger used to kill Billings — a man named Hurst Lemagne — but he claims he misplaced the dagger the day of the ball, and therefore someone else must have used it."

"A logical response. What sort of damned fool would leave his own signature embedded in another man's gullet? Either a very stupid one — or a very smart one, I think." Lincoln's deep-set eyes were grave with seriousness. "But I see you've already come to that conclusion."

"Yes, Mr. Pres— sir. And I discovered something else interesting. Billings was stabbed *outside* of the dance hall, and then dragged inside and left to be found."

"How curious. You're certain of it?"

"Yes, sir. It was no difficulty to track that movement once I had broad daylight to see the footprints in the mud of construction."

"Oh, yes, the mud. It does tend to be everywhere, don't it? At least the ease of tracking one's footmarks is one benefit to living in a city as dirty and filled with offal as a hog's pen." His eyes twinkling again, he added, "And I mean that in more than one way."

"Yes, it does," Adam replied with a grin. Though the president was tall, Adam was one of the few who hardly had to look up at him. "But there were oil smudges too, on the bottom of the killer's shoe — and he left marks from that as well. I can't reckon what that would be from."

Lincoln frowned. "Oil implies the presence of some mechanism, and one that must run smoothly and without hesitation. Not to mention silently."

"I agree. Interestingly enough, I found the smudges only in the area where Billings was stabbed, and then when he was dragged into the building. And one also near the wall in the anteroom where the body was found. They were newer and darker near the location of death. There are no other oil marks anywhere that I could find, either on the plank walkway, inside the anteroom, or even in the foyer of City Hall."

"So the mechanism is related to where and how the murder took place. Or so it seems."

"Even more telling, there were no drops or puddles of oil. Just smudges, from a shoe. As if he'd stepped on something right around the time he attacked Billings. *And,* most importantly, I found an oil smudge on the threshold of the doorway leading to the alcove where Fremark was stabbed."

"Well, that's something, I reckon. Something that definitely connects the two." Lincoln shook his head and rubbed the beard he'd only recently begun to wear. "I must say, I am relieved it's you, young man, who's trying to fit these puzzle pieces together, and not this weary, old brain."

Adam nodded grimly, forbearing to remind him just how that had come to be. "Yes, sir."

"Now I suppose you'd best see what this Doc Hilton is after, and why he's sending for you so urgently. Oh," Lincoln said just as Adam turned to go. "Did you happen to find the whereabouts of the fascinating young lady dressed as a man newspaper reporter?"

"In an — er — matter of speaking, sir, I did. I understand her article about Billings appeared in the *District Herald* under the name H. Altman, but I haven't been able to obtain a copy myself."

"The *District Herald,* is it. Hmm. I'm not familiar with it, but I reckon I'll have to take a gander at the story then, to see how she spins her yarns. A female journalist who dresses as a man." Lincoln seemed particularly tickled by the thought. "Perhaps some day I shall have the pleasure of meeting this unique young lady."

Adam rather hoped he'd have the dubious pleasure himself first — and sooner, rather than later.

"Good night, Mr. President."

"Good night. And, Adam . . . we will see you Friday night, won't we? Dressed in your fine clothes once more, and possibly even shaved again?"

He knew the man too well to take even the slightest offense. "I'm only hoping my new shoes have stretched out by now, for I can't remember my feet ever being so sore after an evening's revelry."

"They didn't seem to be bothering you when you were dancing with the pretty young woman in white," Lincoln added with a wink, then slipped into the study where the others waited.

Adam retrieved his Colt and hat, then bid farewell to McManus at the door.

The brisk March night was dark. Heavy gray clouds filtered across the moon and blanketed the swath of stars. The few gaslights that studded Lafayette Square left yellow pools of illumination spilling around them. On the bite of the air, Adam could smell the dull, earthy scent of the marsh that moldered and stewed just down a small incline from the President's House, and past the elliptical horse corral.

He was pleased to see two guards now standing at the ready near the entrance to the grounds. Though that didn't seem nearly enough security to protect a man half the country seemed to want to kill, at least there was something. He tipped a greeting with his hat and started off into the First Ward, heading north on Sixteenth from the mansion.

Adam's smile faded a little as he left the stately white house behind him. If Hurst Lemagne was found to be the murderer of Custer Billings, Constance would be devastated.

And the handsome, proper Arthur Mossing would just as surely be there to comfort her.

Adam put that thought aside quickly; it made no matter to him what went on between Miss Lemagne and her suitor. He reckoned she would soon be returning to Alabama, especially with war on the horizon and the way she proudly wore her secessionist cockade.

Unless she married the man, and stayed in Washington.

But Adam couldn't put away the possibility of Hurst Lemagne plunging a dagger into a man's chest. His daughter claimed that his bark was worse than his bite, and that he had a temper but wouldn't even whip his horses (Adam had refrained from asking about his slaves), but most certainly the man had had the opportunity to do the job during his disappearance from the ball.

It was Lemagne's weapon — a family heirloom, no less — that had been pulled out of the body and tossed into the closet along with the man's dress coat. And why *had* Billings's dress coat been removed anyway? It seemed like a risk to take the time to do something like that — along with removing the dagger from between the time Fremark had found the body until Miss Gates had come on the scene. Not to mention moving the body inside from where it had originally been stabbed.

And on top of all that, there was the unpleasant fact that Billings and Lemagne had been heard arguing; so there was definitely bad blood between them. That was one question Adam hadn't been able to ask the older man before his daughter returned and he clammed up.

No matter how you looked at it, all facts seemed to point to the man from Mobile, Alabama, being the culprit, and Adam found himself wanting desperately to find another explanation.

And yet . . . if it had been Lemagne who killed Billings, he would have had to be the one who stabbed Lyman Fremark, late yesterday evening.

If Adam could determine where Lemagne had been during the time frame Fremark went to the Willard looking for him and then on to the President's House, that could give Constance's father an alibi . . . or put him into an even worse situation.

The farther up Sixteenth Adam walked, the fewer people he encountered on foot. Several couples, arm in arm — perhaps walking home from dinner at a neighbor's house. A group of three men who'd clearly had a few ales too many, loud and raucous with their laughs cracking and their jeers slapping the silence of the night. Two men standing on a street corner, speaking soberly beneath a gaslight, one of them gesturing vehemently with his hat. An occasional waft of burning tobacco or food cooking filtered through the air, but mostly he smelled the crisp chill of a March night.

As Adam strolled along, the pristine streets of rectangular two-and three-story brick houses with their stamp-sized yards and neat walkways had begun to give way to the raw innards of the interior neighborhoods. The alleys that filled in the spaces behind the residences of the wealthy weren't decorated with gaslights or the steady clip-clop of carriages returning their owners home.

Here the darkness yawned like a big black nothing in the shadows of fancy houses and well-lit rooms. It wasn't even a beautiful darkness, like that of the plains when the sky was dark. Here in this inky world, dark and random shapes spilled over into the narrow grid between shack and shack, sparingly gilded by hints of moonlight. There was little sign of life in this dark bowl of meagerness; the destitute had gone to bed with the sun.

Just as Adam was about to turn onto K Street, he confirmed what he'd suspected almost since he'd left the Executive Mansion: someone was following him.

A little dart of apprehension rushed over him, but he shoved it away coldly. A single man was hardly a threat, even to a one-armed fool like himself.

And this was not Kansas.

This was not the deep, still night in a thrust of thick trees outside Lawrence, where a pro-slavery army of men had been waiting to ambush Adam and his friends.

There wouldn't be the whine and bite of bullet, the searing pain of being pummeled, beaten, kicked, stomped on as he bled into the dirt while trying to get to the house in time, to help Mary and little Carl . . . then the agony of watching the house go up in flames, burying the screams of those inside.

Adam shook his head, forcing the sudden nausea from the pit of his belly, fighting to keep his fingers from trembling as they curled around the metal grip of his Colt. He drew in a deep, clean breath of brisk night air and felt its calmness flow through him.

You've gotten soft, Quinn. Sleeping on a feather bed in a fancy hotel.

Steadier now, he turned into the dark alley, took three quick steps, and dodged into the depths of a shadow. He waited until the figure walked past; then the other man hesitated when he realized he'd lost his quarry.

Adam drew the Colt as he stepped out of the darkness. "Looking for someone?" He held the pistol so the scarce bit of moon highlighted its presence. "Keep your hands where I can see them."

The man turned slowly, his arms out from his sides as directed. He was wearing a hat low on his head, and it shadowed his face. Only the curve of a jaw and the hint of nose could be discerned in the dim light.

"Why are you following me?" Adam said, the barrel of the gun steady and glinting in the dark.

"I have a message for you," replied the man in a low voice. "If you're Adam Quinn."

"And what would that message be?" He didn't allow the pistol to waver.

"You're turning up things better left alone. You'd best stay —"

Adam felt rather than heard the movement behind him, and, cursing, swung around. He pulled the trigger a hair too late, for as he pivoted, the man behind him had swung out with an arm-thick pole. The blow struck Adam, smashing against his upper arm hard enough to rattle his teeth and send him reeling back, and the bullet whined harmlessly through the night.

Cursing, he stumbled and caught himself, just barely managing to hold on to the pistol, and whipped up and around with the gun in his hand. The satisfying *smack* of the metal butt across the face of his first adversary was only a momentary victory, for a second blow from the man behind him caught his shoulder as he came around.

Adam staggered back, then roared and charged forward and low. He dodged another swipe from the wooden club brandished by his attacker, and struck out again with the sharp, heavy gun. This time, he heard the crunch of bone that could have been a nose or even a tooth, and the cry of pain from his victim.

Heaving with effort, he spun back to face another onslaught and caught the sharp gleam of metal arcing toward him in the low light. With a shout, he threw up his false arm just in time to deflect the blow. The blade slammed deep into the wooden prosthetic with a great jolt. Adam stifled a groan of pain, but his attacker cried out with shock and rage as he found he couldn't withdraw his weapon from the new pine wood. Adam used this advantage to pull him into a parody of an embrace, jamming his gun barrel into the man's throat.

"Who sent you?" he panted as his captive squealed for the other man to "Hold off!"

Keeping the Colt pushed firmly into his adversary's neck, Adam eased back a little so he could get a look at the other attacker. He was still restricted by the knife wedged into his prosthetic arm, but the other man didn't know that.

"I'm going to ask you one more time," he growled, shoving the pistol in a little harder. "Who sent you with this message?"

"The-the Association."

Fully aware of the second man standing

barely in his peripheral vision, Adam angled toward him. "What's the Association?"

But before the man could respond, something moved in the darkness. There was a soft squeak from new shoes, and a slight figure emerged from the shadows.

"Mr. Quinn? Is that you?"

No. *Hell. No.* "Get out of here," he snarled, turning toward the boy. "Go! Get the hell out of —"

The club caught him fully across the shoulders this time, knocking the breath from him and whipping his head back. His finger snapped on the trigger and the pistol kicked in his hand as he lost his grip. The man against him cried out and shuddered as the bullet struck him.

Adam wrenched his fake arm away from the knife as the Colt tumbled to the ground, then bounced off into the darkness. Dull pain shot through him as the prosthetic's bindings dragged and burned over his torso and upper arm as the knife blade tore free, even as he was struck squarely between his shoulder blades. His wounded attacker tumbled back, and, breathless and throbbing with pain, Adam roared again as he spun around to face the man behind him.

He was met with the club once more, and this time it was a vicious swipe toward his torso. Already staggering and heaving, he barely managed to fling up his arms to ward off the strike, and the club smashed into his wooden arm with an ugly crunch.

Adam cried out with rage and pain as the shock of the blow reverberated horribly along his arm, but could hardly catch his breath before he was pummeled again.

He heard someone shouting, and the sound of something cracking in the air. . . . Then pain exploded at the back of his head.

Darkness overtook him as he fell.

CHAPTER 13

Adam slowly became aware of his surroundings . . . mainly because someone was shaking him. Whoever owned the hands yanking and pulling at him didn't seem to care that each forced movement sent renewed waves of agony through his body.

"Mr. Quinn! Can't you wake up, Mr. Quinn?"

With a groan, Adam forced his eyes open in the hopes that the incessant shaking would stop. He tasted blood on his lip and areas of his body pounded, but he recognized the slim shadow hovering over him.

"Off . . . me," he managed to grunt. "Brian . . . get off."

The hands stopped. Oh, thank merciful Jesus, they stopped. Now he was just throbbing with pain, instead of being shaken harder into it. Blood dripped from several places and soaked wet and warm in others.

"You're *alive.* Thanks be to the Virgin!

You're alive! He's alive, Mam!"

"Well, it's no wonder, the way you're about doddering the man to his death. He wouldn't have a chance to slip off to either heaven or hell with the likes of you badgering at him, Brian. I told you to wait for me. I hope you haven't hurt him more."

Now Adam could make out an actual circle of people gathered around him. Or maybe his vision was just blurry. There were at least two . . . maybe three. Four? His head hurt.

Feeling foolish and weak — not to mention angry as hell — he struggled to sit up, and suddenly slender arms and hands were helping him, prodding and tugging. "Don't be rushing it, there, now, mister," said the woman who could only be Brian's mother. She had a thick Irish accent and smelled like boiled potatoes and wood smoke.

"I'm fine." The words came out in something almost like a snarl, and he sucked in a breath to stop himself saying something else ungrateful. "Thank you, Mrs. Mulcahey. I'll be fine in a moment."

"Mr. Quinn."

A different voice, heralding a newcomer just coming into view from the shadows, had him looking up at the familiar figure of George Hilton.

Good Christ. Was everyone from the First Ward here, watching him get his arse beat to a pulp?

"I'm fine," Adam said. This time he allowed the snarl in his tone — he reckoned Hilton could handle it — and pulled firmly away from the slender, rough-skinned female hands that fussed over him.

But when he tried to pull to his feet, he realized two unpleasant things: first, he was too weak and a little dizzy to accomplish standing on his own — so he leaned casually against a convenient piece of fence — and, second, his prosthetic arm dangled, battered and useless, from his aching stump.

Damn it all.

"What're you doing here?" he demanded of Hilton in an effort to deflect the attention from himself as he struggled to remain upright. At some point, most of the clouds had been torn away by some celestial being, and now the half-moon shone a bit more light into the night.

"There was a louder ruckus than usual, sir," Hilton replied in a voice that was too formal for the occasion. "And this young man was screeching at the top of his lungs that Mr. Quinn was dead." He shrugged and spread his hands, and when he continued, there was the slightest hint of humor in his voice. "I suppose 'at I could've stayed in my bed, though, sir."

Adam frowned. "Didn't you send for me? What the hell were you doing in your bed, if you were expecting me?" He looked around, suddenly remembering his Colt, even as his head spun and pounded. "And where's my pistol? Did they make off with that?" He wanted to go off and search for it but didn't trust his knees to work properly. Hell. Mrs. Mulcahey was watching him as if she expected him to collapse right there.

Damned if she might be right. He gripped the piece of fence and instructed his knees not to give way.

"I got your gun." Brian offered him the Colt with great reverence. "I shot at them."

Now more details were beginning to filter back into his mind. Adam looked grimly at the boy, suddenly realizing how fortunate both of them were that Brian was still standing on two steady legs. In his brand new boots. "You were there — you saw them. And you shot them?"

"Aye, but I missed," Brian replied matter-of-factly. "But it scared them anyhow. And then I threw Bessie toward them, when they was beating on you. I climbed up there on that lean-to, you see, and tossed her down on them and made a lot of ruckus with the metal roofing — banging on it like it was the end of the world. They saw this big thing with wide, flapping wings coming down on them, and all the noise, and I shot the pistol again and shouted at them — and they were about running away faster 'an Bessie when Mam threatens to make her into soup." He punctuated this speech by swiping his arm across his nose and giving a sharp sniffle.

"Well, I'm much obliged to you and to Bessie," Adam replied.

"And then when you wouldn't wake up, I ran off to get my mam. Because I knew she'd know what to do. She left Erin with Mrs. White so she could come right away, Mr. Quinn."

"Much obliged to you as well, Mrs. Mulcahey. Thank you very much."

"I'll need to be getting back to my Erin now, Mr. Quinn, but I'm wanting you to know I'm obliged to you as well. The pies . . . the boots . . ." She shook her head, and in the dim light he saw her lips purse tightly as if to keep them from quivering. "And you need some tending to, there, I think, or you'll be feeling even worse by dawn."

"I'll see to it," said Hilton, who'd hovered behind the Mulcaheys and the several other bystanders who'd also been drawn from their dark houses.

"I don't need any tending to," Adam growled. He was enraged at being taken by surprise and nearly beaten to death — having been saved by a twelve-year-old boy and a damned *chicken*. And now to be the subject of interest of a half-dozen people standing around, looking at him as he used a scrap of picket fence to keep from landing on his face. His tone must have warned them, for the rest of the gawkers melted away into the night.

"Yes, sir, Mr. Quinn," Hilton said in that bland, formal voice of his. He stepped back even farther into the shadows. "No, sir."

Adam scrubbed his working hand over his face and felt the blood and grit of pain even as his body thrummed and ached. He was being an ass. Besides, there was no way he could get himself anywhere without help.

"Dr. Hilton. Sir. I reckon I could use that wagon of yours — if you'd be willing. Since I don't think this damned piece of fence is going to carry me back to the Willard." In the partial darkness, Adam saw the faint outline of the man's shoulders square up and turn back toward him.

"I don't know if my wagon's big enough," Hilton rumbled as he returned. "For you and that big ole chip on your shoulder. Not to mention the whole barrel full of pride you seem to be carrying around with you."

Adam barked out a surprised laugh, then groaned when it made him hurt. A lot. He caught his breath, still grinning at the man's unexpected wit. "I reckon you can squeeze all of it in if you put me on the bottom."

"Leastways I can try," Hilton agreed. He sounded even more relaxed now. "You want to come with me or wait here? I can treat you in my office at the church."

Adam drew in an experimental breath and decided. "I'll wait. I should return to the Willard as soon as possible, if it's all the same to you." His uncle was leaving in the morning, and aside from that, he wanted to get back where he could try to find out who'd set the two thugs on him. Only one had spoken, but he'd been neither a Northerner nor a drawling westerner.

"Shouldn't take long. Try not to get beat up again." Hilton's white teeth flashed in the dark, and then he went off into the night at a quick jog.

Adam muttered a curse after the man, then, blessedly, allowed himself to sink to the ground. He had his Colt at the ready — how many bullets were left anyway? — if he needed it.

The solitude gave him a moment to think,

and he swiped his own face with a shirt-sleeve, mopping up blood and sweat. Someone had sent those men after him, and how had they known he was coming up to the First Ward anyway? He reckoned they wouldn't have tried to rough him up as he strolled down Pennsylvania Avenue either to or from Willard's, even if it was dark out.

He reckoned, also, that he was a damned sight luckier than Lyman Fremark.

But just as important was the confirmation that *someone* wasn't happy about Adam's investigation into Billings's death . . . and that must mean he was on the right path, doing something or learning something, that made them nervous.

Or maybe they feared Fremark had somehow given him whatever information he had.

Adam tipped his head back against the fence, trying not to think about the incessant throbbing of pain and the fact that his head was light and didn't want to stop spinning. The night air was chilly, and he realized his coat had been torn off during the fracas. It was probably in a heap somewhere in the dark.

His coat.

That brought him abruptly back to the question: Why had the murderer removed

Billings's coat? Why take the time, when he'd already risked so much to stab him outside, then move him — during a public event — when at any moment he could be seen? Why leave the knife in at first, then remove it and the coat?

Adam frowned. His head hurt, but there was something important niggling there. He closed his eyes and focused, ignoring the waves of pain — along with the dark Kansas memories that threatened to erupt in the wake of this violence.

The coat. The dagger . . . yes, that was it. Fremark had seen the dagger sticking out of the dead body, but when Miss Gates arrived in her gentleman's garb, the dagger wasn't there. But when had the dress coat been removed? Was the coat already gone when Fremark found Billings, or had it been taken after?

And again, why?

He closed his eyes once more and leaned back, feeling the useless weight of the wooden arm shifting in his lap. Whether it could be repaired was one question, and how quickly was another. At least the young, supple pine wood had saved him from a knife to the gut. And had helped him put a bullet in the man who'd tried to stick him. Yet it had been too dark and wild for him to know how badly his assailant had been injured. Obviously, not enough that he couldn't make his escape.

After a short, blurry while, Adam heard the sound of wagon wheels and the quiet clop of hooves on dirt. He used his good arm to pull to his feet, pleased that it seemed a little easier this time.

"You got all your baggage there?" Hilton said as Adam took a few staggering steps toward him. "That chip and the barrel o' pride?"

"That's why I'm only walking, and ain't running," Adam managed to joke. "All that extra weight." But he didn't refuse the other man's arm when it came around him for support.

Hilton wasn't as tall as he, but he was muscular and could easily handle the added ballast. Nor did he even make the whiff of a suggestion that Adam might want to ride in the back of the wagon, where his patients obviously did; instead, he helped him climb up to sit next to the driver.

"I told you to come at noon," Hilton said mildly as he clucked to his horse. "That's why I was in bed, bunking at my office — lucky for you. Got too late to go back home."

"Your message said come 'soon,' " replied

Adam. "So I did."

"I surely do know how to read and write, Mr. Quinn," replied the other man firmly. "I wrote to come at noon. And I sent the message to the Willard, like you said, and told them to give it to you in the morning."

Adam curled his lip. Well, that answered the question how his attackers knew he'd be going to the First Ward that night. "Someone intercepted the message and changed it to read 'soon' and brought it to me at the President's House, where I was eating dinner."

That meant someone had been hanging around the Willard both tonight and yesterday, watching and waiting for Adam or anyone trying to reach him.

Yes, he reckoned he was stirring up some nerves in someone.

He was going to have to question Birch a lot more closely about whether he'd seen anyone suspicious loitering about. However, the Willard was a popular place to socialize and eat — and not just for guests. It would be difficult to determine who did and didn't have a reason for being there.

"Eating dinner with the president, were you?" Hilton gave a low hum of interest. "Miss Lizzie said you was a friend of his."

"I've known him since I was a young boy.

My uncle is his close friend. He's a good man." Adam cast him a side glance. "He'll be good for our country . . . no matter what happens."

That comment was left hanging between them, and without having meant to do so, Adam realized he'd subtly broached the subject of their difference in skin color and societal positions. That striking difference had likely been the cause of the sliding scale of Hilton's formality and extreme deference, all the way to the position where he'd actually made a joke at Adam's expense.

Along with that came the realization that he'd been selfish not to go back to Hilton's office instead of making him drive him back to the Willard.

"I've asked too much of you, I reckon," he said, unsure how to raise that subject with the proud man next to him. "It's after curfew, and —"

"It's a ten-dollar fine for a black man to be caught out after ten o'clock," Hilton replied calmly. "I've paid it before, and I reckon I'll pay it again." When Adam began to protest, he continued, "The sick and injured don't wait for curfew to be lifted, Mr. Quinn."

"No, I reckon they don't." Adam chewed on that for a while, which was a welcome distraction from the constant jolting of his aching body from the wagon.

"You're wondering where I got my training," Hilton said. "How I came to learn to read and write and to be a doctor." He guided the horse down a side street, which Adam recognized as an alternate route to taking the more traveled Pennsylvania Avenue, where he'd more likely be seen by the Night Guard. "And how I can pay a ten-dollar fine. More than once."

"I am a curious sort of fellow," Adam replied mildly. "But I can't say it kept me up at night." No, nothing that simple kept him up at night.

Hilton chuckled. It was a dark, low sound that reminded Adam of the distant rumble of thunder when an easy summer storm was rolling in from the western plains.

"So, you gonna put me out of my misery?" Adam said, then sucked in his breath as the wagon hit a large bump. *Christ,* he muttered as his vision went shadowed and dark, then came back.

"I went to medical school in Montreal. It was paid for by my . . . my sponsor, who was a Quaker in Philadelphia. Theodore Raitz was a doctor himself, and he lived next door to a Methodist reverend my momma kept house for. My momma bought her freedom from Mr. Pellman and moved us North to get away from Washington. I was born a free man, and the reverend and Dr. Raitz took an interest in me and my momma." Hilton slanted a glance at Adam. "I started assisting Dr. Raitz when I was thirteen, and he must have seen some promise there. When he died, he left me the money to go to medical school, and a letter of reference to his mentor Dr. Caldwell, who was the founder of the Montreal Medical Institution." He shrugged.

Pennsylvania Avenue glowed two blocks in front of them now, and Hilton eased back on the reins so his horse came to a halt. "I'll help you inside and see what I can do if you like. But I have to find a place for my wagon."

"I'll have them take care of it," Adam said, forcing himself to speak through the pain, though he realized he was fully slumped against his companion. The shadows were closing in on the edges of his vision once more. "The wagon. I reckon . . . I could use some tending after all."

He managed to get down from the wagon with Hilton's help, but then his knees buckled. For the second time that night, his world went dark.

Adam winced as the barber moved his head none too gently in order to get a good, careful scrape around the indentation in his chin.

"Almost done here," said the man as he dunked the straight-blade into a bowl of warm water. "That's some bruising you got there, mister. So tell me, how's the other guy look?" He laughed uproariously and scritch-scritch-scraped the razor over Adam's left jawbone.

Because of the proximity of the blade, Adam couldn't even attempt to reply. He reckoned that was part of the reason barbers as a whole figured they could say whatever they liked while doing their job. He'd experienced many of them over the years who seemed to think they were uproariously funny, spectacularly intelligent, or both. Clearly, no one risked the chance to tell them otherwise.

But what Adam really wanted was to remind the man wielding a frighteningly sharp blade near his jugular that the bruising of which he spoke was tender, and to please not dig his thumb into the black-and-blue marks on his jaw.

Instead, he closed his eyes and tried to relax, even though his thoughts were spinning.

It was Friday morning, two days after he'd found Lyman Fremark in the closet at the President's House. That same day, Adam had eaten supper with the Lincolns then had his life saved by a scrawny Irish boy and his chicken. Yesterday was a blur. He'd gone in and out of a deep sleep most of the day. Hilton had not only put some foul-smelling cream on his injuries, but must have given him something to help him sleep, for Adam had only awakened to use the chamber pot, then succumbed to the desire to rest and sleep off the beating he'd received.

Joshua had delayed his trip home to Springfield by one day to make certain his nephew was all right, and had left earlier this morning.

So, though he was still slow and achy, Adam had had enough of being in bed. He was furious he'd had to spend that much time on his back, but Joshua had insisted and Hilton apparently had agreed.

"You're lucky to be alive," his uncle had said, whistling and then frowning deeper when he saw the extent of the bruises and lacerations decorating Adam's shoulders and legs.

Along with the marks from fists, feet, and club, Adam also had deep, red chafing from where his prosthetic bindings had cut into, twisted, and dragged over his skin during the fight. The widest strap from the contraption encircled his torso, just beneath the armpits. Another one went up and over the opposite shoulder, and there were other, more narrow straps over his left stump arm. Each of them had caused ugly, raw burn-like marks on his skin, tearing out any hair that had grown there and biting into his flesh. The end of his amputated arm was battered and raw as well, especially where the prosthetic fit over it like a shallow cup.

It had actually been a relief not to be able to wear the false limb all day yesterday.

But this morning, when Adam had been clearheaded for the first time since the attack, he hadn't been able to find the prosthetic in his hotel room.

"Hilton took it yesterday," Joshua had told him as he picked up his carpetbag and surveyed the room one last time. "Said he knew someone who might be able to fix it. And that young kid Brian was already downstairs today when I went to get coffee. Was badgering the doorman about you. I told him to come back around noon."

Adam grinned and it didn't even hurt too much. "Brian was here yesterday too, wasn't he?"

"Wouldn't stop talking about someone named Bessie and how they chased off the thugs. Said his mam wanted to know how you were doing. I said I reckoned you'd live." Joshua offered his hand to shake goodbye. "Hope to see you back in Springfield someday, because I don't guess I'll set foot in this city again."

"Soon as I can," Adam replied, responding with a firm grip. "Two weeks, maybe less."

Joshua shook his head with a strange smile. "I wouldn't count on that." He sat his hat on his head and paused before he left the room. "Good luck, Adam."

Now, as the barber pressed a very hot towel over newly shaven skin, smothering his client with steam and relaxing all the muscles of his face, Adam couldn't help but ponder his uncle's knowing smile. *I wouldn't count on that.* What the hell did he mean by that?

"All done there, Mr. Quinn," said the barber as he snatched the towel away. "Smoothest shave in the city, and that swelling's gone down even since I started on you. Won't be scaring away the ladies too much now, then, won't you?"

"Now that's where you're wrong. I reckon my mug scares 'em away every day, shaven or bruised or no," Adam said as he slid off the chair and dug out three pennies to pay the man.

Bathed, shaved, and no longer wincing every time he took a breath, Adam felt better than he had in days. His left sleeve was pinned up from just below the elbow, and one of the first things he meant to accomplish was a visit to George Hilton to find out where his prosthetic was, and what news he had about Fremark — or anything else. He'd not managed to ask why Hilton had sent for him during the tortuous wagon ride back to the hotel.

When Adam left the barbershop — which was on-site at the Willard and also included a bathing area — and strolled out into the lobby, he made his way directly to where Birch stood outside the hotel door, regular as the sunset and 'rise.

"Morning, there, Mr. Quinn," said the doorman. He stood stiff and correct with his white-gloved hands folded at the low of his back. "Mighty happy to see you out and about."

"Mighty happy to be out and about," Adam replied.

"Heard you had a passel o' trouble up to the First Ward t' other night."

"You heard right."

"I understand it was a chicken what come to your rescue."

"Is that so?" Adam might have to have a few words with Brian about spouting off to people about certain things. "I reckon there are plenty of rumors flying about Washington. Perhaps you might choose different gossip to believe."

Birch laughed heartily, obviously seeing the humor in Adam's face. "Oh, you can bet I get my fair share of gossip standing here at the Willard. People waiting for the omnibus or a hack, or their carriage brought around — or just waitin' to cross the street. They don't pay no mind to me, and it's like a long table — their gossip — with all sorts of food on it. I jus' pick and choose what I want to eat — and what I want to listen to."

"Well maybe you can tell me what sort of dishes were on the table the last few days so I can put my hands on the man who stabbed Lyman Fremark in the back."

Birch shook his head and curled his lips, the levity draining from his face. "I done heard about that, Mr. Quinn. In the President's House, yet. Who woulda done such a thing?"

"Took a lot of stones for a man to do it there, but I reckon murder's murder, no matter whose house or which street it's done in."

"Don't got no argument about that, sir."

"Two nights in a row — Tuesday and Wednesday — it seems to me someone must've been hanging around here, picking up information. Tuesday night, he followed Fremark up to the Executive Mansion and managed to get him alone to stab him. He must've heard Fremark asking for me, and reckoned it had to do with what happened to Custer Billings. You did get that bit of gossip from your buffet table, didn't you?"

"I sure did. People's been talking about it."

"Anyone in particular that you notice? Anyone talking about who might have done that to Billings?"

"No, sir, not that I recall. But I go off at six, sir. Don't think George woulda noticed neither."

"All right then. What about the same person being in the area both Tuesday night and Wednesday night? The first night, he would have followed Fremark; the next night, he would have somehow intercepted the message for me from a man named Hilton, then sent a fake message to me up at Mr. Lincoln's house. Then he sent two thugs after me, knowing I'd be going up into the First Ward after dark."

Birch paused to open the door for a trio of well-dressed gentlemen and the cloud of cigar smoke that accompanied them.

When he returned to his position at the outside, he said, "It's hard to say for certain, sir. This place is filled with people all the time, coming for dinner or to have a drink or to socialize or even for those dance hops they have. Not just the guests, but everyone in Washington comes here. Even the women, without their men sometimes." He shook his head, seemingly fascinated by this breach of propriety. "Either way, it ain't possible to tell whether anyone coming in or out has a reason or not."

"Oh, Mr. Quinn!"

A new voice, bright with excitement, drew their attention, and Adam turned. Miss Lemagne was waving at him from across the street, her bell-like skirt swaying with agitation as she waited for the traffic to clear.

"Well, now, Mr. Quinn," said Birch with a grin. "That there girl's one pretty thing. She was here yesterday, asking about you. But she was with that man Mossing, and he didn't seem too pleased about it when your name come up. Not a-tall." His grin was wider. "You want a pretty southern belle, you might have to get him out of the way first. Don't seem like she'd mind too much, there, neither, Mr. Quinn. She ain't no woman in love's far as I can see."

Adam pursed his lips as he watched Miss Lemagne gathering up her skirts in preparation for stepping into the muddy street. "Well, I reckon I don't see Mossing anywhere around today, now do I?" He shot a look at the man and was rewarded with a knowing grin and a little salute.

By the time she was close enough to speak, Adam had subdued the spark of interest, along with his smile. "Miss Lemagne, what are you doing here?"

"Why, Mr. Quinn, I heard you had been injured, and so I came back to see how you were faring. I called yesterday, but a gentleman — he said he was your uncle — wouldn't let me see you. Whatever happened?" Her southern accent was alive and well today and suited her genuine concern and warm smile. If she noticed his partially pinned-up sleeve, she neither remarked on it nor looked at it.

"As you can see, I am well on my feet, Miss Lemagne. Thank you for your concern."

He reckoned he hadn't ever seen a lady

look so fresh and pretty. Like a summer flower: willowy and elegant, and all creamy skin and roses in her cheeks and cornflower eyes.

She was dressed in a pale blue dress with tiny white flowers and green leaves sprinkled over the fabric. There was an inordinate amount of lace trimming along the hem of her ungainly skirt, and from beneath the cloak she wore, he saw that the sleeves of her bodice dripped with lace as well. She wore gloves and carried both a parasol and a small reticule. Her hair was piled up beneath a proper hat dripping with false flowers, exposing those smooth golden swoops that covered most of her ears. Miss Lemagne's cheeks were flushed pink, and her lips matched. To Adam, she looked as if she were going to a party or a formal dinner.

"I declare, I'm delighted to see you on your feet. I was hoping," she said, easing closer and bringing a sweet scent along with her, "to find out if you had any more information about the . . . er . . . matter related to Mr. Billings." She glanced at Birch, whose expression was blank as he watched up and down the street. "My daddy has — well, *I* have been worried sick about all of this."

"As a matter of fact, I was just leaving to attend to a matter related to Mr. Billings."

As soon as he said those words, Adam realized he shouldn't have added the last bit, for her eyes lit up. But those same crystal blue eyes seemed to have loosened his tongue and now he'd put the pan in the fire.

"If it's related to the investigation, I must insist upon accompanying you," said Miss Lemagne. "After all, it's my father who you have put in the sights for this crime."

"I'm sorry, ma'am, but it would not be advisable for you to accompany me. I'm going to be speaking with a doctor who did a very thorough . . . er . . . medical examination of Mr. Billings's body. It would not be seemly for a young lady to be present in such an indecorous situation."

"I wish to accompany you, Mr. Quinn." All at once, the southern allure was replaced by steel. It was steel covered in velvet, but it was steel nonetheless.

"I must decline, Miss Lemagne. It would be very unseemly, and —"

"And I find it unseemly that my father is suspected of murder, Mr. Quinn." Miss Lemagne looked at him from beneath an arched brow. "If I can handle the knowledge that he could be imprisoned — or *worse* — for a crime he didn't commit, surely I can handle whatever it is this doctor might have to say." She leaned forward. "And, if you refuse to allow me to accompany you, Mr. Quinn, I promise you I will simply follow on my own."

Adam resisted the urge to scrub the crease between his eyebrows with the palm of his hand. How on earth would his mother expect him to handle this? He suddenly felt a stirring of sympathy for the haughty Mr. Mossing.

"Very well, then. It's settled." She smiled brilliantly up at him before he had the chance to respond, then slipped her fingers around his forearm.

And that explained why, shortly thereafter, Adam Quinn found himself strolling north-westerly along the avenue accompanied by the lovely, chatty Miss Lemagne.

But several blocks north of Lafayette Square, when they turned onto the alley off K Street, Adam felt Miss Lemagne's fingers tense through his sleeve. Indeed, merely by turning off the main road into the smaller throughway, the entire world seemed to shrink, darken, and simply become gloomier. Miss Lemagne gathered up an even bigger handful of the front of her dress in a vain effort to keep its hem from getting soiled.

He once again observed the ramshackle shanties, sagging roofs, and scraggly buildings anew — this time, through the eyes of a young woman who'd likely never before been exposed to such impoverishment. Though there was muck and refuse lining the main streets and avenues of Washington, the trash and offal here in these putrid, dingy walkways was even worse.

They were only several yards into the short, offshoot alley when Adam came upon the place where he'd been attacked. Releasing Miss Lemagne's arm, he crouched to examine the ground, hoping to find some new information that might lead him to his assailants, even though the area had surely been trod upon.

"What is it?" she asked, standing close enough that her skirt encroached upon his view.

"Please step back, Miss Lemagne," he said, ignoring the ache from his battered body as he maneuvered around awkwardly.

But there was little to see. Other than a random chicken feather from the heroic Bessie, the evidence of his attack had been obliterated. Stifling a groan, Adam pulled slowly to his feet, finding it more difficult than usual, missing his prosthetic as he was.

"What was that all about?" Miss Lemagne

asked. "What were you looking for?"

"Clues as to who tried to kill me Wednesday night," Adam said matter-of-factly.

"Oh." She breathed in a quiet gust of air. "Were they really trying to kill you?" She looked around as if to ensure the thugs weren't lurking in the shadows.

"I don't reckon they were inviting me to tea," Adam replied. "Shall I escort you back now, Miss Lemagne? I can see to my task another time."

"Certainly not," she replied. "You'll not get rid of me that easily, Mr. Quinn."

But he noticed the way she warily eyed the activity on the narrow street as they continued to Great Eternity Church.

A woman with frizzy red hair and pale skin looked up from where she was scrubbing clothes in a wash basin between two wilting buildings, and where three toddlers sat in a broken-down, wheelless wagon. It seemed to serve as a sort of pen to confine them and keep them out of the muck as they screeched and babbled.

Across the pitiful excuse for a street — barely wide enough for a horse to pass through — a Negro woman wearing a kerchief was hanging laundry on a sagging line. She was accompanied by a young girl of six or seven who handed her the clothes-pins.

A scrawny man with skin the color of weather-beaten leather was chopping wood next door, and in the distance there was the sound of someone hammering. Beneath it all was the unrelenting stench of waste — human, animal, plant — and smoke.

"Who are these people?" she asked softly. "Why do they . . . ?" She didn't seem able to form a reasonable question. Because there was a simple answer to "why": Why did they live in such hovels? Why did they live in such poverty and depravity?

Because they had no choice.

"Some are Irish immigrants," Adam replied in a similarly low tone. "Others are free Negroes. Some are slaves. Many of the houses — if you can call them that — are for the slaves of the big houses that face the main streets like J and K, and the number streets. They were built by the owners of the mansions to rent out to the free Negroes or immigrants, or to house their servants."

Miss Lemagne seemed quietly stunned by this revelation, and Adam wasn't certain whether he should be proud of the lecture he'd given her or ashamed.

"We're nearly there," he said as Miss Lemagne paused to adjust her parasol so she could dig into the small drawstring bag that hung from her wrist.

When she extricated a handkerchief and pressed it to her nose and mouth, Adam noticed a fresh wave of floral essence — likely from the scrap of lace-trimmed cloth.

Good luck in keeping the stench away once you get inside Hilton's office, he thought grimly.

They went around to the backside of Great Eternity Church, with Miss Lemagne once again hiking up her skirt, petticoats, and hoops while managing parasol, handkerchief, and drawstring bag. This necessitated her releasing his arm, as well as giving Adam a pang of fury that he didn't even have a second hand to offer for assistance.

Damn it.

He put away the surge of pride and, against his better judgment, assisted Miss Lemagne and her attire down the narrow five steps from grass level to cellar door. It was a ludicrous proposition, attempting to manipulate her, her stiff hoops, her wayward parasol, and her dainty, mud-slicked feet down the stairs, especially when she slipped on the edge of one step and nearly took a tumble.

Adam smothered a curse and easily caught her with his one working arm, but he was still furious: at himself, at the situation, at the damned steps.

"Hilton," he called, ignoring the sign that said CLOSED. The man had better be there, after all this. He didn't wait for a response before shoving open the door.

Miss Lemagne walked through, spine-straight and handkerchief over her nose and mouth, and stopped dead still.

"Good heavens," she said faintly.

Oh yes, Hilton was there . . . and so were Fremark and Billings.

CHAPTER 14

Constance could hardly believe her eyes, not to mention her nose.

But she wasn't about to admit to Mr. Quinn how much she did not want to take another step into this . . . chamber of horror. Instead, she forced herself to walk in . . . just far enough to let him slip on past as she gaped at the scene in front of her.

Now she understood why Mr. Quinn had been so determined not to bring her.

The place . . . it was beyond morbid. The large, open room with whitewashed brick walls was lit by a remarkable number of kerosene lamps. Shelves and worktables, along with a desk and chair, lined two of the main walls — which were topped by small windows at ground level and near the ceiling. Two forlorn curtains hung at right angles to each other in a corner, effectively cordoning off a private area. Beneath the barrier, she could see what appeared to be the legs of a bed and chair.

But it was the long table in the center of the room that drew — and kept — one's attention.

The man standing behind it was staring at them — no, at her — with the same sort of shock she seemed to feel, stepping into this makeshift morgue.

He was a Negro, with medium-dark skin and a cropped beard and mustache. His hair was very short, as if it had recently been shaved off and only begun to grow back. He had a handsome face, carved from walnut, with full lips and skin that shone faintly with perspiration. A butcher's apron covered him from chest to knee, and his shirtsleeves were rolled halfway up his muscular upper arms.

But more shocking than that was the dead body lying on the table in front of him.

Constance realized her mouth was hanging open, and she closed it.

"What on —" the man began, then made a sound of disgust as he flung a blood-stained sheet over the pale, lifeless body on the table in front of him. "Good afternoon, madam," he said in a strangled voice as his attention snapped to Mr. Quinn. He wasn't even attempting to hide his vexation. And — good heavens — his hands and most of his exposed forearms were slick with blood, and there was a shiny streak of the same on his face.

She felt a little faint.

"Dr. Hilton, this is Miss Constance Lemagne," said Mr. Quinn as he removed his hat.

Doctor Hilton? Constance couldn't contain an audible reaction of disbelief. A Negro doctor? How could that be?

"She insisted on coming with me." The tone of Mr. Quinn's voice clearly indicated his own dislike of the situation. And the bruise he'd acquired on one clean-shaven cheekbone, along with a nasty scrape and two-inch cut across his jaw, merely emphasized his displeasure. "And barring the option of Miss Lemagne insisting on making her own way here, I could see no choice other than to allow her to accompany me."

"I see. Apparently the 'closed' sign made no difference to you, either," replied the man in what Constance felt was a discourteous tone.

But Mr. Quinn didn't seem to be offended. "I didn't believe it referred to me," he said in a mild rebuke. "Considering the work I've sent you."

"Miss Lemagne, there are chairs over there." The black man — she couldn't really accept the fact that he was a doctor — gestured to a trio of them lined against the wall next to the door. "Please make yourself comfortable."

Dr. Hilton spoke with smooth diction and grammar. He didn't sound like any other Negro she'd ever heard. His grammar was perfect and his diction clear. He even sounded a little exotic, and there wasn't a trace of southern accent.

But he seemed extremely ill at ease as he stood there in shirtsleeves covered by a heavy butcher's apron. Both were marred by dark, rusty stains, and Constance averted her eyes when she realized there were more bloodstains on the dirt-packed floor. Big, sprawling stains that appeared to have run off the far edge of the slightly tipped table.

And then there was the *stench.* The heavy, cloying smells: the metallic essence of blood was so thick she could taste it on her tongue, and there was the wild, meaty aroma of exposed organs — the very beginning odor of age and decay — all mingled with the astringent scent of whisky and the earthy perfume of damp, dark overturned soil.

She didn't take a seat. Instead, she moved the handkerchief away from her mouth and nose to speak. "Mr. Quinn believes my father killed him — Mr. Billings."

She hated that her voice shook a little, but this situation was quite untenable. Mr. Quinn had been correct: it was unseemly for her to be there. Nevertheless, she was glad she'd come. She couldn't just stand by and do nothing. The fear of what would happen if her father was jailed, tried, and even convicted of killing Custer Billings had kept her up at night. "I insisted upon accompanying him today because I want to help prove that my father wouldn't do any such thing."

"I haven't accused your father of killing Custer Billings," Mr. Quinn said firmly. "Though his knife was found near the body — and seen sticking out of it — I reckon he wouldn't have been so foolish as to leave it at the place of the crime if he'd committed it."

"Is that not what I've said all along, Mr. Quinn? That my father wouldn't have been that foolish?"

"Yes. You've mentioned it a number of times," he replied wearily as he lifted his good arm so he could rub the creases between his eyebrows. He'd moved rather stiffly during their walk here, and had emitted an audible groan when he rose from his examination of the tracks in the alley. How badly had he been injured?

"Regardless — I'm not certain what you expect to find here. This place is not fit for a woman, as you can easily see," Mr. Quinn added.

Though Constance privately agreed, she wasn't about to admit it. Instead, she edged to a counter at one side of the room — thankfully far from the long table bearing the corpse. There were a number of items laid out on it, including men's clothing and a pocket watch.

"I heartily concur," Dr. Hilton replied, sounding slightly relieved. "Maybe you'd like to step outside —"

"Are these his personal belongings?" she interrupted without thinking. "Mr. Billings's?"

"Yes." The doctor sounded harassed. "My apologies, ma'am, but I really don't think you —"

"All of this is his?" Constance frowned as she looked at the articles of clothing: formal trousers, dress coat, waistcoat, shirt, cravat, underbreeches (at least, she assumed that was what they were), gloves, and stockings. In a small pile next to them, there was also an expensive pocket watch, a wrinkled business card with her daddy's name and address on it back home, an invitation to the

Union Ball, a crumpled Union cockade (at which she couldn't help but sneer), and a few coins.

"Yes," Mr. Quinn replied. He sounded slightly mollified; perhaps because she wasn't looking at the body any longer.

"I removed everything that was on the body. It's all there," added Dr. Hilton.

"But where are his shoes?" Constance asked curiously.

"I have them," Mr. Quinn replied. "Back at my rooms."

She nodded, then picked up the dress coat and brought it closer to one of the lamps. She examined it closely, comparing it to the trousers in the better light, then straightened, frowning. "Are you aware this isn't Mr. Billings's coat?"

"What are you talking about?" Now Mr. Quinn was looking annoyed again. Unfortunately, he still looked quite attractive even when irritation was darkening his face. Arthur Mossing, Esquire, couldn't hold a candle to this tall, lanky, broad-shouldered frontiersman.

"Of course it's his coat," Mr. Quinn said. "Mr. Billings was missing his when he was found, and this coat was in the broom closet with the knife. It's got blood on it."

"It's not his coat," Constance said clearly.

"It doesn't match his trousers. A man — especially one of Mr. Billings's wealth and taste — would have trousers and a dress coat made to match for a formal occasion like the Union Ball. Even my daddy did, though he only had a short time to have it done once we arrived here."

Mr. Quinn strode over and took up the coat and trousers in question, bringing them close to the lamp as she'd done. "What do you mean, they don't match? They're both black." He lifted his eyes, frowning in bewilderment.

"Yes, Mr. Quinn. They're both black, but they're not the *same* black."

"The same black? Isn't black . . . just black?"

She found his bafflement amusing. "There are different shades of black, Mr. Quinn. Especially when it comes to fabric. And I assure you, no self-respecting man would wear mismatched black trousers and coat to the inaugural ball. You may trust me on this — these coat and trousers definitely did not come from the same ensemble, but from two different men."

"You're certain of this?" Mr. Quinn said thoughtfully, still peering at the two articles of clothing.

"Quite certain." Constance took back the

trousers and turned them over in her hands. "The fabric not only looks different, subtle as it is, but it feels different as well. And — what's this?" She leaned closer to the lamp by Mr. Quinn. "Look. On the back of the trousers — there's a faint smear of white on them. Hardly noticeable."

"Yes," Mr. Quinn said. "When I saw that, I reckoned Billings was backed up into the freshly whitewashed exterior of the dance hall when he was attacked."

"But look — it stops suddenly. Where the tail of the dress coat would have hung." She traced her finger over the area in question, her pulse leaping. This was quite fascinating, this investigating a crime. "Let me see the coat."

But Mr. Quinn had already picked it up and was examining the back of it, near the hem. "There's no white smudge here, damn — er, blast it. There should be, if he backed into the wall."

He put the clothing back on the table slowly. "So I reckon that means the killer might have switched coats with Billings. Why would a man move a body, then switch coats with him?" He turned away, clearly talking to himself. "He didn't put the coat back on Billings. He just took the dead man's coat — to wear it, I suppose — and threw his own coat into the broom closet, along with the knife. One thing it does tell us, though," he continued, appearing not to notice that he'd somehow included her in his use of the word *us*, "is that the murderer was dressed in formal clothing. So he was an attendee of the ball — not a server, or a reporter," he added, "or even a curiosity seeker. He was *at* the ball. And most likely needed to return — which is why I reckon he had to exchange coats. Couldn't walk back in with blood on his sleeve."

"And regarding these belongings" — Constance gestured to the pile — "could any of them belong to the murderer and not Mr. Billings? Were any of them found in the pockets of the coat?"

"No. The pockets of the dress coat were empty," Mr. Quinn replied. "Those items were in his waistcoat or trouser pockets."

"Well, then. It's very simple to prove that my father came home wearing his own dress coat, Mr. Quinn. In fact, Mr. Billings's coat wouldn't fit my father, and this one wouldn't fit him either. As you've surely noticed, he's a bit portly. This is proof my father didn't stab Mr. Billings. Even though his knife was used to kill —"

"I beg your pardon, Miss Lemagne, but that's not true," Dr. Hilton said in a low

"The dagger didn't kill billings?" Adam said, wondering if he'd heard the man correctly. First coats and now daggers — and everything was not what it had seemed. What on earth was going on?

Hilton met his eyes with clear understanding for the predicament. "I think you'll find what I discovered very interesting. I know I did. I'd like to show you something if you'll come closer." He looked hesitantly at Miss Lemagne, who, fortunately, seemed to have little intention of accepting his invitation and was still standing over the two different articles of clothing. Both of which still looked black to Adam.

Curious, he went to stand on the opposite side of the long table from Hilton. With a dubious glance toward Miss Lemagne, Hilton slid the sheet away from the torso to reveal a pair of triangular flaps of skin that had been pulled away to expose two white ribs and a mass of red-purple insides. Adam couldn't identify anything but the ribs himself, but assumed the heart was behind there somewhere, and maybe a lung.

"Well?" he asked, a little stridently as he felt the attention of their unwanted female guest on them, followed by the thought of the pale, weak Althea Billings in her frilly bed. There was something almost blasphemous about treating the dead so callously, especially when a loved one was only a few blocks away, mourning the loss.

Hilton flipped the triangular pieces of skin back into place, covering Billings's insides. "You see he was stabbed twice. Here, just below the ribs in the gut, and again here, at the base of the sternum. But what bothered me was the amount of blood — or, to be more specific, the lack of blood. Someone stabbed there should have bled quite a lot. But there wasn't much at all."

"And so . . . ?"

"I kept telling myself it's not right. There's something not right here, and that's why I wanted to cut him open." His voice dropped as he glanced at Miss Lemagne. "And when I did, I understood why he hadn't bled out so much."

"Why?"

"That knife." Hilton said soberly. "That

knife you showed me on Tuesday . . . it's not what killed him."

"But Fremark saw it sticking out of the body. And it had blood on it."

"That wasn't it that killed him, Quinn. It was something much longer than the knife blade. And more slender."

Adam took in these words with a wave of dismay. Maybe he hadn't done the right thing giving this job over to George Hilton. He spoke carefully, trying not to sound as frustrated as he was. "A man saw the knife sticking out of his chest. It had blood on it. How could it not have killed him?"

"Look here. Not too close or you'll block the light. See this?" Hilton pointed to the gash at the base of the corpse's sternum.

"Looks like he got stabbed with a dagger," Adam said stubbornly. Good God. What was he going to tell Lincoln — and Mrs. Billings — about what this lunatic doctor had done to the body? Not to mention the fact that Miss Lemagne was witness to this debacle.

"Billings *did* get stabbed with the dagger. I ain't arguing that. But that isn't what actually killed him." Hilton was still pointing at the lower gash. "Remember when you asked about the middle of this cut? About why it's wider than the other laceration, just here in the middle? I told you I was gonna cut him open to look and see what happened inside. And this is what I found."

Once more, Hilton hesitated as he glanced over at their feminine audience. She was now watching with interest, but from a safe distance.

With an audible grinding of his teeth, Hilton flipped open the large flap of skin that contained the gash in question. "Now look here, Quinn. This is where the dagger blade went into the body — right into the soft part below the sternum. Into the diaphragm — that's that thin muscle right there, looks like a plate holding up the rib cage. But look here. Just above the lung, to the center more."

To Adam's shock, Hilton pulled apart the ribs and pointed with an index finger into the glistening red mess. Miss Lemagne gasped behind them, and Adam turned to see her drop straight down, into a chair, as if her knees had given way. She was dead-white and her eyes looked liable to pop out of her face above the handkerchief pressed to her nose and mouth.

Adam refrained from saying anything. He reckoned she'd made her decision to come and now had to make do. However, he did shift his body so as to block her view as much as possible as he leaned closer. His mouth was open now so he could breathe through it during this close proximity to death, and tried to forget that it was a man who was being disgraced — albeit gently — in front of him.

And then he saw it: what Hilton's dark, wet hand was pointing to. And with a rush of illumination, he understood.

"That's not a cut from a blade," he said, straightening up. "It's more like a — a puncture."

"That's right. He was stabbed up through the diaphragm, directly into the heart. Then, you can see, he jammed the weapon — whatever it was — around in there. Pretty much destroyed the organ. Woulda killed the poor sot instantly; he'd've slumped in his arms. Probably got some blood on his killer's coat sleeve that way," Hilton said meaningfully. "But the important thing is, the diaphragm would've caught most of the blood from spilling out, with the hole kind of closing up from the pressure above."

"You mean all the blood from the . . . the sliced-up heart would have just been trapped inside the rib cage?" Adam was feeling a little queasy, especially now that he realized the shiny mass of purplish red organ between the white bones of the rib cage was a pulverized heart. He looked away.

"Yes, sir. There was nowhere else for it to go, so it stayed trapped inside the torso. The other stab, the one in the gut, didn't go deep enough to let much bleeding out there. And the heart had already stopped. I figure it was just for show, just to confuse us — that stab in the gut. Because soon as I opened him up, all the blood came out." Hilton made a sound of satisfaction, then jolted when he obviously remembered a lady was present. "What the hell were you thinking, bringing the likes of her here?" he muttered.

Adam merely shook his head, for he had no response other than, "There are many shades of black fabric, Hilton."

The doctor snorted a surprised laugh, then continued, moving around to stand next to Adam in order to further block her view — and possibly even obstruct what she could hear.

"Seems to me someone tried to make it look like he died from the knife blade by stabbing him with a dagger right where he'd been punctured. But he was really killed by something long and pointed. And that's why the cut you noticed is thicker in the middle — because the dagger went in through the same laceration, but that blade is flat, not triangular. He was killed with something shaped like a fireplace poker, but longer and more slender even. Long enough to go deep — up through the diaphragm in one sharp thrust. You can see evidence of that shape of puncture-like cut here . . . and here."

Adam didn't bother to look that closely; he believed the doctor. "Someone skewered him. Like a damned rabbit." He kept his voice down due to the lady present but he met Hilton's clear dark eyes over the corpse.

"Right. But then someone stabbed him afterward with the dagger."

It was like someone brushing away tracks in the snow, then using a branch to skitter over the top of it and make a different pattern.

"The killer wanted to make it look like Billings died from the dagger wound." Adam stepped back from the table. "Why? To either throw off suspicion — because the way he was killed is important or incriminating? — or to make it look like someone else killed him."

It really did appear that someone *was* trying to frame Hurst Lemagne. Or was the Southerner simply a random choice — a convenient one, because the killer had found Lemagne's dagger and decided to use it to throw off suspicion?

Either way, one thing was certain: if

George Hilton hadn't done such a thorough job of examining the body, no one would ever have known.

"And then there's Fremark," Hilton said in a low voice. He glanced over toward the dividing sheet, giving Adam to understand the other man was similarly displayed on that side.

"Oh, yes, you received the package."

"To the dismay of my patient at the time. That's why I've been closing up the office part of the time since Wednesday. If I'm not careful, there'll be rumors that Doc Hilton's opening a human butchery down here." He was joking, but Adam also reckoned there was a bit of truth — and wariness — in his tone.

"Well, did you find anything of interest?"

"Far as I can reckon, Fremark was stabbed by the same triangular-shaped ice pick–like weapon that did in Billings. But the killer wasn't as careful about hiding his tracks; he just wanted the man dead. Seven wounds, all in his back. Probably killed him with the one to the heart from behind, which one of the earlier ones, far as I can tell. But he wanted to make sure the man was dead, and he didn't want to waste time."

"So there would have been blood everywhere, unlike with Billings."

"Wasn't there?" Hilton looked at him curiously.

"Yes, yes, there was. But it should be on the killer's clothing too, right? With all that stabbing?"

"Yes. Would have been impossible to hide it."

"What about Billings? I understand he was stabbed quickly up through the center of the torso, and that contained the blood — but how much blood would there have been?"

"Enough that he had to switch coats, I reckon. Probably realized he got it on his sleeve. Billings didn't bleed that much, and with the cutaway style, the only blood would have got on his waistcoat and shirt. Man was smart to switch coats."

"He just didn't reckon on two different shades of black."

Hilton barked a laugh. "I guess not."

Adam was about to take his leave, figuring Miss Lemagne might have had enough of her visit to the makeshift morgue, when he thought of another question. "Have you found any trace or smudge of oil on either of them? Their clothing, bodies, anything?"

The doc shook his head. "No. Why?"

Adam explained, "I reckon it might have something to do with the murder weapon, or how he killed them. But I'm not sure how it fits."

"Oh, and one more thing. The killer is right-handed. Both men were stabbed by a man with his right hand."

"Right-handed? How do you know that?"

"The way the weapon was shoved up inside Billings — its blow leans slightly to the left, as it would if a right-hander was doing it." He demonstrated with a thrust of his right hand. "It's not going to angle to the right if he's right-handed."

Adam nodded. That made sense.

"And for Mr. Fremark, he struck down from above, behind him. Must've been holding it in his fist, pointing straight down, because that's the angle of the blows. Again, the angle bears this out — but he was attacking more recklessly and wildly the second time. And . . . based on where the highest blow is, and its angle, I can also tell that the killer was taller than Fremark. Maybe three, four inches. I could do some calculations and try to get more specific, if you want."

"A right-handed man who is slightly taller than the below-average Fremark . . . well, that does narrow it a bit, then, doesn't it?" Adam said dryly.

"Well, you do have the color of his dress

coat to go by," Hilton replied with a quick grin. "Just find the right shade of black trousers."

Adam took all of Custer Billings's belongings with him when he and Miss Lemagne left Hilton's cellar office.

One thing he did not have with him, to Adam's great disgruntlement, was his prosthetic arm.

When he asked after it, the doctor replied, "My friend Marcus can repair it, he says, but he'll need a little more time."

Adam had to bite his tongue to keep from commenting on the fact that he hadn't even been able to assess the damage to his wooden and mechanical arm — and that it would have been better to at least have something strapped to him, broken or not, rather than a stump that wasn't even useful enough to offer a young lady for escort.

Having to pin up his sleeve took him back to those early, ugly days after the attack near Lawrence, and all the pain, loss, and strangeness that had come with it.

"Very well. I hope this Marcus can make it work properly again." Otherwise, he'd not only have to buy a new prosthetic for more than a hundred dollars, but he'd have to wait weeks for it to be made.

To Adam's relief, Miss Lemagne seemed unusually subdued as they walked back along to the avenue. She hardly spoke at all, and he appreciated the fact, for that gave him the opportunity to think about what he'd learned from George Hilton, as well as from his female companion.

Yet it seemed that although he'd determined several interesting facts, the answer to the problem of who'd killed Custer Billings and Lyman Fremark felt as elusive as ever. As they passed by, he glanced toward Lafayette Square and beyond, where the President's House sat like a taunting reminder of Adam's task.

Tonight was the levee being given by the Lincolns, and Adam would need to attend. He'd likely be expected to give the president a report then as well. He sure as shooting hoped he had something to tell him.

One thing he intended to do as soon as possible was to speak to Billings's manservant, and possibly his wife, in order to determine whether the dress coat belonged to him or not. If it didn't, then Adam had a definite lead to follow. Tracking down the owner of the coat could be a direct path to identifying the murderer. Unfortunately, he wasn't familiar enough with the tailors in Washington to identify who'd sewn the coat.

And being an out-of-towner, Miss Lemagne likely wasn't either.

He escorted Miss Lemagne to the St. Charles, then walked back another four blocks to the Willard. He was still achy and weak from his injuries, and he wanted some time to think before he took his next step.

He found solace in his hotel room, empty now of his uncle's belongings. That brought to bear another question: How much longer could he afford to live here, now that Joshua was gone and no longer shared the expense?

Not very long. Which gave Adam an even greater inducement to solve this crime and leave Washington forever.

After a brief rest, Adam departed the Willard once again. This time, he took the trousers and dress coat found by Custer Billings's body. He nodded to Birch as he exited the hotel, feeling both relieved and mildly disappointed not to find Brian Mulcahey waiting for him.

Although he meant to take the clothing to the Billings household, Adam first made a detour back to the scene of the crime. He needed to see it once more in light of the new information he'd received.

It was well past noon, and although people were going in and out of City Hall from both the Judiciary Square entrance and the street-facing one, no one was near the temporary building that had been erected for the ball. Now that its purpose had been fulfilled, the building would be torn down sometime within the next month or so, and its lumber used for some other purpose.

Now, as he stood there near the entrance to the hall, he reimagined the murderer's actions once again.

Mr. Billings standing there. He must have known the murderer well enough to step off the wooden walkway, to move out of the way of any foot traffic going from City Hall to the dance hall, to speak with him. They stood right next to the freshly painted wall. The murderer steps toward him and shoves his pike-like weapon up into Billings's diaphragm and rib cage.

One smooth, quick, perfect blow.

Adam frowned. But the tool with which the man had skewered Billings . . . it had to have been several inches long. Seven or eight at least — definitely longer than the dagger belonging to Lemagne. It was not the sort of instrument easily hidden, and certainly not readily withdrawn from some hiding place and then plunged into a man's torso without him noticing or reacting. . . .

Billings had been stabbed from the front, and yet there were no defensive wounds on his hands — no blood on his gloves, no cuts. If he'd been threatened, surely there would be deep heel marks here, and a twist and step to the side, too . . . but there was no evidence of it.

Adam tried to picture it.

The two men standing here, talking, facing each other. It's shadowy but not dark; a single lamp hangs near the doorway of each building.

The murderer reaches into his . . .

Where? Where could he have secreted a long, straight, *sharp* weapon like a large ice pick — and how could he have withdrawn it, then struck without taking Billings off guard?

The sleeve of his coat?

The two men talking, Billings with his back to the building, the other man reaching up into his sleeve to pull out the weapon, then thrusting it up . . .

No. That wouldn't work, for either the pointed part of the weapon would have had to be stored aiming toward the elbow, which would be dangerous and likely cause an injury, or the pointed end would have had to poke out from the sleeve, which meant the murderer would have had to withdraw the weapon and *turn it around* facing the other way — or switch hands — in order to utilize it. Doing this maneuvering smoothly and without Billings noticing and reacting?

Not likely.

And the weapon would be too long to fit into a pocket.

And then there was the other issue: Had the murderer carried Lemagne's dagger on his person as well? If so, that meant he'd had two weapons secreted on himself, while wearing formal clothing — which was well tailored and close fitting, as Adam had cause to know.

Then it struck him: a walking stick.

That would be the logical place to hide such a weapon.

Adam imagined it, working it out in his mind and with his own actions.

The murderer standing there, speaking to Billings. Walking stick in his right hand. He lifts it, yanks or screws off the bottom half with his left, and reveals the stake-like weapon and thrusts, up and into Billings —

No.

He opened his eyes. No. Again, that obvious movement of unsheathing the spike in the bottom of his walking stick would be too obvious for Billings not to react, to hold up his hands or call out or otherwise turn away, prohibiting the murderer from making that one perfect strike that killed him instantly.

Adam propped his good hand against the dance hall's wall as he lowered himself into a crouch once more. Had he missed anything in the mess of footprints? Could he have mistaken the movements he'd discerned?

No. The activity, the story was still as clear as it had been: two men standing there, facing each other hardly a foot apart, and then Billings slumping, then being caught and dragged away.

No other unusual movement.

Adam rose, stepped back, and stared again, reviewing it in his head.

What was he missing?

He knew the weapon. Reckoned how it had been used: in a single, perfect stroke. The murderer had to have been fairly close to Billings — close enough to share a secret, shake hands, or even embrace him.

A sharp thrust, and the man collapses, the murderer catches him. . . .

But that still didn't explain how he got the weapon in his hand and positioned it properly, quickly, and without alarming his victim.

That was, Adam thought once more, a cornerstone to this puzzle. When he figured out the weapon, he'd know much more about the murderer.

But what he still didn't know was why. Why Custer Billings, why Hurst Lemagne's dagger, why the Union Ball?

Lemagne wouldn't have left his own knife as a signature in killing the man, so it seemed as if whoever had planted his knife at the crime must be aware of the argument between the two men.

And once again — why all the manipulation and jockeying about in such a public place, at a most public event?

Opportunity? Camouflage?

Or the opposite: Could the killer have wanted to make a political statement by doing the deed at the inaugural ball of the Southern Contingent's most hated man?

He thought again about the motives the Megatherium Club members had thrown out. Love, greed, revenge, hatred . . .

Love. If Billings was in love with Annabelle Titus, and vice versa, her husband would have a strong motive to get rid of his rival. Tomorrow, he would pay a visit to the Latney House to see if anyone recognized a man of Billings's description visiting there.

Revenge? Adam had found no evidence that anyone disliked Billings, let alone hated him enough to kill him.

Greed? The man was wealthy, but his wife

would inherit his money. Billings had no business partners at the bank, so it would have to be sold or merged with another institution. They had no children.

Adam quickly covered the ground from Judiciary Square and City Hall toward E Street and the Billings house. He hadn't pinned up his sleeve this time, and the empty portion flapped easily against his hip, reminding him of his liability. He hoped George Hilton's friend was correct — that he could fix the arm, and get it back to Adam quickly.

Missing arms and legs weren't all that rare. Men — and less commonly women — lost limbs in farming accidents or mechanical ones, so it wasn't unusual to see an empty sleeve or a pinned-up trouser leg. But that didn't mean it was simple or easy to get a new prosthetic, or to fix a damaged one. However, empty sleeves didn't generally invite comment, and hardly a glance most of the time — although the owner of the loss might feel self-conscious about it.

Replacing an amputated leg was, in some ways, simpler than replacing an arm — for a prosthetic leg mainly needed to hold weight and to swing fairly simply at the hip, and possibly ankle, rather than all of the other fine movements conducted by wrist, hand, and fingers. A wooden peg leg was not only inexpensive and could be home-made, but was also more easily disguised beneath trousers and shoe than a missing hand and arm.

Adam was fortunate enough to have acquired one of the most functional false arms and hands currently available, made by Mr. Palmer in New Hampshire. There were other options, as well as far more simplistic ones — which consisted of a carved wooden hand that was completely immobile, or even a fake forearm that allowed for different "fixtures" to be inserted in the place of a hand, depending on what one was doing: a hook, a fork, a knife —

Adam stopped dead in the middle of the sidewalk.

A lethal ice pick.

Could the murderer have such an apparatus — a false arm or hand — that held a long, slender, triangular blade?

That would be one way to hide such a weapon inside the sleeve of his dress coat — as part of a prosthetic arm.

The idea was so fascinating, Adam continued to stand there on the street for a moment, turning it around in his mind to see if it worked.

It was possible, but —

"Mr. Quinn!"

The sound of flat-footed running and an excited voice drew his attention to none other than Brian Mulcahey.

"Mr. Quinn! Are you all right? What are you doing?"

Adam noted with no small relief that Brian was without Bessie this time. "I was just thinking," he told the boy as he stood there, catching his breath. "What are you doing over here on this side of town?"

"You told me to keep an eye on that Mr. Lemagne, and I was about doing that for you all day today. I followed him and I was on my way back to the Willard to tell you, when I saw you just standing here." His eyes widened, having settled on the flap of a sleeve on Adam's left side.

"Very good, son. I reckon you could walk with me while you tell me what you learned about Mr. Lemagne." And maybe he could make an excuse to stop for a bite to eat on the way.

Brian trotted along next to him, and though he didn't say anything about Adam's missing arm, his attention continued to wander to it. "Mr. Lemagne took his horses — he drove himself, and I had to run to keep up with him, but with so many carriages and buggies, it wasn't too hard. And his horses, they're about being the best beauties I've seen. One is white — that's Delilah. Whiter than a bleached cotton rag, my mam says. And Samson, he's all black. I'da done anything to get close to them, but I didn't want to give myself away to Mr. Lemagne, like you said."

"That was good thinking, Brian. Will you look at those apple tarts? I reckon I forgot to eat today." That was only half a lie. He walked into the bakery without waiting for a response and bought four of them and a cup of milk.

As Brian wolfed down two tarts — not that Adam blamed him, for they had just the right amount of cinnamon and sugar sprinkled on top, and the crust was golden brown and flaky — he told him more about what he'd seen.

"He drove himself to a big house on F Street and tied up the buggy out front while he went in. A black man came out and brought the horses around to the side, and he was really good with them." Brian spoke earnestly, his freckles standing out in a cream-white face like cinnamon dots above a milk mustache. "If I had my own horses, I'd trust him with them. He knew how to speak to them, and even rubbed them under the trappings, where they really like it."

"Do you remember which house it was that he visited?" Adam asked, brushing off the last bit of crumbs from his lap. "Can you show me?"

"Yes, sir, I can. He was still there when I left to find you, and even if he isn't there, I know which house it is. Are you going to eat that one?"

"I don't reckon I could take another bite," Adam replied, handing over the fourth tart.

"My mam says I got hollow legs," Brian informed him. "The house is down this street. Do you see, his carriage is standing there in the street. The man must have brought it around for him. Maybe he's about to leave."

"Well, isn't that interesting," Adam muttered to himself as he recognized the house where Lemagne's carriage was parked.

It belonged to Custer and Althea Billings.

CHAPTER 16

Adam strode up to the door of the billings residence and knocked. Since he'd been here three days ago, the house had been draped with black crape — mainly over the door and front windows. The knocker was covered with black fabric as well, and the curtains or shutters were drawn over every window. As it was meant to do, the decor gave the stately house a sober, empty look.

He had sent Brian off, unwilling to risk anyone connecting the two of them. So far, the Irish lad had been very helpful in a number of ways, but in light of the attack on Adam, he had a niggling concern that any animosity toward him could be directed elsewhere. Best to keep the boy out of harm's way as much as possible.

When the door opened, Adam was greeted by a Negro servant he hadn't met on his previous visit. The man was at least a decade older than James — the Billings's butler —

and had frizzy gray hair along with a short stature. He wore a black armband around one upper sleeve. "Are you Stanley?" he asked.

"Yessir. Who are you?" Obviously taken by surprise, and possibly alarmed, the man nevertheless maintained a polite demeanor.

"My name is Adam Quinn. I spoke to Mrs. Billings, along with James and Louise, on Tuesday about your master's death. I'd like to come in."

"Yessir. They tol' me about you, sir." Stanley stepped back into the dim foyer. A single lamp offered the only light in the shrouded room.

As Adam crossed the threshold, he glanced up the stairs to where Althea Billings had been when he visited last time. He heard no sounds of any voices, or anyone taking their leave. "Mrs. Billings has a guest?"

Stanley glanced up the stairs. "Yessir. Yes, she does." His voice dropped low and he looked around. "He'll be leaving soon."

Adam's curiosity was aroused, but he had other fish to fry first. "I'm sorry about your master, Stanley. I reckon you're mighty disrupted over the news."

"Oh, yessir. Yes, I am."

"You were Mr. Billings's manservant, weren't you?"

"Yessir. For twenty years, sir, since he moved here from down south. I'm a free man, sir," he added. "I've got my papers."

Adam smiled and gave a brief nod. "I wanted to return his clothing and other personal items. Would you take a look at them and confirm for me that the coat and trousers are his, and that he was wearing them on the night of the inaugural ball?"

"Yessir. Of course, sir. I dressed him myself. Wouldn't let him off to such an important party without making certain he was perfect."

Stanley began to dig through the sack, drawing out first the trousers, then the shirt, waistcoat, tie, and finally the dress coat. The bag still sagged from the weight of the shoes and pocket watch left inside, and he set it down on a side table as he lifted the clothing in question to examine it.

"Yessir, this is what he was wearing." Stanley laid the trousers, the shirt, and the waistcoat and tie, one at a time, over a chair.

"And the coat as well? You're certain that was his?"

"Yessir . . . wait." The manservant frowned as he took another look at it, bringing it nearer the lamp. When he turned up the kerosene and examined the coat closely, his brows shot up. "No, sir. No, this isn't Mr.

Billings's coat. It's most certainly not his coat —"

The front door opened suddenly behind them, spilling a wave of sunlight into the gloomy house.

"Who are you? Is that your carriage out front? Don't you know this house is in mourning? It's not the time for social calls."

Adam turned to the newcomer: a man of about forty with an untrimmed brown sugar beard, straggly mustache, and angry dark eyes. Like the house, he was dressed in black from head to toe.

"I do," Adam replied calmly. "I had the unhappy task of bringing the news to Mrs. Billings on Tuesday. Adam Quinn," he said, offering his hand to shake.

The man ignored his proffered hand in favor of shoving his hat, cane, and coat at Stanley as if he were a humanized coat rack. "Then what are you doing back here if you've already delivered the news? Poor Althea's already weak as a kitten, and she doesn't need any visitors bothering her. Whoever they are."

Adam glanced at Stanley and was surprised to see a horrified, arrested look on his face. He gave a furtive look toward the upstairs, then spun to put away the coat and hat. But that didn't hide the fact that his eyes were so wide Adam could see white all around the irises.

"I'm here because I'm investigating the murder of Mr. Billings," Adam said.

The man's temper deflated slightly. "Investigating the murder? But why — Althea didn't mention anything to me about that."

"I was given the task by Mr. Lincoln, since Mr. Billings was stabbed at his inaugural ball. He wants to set things right. I reckon you must be Mr. Orton — Mrs. Billings's brother?"

"Yes, I'm Alan Orton. You say Mr. Lincoln sent you?"

"He did, in a matter of speaking. I was returning your brother-in-law's personal articles, found with his body. I reckon Mrs. Billings would prefer to select his clothing for . . . for burial."

"Yes, yes, I'm sure she will. If she's feeling up to the task. Been mostly bedridden for over a year, and now this." Mr. Orton shook his head, his face saddening. "I don't know how much more grief she can take. First the boy, now Custer. She's always been a weak one." He rubbed his forehead in a gesture similar to the one Adam made when he was frustrated. "How is the investigation coming? Have you any suspects? Learned anything? Any news would help Althea, I'm sure."

"I've got quite a bit of information," Adam told him. He happened to be facing the stairway and thought he saw a bit of movement up there. The flutter of a skirt hem, a shadow flitting away from the overlook. Curious. "But I haven't drawn any conclusions yet."

"Good. What I mean to say is, I'm glad you've gathered information, and I certainly hope you have some good news soon. We want the culprit caught and hanged."

"I'd like to ask you a few questions, Mr. Orton," Adam pressed, just as James appeared from the back of the house. He looked harried as well.

"Pardon me, Mr. Orton. Perhaps you and Mr. Quinn would like to sit in Mr. Billings's study."

Orton pursed his lips, then relaxed. "I could use a brandy. And I hate to bother Althea when she's resting. There's no need for her to hear any of this madness."

Adam remembered to remove his hat as he walked into the study. He saw no reason to refuse a glass of brandy, and he made certain to sit in a tall-backed chair so he could see the hallway beyond the study door. Something strange was going on here, and the best he could reckon was that the servants were trying to keep Orton from knowing his sister had a guest.

"I won't keep you long," he told the other man. "I understand you're staying here with Mrs. Billings in light of her husband's death."

"Yes. Can't stay alone, can she?" he grumbled, then sipped from his drink. "Came right away. Been here two days. Wife's set to arrive on the train tomorrow. Can't come soon enough." He looked around the neat, well-appointed study in disgust. "Will put this household to rights in no time."

"You don't live here in Washington City?"

"Mostly in Baltimore, but I have business here often — I work with the patent office, representing inventors — and usually stay at the Willard or the other one — the St. Charles, though it's not my preference — when I do. Only a couple hours' train ride to get here. Just like the one Lincoln took to get here in the dead of night." He frowned. "What does that have to do with Custer's death?"

Adam shrugged. "I reckon if you live nearby or see your sister and her husband often, you might know if he had any enemies, or business problems that might have led to someone being angry enough to stab him."

"Oh, yes, of course." Orton thought for a moment, staring off into space. Then he came back to the moment, shaking his head sadly. "I can't really think of anyone Custer didn't get along with — other than Mortimer Titus."

At last. Adam lifted his glass and sipped, waiting for the other man to give more information. The brandy was excellent — warm and lush, pleasantly heating his body and taking the edge off the lingering discomfort of his injuries.

"Titus and he went a few rounds some months back, right after the election. My brother-in-law was an abolitionist, Mr. Quinn, and that didn't make him very popular in this town — especially after the election. Washington City might be the capital of North and South, and people come from all parts of the country to live here, but it's still below the Mason-Dixon Line. Washington's a Southern town, a slave district — and if it were a state, I don't doubt it would follow South Carolina and Alabama and the others and secede. Virginia's about to do so — everyone knows it — and it's just across the river there." He took a drink, thoughtfully sucking in the brandy between his teeth. "Though when it came time for Billings Bank & Trust to loan them money or finance their cotton crops, not one of those Southern slaveholders minded where their funds came from. They took it from the abolitionist gladly."

"So Mr. Billings did a lot of business with Southern and secessionist businessmen. Did he loan money to Mortimer Titus? Or were their differences only of a political nature?"

"Titus is a hothead. And a die-hard Democrat. Loathes the Republicans, especially the rail-splitter and his followers. But he's also got a very handsome wife named Annabelle." Orton settled back into his chair and lifted his brows as he set his drink on the table next to him. "My sister's been poorly for over a year now, Mr. Quinn. And my brother-in-law . . . well, he's always been one for female companionship. Of all sorts."

"I see." Adam didn't look toward the hallway beyond the door, which had been left open, but he could hear the sounds of movement out there.

Orton leaned forward, his voice dropping. "I wouldn't be surprised if Titus got mad enough to run Custer through with a sword over being cuckolded. Wouldn't be the first time a man had to take matters into his own hands. You ask me, Barton Key was asking for it — being shot down by Senator Sickles for tupping his wife. Was a year — no, two years ago. Shot him right on the street."

"Are you saying Custer Billings was . . . er . . . dallying with Mortimer Titus's wife?" Adam said.

"I'm saying it's more than possible. They socialized in the same circles — with the upper crust of Washington. The elite of Lafayette Square." There was the slightest sneer in his tone. "They certainly had the opportunity to know each other."

Adam wondered how a man like Orton, who didn't live in Washington, would know this gossip with such certainty, when hardly anyone else Adam spoke to had given off even a whiff of it. "Mr. Orton, did you like your brother-in-law?"

"What sort of question is that?" He straightened up in his chair, the drink sloshing on the table next to him. "Are you accusing me —"

Adam held up a hand and shook his head. "I reckon if I thought my sister's husband was stepping out on her, I'd not be very pleased with my brother-in-law."

"Oh, yes, right. Well, Mr. Quinn." Orton had eased back in his seat with a wry smile. "I don't know if you're married, and I'm not one to cast judgment on the actions of a man who is, but I suppose if a husband's going to look elsewhere, he'd best do it on the sly and not call attention to it. Use a fancy girl or visit Mrs. Hall's." He shrugged. "But if you're going to be bold about it, embarrass your wife and friends, then you deserve what comes your way."

Adam was finishing his brandy when Orton said those words, and that last sip almost went down the wrong way. That was, he supposed as he swallowed hard, one way to look at it.

"I'm much obliged for your time, Mr. Orton," he said and rose. All of a sudden, he felt a little dirty.

"Yes, of course. I'll want to know anything you learn about who killed Custer. If I'm not here, I'll be at my office. Four-fifty K Street, third floor."

Adam picked up his hat and made his way into the hall, leaving Orton and his rather flexible morality sitting in the office of his brother-in-law.

Something Orton had said stuck in his mind. *Embarrassing your wife and friends.*

Could Althea Billings have known about her husband's philandering? And told her brother? Perhaps that was how Orton knew something others only conjectured on.

James had taken Stanley's place in the

foyer to see him out. Adam was just about to request a meeting with Mrs. Billings when he glanced out the front window. Hurst Lemagne's carriage and remarkable pair of horses was gone.

"Who was Mrs. Billings's visitor?" Adam asked in a low voice, setting the hat on his head.

James merely shook his head, flattening his lips as if they were sealed. "Good day, sir." He opened the door and lifted his brows meaningfully.

"Why was it a secret Hurst Lemagne was here?" Adam pressed. "Why didn't she want her brother to know?"

James's eyes flared with surprise, and he stepped closer to the door — and farther from the hallway leading to the study. "It's Mrs. Billings's business, sir. I ain't going to talk about that. She's had enough grief this past year, Mr. Quinn."

Adam stood on the threshold and looked out at the gray March afternoon. "At least tell me this: Do you think Mr. Billings was romantically involved with a woman not his wife? Maybe a Mrs. Titus, the wife of the man with the fancy carriage?"

James's eyes were dark and sober. "I never saw nothing like that, Mr. Quinn."

Adam nodded, hiding his frustration. He

was certain the man was lying. "Very well. Thank you, James. My best to Stanley and Louise, and also to Mrs. Billings. Please tell her that when I have any news, I'll be back."

As he left the black-draped house slightly warmer and less achy, due to the brandy, Adam pondered what he'd learned. The staff was trying to hide Lemagne's visit to Althea Billings from her brother. Why? Did Orton know Lemagne? But how could he? Orton lived in Baltimore; Lemagne lived in Alabama.

But they both traveled to business in Washington. So they could know each other.

Orton stayed at the Willard sometimes — as well as the St. Charles — and Lemagne was at the St. Charles.

Was Orton simply trying to protect his weak and ill sister from Lemagne for some reason? He didn't seem to be a particularly warm and sympathetic person. In fact, he made Adam feel as if he needed to wash his hands.

He sighed. Thanks to the brandy, he might feel warmer now, but Adam was certainly more concerned and confused with the puzzle than when he'd arrived.

Though Adam knew he needed to speak with Mortimer Titus, he had to wait until tomorrow. It was getting late, and he was expected to be shaved and formally garbed, and at the levee, in less than three hours.

However, he stopped at the St. Charles Hotel after he left the Billings household. He reckoned he and Mr. Lemagne needed to have another talk — and hopefully without the assistance of his daughter.

It was late in the afternoon, approaching supper time, and the hotel entrance and lobby were filled with guests coming and going. The St. Charles seemed as busy with the crème de la crème of Washington as the Willard did.

Down the hall from the gilt and red lobby was the bar room, and loud voices and laughter spilled out from there into the rest of the corridor. Beyond was the restaurant, which was quieter so early in the evening.

Instead of stopping at the front desk where the palmetto cockade–wearing manager was busy shuffling keys, mail, and guest requests, Adam strode past and toward the sounds of revelry. If he was lucky, Lemagne would have stopped in the bar for a drink before collecting his daughter for dinner, and that meant Adam could corral him alone.

The room was filled with people — mostly men, but a few well-dressed women sat at tables with their companions — noise, and cigar smoke. The underlying scent of liquor fought with smoldering tobacco and balsam pine cologne. In the corner, a pianist attempted to provide entertainment, but his efforts were dampened by bursts of laughter, amiable shouting, and loud bellows to the bartender for more rounds, or "a tall one, if you please."

As Adam skimmed the room with his eyes, he recognized several people he'd seen or met over the course of the two weeks he'd been with the president's entourage in Washington. There were some he avoided eye contact with, such as Browning and Thatcher — for they'd be the ones to presume upon Adam's relationship with Mr. Lincoln, and he reckoned the president already had enough people lining up asking for favors.

There was a group of men who'd met with the president the morning after his arrival in the city. Wellburg, Martindale . . . and the third one's name escaped him. They'd been asking about his stance on import taxes, and now that Adam thought about it, he remembered seeing one — Martindale — at the Union Ball. He'd had the impression the three men were from somewhere down south, but he reckoned he must have been wrong about Martindale, for the man had been wearing a blue and white Union ribbon.

Adam navigated around two tiny tables and past a prominently placed spittoon that, despite its central location, seemed to have been ignored, and sidled up to the bar. Adam purposely squeezed in next to Martindale and his friends, then set to work on getting the bartender's attention.

"Worse 'n trying to snatch a leaf in a windstorm," Martindale commented amicably after he jolted Adam with his elbow in the close quarters. "Trying to get Bradley's attention at half past five on a weekday. But he pours 'em tall and replaces 'em fast, and I ain't got no complaints about that." His eyes narrowed with recognition, then cooled as he looked up at Adam. "Name's Quinn, ain't it?"

"For thirty years and change." He gave a brief grin and removed his hat. "Evening, Martindale. Wellburg, is it?" Adam turned so he edged into their little trio. He nodded at the third man, whose name suddenly dropped into his memory. "Evening, Littleton. What tall and fast pour do you recommend?"

"A Kentucky bourbon always hits me right," Wellburg replied, but the smile didn't reach his eyes. "You're the one working for the rail-splitter, ain't you?" He fairly spat the reference to Lincoln, giving the words an ugly, pejorative flavor. "Something about a murder."

"Not a very pleasant way to occupy a gentleman's time," Martindale added with a faint sneer. He'd made no effort to adjust his position to allow Adam to join their group. Hmm. So much for the Union sympathies. Maybe Adam had been wrong about his ribbon at the ball. "Murder."

"I reckon Custer Billings and Lyman Fremark both feel the same about now — each having been right in the thick of a murder himself." Adam caught Bradley the bartender's eye and said, "Bourbon. Whatever he's drinking." He nodded toward Wellburg.

"Make it a full round for the gentlemen here," he added, wondering briefly how much it was going to cost him. The way these men were dressed, he reckoned they didn't hold back on their liquor expenses either. Between this, the possible expense for a new prosthesis, and his hotel bill at the Willard, he might find himself plowing through funds faster than a drunken cowhand.

"Playing Pinkerton don't sound like much fun. In fact, it could be downright dangerous," Littleton said, swiping a hand over lips glistening with whatever he'd been drinking. He held Adam's eyes a trifle too long.

Adam looked at him blandly. "I reckon it depends what you call dangerous. Searching out the truth of who killed a man in his prime is worth the risk. Standing up for what's just and right." He lifted his drink in a brief toast and watched them all over the rim as he sipped. "I reckon I'd rather be on that side of things than be a coward who kills an unarmed man like Custer Billings . . . or anyone else he might have a political disagreement with."

"There's a whole hell of a lot of people who don't see it that way, Quinn," Wellburg said. "People who got to make a change in this country. Do what needs to be done even if it causes bloodshed and division."

"There are those types — hiding behind packages of dried apples laden with arsenic, and adding castor bean oil to a bottle of rum, then sending them off to the president. Trying to get their way on the sly, instead of the way this nation was meant to be run." Adam stood, sensing the growing ire from the others. He wasn't about to get into a brawl here, with only one functioning arm — and possibly losing his chance to talk to

Hurst Lemagne. "I'd happily meet my enemies face-to-face, hand to hand — if they've got the stones to do it. Too damned bad Custer Billings didn't have that chance."

He looked around at them and finished, "It leaves me wondering who might've given the man a hand into his grave — staunch abolitionist he was, and celebrating the oath-taking of the man who means to preserve this country."

Wellburg's hand moved as if to an invisible weapon at his waist, but Littleton nudged him aside. His eyes were filled with a dark light as he looked at Adam. "It would be one hell of a statement, that's for damned sure. One I'd happily sign for."

Adam tossed a half-dollar onto the counter, hoping it was enough to cover four bourbons. Cocktails were ten cents at Willard's, but who knew what the price was at the St. Charles. He kept his half-finished drink in hand as he gave a brief bow. "Evening, gentlemen."

He felt their six eyes on him as he made his way across the bar room. Nothing prickled over his shoulders like his skin would have done if someone had made a move on him, but he wasn't foolish enough to think he hadn't set out a challenge —

and a warning.

Yet, somehow, he felt more exhilarated than he had for days. There was something about calling out a coward — and the three had made it clear they were just that sort — that made a brave man feel alive.

He was just walking out of the room when he came face-to-face with Hurst Lemagne.

"What are you doing here?" the man demanded after a moment of shock. He looked as if he wanted to brush past Adam and seek solace in the bar room.

"Time's past gone for us to have a private talk, Lemagne," he told him, and set down his drink. "Might be best for it to happen somewhere we aren't seen together."

"If you don't stop harassing me, I'll —"

"You were visiting Althea Billings today. Secretly. And I reckon there's more to the story than you've been telling me. I suppose you'd better take a few minutes to talk to me now, because the next time I see you, your daughter might try to interfere. I don't reckon either of us want her involved."

Lemagne's jaw moved as he ground his teeth, but he stepped back from the threshold of the room. "All right. There's a small parlor around the corner."

They'd barely stepped into the room in question and Adam had closed the door when Lemagne began to talk. "Yes, I was with Althea today. And the night of the ball."

Adam was only mildly surprised by this revelation, and he remained silent.

"She and I . . . we . . ." The normally blustering man was suddenly at a loss for words. He paced the room, hands clasped behind his back. "Custer Billings didn't *deserve* her!" he exploded. "He didn't deserve to touch the pinkie of her gloved hand. I told her that, years ago — but she chose him. Or I thought she did. I found out later — when it was too late — her father forced her into it. She told me she chose Custer, but really she didn't have a choice — and she didn't want me to do . . . to do anything about it. So she lied." He shoved both hands into his hair. When he removed them, his wiry, brown-gray curls stood out like a wild nimbus. "Dammit, I need a bloody drink."

"You and Mrs. Billings were . . . involved?"

"Yes, dammit. Yes, we were in love — grew up in the same parish. But my family had only a small tobacco farm, and cotton was the crop of choice. The one of wealth and success. Althea's father wouldn't approve the match, and he wanted her to marry Custer. She agreed, and . . . that was it."

"But it wasn't it," Adam prompted. "You saw her the night of the ball. And you were heard arguing with Custer Billings earlier that day. You even told me Billings hated you."

"Damned right he hated me. He knew Althea never loved him, and he knew *I* knew how he'd been mistreating her. Carrying on while she lay wasting away in her grief. Month after month after month." His voice had grown rough and unsteady, and Adam wished he'd bought this man a drink instead of wasting his money on three secessionists back in the bar room. "How *dare* he treat her that way."

"How did you find out Billings was involved with another woman? If you live in Alabama? Did her brother tell you?"

"Her brother? Alan? No. I've . . . I've been in touch with Althea for months now. I was here in November, just after the election, and I learned Custer was out of town. So I called on her. My sister is her close friend, and they write each other all the time. When Althea lost the baby" — his face became pained — "I heard about it, but I didn't contact her. It just wasn't right. But I made certain I asked my sister about her — casually — whenever I had the chance. So when I was here on business, I found out Custer was gone, and nothing could keep me away. I knew she was hurting. I just didn't know how much." His voice broke and he turned away.

But when he looked back up, his eyes glittered with hard fury. "How could he do that to her? Leave her to waste away, leave her to grieve — and be out skirt chasing?"

"Mr. Lemagne, did you kill Custer Billings?"

"No. But I damned well wish I had."

Adam's feet in their fancy shoes didn't hurt quite as much as he feared they would by the time he walked up the incline to the President's House — or the White House, as Mr. Lincoln had begun to call it.

It was almost eight o'clock as he passed through the opening in the big iron fence, striding past the statue of Jefferson. He was right on time.

However, everyone else seemed to be early. The entire drive and avenue leading up to the house was so packed with carriages, he reckoned they'd been lining up and jockeying for position for at least an hour, maybe even longer. The sheer number of people spilling out of carriages and moving up the walkway made him wish he could turn around and slip away, unnoticed and anonymous, and head back to his hotel room.

However, duty called, and he pressed on. Adam had misplaced his top hat on Monday night — left it in City Hall during his questioning of James Delton and had never bothered to retrieve it, so he was one of the few — perhaps only — hatless men. Since he was also missing his fake arm, and had pinned up the bottom third of his left sleeve, he couldn't help but feel a little self-conscious.

But once inside the house — after being greeted, of course, by a bright-eyed Mc-Manus (did the man ever sleep?) — Adam found himself swept up in the society of hundreds of people who only seemed to care about Mr. Lincoln, not a different rough-looking man from the frontier.

"Adam, darling," said Mary Lincoln when he came through the receiving line. She stood on her tiptoes to embrace him — something she was obviously used to doing, considering the height of her husband. "I'm so glad you could make it tonight. Mr. Lincoln says you're healing up nicely from your accident, but I daresay that cut on your chin looks painful. And those bruises!"

"Thank you, Mrs. Lincoln," he said, bowing. "You look lovely. I understand Mrs. Keckley made your gown."

Mrs. Lincoln was wearing a bright pink

dress made of some fabric he thought was called antiqued silk. Regardless of its name, the material seemed luxurious and shiny, and was probably very rich to the touch.

"She did indeed, although it was a very close thing." Mrs. Lincoln leaned closer. "She didn't arrive here with it until it was just time to get dressed — and I feared she had fallen back on her word!"

"Well, it is certainly beautiful. Quite worth the wait, I reckon." Adam moved on to greet the president, who stood next to his diminutive wife. "Mr. President."

As he shook his offered hand, Lincoln peered owlishly at Adam's face. "I reckon you've looked better, my boy, but I've also seen you look worse. Reminds me of the time you fell off the apple wagon when you were reaching round back to steal a nice red one, and the wagon hit a big bump."

Adam laughed ruefully. "That was a painful moment — in more than one way."

"As I recall, you were showing off for that pretty young girl. Mary Elizabeth Letterman, wasn't that her name?"

"It was indeed. I was heartbroken when her family moved to Kentucky." Adam was still grinning.

The president's chuckle was loud and free, and Adam was relieved to see that at least some of the tension had ebbed from his craggy face. "Before you disappear into the jam," said Lincoln, "Pinkerton needs a word." He jerked his bushy eyebrows toward the man in question, who was standing with the wall behind him, watching the proceeds with sharp eyes.

"Thank you, sir."

When he approached Pinkerton, the man nodded as if to confirm that he needed to speak with him. After a few brief words with the two men standing next to him, the detective asked Adam to follow him.

"Evening, Quinn. I know you have other things on your mind — as do I — but I wanted to take a moment to thank you for your assistance today."

Adam looked at him curiously. "I'd be happy to take your thanks, but I reckon I don't know what for."

Pinkerton grinned. "That's a good answer, my boy. Very good. You see, you helped us make two arrests today in relation to an assassination plot against the president."

"Again," Adam said, thoroughly baffled, "I'm obliged, but —"

"But you don't know what the hell I'm talking about. And that's all right. You weren't intended to. You see, one of my men — who's been working here in Washington for two weeks now to help expose some of the plots against the president — was witness to a conversation of yours at the St. Charles today. You might remember him. His name is Martindale." Pinkerton grinned proudly.

"He's one of your men?"

"Indeed he is. It worked so well in Baltimore, when I sent Kate Warne and Harry Davies into the city to pretend they were Lincoln haters and secessionists, that we did it again here. Martindale befriended Wellburg a few weeks ago, and he'd been sticking to him and Littleton as they made their violent plans for our president."

"They were going to blow up the platform where Mr. Lincoln was being sworn in," Adam said.

"No, no . . . that was a different plot." Pinkerton laughed, but it was rueful instead of jolly. "There's more of 'em than I can count, unfortunately. This one that Wellburg and Littleton were involved with was a little less crude than setting dynamite under a scaffolding. They meant to take advantage of a distraction at the ball, and then use the resulting disarray to make their move on Lincoln."

"If the distraction was the murder of Custer Billings, that didn't work," Adam said. "It didn't cause a fuss because we kept it under wraps, and the president left early."

"Precisely."

"But are you saying Littleton and Wellburg were responsible for the murder of Custer Billings?" A bit of the tension he'd carried for days started to dissipate.

Pinkerton shook his head. "Can't pin that on them, no. From what my agent Martindale got, the 'distraction' was being carried out by a fourth person whose identity we haven't been able to determine."

Another person. The fourth person the groom at the back of the Willard mentioned he'd seen. While Miss Lemagne had seen only three. "Did they give any indication, any clue about who that person was?" he asked.

The detective shook his head. "All Martindale was able to learn was that the culprit was an acquaintance of Wellburg's, but not involved in their so-called organization."

"What sort of organization?" Adam asked. "Was it the group known as the Association?"

"Well, there're more than a few springing up, to be honest, there, Quinn. Secret clubs or societies that want to break — or preserve — the Union. At any cost. There's one called The 1860 Association. It started last autumn, after the election in South Carolina. It's an organized group promoting secession among the Southern states. They've published pamphlets and written letters to the state legislations in the South arguing for secession. And possibly creating militias in that support as well, but we've seen no evidence of that yet."

"The 1860 Association. The men who attacked me claimed they were sent by 'the Association.' I reckon that's no coincidence," Adam mused.

"But there does seem to be an offshoot of the Association that leans more toward the violent route. They call themselves the Black Dots because they secretly identify themselves to each other by wearing cockades — Union or Southern."

"Everyone in the city is wearing a cockade," Adam said dryly.

"Exactly. But the members of this branch of the Association put a black ink dot somewhere on their ribbon — regardless of which sympathy they are wearing. Apparently, a number of them wear the blue and white of the Union, further obscuring their sympathies. But the black dot — it's not very noticeable, unless you're looking for it. That's one of the most important things Martindale was able to learn for us."

Adam nodded. "Martindale was wearing a Union cockade at the ball. I reckon it had a dot on it." Then he frowned. "You arrested Littleton and Wellburg. But how was that possible, since they didn't actually carry out their plot to murder the president?"

"As I said, we have you to thank. It was because of your conversation with Littleton and Wellburg. We were able to arrest them afterward. From what Martindale told me, you were practically baiting the two men into admitting what they intended to do, but after you left, when they were still furious and rattled, was when they spilled their guts — about both the previous plan at the ball and the next steps they had in mind since the *first* plan hadn't worked out. See, they'd been careful about saying too many things — maybe they'd learned from what happened in Baltimore.

"And it seems they never run out of ideas, or the zeal to carry them out. Of course, they were complaining with loose tongues, not knowing, you see, that they were talking to a Pinkerton agent." The detective slipped his thumbs behind the lapels of his dress coat and pulled on them proudly. "That was the last bit of evidence we needed, and I had my man and some of the federal marshals pick them up around half past six today."

"Congratulations," Adam told him, and they shook hands.

"If we get any information from them about who killed Billings, I'll be sure to pass it on as soon as possible."

"Thank you, sir."

As he and Pinkerton finished their conversation in the hall, Adam noticed Mrs. Keckley standing a short distance away, lingering outside the East Room. She smiled at him but remained where she was.

He made his excuses to Pinkerton, who was ready to return to his post, and walked over to meet her.

"Good evening, Mrs. Keckley. Congratulations on such a fine turnout for Mrs. Lincoln. She seems very pleased with the gown you sewed for her."

She beamed up at him from beneath a hat that was almost as fancy as her client's dress. Mrs. Keckley was also wearing proper white gloves and a pale gray dress decorated by zigzag black ribbons. "I just had to peek into the room and see how things were lookin'. She is turned out beautiful, ain't she? And all the people! Laws, I don't think I ever seen so many people packed in one room before. Some of them are other customers of mine, too. I know pride's a sin, but it makes my heart warm to see Mrs. Blair and Mrs. Titus —"

"Mrs. Mortimer Titus?"

"Yes, sir. She's a very handsome woman, and it's a pleasure to sew for her."

"Mrs. Titus is here tonight? Did you see Mr. Titus as well?" Perhaps he'd be able to speak to the man after all.

"Why, yes, sir, he just walked in with her not thirty minutes ago, Mr. Quinn. An odd-looking couple, they are, with her so beautiful and him so . . . well, *not.* It's the lack of eyebrows and his pasty skin, I think, that does it. Makes him look like a — oh." Mrs. Keckley's eyes went wide and shocked as she realized how she was speaking. "I beg your pardon, Mr. Quinn. How I do ramble on. . . ."

Adam merely smiled. Now that he knew the Tituses were here, he'd be able to find them. But in the meantime, he thought it best to alleviate the seamstress's discomfort. "I reckon I don't mind your rambling at all, Mrs. Keckley. And did I mention I don't believe I've ever seen Mrs. Lincoln look so fetching — and I've known her for many years."

"That's very kind of you, Mr. Quinn, and also very kind of you to be keeping my

George busy."

Adam was mildly surprised. "I reckoned he was busy enough with all the patients he has. I was feeling rather guilty about adding to his responsibilities."

She laughed, her cheeks curving like plums beneath mirth-filled eyes. "Oh, he's busy all right, but that boy allus needs something else to occupy his mind. Haven't known him more than two years, but that boy's brain never stops working. You give him a puzzle or so and he'll work 'em between all his other patients." She stepped closer, her eyes now glinting with some other emotion. "He's *honored* that you and Mr. Lincoln should trust him with what you done. He's honored and humbled. Thank you."

There were layers upon layers of meaning and emotion in her words, and Adam found himself feeling a little soft inside.

"He's been a great help to me, Mrs. Keckley. I'm only obliged that he's been willing to do so."

She smiled up at him as if it were her own son she was speaking of, and then her expression became more serious. "Have you come any closer to identifying the man who killed that Mr. Billings? And the other one?"

"A little closer every day," he replied,

thinking of how many pieces of information he had, and how none of them fit together quite perfectly yet.

Would they ever do so? Love, revenge, power, greed —

Adam stilled. Greed. Money. Billings had a lot of money, which his wife would inherit when he died. But what happened when Althea Billings died? She was surely not long for this world herself.

"Oh, I nearly forgot. George told me that if I saw you, I was to tell you Marcus done fixed up your arm and he'll be bringing it tonight when he picks me up to take me home. Fine boy, insisting on driving me."

"That's very good news," Adam replied, resisting the urge to touch his empty sleeve. "Thank you."

He made his apologies, then returned to the reception, wondering how difficult it would be to locate Mr. Titus in this crush. In the meantime, having a bite to eat sounded like a good diversion.

As he began to weave his way through the crowd, he glimpsed William Stimpson and Robert Kennicott standing near one of the long food tables — no surprise there. He was surprised and pleased to see that neither of them were wearing a top hat, or, for that matter, the same type of formal dress coat and trousers Adam had donned. For the first time since arriving, Adam felt like he might actually find a way to enjoy the evening after all.

"Quinn!" Stimpson greeted him readily, though he didn't shake his hand because he had a drink in one and a plate in the other. "Darned pleased to see you. I was just saying to Kenny here how you and that Altman fellow were a nice addition to our club. Hope you'll come back again."

"Without a doubt," Adam replied. "Do either of you happen to know a man named Mortimer Titus?"

"Can't say I know the man, but I've seen him. High up at the Treasury's what I know," Kennicott said. "Guess he likes to fondle the money."

Stimpson laughed, then choked it off. "Oh, blast, here comes the big gun, and here I've got my hands too full to shake his."

Adam turned to see a distinguished-looking man of about fifty pushing through the crowd toward them.

"Good evening, Dr. Henry," chorused Stimpson and Kennicott. The latter snagged Adam's arm before he could slip away.

"Dr. Henry, meet Adam Quinn — quite a raucous, er, I mean, interesting fellow who has a very strong knowledge of the flora and fauna in Lake Michigan. Quinn, allow me to introduce you to Joseph Henry, the director of our fine Smithsonian Institution — or the king of the castle, as we often call him." Kennicott spoke lightly, but as soon as Adam turned to greet the older man, he and Stimpson gave him unapologetic smiles and slipped off into the crowd.

As Adam shook Dr. Henry's hand, he wondered if he was aware of the meetings of the Megatherium Club late into the night — or if he didn't, and that was why the two naturalists had dodged off.

"It's a great pleasure to meet you, sir," he said.

And it truly was, for Joseph Henry was known as the preeminent scientist in the United States, and his appointment as director of the institution had come as no surprise. His name was as familiar to the masses as Eli Whitney, Jefferson Davis, and Abe Lincoln himself. In fact, although he'd not been publicly or professionally credited for it, Joseph Henry's experimentation with creating powerful electromagnets at Princeton University had paved the way for the invention of the telegraph. Though Samuel Morse had invented the telegraph machine, he couldn't have done so without Dr. Henry's work.

"Quinn, you say?" Dr. Henry frowned slightly as he looked up at him. "Adam Quinn. Yes, yes, I thought that name was familiar. I understand you were at the meeting Tuesday night with the other boys. Who, I see, have just slipped off — to find more food, if I know them."

Well, that answered one of Adam's questions. "I was, sir. It was quite enjoyable — and enlightening. I wasn't certain you were aware of the . . . er . . . club."

"Oh, there's nothing that goes on at the institute that I don't know about — even Baird's little gimmick. I suppose I should have no real complaints, considering the amount of work those boys do — all for free. I merely give them a place to bunk and a lab in which to muck about with their specimens, and Baird keeps them in line. Most of the time."

He looked beyond Adam as a female voice spoke right at his elbow. "Uncle Joseph, thank goodness I found you. Mr. Farley was asking about — *oh*. Excuse me."

Adam politely edged back to allow her to ease into their group as Dr. Henry said, "You'll have to excuse my niece, Mr. Quinn. She's smart as a whip, but rarely remembers to think before she barges in to speak."

Adam looked down at the young woman,

whose face was blushing very pink. She had mink-like brown hair, a pert nose, and startled gray eyes that he recognized immediately.

"This is my niece, Sophie Gates," Dr. Henry was saying.

Or, as Adam knew her, Henry Altman.

CHAPTER 17

Oh . . . Fiddlesticks.

Sophie caught her breath, goggling up at the all too familiar man standing before her.

Of all the bad, bad *luck.*

"Pleasure to meet you, Mr. Quinn," she managed to say. She might have tried to bluster her way through by pretending there was nothing out of the ordinary, but the moment their eyes met, she'd seen the flare of recognition therein. Her only hope was that he'd be as circumspect tonight as he'd been on Tuesday at the Megatherium Club.

And considering the fact that she'd dodged him then, she doubted the chances were high.

Fiddlesticks.

"The pleasure is all mine, Miss Gates." He spoke in that sort of easy drawl that was different from a southern accent, but much slower and more deliberate than the way people spoke back in New York.

Uncle Joseph had turned away to greet Mr. Farley — who, drat it, had caused this whole thing in the first place, since he'd had a box of rocks or bones or some such thing he wanted to donate to the institution — and Sophie decided her best course of action was to slip away and find her cousins, the Henry girls.

But Mr. Quinn was too quick and he stepped directly in her path, then took her arm. "Although you do remind me of a young man I've met once . . . or twice. What was his name again? Ah, yes, Henry Altman. He seems to always be sneaking off whenever I want to speak to him. Shall we?" he said in a tone that warned her not to argue. "It's a bit less crowded over yonder."

"I think it's fine right here," she said, just as someone pushed past behind her, fairly shoving her into his tall, lanky body.

That caused him to crack a smile, which, along with the subtle cleft in his clean-shaven chin, made him look less rugged and more handsome than she'd first thought — even with the cuts and bruises on his face. He hadn't had them at the club meeting, and she wondered how he'd obtained them. And why his sleeve was pinned up. She'd touched his arm at the club and realized it was a prosthetic — but now it was missing.

The fact that she cared enough to wonder annoyed her even more. "It's been a pleasure to meet you, Mr. Quinn, but I —"

"Come now, Miss Gates. I did you a favor — quite a favor — on Tuesday night. I reckon you can spare me a bit of your precious time in return."

Sophie sighed. She was nothing if not fair, and he did — blast him — have a point. "Very well, Mr. Quinn," she replied primly. "And I suppose it *is* in my best interest as a reporter to speak to as many people as possible."

"Ah, yes. Your story for the *District Herald,* is it? The paper no one seems to know about? I begin to wonder whether it even exists — other than in your imagination."

She snapped a startled look at him, then couldn't hold back a grin. "Well, it's a very *small* paper. With low circulation." Which was mortifying, but true. With those words hanging there, she took his arm and allowed him to lead her to a far corner of the packed room.

Was there a small part of her that was disappointed Mr. Quinn didn't attempt to take her to a more private place — such as the corridor, or even the far side of the main foyer? No, there certainly was not. He was being quite proper, keeping them both in

430

full view of everyone at the levee.

"I wanted to speak to you, Miss Gates, because I've been asked to discover who killed Custer Billings at the Union Ball, and I —"

"By whom?"

He hesitated. "Mr. Lincoln."

Sophie couldn't control her reaction. "The president? Why would the president ask *you* to investigate?" She couldn't help but glance in the direction of the man himself, the tallest one in the room, and boxed in by so many people it was a wonder he could breathe.

Too late, she realized how rude she sounded, and held up a hand to ward off Mr. Quinn's response as she fumbled to explain herself. "What I mean to say is, how do you know the president that he should put you on such a delicate task? Who *are* you?"

Any journalist worth his — or her — salt knew all of the major (and most of the minor) political players in Washington, along with those people with whom the president surrounded himself. In fact, Sophie had been testing herself by identifying as many people here tonight as possible — which was a great number — and mentally reviewing their politics, occupation, and connection (or lack thereof) to the president.

But before Monday night, when he'd accosted her, she'd never seen nor heard of a man connected to the president named Adam Quinn. And even afterward, there'd been no mention of him in any of the papers, though he'd been at the president's side during the ball. Who *was* he?

Mr. Quinn gave her a small smile that was almost embarrassed. "I don't reckon it matters who I am, Miss Gates. Nevertheless, the president has set me to the task, and I won't disappoint him."

His prevarication didn't bother her. Sophie had ways of finding out. She wouldn't be much of a reporter if she didn't, would she?

"So," she prompted, looking up at him, "you're working for the president — are you a Pinkerton agent, then?"

"No, I'm not. But I'm recently from Kansas." Again he almost smiled, and Sophie realized he was gently teasing her.

"Very well, then. Enough about you. You're investigating the murder of Custer Billings and you need my help."

"And Lyman Fremark. Were you aware that a second man has been killed?"

Sophie covered her mouth with a gloved

hand. "No, I didn't know. That's horrible." Her last bit of lightheartedness evaporated. "Absolutely horrible."

"He was stabbed in this very house. I believe — I'm quite certain — it was the same man who killed Custer Billings."

She nodded, suddenly fully cognizant of how serious and dark the situation was. "I'll assist you however I can, Mr. Quinn. But it might be helpful if you were to tell me what you know. I'm . . . well, I'm rather good at puzzles." She half expected him to pat her on the head, at least figuratively, and tell her to leave the puzzles to the men — but he didn't.

And perhaps that shouldn't have surprised her, since, after all, this was the man who — for some unknown and happy reason — had not only *not* dissuaded her from attending the Megatherium Club meeting, but also hadn't given her away during the whole event.

Which had been, she had to admit, one of the most fun and enlightening, and even eye-opening evenings she'd ever spent.

"I reckon there's no reason not to tell you what I've learned, Miss Gates. It might even help me to unravel the twisted ties of this crime a little faster.

"Custer Billings was stabbed when standing outside the entrance to the dance hall by City Hall. And then his murderer dragged or carried him inside the building, where he was found. Which is why," he said, looking at her with a glint of humor in his expression, "I've eliminated Henry Altman from suspicion — although he was found with the bloody knife and Billings's coat in the closet. Mr. Altman was far too slight of a person to have been able to hold up, let alone drag, the dead weight into the building without a lot of difficulty."

Sophie huffed. "Well, I should say so. I told you I didn't have anything to do with it."

"But you also told me your name was Henry Altman."

She scowled. "Go on."

"I'd like to know what you saw when you came into the room, and what happened — how you came to be hiding in the closet with the murder weapon and the man's coat."

"All right. Let me see . . . I left the ball, and I had just left the ballroom to go back through the hallway that led to the anteroom when a man came running toward me. Nearly knocked me over, and he was babbling something about a body. So, of course, I wanted to find out what he was talking about —"

"Being the journalist that you are — or aspire to be."

"Yes, of course." She shot him a dark look. It was hard enough being taken seriously as a reporter, but it was impossible to be taken seriously as a reporter who was also a woman. "I wasn't going to miss the chance for a story like that."

"I reckon I can understand that. What did you see when you got there?"

"He was lying on the floor, off to the side. I didn't see a lot of blood, so I thought perhaps the man who ran past me had made a mistake. I went over to him and knelt down to see if I could help him. Then I saw that the front of his waistcoat had two bloodstains on it. The man wasn't breathing. I put my ear next to his mouth to check, and then I felt for a pulse. There was nothing."

"Where was the knife?"

She shook her head. "There was no knife. I told you, I saw the bloodstains on his chest, but there wasn't a knife anywhere."

Mr. Quinn was looking at her as if he didn't actually see her. "Lyman Fremark — the man who found Billings, and who was stabbed Tuesday night — said he saw a knife sticking out of the man's chest. Are you certain there wasn't one anywhere?"

"I'm not an idiot, Mr. Quinn. I do believe I would have noticed if a dagger hilt was sticking out of a man's chest, especially since I *knelt over him.* I didn't see a weapon anywhere, and as I said, I didn't even think there was all that much blood for a man to be *dead.*"

Mr. Quinn's voice dropped as if he were speaking only to himself. "Then someone — probably the murderer — had time to take the knife out of Billings's chest and hide it, along with his dress coat, in the closet between when the body was discovered and when you came on the scene. Did you see or hear anyone before you came into the room?"

"No." Sophie thought for a moment, trying to relive the moment. "I was running — astonishingly enough, one can actually run when one isn't encumbered by hoops, petticoats, and high-heeled shoes," she added, purposely tilting the ungainly cage that exploded out from her waist, "and both my feet and the other man's feet were making pounding sounds as we ran down the hall in opposite directions. And, of course, the party was very loud."

"You tried to determine whether Mr. Billings was really dead . . . and then you hid in the closet."

She nodded. "That's right. I heard you — someone — coming down the hall, and I wanted to . . . well, I didn't want to lose my chance on the story, but I also couldn't . . . didn't . . . want to be recognized."

Mr. Quinn nodded, but his expression was grim. "Miss Gates, didn't it occur to you that whoever killed him might still have been nearby? Even hiding in the closet?"

Sophie felt her face lose color. A faint queasiness that had no business living in the belly of a good reporter bubbled up. He had a point. She could have really stepped into the fire. "No. I-I just wanted to hide, and I was hoping that I'd overhear enough to get enough details for the story."

She'd seen her opportunity and taken it — as any journalist would have. To be the first (well, second) on the scene of a big story, to have the chance to scoop all the other papers. The *Daily Intelligencer* or even the *New York Times* would have to pay attention to Henry Altman then. She'd imagined the headline on the front page of the *Times:* MURDER AT THE UNION BALL, BY WASHINGTON CORRESPONDENT H. ALTMAN.

Of course, they wouldn't know — at least not for a while — that H. Altman was really

Sophie Gates. She'd have to write more than one good story to prove that a woman could be just as solid a journalist as a man.

"Miss Gates, Lyman Fremark is now dead — and I reckon it's because he saw or thought he saw something that might help identify the murderer."

He didn't need to say any more; Sophie's belly was already churning — and that just made her even more light-headed and breathless beneath her corset.

"If there's any chance he saw you — even in your disguise —"

"Yes, yes, Mr. Quinn. You've made your point quite clear. However, there was no one there when I went into the room. I'm certain no one saw me."

"So, when you went into the closet, did you notice where the knife and coat were? Did you step on them?"

"There were other things in there — a broom and mop, a coal bucket and its shovel, and it was all a jumble, so, no, I didn't notice them." She'd knocked over the broom and mop, barely catching them before they fell to the ground with a clatter. "Nothing unusual. And the rest of the room was empty — only the body and the walking stick."

"A walking stick." Mr. Quinn's eyes narrowed. "There was no walking stick in the room when I got there."

"Right. Well, there was a walking stick leaning against the wall by the door. I assumed it belonged to Mr. Billings." She frowned, thinking, remembering. She'd rushed into the room, seen the dead body, tried to revive him . . . then when she heard the sounds of voices coming down the hall, she bolted into the closet —

"*Oh!* That's what happened." It was clear now. "I heard you coming down the hall — voices, footsteps — and I ducked into the closet. But then I thought I heard the *outside* door open. I remember expecting someone was going to scream or shout from seeing the body . . . but they didn't. And I thought, well, maybe whoever it was already knew about the body — like you did — and was just coming from a different direction. To help. But then I nearly knocked over the broom and I had to grab it, and the pail, because I didn't want to make any noise. It — er — took me a minute to settle things down." Including the roaring in her ears and the pounding of her heart. She opened her eyes to find Mr. Quinn looking steadily at her. He had very dark brown irises, almost black, and his eyes were ringed with blond-tipped lashes. That made her heart

439

beat a little faster now.

"And then?" he prompted.

"And then you and Pinkerton came into the room — quite loudly and obviously, I must say. There was no mistaking your entrance. So I thought maybe I hadn't heard the outside door after all, or that the person was part of your group. But I'll bet I was right — he took the walking stick," she said. "He opened the door, reached in, and retrieved his walking stick." She suddenly felt a little light-headed. "It must have been the murderer." *What if he'd opened the closet? What if he'd needed to hide in there — when she was already there?*

After a beat, Mr. Quinn nodded. Satisfaction gleamed in his eyes. "Miss Gates, you've been extremely helpful."

"It was my pleasure, Mr. Quinn. I only wish I'd realized it sooner — but when you found me and pulled me out of the closet, the moments following were a bit . . . untenable." She gave a rueful smile.

"Thank you," he said again, then lapsed into that thoughtful silence once more.

Sophie knew she could make her excuses and return to the party, and he'd no longer detain her, but . . . She drew in a deep breath. "Mr. Quinn, I want you to know I'm grateful for your confidentiality on

Tuesday, at the club meeting," she said quickly.

"It was quite an enjoyable evening," he replied, looking down at her with those serious dark eyes once more. "But I intended to see you home. Miss Gates, it's not at all safe for a young woman — even dressed as a man — to be wandering all about the city at night, alone. Especially with a murderer on the loose."

She bit her lip and looked down, then supposed it didn't matter any longer if he knew the truth. "I appreciate your concern, Mr. Quinn. Will it ease your mind to know that when I left the club meeting in the laboratory, I merely went down the institute's corridor to the East Towers and took the stairs to the second floor — where I live with my Uncle Joe and his family?"

His eyes widened. "Well, I reckon it would, Miss Gates. Quite a bit, in fact. And that explains why you were able to throw off Agent Pierce on Monday night when he was following you after you . . . er . . . got away from me. You were just going home."

"Exactly." She smiled up at him and felt a surprise stab of warmth when he smiled back. Her heart did a little off-rhythm thump.

"Your uncle had just finished saying he

knew everything that goes on inside the Smithsonian, but I reckon he didn't know about Henry Altman, did he?"

Sophie shook her head. "And I beg of you not to tell —"

"Mr. Quinn." A female voice filled with the South spoke behind her. Even before Sophie turned, she recognized a layer of steely fury beneath it. "I must have a word with you."

Sophie turned to see a strikingly beautiful blonde whose hair was twisted into an intricate design that must have taken hours to create, and a dress that had at least twice as many rows of flounces as it needed. The woman's broader hoops bumped into Sophie's as she pushed closer, requiring Sophie to step aside and give the other woman space to move closer to Mr. Quinn.

"Miss Lemagne," he replied, then glanced beyond as if he expected someone else to be with her. "Good evening."

The woman looked at Sophie with a cool blue gaze. "I hope I'm not interrupting anything," she said, sounding as if she definitely did, "but I must speak with Mr. Quinn. Immediately. About a private matter." She was pushing the words out from between her teeth.

Mr. Quinn, for his part, seemed baffled

by and yet acquiescent of the blond woman's rudeness. "Miss Sophie Gates, this is Miss Constance Lemagne. She's visiting from Alabama."

But though she would have given anything to stay and hear what the vibratingly angry southern belle wanted to say to him, Sophie decided to take matters into her own hands before Mr. Quinn could ask her to leave — which would be mortifying.

"Oh, thank you, Miss Lemagne — I need to speak with Mr. Stimpson, and I was loathe to leave Mr. Quinn alone. I'm certain he'll be content to speak with you. Good evening, Mr. Quinn. And good luck — with everything."

Without a backward look, she flounced off.

CHAPTER 18

The irritatingly pretty Miss Gates had hardly turned away when Constance launched into her attack. "Mr. Quinn, how *dare* you continue to harass my father! Why, it's un*conscionable* the way you've been questioning him — accusing him and hounding him day after day."

Despite her fury, he kept his expression blankly polite. This made her even angrier, causing her to curl her fingers tightly into her gloved palms. Her breath was short, thanks to the tight lacing of her corset, and she knew she had to get control of it before she became light-headed and swooned in front of him.

That would be the worst.

"Miss Lemagne, as you know, I have a task set before me, and, unfortunately, your father is a suspect in this case."

It irked her that he didn't even *try* to appease her like any normal gentleman would.

"I told you we could easily prove he wasn't the murderer by checking his clothing from that night. To make sure he had the same dress coat," she said from between gritted teeth. "But you still have to keep nagging him, questioning him, *stirring up* everything! He came back to the hotel room tonight devastated and angry — practically livid — and it's all because of *you*!" She wasn't going to confess how upset her daddy had been, how he seemed beside himself — not so much with anger, but with sorrow and grief. And those were emotions she didn't understand, coming from him.

But despite her pleadings, her father had refused to tell her what was wrong — and where he'd been all afternoon. The only information she was able to glean from him was that Adam Quinn was involved, and that he'd just come from an upsetting conversation with the frontiersman.

Therefore, Adam Quinn was going to feel the sharp side of her tongue as she skinned him with her words.

At least that would make her feel a little better.

"Miss Lemagne," he said, glancing around as if to make sure no one was close enough to hear, "like it or not, your father has a very strong motive for killing Custer Billings. He was missing during the time of the murder, so he had the opportunity to do so. His knife was found at the scene — and was used to stab him. And he as much as admitted to me that he would have liked to have done it." He held up a hand when she would have started back at him, shocked that her father would have made such an admission. "He lied to me several times about this situation — and if he had nothing to hide, why would he do so? And although we can look at his clothing, there's nothing to prove what I'm shown is what he was actually wearing the night of the Union Ball."

Her cheeks were hot with fury, and she drew in a deep breath — ready to explode — but he trundled on.

"If it makes you feel any better, I'm not the least bit certain he is the culprit. But I'm not going to hold back on doing my duty simply because it upsets you — or your father. Two men are *dead,* Miss Lemagne. I reckon finding out who did that is more important than upsetting a man by asking him some serious, reasonable questions."

She was calming down a little now, slightly mollified by his admission that he didn't truly believe her daddy would have killed a man. But still, the fear that her father would be arrested, taken off to jail — maybe even *hung* . . . she couldn't bear it.

"I thought you'd given up on my father after our — after the visit to the — to Dr. Hilton," she said stubbornly.

"There was more information that came to light after that," he told her. "I spoke with your father about it, and I'll continue to do so until I'm either satisfied he isn't guilty or I find the murderer."

"Constance."

A low, furious voice made her heart plunge and her stomach flip. Oh, dear. Oh, *no.*

She turned to her father, who'd stormed up to them. He certainly didn't look like a murder suspect — for he was dressed in smart, formal evening clothing with pristine gloves, shiny top hat, and the requisite walking stick gripped in his hand — almost like a weapon. But his demeanor was anything but sleek, slick formality.

He nearly shook with rage as he spoke to her. "I instructed you not to speak to Mr. Quinn, did I not?"

"But, Daddy," she began, then clamped her mouth shut. Her cheeks were burning, and once again the restrictions of her corset made it difficult for her to draw a breath.

"Mr. Mossing and I have been looking everywhere for you." His grip on her arm was firm and very nearly painful, but she supposed she should have expected it after so blatantly disobeying him.

She shouldn't have approached Mr. Quinn in such a public place — where she could be seen.

"Excuse me," said Mr. Quinn, clearly desirous of making his escape. "Good evening, Miss Lemagne. Mr. Lemagne."

Neither of them bothered to respond. Constance was near tears. She hated upsetting her father, especially when he was already upset. But didn't he *see*? Someone had to *do* something.

Someone had to figure out who was behind the murders, and who had framed him.

She blinked rapidly and suddenly a handkerchief was thrust into her line of vision.

"Wipe your eyes," her father muttered.

"Daddy, I'm sorry I disobeyed you, but I'm just so angry with Mr. Quinn. He has no right —"

"I told you before, Constance, this is none of your affair. You need to stay out of it." His voice was firm, but the blazing anger had eased.

"But, Daddy, I'm afraid — what if they arrest you?" She looked up at him, not caring that her eyes were filled with tears — in fact, glad they were. He needed to understand how much she'd had this worry bottled up inside her, how much she feared what could happen here in this unfamiliar city where they hardly knew anyone. "What will happen to you — and to me? How will I pay for your lawyer, and where will I stay? And what if the war comes?"

His face softened a little more and he chucked her under the chin. "I won't be arrested, poppet, because I didn't do it. That damn — er, that blasted Mr. Quinn is a smart man — too smart for his own good — even if he's working for the damned railsplitter. He's not going to make a mistake like that."

"But, Daddy . . . the *knife*. They found your knife there. And — and you won't tell me what's wrong. What's going on. I know there's something wrong, and you won't tell me. Why not?" Her eyes stung again and now her nose was beginning to run — which was not attractive, even on her.

He sighed. "It's nothing you need to be concerned about, Constance. It's something that happened a long time ago. You needn't worry about anything. But," he said, holding up a hand when she would have argued further, "if the worst should happen and I am arrested — which I *won't* be — you know Arthur will take care of you." He smiled affectionately at her. "I know you aren't all that fond of Mossing, but he wants to marry you."

"And you want me to marry him because he's the son of your friend," she added dryly.

"Constance, please. You know it's more than that. And you've hardly given the man a chance. We've been here hardly more than a week, and you barely know him. A few walks down the street aren't enough to know."

She drew in a shaky breath. "I don't really understand your reasons for wanting me to marry Arthur. Yes, he comes from a good family and you were friends with his father. I know you always talked about merging our families, and creating an empire — but you already own the business Mr. Mossing started. And doesn't it matter what I want? Shouldn't *I* get to choose my husband? You and Mama got to make your own decision, your own choices. I shouldn't be forced into marrying someone I don't love simply because you want me to. Please don't take away my choice. Please don't force me to marry someone I don't want to."

Her father had stilled, the ruddiness in his cheeks fading to pale. "Constance . . ." His voice trailed off. "Of course, I wouldn't ever *force* you. I only . . . I won't force you. I never meant you to think that."

He reached for her hand, squeezing it softly — but, as was his way, he wouldn't actually say soft words or apologies.

But the hand squeeze — it was enough.

Adam gave the Lemagnes the space they obviously needed, but he lingered within sight of them. Just to make certain.

He didn't reckon Hurst would do anything to hurt his daughter; despite the anger and bluster he showed, it seemed wrapped around sincere concern and affection for her. And the fact that the man still desperately loved a woman from his youth gave Adam the impression that Hurst Lemagne's adorations were firmly and deeply rooted, and that he was more bluster and bark than anything venomous.

Which was why he really didn't believe the man had killed either Custer Billings or Lyman Fremark.

But someone had, and standing in a corner tucked behind two large urns of graceful palms (he had no idea where Mrs. Lincoln had obtained them on such short notice, but there they were), Adam was grateful for a quiet moment to think about all the possibilities. Including what Pinkerton had told him.

It seemed that some members of the 1860 Association were no longer content with merely printing pamphlets and convincing states to secede. The Black Dot faction of the group — which seemed to include the men Miss Lemagne had overheard in the courtyard, plus the other one seen by the groom — had planned a distraction at the Union Ball in order to make their move to assassinate Lincoln.

The next question was: Why choose Billings?

Was he a random choice as victim? If so, then that put Adam even further away from solving the murder . . . unless he could figure out the clue of the oil smudges. Based on what Miss Gates had told him tonight, he'd become certain that the weapon had somehow been secreted in the walking stick she'd seen — *the walking stick the murderer had come back to retrieve.* And that the oil drips were related to it.

It made sense. There had to be some sort of mechanism, for the oil appeared only at the approximate time and location where the murder was committed. And there had been an oil stain on the floor near the closet — just where Miss Gates said the walking stick was leaning against the wall.

So he could follow that trail — somehow.

Not that it would be easy — every man of the upper class carried a walking stick.

But back to Billings. If he as the victim hadn't been a random choice — if it was a purposeful one — what would the reason be?

Well . . . Billings was a staunch abolitionist. It would be a strong statement to kill him at the ball celebrating an antislavery president. That alone could be the reason — and perhaps Wellburg and Littleton *had* known more than they were telling, and the death of Billings in particular had been the plan all along.

Or . . . Hurst Lemagne could have killed him in retribution for the way Billings treated the woman he'd loved for decades. And left the knife purposely, so as to make it appear that no one would be so foolish as to leave such blatant, identifying evidence behind. That would make Lemagne a very clever man, and Adam . . . well, he wasn't certain Lemagne was *that* clever. But it was a theory that couldn't be dismissed.

Or someone could have known about the bad blood between Lemagne and Billings — after all, Miss Lemagne had heard them arguing, so others may have as well — and decided to use their history as a cover for the murder of Billings. And then framed Lemagne for the crime.

But if that were the case, then the choice of Billings couldn't be completely random. Someone would have had to have brought Lemagne's dagger in order to plant it near the scene.

Once again, that could lead back to the Black Dot Association . . . but there were other reasons to kill Billings.

Mortimer Titus, for example. If he'd learned that Custer Billings was dallying with his wife, he might have decided to take matters into his own hands. And if he were also a member of the Association . . . that would make everything nice and tidy.

Adam stood on his toes, looking for a man with pasty skin and insignificant eyebrows in the hopes that he might find Titus himself.

Who else would benefit from Billings's death? There was always the motive of money. That and love, the members of the Megatherium Club seemed to have agreed on, were two of the most common motives. Love and money.

He'd already figured if Billings died, his wife would inherit all of his money.

Adam's eyes widened. And if Billings was dead, that would leave Hurst Lemagne free to marry Althea Billings . . . and then *he* would have Billings's wealth along with his own.

He shook his head. Either Lemagne was very, very clever, or someone really knew his history and had set him up very neatly.

He frowned. Althea Billings was weak and ill. Would she even live long enough to marry Lemagne after her required period of mourning — at least a year or two? Or would she even *want* to marry him, after so many years? Adam only had Lemagne's word that Althea had loved him all those years ago. . . . Maybe that wasn't true after all.

He rubbed the crease between his eyebrows and tried to make sense of the whirlwind of thoughts. Who else might benefit from Billings's death?

Then it struck him. The brother. Althea Billings's brother. Because when she died, Orton would be her heir, and —

"Mr. Quinn."

His eyes flew open — he hadn't even realized they were closed — and he found himself looking down at Miss Gates.

"I see you came through your interview with Miss Lemagne unscathed," she said.

"Most of my hide remains intact," he managed to say with a rueful smile.

"I'm sorry to intrude," she began, "but I

wanted to make certain you didn't have any more questions for me — since we were . . . er . . . interrupted."

He thought for a moment. "Only if you can remember what the walking stick looked like; I reckon that would be helpful."

"If only I could," she said with a sigh. "I've been racking my brain trying to picture it in my head, but I can't."

"I appreciate your persistence. And I want to remind you, Miss Gates, that there is still a murderer wandering about. Please don't go anywhere alone, especially at night."

"I'm not a fool," she retorted, her eyes flashing.

"I cannot argue with that," he replied gravely.

She lifted her dainty, pointed nose as if she wasn't certain whether he was joshing her or not. But before she could speak, they were invaded — which was the only word to describe it — by William Stimpson and Robert Kennicott, their full cups, and their laden plates.

Miss Gates threw him an apologetic farewell, then slipped away as the two new arrivals began to pepper Adam with questions. Clearly she wanted to take no chance they'd recognize her as Henry Altman.

"Where'd you get off to? We were looking

for you. Had a question, and now can't remember what it was. What was it, Stimpy?" Kennicott rattled off.

"Damned if I know," replied the other, then popped what looked like a fried oyster into his mouth. "Must not have been important."

"You set us up with that challenge on Tuesday, didn't you, Quinn?" said Kennicott good-naturedly. "Nice job on that. There wasn't a hair swatch to match after all, was there?"

Maybe it was that he had so much information in his head that Adam decided to tell them the whole of it.

"The truth is," he said, yanking them closer into the corner that had seemed secluded but kept being invaded, "I'm investigating the murder of the man who was stabbed at the Union Ball."

"You're mad," Stimpson said, crumbs flying from whatever he'd just stuffed in his mouth.

"What're you, a Pinkerton?" jumped in Kennicott. "That'd be a great time, being a detective, Stimpy. It'd be like following tracks in the woods."

Adam laughed, because that was exactly what it was like . . . and yet it wasn't. And because the two slightly inebriated, very enthusiastic men were willing to hear more, he told them all of what he knew about the way the murder had actually happened. He didn't name the names of any suspects, however, simply sticking to the way the murder had been committed.

"It has to be a walking stick," agreed Kennicott, after tossing back a big gulp of ale. "With some kind of mechanism in it."

"I reckoned for a time it might have been part of a prosthetic," Adam said, gesturing easily with his half-arm. "An implement that was, maybe, inserted in the end of the prosthetic. That made sense for how Billings died — as the wounds came from below and went up. But Fremark was killed with blows from slightly above, stabbing down."

"He could have been sitting," Stimpson said. "Or bending over."

Adam considered that, then shook his head. "No, even that wouldn't help. And the location is wrong. But it's the way the weapon would have to be — sticking straight out from the arm like this." He demonstrated. "You'd always be stabbing up from that angle. Impossible to make it angle down without really contorting yourself."

"So it makes sense it's part of a walking stick. Easier to handle and hide, anyway, I reckon," Kennicott said. "I mean to say, a man wearing an ice pick for his hand would be noticeable."

The three of them chuckled a little, then sobered.

"Wouldn't be difficult to put a sword tip inside a walking stick. It's been done before," commented Stimpson.

"Agreed. But it's the getting it out unnoticed — the motion of unsheathing a knife of any size is broad and obvious — and using it without the victim realizing it — and reacting — that bothers me," Adam said.

"There was a man — saw him earlier tonight," Stimpson said slowly. "He had his hands full, with a plate and a drink, and what do you do with a walking stick then? Can't slide it under your arm, or it sticks out from behind and snags on the skirts or sleeves of anyone walking by, trips 'em, and causes a problem. Imagine if everyone did that."

"What's your point, Stimpy?" Kennicott said.

"Right. The man's stick was standing next to him, upright all by itself. I noticed because, well, hell, it looked strange and yet useful."

"How was it standing up?" Adam asked,

feeling a strange little buzz in his belly. "Did you notice?"

"Hell yes I did — I was curious. He was stepping on a small metal plate that had flipped out from the bottom of the stick. I've never seen anything like that before."

"Neither have I." The buzzing in Adam's middle became stronger. "I think that's it," he said, his voice tense with excitement. "There's a mechanism that causes the plate to flip out — maybe in the handle or on the side. The murderer steps on the metal clip and then only needs the one hand to pull off the top of the walking stick and expose the weapon." He showed them how it could be done with spare, hardly noticeable movements.

"And if he does it as he's moving forward to, maybe, embrace Billings, or speak to him in a low voice, then it wouldn't be noticeable at all. He'd pull out the top half or top third of the stick, his arm moving slightly behind him as he angles forward . . . then as he steps back, jabs his arm up and forward — *ugh*! Right in the gut."

Adam could see both enthusiasm and confirmation from his companions.

"And the oil smudge is from the plate flipping open — it has to move quickly and silently in order to be effective," Stimpson said. "So it must be lubricated."

"Exactly."

"Right you are," Kennicott said, his words uncharacteristically sober. "And how many walking sticks are like that? Such a useful invention, though — it should become quite popular. Age-old problem of what to do with your walking stick while at a party."

Invention.

Adam stilled, his brain fumbling for something he'd heard, something someone had said —

Mr. Orton. Althea Billings's brother. He was a lawyer — who worked with inventors filing their patents.

Althea would inherit Billings's money, and *Orton would inherit from Althea when she died.*

Which was likely to be sooner rather than later.

And Alan Orton lived in Baltimore. It came to him in a flash — the groom at the St. Charles mentioned the fourth man didn't have a southern accent. He sounded like he was from the North.

"Where's the man you said you saw with the walking stick like that?" Adam said, looking around. "Would you know him again? Did you see his face?"

He hadn't noticed Orton present himself,

but there were probably at least a thousand people here, and he'd been cloistered in corners and alcoves for most of the evening.

"Yes, of course." Stimpson, obviously anticipating the demand, had already begun to look around, turning in a slow sweep as he scanned the room. "I don't see him . . . at the moment."

"Find him," Adam said flatly. "Find him before he kills again."

And then he began to search for Miss Gates. Just in case.

CHAPTER 19

"Is everything all right, Constance?"

She looked up into the concerned eyes of Arthur Mossing, Esquire, and tried not to be irritated that he'd taken to calling her by her familiar name. He clearly assumed their marriage was a foregone conclusion, regardless of her lack of interest in him. She couldn't completely cut him off socially, but couldn't he tell she didn't care for him? At all?

"I'm just a bit warm," she lied, seizing on a handy excuse. She noticed that he'd not offered to obtain any refreshment for her tonight — likely due to an effort to keep his waistcoat from getting drenched with lemonade again — and that he'd stuck to her side like a burr since her father had returned her to their group after their conversation with Mr. Quinn.

She'd gotten the definite impression that Arthur Mossing didn't like Mr. Quinn. The one day she'd been unable to politely extricate herself from going for a walk with her unwanted suitor, she'd manipulated it so they stopped by the Willard for luncheon. She'd hoped to see Mr. Quinn, but she learned he'd been injured by an attack by thugs the night before. And Arthur had seemed almost smug about the fact that the man was laid up. He was such a prig.

But Mr. Quinn. Now if *he* were interested in her sticking to his side all night, she wouldn't dream of spilling lemonade on him. For all his rough manners and less than polished dress — and even his lack of wealth — he was far more attractive to her than the prim lawyer stuck to her side.

"It is rather warm in here," Mr. Mossing agreed. "But I am still hoping to shake the president's hand."

He frowned as he adjusted his coat sleeve and the shirt cuff beneath it, looking along the line that had been never-ending since their arrival. He'd jockeyed them into place near the curve in one corner. "All those foreign dignitaries. You'd think the president's first levee would only be for *his* countrymen."

"I'd be very grateful for something to drink, Mr. Mossing," she said firmly. "Even just a cup of water."

He sighed. "Very well, but promise me you'll wait here and save my place in line. The table is only right there; I won't be gone long."

"Of course," she replied, mostly meaning it. She wouldn't mind shaking the hand of the president — even though she was a Southerner. Her father might despise him and the Republicans, but Constance didn't have such strong opinions. Besides, he was, no matter how you looked at it, the *president of the United States.*

From everything she'd heard and seen about Mr. Lincoln, he was a fine man. A little rough and uncivilized like someone else she knew, but that wasn't all bad.

The line had hardly moved by the time Arthur returned (Constance supposed it was permissible to think of him by his familiar name at this point), carrying two cups, and with his walking stick stuck under his arm.

As he slid into place back in line, handing Constance her cup, he bumped the person behind them with the end of his walking stick, and turned to offer his apologies.

When he pivoted, Constance noticed a subtle streak of white on the back of his coat. "You've got a bit of chalk on the back of your dress coat," she murmured as he turned back around, walking stick safely back in hand, cup in the other.

It would be awkward for her to brush it off — considering where the dirt was located — but it was here in public and he couldn't remove his coat nor reach it.

"How noticeable is it?" he asked, then drained his drink and set the cup on a nearby table. "Should I leave and find a lounge so I can attend to it?"

He sounded tense and concerned, which was no surprise. He was all about appearances and propriety. She doubted he would risk meeting the president with chalk stains on his coat, even though Mr. Lincoln would surely be oblivious.

In fact, she rather hoped he *would* go off and take care of it, so she could be rid of his company. Perhaps she could help him on his way. . . .

Doing her best not to appear to be staring at his behind, Constance angled around to take a better look. And that was when she noticed something strange.

"Your dress coat is different," she said without thinking.

"Pardon me?" Arthur turned abruptly, spearing her with his eyes.

Constance suddenly felt as if she couldn't draw in a breath — then she expelled it.

How silly. "I just noticed — your coat . . . it's different. From your trousers." Even as she said the words, icy disbelief and confusion gripped her.

No.

Don't be a *goose.*

She couldn't contain a shiver.

"What on earth do you mean?" Arthur had stepped very close to her, and somehow, over the dull roar of the packed room and the louder roaring in her ears, she heard a faint, metal click.

"Nothing," she said quickly. But her head felt light, and her cheeks were clammy, and her insides were churning. "I need —"

"I think you need some air, Miss Lemagne," he said, taking her by the arm and drawing her very close to him. "Right now."

She would have declined, pulled away, made some sort of protest, but all at once, she felt something sharp poking her between the boning of her corset.

"Now, Constance," he said quietly. "Walk with me now, and everything will be all right. I promise."

CHAPTER 20

Adam looked everywhere for Miss Gates, but the reception was so crowded it was like wading upstream while the fish were all swimming down — and it was made even worse by obstacles such as stray walking sticks and stiff, broad skirts.

He was also watching for Orton as he pushed through the people. He noticed Miss Lemagne standing in the reception line with Mr. Mossing, waiting to shake the hand of Mr. Lincoln, but she didn't notice him.

Pushing through the crowd left him sweaty and irritated, as it seemed as if he could only take three steps at a time, then had to change his direction to get past nonmoving obstructions — usually a cluster of skirts — and then take only a few more steps. He didn't think the Union Ball had even been this crowded. He wondered how everyone was going to retrieve the coats and wraps they'd left in the coat room when the party was over. It was going to be a mad scramble.

"Quinn!"

He heard his name over the constant buzz of conversation and laughter, and turned to see Stimpson and Kennicott plowing their way through the crowd toward him. The two of them seemed to pay no mind to the ladies as they pushed and inserted themselves between and around gossiping partygoers.

"I saw him," Stimpson said when he got close enough. "He was just over there, getting something to drink."

Adam turned to look where he'd pointed — a futile effort, for it was on the other side of a decorative screen that was intended to help break up the room — and then started off in that direction. The other two remained with him. "Where is he? Do you see him now? What does he look like?"

Stimpson brayed a laugh. "Like every other damned man here — wearing a top hat, a black dress coat, and carrying a walking stick. Brownish beard, light brownish hair — he was right there, getting two cups of lemonade. I don't see him anymore." He paused, stopping stock-still in the middle of the room so that someone bumped into him from behind.

"Stimpy, here," called Kennicott. He'd

somehow obtained a chair, and he wrestled it through the crowd, plopping it right where his friend was standing.

Adam waited impatiently as Stimpson climbed up and looked around the room, making a small circle on the chair. "Why didn't we think of this before?" he asked, still circling — and oblivious to the stares and comments he raised from the spectators around him. "I don't . . . wait. Is that him? No . . . damn."

The chair was jostled by someone walking past, and Stimpson barked down at Kennicott, "Hold it steady, will you?"

Adam chafed at the delay and was just about ready to knock the man off so he could look himself — for both Orton and Miss Gates — when Stimpson said, "There he is. Right there. Looks like he's got a very pretty lady on his arm too — saw you talking to her earlier tonight, there, Quinn," he said, sending Adam's heart into a sharp lurch.

A lady he'd been talking to earlier? How had Miss Gates gotten herself into such a mess?

"Let's go," Adam said.

Stimpson leaped down from his perch without regard to the crowd that had begun to fill in around the chair. As he landed, he bumped into a man who knocked into another man and sloshed his drink all down the back of a woman's gown.

Adam didn't wait to see how that mess was resolved. He took off in the direction Stimpson had indicated, hoping he was behind him — but now he was more terrified that Miss Gates was in the hands of the murderer.

"Where is he? Do you see him?" he asked, stopping when he was nearly across the room. He hadn't seen either Orton or Miss Gates, and he was getting concerned.

When no one responded, he turned to look and realized he'd lost Stimpson and Kennicott during his breakneck crossing of the room. Dammit. *Dammit.*

He was balancing on his toes, turning in a small, desperate circle, when someone bumped into him from behind.

"Mr. Quinn!"

He staggered, catching himself, as he turned to find Miss Gates standing there. He had a moment's rush of relief that she was there, and safe, before he registered what she was saying. Her eyes were bright and her cheeks were pink with excitement, and she was holding a slender black dowel decorated with brass fittings.

He knew immediately that it was the bottom half of a walking stick. *The* walking stick.

"I'm so relieved I found you," she gasped, out of breath with exertion. Worry and fear shone in her eyes as she thrust the wooden object toward him. "This is it, Mr. Quinn. I recognized it; I saw it and I recognized it. Because of all the decorative fittings — see?"

"Where did you get this?" he demanded, looking around. "And where's the other part?"

"I just saw it on the floor, just now, over there," she said, pointing in the direction Stimpson had indicated.

"Did you see who had it? Who was holding it?"

"No, I don't think so, but I found it near where Miss Lemagne was standing in the receiving line. She was with a gentleman."

"Quinn, they're gone." Kennicott pushed through the crowd, his eyes dark and concerned. "Stimpy saw them — they just went out that door. He was walking with that blond woman you were speaking with. They were walking quickly, that way."

That blond woman he was speaking with? *Miss Lemagne.*

"Get Pinkerton." Adam started toward the door, still holding the bottom half of the walking stick, pushing rudely between the guests.

The murderer had the top half of the walking stick — and Adam feared he knew exactly what he was going to do with it.

Cold fear rushed through him, but his mind was clear. He had to find her.

It was well past the ten o'clock curfew, but that didn't stop George Hilton from parking his wagon on the muddy, straggling grass down the hill from the President's House. There was nowhere else to park, for the roads and areas along them were clogged with vehicles for at least a mile in every direction.

He'd driven Miss Lizzie earlier today, when she came to deliver Mrs. Lincoln's dress — she could never have managed the beautiful, bulky garment without a ride — and now he was here to pick her up.

But she'd never find his wagon in the dark, amid all the other carriages and barouches and landaus, he reasoned. And he didn't like the idea of her walking out by herself, at night, after curfew, and around a lot of men who'd likely been drinking.

So he tied up his horse to a tree and turned to his companion. "Stay here."

Brian Mulcahey, the twelve-year-old Irish

boy who'd been befriended by Quinn, looked up at him with mutiny in his eyes. "But can't I come and look at the house, mister — I mean, Doctor?"

Somehow — George wasn't certain precisely how — he'd acquired a shadow in Ballard Alley.

He and Brian had first encountered each other on the night Quinn was beaten up, and then, the next day when he came to see to his patient at the Willard, the boy had been loitering about. He'd been desperate to see how his mentor was faring, and George didn't have the heart — or the strength, because the kid was damned determined — to turn him away.

Since then, he'd seen the kid around the alley and had given him a few things to do to earn a few coins. Mainly so he'd quit bothering him. George thought tonight he'd leave Brian with the wagon and horse while he went up to get Miss Lizzie, but now that was in jeopardy.

"Someone's gotta stay here with Hellman," he told the boy. His voice was gruff because, well, hell, he knew how the kid felt. He wanted to see the house too.

"Fine," said Brian, sulking and scooching down in his seat in the wagon. "Thank you, mister-doctor," he added belatedly, as if the thought of his mother had reminded him.

"I'll be back soon." George tucked away the slight bit of guilt — the horse really wasn't going anywhere — and started his way toward the majestic house, raised up on a small incline.

Though it sprawled like a scattering of wooden blocks at either end, the main part of the mansion was just about one of the most awe-inspiring things he'd ever seen. Its white exterior picked up an ice-blue shine from the moon, making it look pristine and powerful. Even pure, though he knew, of course, that nothing related to politics was pure.

Still. He sure would like to have a look inside someday.

A look inside the house of the man everyone said would free the slaves.

Because there'd been no room to park on the main driveway that led up on the north side of the house, from Lafayette Square, George was approaching the mansion from the southwest — an angle that was dark and deserted, for everyone had entered from the north, main side of the house. He hoped that would help keep him in the shadows and unnoticed by anyone who wanted to give him a hassle.

But as he drew closer, he saw the shadows

of two figures coming from around the far side of the mansion. It was easy to discern the shapes of a man and a woman in the moonlight.

George hesitated, keeping to the shadows of the beautiful landscaped gardens that surrounded the house. It was best if he wasn't seen . . . and likely the couple would prefer not to be observed as well — for there was only one reason a man and woman sneaked out from a party, into the dark by themselves.

He smiled, suddenly reminded of the sweet and soft Marie-Louise Carpier from . . . well, from years ago in Montreal. He didn't like to think about her too much because it made his heart hurt, but there had been good memories too.

As he made his way closer, he could hear that the couple was in a fervent conversation. Once again, he hesitated. He didn't really want to be privy to anyone's personal conversation — or private activities.

That never led to anything good, his mama always told him.

Yet there was something about the couple that drew his attention. Something was wrong. . . . It was the way they were moving. She seemed agitated, and the man with her seemed almost threatening.

George swallowed his concerns and edged around a low brick wall, moving silently and carefully. The last thing he needed was to be caught — a black man, after curfew, sneaking around the President's House, spying on someone — but his instincts urged him on.

"It was you," said the woman in a voice that sounded vaguely familiar. Hers was a southern accent, cultured and with a hint of gentility despite what seemed to be a moment of tension. "All along, it was you. And you made it look like my father was guilty of stabbing that man."

With a shock, George not only recognized her voice now — it was Quinn's Miss Lemagne — but he also realized what she was talking about.

Oh, Christ Jesus. His heart nearly stopped.

"They wouldn't have hanged him," said the man roughly. "I'd have stepped forward and given him an alibi when he needed it. And then I would have been a hero. *Your* hero."

"But why did you do it, Arthur?" Miss Lemagne's voice shook, and it was high and tight, but it wasn't hysterical.

"Partly because of you, Constance. You weren't giving me the time of day, and you've been promised to me for years."

"Me, and all my father's money," she said in a bitter voice that wafted to George's ears from across a bed of low-cut shrubs.

"Your father." His voice was bitter. "Half his money belongs to *me*. If they hang him, I won't shed a single tear."

"What — what do you mean?"

"He forced my father to sell the textile business to him, instead of letting me keep it. *I* should have been running Mossing Textiles, instead of being a drudge-working lawyer. But my father made some bad investments in '58 — with the financial help of Custer Billings — and your father bought him out and obtained a controlling interest in Mossing Textiles. I didn't even know about it — that my future, my inheritance, was caught up in Hurst Lemagne's pockets — until my father was on his deathbed. Father said it would be fine, that I'd get the business back when I married you. So, yes, I'd been promised you — and my inheritance — for years. But don't misunderstand, my dear. You are a fetching reason to marry, all on your own." He pulled her close and kissed her so roughly she bent backward.

George curled his fingers into furious fists and took the chance of dashing across an exposed expanse of garden path while the couple struggled. His movement brought him closer . . . close enough to see that this man named Arthur had a long, slender, shining blade pressed against Miss Lemagne's side, just above where her broad skirts erupted.

Which meant that he couldn't just lunge out of the dark for fear of startling the man, for that blade could slide home in an instant.

He knew. He'd seen the man's work on two dead bodies.

Lord Jesus. A trickle of perspiration ran down George's back. Arthur had murdered two men already — he certainly wouldn't stop at killing a third time. And if George were found in the vicinity. . . . He was no fool. He knew exactly how it would all evolve.

But he wasn't about to do nothing.

The man finally released Miss Lemagne, and they were both gasping for air; him with lust, and she with anger and fear. George could see tear tracks glistening down her cheeks. Heart pounding in his throat, he crept forward, watching them through the bushes and praying whatever he did next wouldn't end up getting him hanged.

George was just about to ease forward when he felt, rather than heard or saw, something behind him. Heart thudding, he spun to see a small, lithe shadow sprinting across an expanse of lawn.

Brian.

Oh, Jesus, *why*? Why couldn't the kid stay put for ten minutes?

George's attention was split between hoping the Irish boy wouldn't be seen or heard in his new, squeaking boots, and his fear for Miss Lemagne. He gritted his teeth and stared into the darkness toward Brian, willing the kid to be quiet and not call out to him before he got there. Quickly, he moved back, away from the arguing couple, in order to apprehend Brian.

"Not a damned word," he breathed into the boy's ear as he clapped a hand over his mouth. "Or movement."

The kid struggled briefly before realizing it was George who had hold of him, then relaxed as he listened to the older man's explanation.

Brian's eyes went wide, gleaming in the moonlight, and George could almost read the *"Gor!"* in them.

He explained carefully and quickly what he wanted Brian to do and watched while he removed his new boots.

Then, filled with both misgivings and hope, he released the brat into the darkness. And prayed.

Only after he saw the skinny kid slip along the edge of the porch walkway that ran along the side and rear of the mansion did George return his full attention to Miss Lemagne and the man named Arthur.

George carefully crept closer.

"Now, Constance, darling," the man was saying, "everything is going to be all right. I'm going to clear your father's name, very easily. It won't take anything but a statement from me, and all will be well . . . but in return, you are most definitely going to marry me, Constance. No more of this hesitation, this coolness. And definitely no more of that uncivilized frontiersman Quinn. I was damned disappointed he didn't die that night I set those thugs on him. But you're going to stay away from him, and I'm going to make everything all right."

"I'm never going to marry you, Arthur. You're mad to think that after what you've told me, after what I *know,* I'd even consider —" Her voice went to a strangle as the slender silver blade gleamed its movement, prodding her through her clothes. She squeaked in pain, and even from his position, George saw her shudder.

"Oh, you will, my darling. Because if you don't, your precious father is most certainly going to end up at the end of a noose. I intended for him to be arrested — I wanted revenge on him for stealing my father's business, and I didn't care if he hanged. An added benefit was that you'd have to come to me for support — where else would you go in a strange city, with no resources? — and you'd see how well I would take care of you. And when — *if* — I chose to save your father from the noose, well, of course you'd be delighted to marry me. And I'd have the family business back, a full bank account, *and* a beautiful wife on my arm. Not to mention the everlasting gratitude of Hurst Lemagne." His voice had gone to a sneer.

George was very close now . . . close enough to see the terror in Miss Lemagne's eyes and the way her hand shook in the moonlight.

To his relief, he could also see, in the shadows just below them, the boy slipping around a small, staked fruit tree. Only another minute or two until Brian was in position.

He just hoped the boy would wait long enough. . . .

George edged carefully into position next to a massive stone urn arranged on the bottom of a short flight of steps.

"I'm *never* going to marry you, Arthur.

I'd rather die than marry you. So you might just as well kill me, right here, because otherwise I'm going to tell everyone what I know."

Good God, no! Don't threaten the man like that!

His heart thudded, and then, with relief, he saw a skinny arm lift from the bushes on the far side of Miss Lemagne. The kid had moved fast, and —

The arm moved and George was surely the only person to see the rock fly through the air, up and onto the walkway behind Mossing and Miss Lemagne.

When the stone landed with a skitter, the murderer stiffened and whipped around, bringing Miss Lemagne with him.

"Who's there?"

George dashed, fleet and silent footed, up closer, so he was within two feet of them now, behind a bench next to the walkway, overlooking the garden. It wasn't the best cover, but it put him close enough to do something.

Everything was quiet and still, and George held his breath, waiting to see if Brian would follow through on the second direction. He needed one more distraction in order to get closer. . . .

Once Mossing assured himself no one was

there, he turned his attention to Miss Lemagne as he loosened his grip to look down at her. His back was to George, but he could still hear the man say, "Kill you instead? Why, that's not a bad idea, my darling. I could slit your throat very, very quickly. It would be painless . . . but then you'd get blood all over me, and this time I wouldn't have a coat to change into."

Her voice was strained when she replied, but she was *looking right at George* through the darkness. "I'd rather die than marry a cold-blooded murderer, Arthur Mossing. So do your worst. I just —"

Suddenly, she collapsed in Mossing's arms.

Her movement was so unexpected the man staggered, and his blade hand shifted — and that was when Brian gave a loud, bloodcurdling Indian whoop.

George vaulted from the bushes.

He crashed into Mossing and Miss Lemagne, and they all tumbled to the ground on the narrow stone patio, tangled in skirts and stiff hoops. George felt a burning sting on his arm as he landed, but he had hold of Mossing's shirt so he couldn't get away. As they grappled, he managed a powerful punch square into the man's face. His foe gasped and his head whipped back, slamming onto the stone walkway with an ugly crunch.

And then he didn't move.

Somehow, Miss Lemagne had maneuvered herself away from them, and George heard her gasping and struggling to rise — which was nearly impossible, enclosed in the ridiculous cage that she was.

"Brian! Go find Mr. Quinn!" George shouted.

Arthur Mossing seemed to rouse at the sound of his voice, so George slammed an elbow sharp to his gut and followed it with another right-side blow to his face.

Obviously, the man was nothing more than a dandy. He looked good in his fashionable clothing, could use a knife when necessary — but was helpless as a woman without a weapon.

Only slightly out of breath, George pulled to his feet, snagged the dropped knife, and went over to offer his hand to Miss Lemagne. He came around behind her so he could ignore the fact that her skirt and petticoats were tilted up so high they looked like an overturned bell with two legs as clappers.

He kept an eye on Mossing. "Are you all right, miss?" he asked as he helped her to her feet.

She was barely upright when she lunged into his arms, shaking and sobbing — a whole mess of woman: soft, sweet smelling, shivering. . . .

And, for him, completely and utterly untouchable.

George was trying to decide whether to pat her on the back to comfort her or put her *far* away from him when Adam Quinn came running around the corner.

CHAPTER 21

"Well, well, Arthur Mossing. *Esquire,*" Adam said as he wrangled the man to his feet and slammed him against one of the great columns holding up the portico. An easier feat when one had both hands intact, but galvanized as he was by fury and fear for Miss Lemagne, he managed it with the one and used the elbow of his stump-arm to pin the bastard in place.

It helped, he reckoned, that the man had obviously already been pummeled by George Hilton and was a bit unsteady on his feet anyway.

Adam — with Miss Gates on his heels, of course — had just rushed out of the East Room and was heading into the foyer of the mansion when a bloodcurdling whoop filled the air. Though it didn't sound like Miss Lemagne, he ran through the front door and bolted toward the source of the noise — nearly running into Brian Mulcahey as he careened around the corner.

"Mr. Quinn!" the boy gasped, dodging just in time. "Mister-doctor needs you!"

By the time Adam had Arthur Mossing shoved up against the column, the murderer's head lolling and his nose bleeding profusely, Pinkerton and two of his men had arrived, and Miss Lemagne was being comforted by Miss Gates.

Hilton held back and remained silent, lingering in the shadows as if attempting to remain unnoticed. Adam met his eyes in the dim light and allowed his gratitude to shine through. He also realized what an untenable position the Negro man could find himself in, all things considered, and chose not to say anything to draw attention to the doctor. But his expression told him everything.

With the help of Pinkerton to clear the way, Adam muscled Mossing through an unobtrusive side door into the mansion, taking care not to draw attention from the guests. If any of them had heard the war whoop over the raucous noise of the levee, it would be explained away by the agent Pinkerton had sent back inside.

Adam flung Mossing into a chair, then, for the first time, turned to speak to Miss Lemagne. "Are you hurt?"

"No," she said, though her voice was shaky and her eyes bloodshot. "I'm *furious.* That man killed two people — and framed my father for it — because he wanted to marry me." Her voice rose, shrill and tight and very southern as she continued. "As if I would ever have considered it. I told him I'd rather die first!"

Adam, though he'd not actually suspected Arthur Mossing of being the murderer, had never liked the man. In fact, his instinct had been strong antipathy from the first time he'd met him; but he'd tried to submerge it, assuming it was because the man was the beau of the lovely Miss Lemagne.

Perhaps if he hadn't tried to ignore his instincts, he might have figured it out sooner. Ishkode would have been disappointed in his friend.

And even now, Adam still had questions about why, but he had reckoned out the how.

Adam had retrieved the weapon Mossing dropped during the altercation on the quiet, west side of the house, and now he fitted the two parts of the walking stick together. "This is how you did it." He stood in front of Mossing, who sat there sullenly, staring through a swollen eye.

The others watched as Adam demonstrated, clicking the ice pick blade into place inside the walking stick, then removing it again. As he'd suspected, the weapon was short — only the top quarter of the walking stick. It took him only a moment to find the catch that flipped out the metal stand on the bottom with a little *snick,* and he stepped on it.

The walking stick remained upright without being held, very close to his body, and Adam twisted the weapon part off once more with a smooth, abbreviated, one-handed motion. "Very simple to do as you lean forward to speak quietly to a man, or even to shake his hand."

Adam continued, "And this is how I — we" — he glanced at Miss Gates — "figured it all out." He pointed to the smudge of oil on the floor next to his foot. "Every time you opened that metal catch, you left a tiny oil stain that clung to your shoe."

Mossing said nothing, merely glared from behind a rapidly swelling eye.

"One thing I would like to know," Adam said pleasantly, "is where and how you hid Lemagne's dagger."

At first Mossing didn't respond, but when Pinkerton cuffed him on the side of the head and growled, "Answer the bloody question," the man forced the answer from his equally swollen lips. "In my stocking."

"And why did you choose Billings? Was he always the target, or was it only convenience?"

Mossing sneered a little at that. "More than mere convenience. He was our family banker, so I knew him well. But he got what was coming to him — damned abolitionist. Always talking about how the slaves should be free, without any realization of how it would affect the lives of others. How many families it would put out of business. And it was he who kept loaning my father money for his investments. If he hadn't done so, my father wouldn't have had to sell to Lemagne."

"But the plot to kill Billings was part of a larger one, wasn't it?" Adam said, leaning back against a table. He exchanged glances with Pinkerton, then got the nod to continue. "Littleton and Wellburg were arrested earlier today for the Black Dot plan to assassinate the president at the Union Ball."

"The Black Dots. How did you learn about that?" Mossing was startled.

"I reckon you're a member of that secret society, aren't you?" Adam glanced at Miss Gates, who'd nearly snapped to full attention at that comment. He could almost see the wheels turning in her journalist's mind and he smothered a grin as she spoke up.

"A secret society? To assassinate the president? Why are they called the Black Dots?" Miss Gates was fumbling about her person for a notebook that wasn't there.

"The members identified themselves to each other by placing an ink dot on their cockade ribbon," Pinkerton replied.

"Did you say Mr. Wellburg was part of it?" asked Miss Lemagne suddenly, sitting up straight in her chair.

"He was. An undercover agent of mine helped to identify those responsible for the Union Ball plot — well, most of them," Pinkerton added, looking at Mossing. "The three main plotters who meant to actually carry out the assassination. But they were relying on you to create the necessary diversion by killing Custer Billings. Fortunately, that part of the plan didn't work."

"I noticed a black dot on Mr. Wellburg's cockade at the St. Charles. I had no idea it meant anything," Miss Lemagne said. Then she gasped and spun to Mossing. "Your cockade! The night of the Union Ball — it had a black spot on it. I thought it was amusing that *you* would be wearing something so imperfect. But it was on purpose! And then it was gone. I thought you'd removed it, but instead it must have been pinned to your dress coat — the one you left in the closet after you killed Mr. Billings." Her lips flattened. "If I'd looked more closely at the cockade at Dr. Hilton's, I might have noticed the spot then. And this would have all been over much sooner."

Mossing glared at her. "That was my one mistake — taking the time to change those damned coats. But I got blood on mine, and I couldn't go back into the ball with it looking like that. And his blasted coat didn't fit me quite right, so I was constantly having to adjust the sleeve and hem."

"How did you manage it all, without getting caught?" Adam asked. "You were taking a great risk being seen in the first place. And why did you remove the knife after Fremark saw the dead body?"

It seemed that Mossing was getting over his hesitation about talking, for he answered — albeit grudgingly, "I was going to leave the body in the anteroom with the blade in it — the one I placed there to draw attention to Hurst Lemagne. That was just plain luck that I'd come upon his knife in the stable that same day; I was just going to put Lemagne's business card in Billings's pocket and then carefully direct any questioning to the fact that the men didn't get along. But finding the knife was pure luck on my part."

"So why did you remove the blade from his body?" Adam pressed.

"I had to switch coats because of the blood, and then I heard someone coming from outside — the plank near the door is loose, and it made a little bump as he stepped on it. I ducked into the closet, figuring he'd see the body and run for help — which is precisely what happened. Lyman Fremark took one look and screeched like a girl.

"As soon as he bolted from the room, I came out of the closet — I'd already taken off my coat, and I knew I didn't have much time to make the switch — and I certainly didn't have time to put my coat on him. I was removing Billings's dress coat when the knife fell out of his body. I thought it might add to the drama — and make it less obvious the knife was planted — if I wrapped it in the bloody coat and shoved it in the closet so it wouldn't be found immediately. Then I heard footsteps coming from the corridor, and I ran outside, holding his coat. It was only after I was outside that I realized I'd left my damned walking stick."

"I was the one who came into the room after you left," Miss Gates spoke up. "And when I heard everyone coming, I hid in the closet. For reasons of my own," she added pertly when Pinkerton seemed about to question her. "I heard you open the outside door, but I didn't realize you'd taken the walking stick until Mr. Quinn mentioned it was missing."

"Why did you kill Lyman Fremark?" Adam asked. "And why did you set those thugs on me? It was you, wasn't it?"

"That was Wellburg's idea — the thugs. Not that I argued against it. You were snooping around, asking questions, and at the least, we wanted you laid up — and at the most . . . well, I wouldn't have minded if you ended up dead." He gave Miss Lemagne a pointed glance, then turned back to Adam. "And as for Fremark — I knew someone had walked by me and Billings when we were talking outside the hall just before I killed him, but I didn't know who it was who'd seen us. Once I found out his identity, I knew I couldn't risk that he'd remember something or that he might have recognized me. I followed him until I had the opportunity — and it was a good thing too, because he was coming here to speak to that damned rail-splitter. Man has no right to be president," he spat. "He'll ruin this nation."

Silence fell for a moment, and then Adam exchanged glances with Pinkerton. He nodded, then rose to open the door.

"No sense in letting the president know about this tonight," Pinkerton said as Agent Pierce and one of the U.S. Marshals came into the room. "Let's get this bast— er, this bloke off to jail tonight. There'll be time enough to break the news to Mr. Lincoln tomorrow. Let him keep shaking hands tonight."

CHAPTER 22

"Arthur Mossing?" said Mr. Lincoln. "Of Mossing Textiles? That's quite a reputable company, if memory serves."

Adam nodded. "Yes, sir, although his family no longer owns that business. Mossing is currently a partner at the law firm Strubert, Blackmore, and Mossing."

It was the morning after the levee, and he'd insisted George Hilton come with him to report to the president in his office, bright and early.

"None of your kind is up this early," Hilton had grumbled good-naturedly as they met at the front door of the White House. Lincoln had been heard calling it by that moniker, and the name had begun to stick.

But then the doctor had fallen into almost reverent silence as the ever-present McManus waved them across the threshold. He paused, just over the entrance, and looked up and around in all directions.

Because of the levee last night, no one had come this early, and the foyer, for once, was silent and empty.

He gave a brief nod to Adam, as if letting him know he was finished with whatever had halted him, and started toward the stairs.

"There's one more expected," Adam said to McManus as he followed.

"Yes, sir," replied the doorman with a little salute. "I'll send him up."

Now, they were in the office with the president. Hilton had caught his breath audibly as they entered that chamber as well, and Adam could feel something like tension, and perhaps wariness, reverberating from him as he introduced the two men.

Mr. Lincoln shook Hilton's hand and cordially patted him on the arm. "I'm obliged to meet you, Dr. Hilton, and I'm all ears, waiting for Adam here to explain what happened last night."

"Pinkerton and I thought it best if we didn't disrupt your evening, sir, and so we took care of everything on our own. I reckoned morning would be soon enough to tell you the tale."

"Indeed. My hand — actually, both of them — appreciate it. I'm told I shook hands without pause for three hours last night. I do know I had to use my left hand occasionally, because this one was getting sore from all the congratulating," he said, lifting his right paw. He looked meaningfully at Adam's restored prosthetic arm but didn't mention it. Instead, he commented, "And from what I understand, it was a damned mess in the coat room last night. No one could find their wraps or overcoats, so they just took what they wanted." He shook his head. "But that's going to be Mrs. Lincoln's problem, I think, for future parties."

"I think it's best if that sort of thing is left to her, sir," Adam said.

"Well, now, why don't you tell me more about it. The only information I was able to squeeze from Pinkerton was that the events of last night didn't involve a threat to me — happily — and that Arthur Mossing — the son, was it? — was involved."

"Yes, sir. Mossing killed Custer Billings and Lyman Fremark. He also framed Hurst Lemagne for the first murder."

Lincoln merely lifted his brows, waiting for Adam to continue.

"Mossing was angry that his father had been forced to sell the textile business to Lemagne. Apparently there were some bad investments in eighteen fifty-eight, and Mossing senior had borrowed against the business to pay them — coincidentally, using Billings Bank & Trust. Lemagne bought him out, leaving Arthur Mossing with no choice than the lowly option of practicing law. Apparently, he felt that was a step down from his previous situation." Adam gave Mr. Lincoln a wry smile. "Mossing wanted revenge on Lemagne for what he considered the theft of the business from his father, as well as to regain the company — *and* Miss Lemagne's hand in marriage. Mossing knew if her father was imprisoned and in trouble for the crime, she'd have no choice but to turn to him for help — knowing no one else here in Washington, and being far away from home."

The president shook his head. "Well, I reckon that's one way to get a wife. Rather risky one, though, if you ask me. Flowers or a bit of pretty lace generally work better, I'm told." Then he became grave. "But to kill two men over it? Appalling."

"I agree, sir. Appalling is not a strong enough word," Adam said. He glanced at Hilton. "I couldn't have solved the crime without the assistance of Dr. Hilton, sir. He was invaluable, sir, in helping to determine how the two men were killed — what sort of weapon, which was very unusual — as well as certain information about the killer."

"What sort of information?" Lincoln asked.

Adam let Hilton explain about the different blades used on Billings's body and how he determined the real cause of death, as well as the fact that the killer was right-handed.

"Quite remarkable," the president said once Hilton had told his story. "An excellent example of perseverance and creativity. Thank you again, Dr. Hilton."

"I agree, Hilton. Thank you again for your assistance."

"And this weapon. Tell me about it, and how you came to solve the mystery because of an oil smudge."

Adam smiled. Apparently, Lincoln had gotten a little more information from Pinkerton than he'd let on. He explained about the walking stick. "And if it weren't for a witness who actually saw it, and helped me put the details together —"

He stopped when there was a knock at the office door. Nicolay stuck his head in. "Mr. President? This young woman says she is expected."

The door opened and Miss Gates came in — a little hesitantly for her, Adam thought.

She was dressed neatly in a medium blue dress with a skirt of reasonable circumference, a fairly subdued hat, and gloves.

"Mr. President," she said in a clear voice. "It's an honor to be here. Thank you for having me."

"Well, come in, Miss Gates." Lincoln squinted at her a little. "Have we met before?"

"Yes, Mr. President, very briefly. My uncle — Joseph Henry — introduced me to you last night."

"And you're the young woman who fancies herself a reporter, and has been known to dress in trousers in order to do so?"

Miss Gates flung a mortified look at Adam, who swallowed a smile. Then she looked back at the president. "It's much easier to move about in trousers and a coat than in skirts and a corset. And editors tend to take male journalists more seriously than female journalists."

"I cannot argue with that," Lincoln said in his calm, serious way. "When Adam told me about a female journalist dressed as a man, I was intrigued. And now, I'm having the opportunity to meet you. I'm much obliged, young lady, for your assistance in the matter of the Billings and Fremark murders — and you as well, Dr. Hilton. I set Adam to the task, knowing full well he'd succeed at it. Part of what makes a man successful at his undertakings is surrounding himself with men — and in this case, women, as my dear wife would remind me — who complement his own skills and abilities. It sounds as if you have done precisely that, Adam."

"Yes, sir. I reckon I did my best. Some of it was just pure luck, though," he replied candidly.

"Luck simply means you're aware of and prepared to take advantage of whatever comes your way," Lincoln said. "Which you did."

"Yes, sir."

He looked around at the three of them. "I'd like to thank you all again for your help in putting this matter to rest. Arthur Mossing will stand trial, and, presumably, be sentenced for the murders of Custer Billings and Lyman Fremark and the attempted murder of Constance Lemagne. Justice will be served, and I cannot thank you enough for that."

They took this little speech as the gentle dismissal he obviously intended and said their farewells.

"Adam, a word, please."

Once Hilton and Miss Gates were gone,

Adam closed the door.

The president steepled his hands together, looking at Adam closely. "So now I reckon you're wanting to return to Springfield with your uncle and aunt."

"Yes, sir," Adam replied. "I've had enough of Washington and the crowds." Although he meant it, he felt a little pang over not seeing Brian Mulcahey and his Bessie again, or meeting with Stimpson, Kennicott, and the others at the Smithsonian at night.

"Hmm." Lincoln walked to the window and looked out over the lawn. "And what if I asked you to stay."

Adam straightened at this unexpected request. "I'd . . . I'm not sure, sir."

"Adam, I need someone like you. Someone who doesn't want anything from me," he said, flexing the fingers of his sore right hand. "Someone who doesn't give a damn about politics. Someone who's loyal and whom I can trust. I need someone I can call on for . . . whatever comes along. Hopefully, it won't be something as terrible as murder next time . . . but one can never tell — especially over these next few months." He sighed quietly, as if trying to hide his sadness. "I would consider it a great favor if you would stay here in Washington and continue to work for me."

Adam couldn't say no.

In light of what this man was sacrificing, in light of what changes would soon come to this country — this city — in light of all the hatred and vitriol directed at this one man, who nevertheless would put the good of the nation and his people ahead of himself . . . in light of all that, and the fact that Adam loved and respected Abraham Lincoln, of course he couldn't say no.

"I would consider it an honor to remain in your employ," he said, his voice rough with a sudden onset of emotion. "As long as you need me, Mr. President."

Lincoln's shoulders lowered a bit, and he turned from the window. "I cannot tell you how happy it makes me to hear you say that, Adam. Thank you." He smiled — and it was a genuine smile, almost lighthearted. "But you cannot afford to continue to live at the Willard."

Adam gave a short bark of laughter. "No, I reckon I can't."

"I could put you up here, like I have with Nicolay and Hay — but I suspect you'd prefer not to be in such a busy place. So may I suggest Mrs. Sprigg's boardinghouse? She would welcome you as a boarder — I've already put in a word for you. Mrs. Lincoln and the boys and I lived at Mrs. Sprigg's when I first came to Washington, as a congressman in '47. It's a fine location, and close to this old white house."

"Yes, sir," Adam said. "I reckon I can't do any better than that."

"Not unless you want to bunk in the North Tower at the Smithsonian. I hear it's quite drafty, and a little loud, but then again, you might enjoy that."

Adam hid his surprise, then laughed. "Well, sir, I suppose I'll have to look into both options."

"Excellent, then, Adam. Now, I have one more question for you, if you have a moment."

"Of course, Mr. President," he replied.

"Can you explain to me how it happened that a chicken saved your life?"

NOTE FROM THE AUTHOR

Researching this book was a complete joy and eye-opener — if not sobering — at times. I've done my best to re-create the world of early March 1861 in Washington, D.C., as authentically as possible — even when the facts seemed unusual or surprising.

For example: Yes, there was a Megatherium Club in the Smithsonian Institution, and William Stimpson and Robert Kennicott, as live-in naturalists cataloguing specimens, were the ringleaders. Their parties, though raucous and wild, were permitted by Dr. Joseph Henry as long as the "boys" didn't serenade his daughters — who did live with him and his wife in the East Tower of the Castle. (As far as I know, Dr. Henry did not have a niece residing with him at the time.)

The information about the free woman and seamstress Mrs. Elizabeth Keckley, who eventually became one of Mary Todd Lincoln's closest confidantes, is also true — drawn from her autobiography. Although Dr. George Hilton is a figment of my imagination, the story about how he became a physician is based on the experience of Dr. Alexander Augusta, who was eventually appointed surgeon of the United States Colored Troops by Abraham Lincoln.

Additionally, the description of alley life in Washington, whereby the more wealthy lived facing the streets and the poor (generally Irish and German immigrants, free and enslaved blacks, often jumbled together) lived behind them in hidden alleys, is as accurate as I can make it.

Many of the slaves from elite families, as described herein, were allowed to negotiate their own rates for rental — and keep whatever was left over. I found it most interesting that their owners allowed them to handle all of the business related to that subleasing.

Allan Pinkerton and his staff of agents were instrumental in getting Lincoln safely to Washington, and the description of their unveiling of the Baltimore Plot is accurate — including the fact that Pinkerton employed the first female detective, Kate Warne, as part of that undercover work. As well, the number of constant death threats made to Lincoln — both overtly and through "gifts" in the mail — are both accurate and eye-opening. Especially when taken into account that the White House was, in fact, open for pretty much anyone to walk in at any time.

The 1860 Association was a real entity of legislators and other movers and shakers who were determined to organize secession from the Union after Lincoln was elected. Its actions were mostly limited to letters attempting to garner support for that movement. Thus, the Association's violent offshoot and its black dot identification process is my own creation and was in part inspired by the Knights of the Golden Circle — the most famous of secessionist secret societies during the Civil War.

And, finally, until Lincoln came into office, the president's home was known as the Executive Mansion or the President's House. It was he who began to use the term *White House,* and eventually the name stuck.

I hope you enjoyed this slice of life in antebellum Washington, D.C.! I'm already beginning work on the next Adam Quinn mystery.

— C.M. Gleason

ABOUT THE AUTHOR

C.M. Gleason is a *New York Times* and *USA Today* bestselling and award-winning author. She lives in the Midwest with her family and two dogs, and is hard at work on the next Lincoln White House Mystery.

The employees of Thorndike Press hope you have enjoyed this Large Print book. All our Thorndike, Wheeler, and Kennebec Large Print titles are designed for easy reading, and all our books are made to last. Other Thorndike Press Large Print books are available at your library, through selected bookstores, or directly from us.

For information about titles, please call:
(800) 223-1244

or visit our website at:
gale.com/thorndike

To share your comments, please write:
Publisher
Thorndike Press
10 Water St., Suite 310
Waterville, ME 04901